Jane Seaford has had a number of careers: mother, academic, IT consultant, bakery manager. She currently focuses on her writing. Her short stories have been placed highly commended or short-listed in international competitions. Many have appeared in anthologies or magazines. Several have been broadcast. She has also worked as a freelance journalist. Her first novel, *Archie's Daughter*, was published as an e-book in 2012, and a collection of short stories *Dead is Dead and Other Stories* is due out in 2016. Jane is joint fiction editor for *takahē*, a New Zealand literary magazine. Her website is janeseaford.com.

Also by Jane Seaford

Archie's Daughter

Praise for Archie's Daughter

'This seems at first a mystery story uncovering the truth behind the disappearance /death of the main character's mother, but it is more than that. It looks at communication between family members, the differing interpretations of significant events within the family and - most heartbreakingly - the impacts of mental illness on marriages. It left me thinking how little we know about how mental illness has affected marriages and other relationships in the past and how little we still know about how to deal with mental illness within our own relationships today. A great read. .' Mpg, Amazon UK review

'Archie's Daughter really is an admirable piece of work; I'd definitely want to read Seaford's next novel.' Ije Kanu. Editor, LiteraryFiction.bellaonline.com

'Excellent narrative of daily life, including the blight of depression, that holds the attention till the end.' Doc Lyn Saunders, Amazon UK review

'This is one read that you won't want to miss.' http://www.mentalhealthy.co.uk

The Insides of
Banana Skins

Jane Seaford

Copyright @ Jane Seaford

First published in 2016

ISBNs

   978-0-473-37119-7 (softcover)
   978-0-473-37120-3 (Mobi)
   978-0-473-37322-1 (epub)
   978-0-473-37323-8 (pdf)

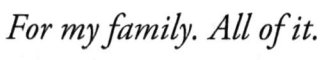

For my family. All of it.

Thanks to Rocky Hudson for her excellent proofreading, to Karen Baker for her wonderful cover, to Janet Wainscott for giving wise and considered advice on the publishing process, to Juliana Feaver for her support and assistance on many aspects of producing this book, to Shirley Eng for endless discussions on writing over the years and to the other members of my various writing critique groups: Hikatea Bull, Felicity Cutten, Joan Eddy, Janice Healey, Pat Land, Mary Fitzgerald. Wendy Williamson and Karen Zelas.

Chapter 1
October 1966: Sukey

Sukey knew it. When she thought about it, she knew it was over. But Rick said nothing. They still saw each other, slept together, too.

He came to dinner on the Saturday he and his friend Paul moved into their new flat, but he didn't stay, told her he must go home, there was so much to do the next day.

'OK,' she said, wanting more and not knowing how to ask for it. She watched from the front step as he walked away. He'd call in a few days, she was sure. He'd promised to tell her when their phone was installed.

It was Sunday, just over a week later, and Sukey knew that Rick wouldn't be ringing her or coming over that weekend. Looking through the window at the damp, grey, lonely London street, she felt strange, absent, as if she was hollow. She wondered why she had to depend on another person for how she felt.

The first time Sukey slept with Rick, they hadn't had sex. There'd been a fight, a small fight in the bar and Sukey had left with Rick, who'd won. That had been in early May. Sukey was then a student at an arts college set in the Devon countryside where introductory courses in music, painting and drama were taught. Somehow in her last year at school she'd decided she wanted to be an actress. Rick worked in the nearby town. They came to the Saturday night dances at the college, these local men, lured by tales of young girls, no rules, beatnik freedom.

After the fight, after the two of them had left the bar together, Sukey unlocked her room and let him in. He sat on the bed, leant back on his elbows, looking at her from under his fringe of dark hair. Sukey stood at the window, saying nothing, trembling slightly.

'Come and sit down,' he said and she obeyed. He put his arm round her and started to kiss her. She kissed him back, let him unbutton her blouse, but when he groaned, saying he wanted her, she gently pushed him away. At first, he ignored her, holding her tightly. She struggled and he released her.

'Let's go to bed,' he whispered, pulling his wallet out of his pocket. 'You'll be OK; I've got what's needed.' He took a small packet out of the wallet and held it up.

'No,' Sukey said and moved away. He frowned.

'I can't,' she said, not knowing how to tell him she was only sixteen, still a virgin.

He looked at her, sighed. 'Why didn't you say before?' he asked.

'How could I?' she said, almost crying.

He nodded, he understood. 'OK. But could I sleep here,

2

with you? Will that be all right?'

Sukey swallowed, nodded. It was all right. They lay in bed and he talked, telling her about the girlfriend he'd had for four years who'd left him for his best friend in December, just before he turned twenty-one. He told her how much he'd loved this girl. How hurt he'd been.

'But I'm getting over it. I've applied to University, going up to London in September,' he said.

'I'm going to London, too, when this course is over,' she told him.

'To another college?'

'No, a year out, to decide what I really want to do.' She thought it sounded grown-up as she said it.

The next time he slept with her, she'd already decided that they would have sex. Although the thought of it made her feel quite strangely breathless, it was something she knew she wanted to do. She wanted to know what it was like and she wanted to be the same as the other students at this odd college she'd stumbled into.

Sukey had arrived the previous September by train, and a mini-bus had picked her up from the station along with several other students, all of them sophisticated and experienced, Sukey thought. Shy and awkward, she was almost completely silent, both then and in the following days. Her clothes were wrong, the way she thought and felt was wrong. She didn't know about drugs, could drink only a glass or two of alcohol before she felt ill, had nothing to say that would interest anyone. She sat with the others and practised smoking their cigarettes until one of them told her that she should buy her own. She listened and watched and sometimes she began to feel that she might fit in, given time. She learned to drink and what to do with dope and even LSD. And now it was just having sex that would make her the same as the others.

So she whispered: 'Rick, you can, you know, if you want to.'

'You sure, really sure?'

'Yes,' she whispered, 'yes.'

Even so, before he penetrated her for the first time he asked again: 'Are you sure?'

It was, she believed, the most remarkable thing to have ever happened to her. It was not so much the act itself as the fact that it had happened; a man's body had entered hers. At the same time, while it was intensely intimate, she'd not known what Rick was feeling as he came or even what she was supposed to feel. She spent all the next day thinking about it and when she opened her door that evening, he was there.

All through the summer term, she slept with Rick, several times a week. He talked of the holiday he was planning, a trip to Greece with Paul, his new best friend. They were renovating a van to take them there and to live in. They were looking for a third person to travel with to make the costs lower.

Sukey waited. She waited for Rick to ask her to come to Greece. She waited for Rick to tell her that he loved her. She knew she loved him; of course she did. She loved being in bed with him, sometimes waking in the night to find him

4

wanting her again. She loved the way he paid for her when they went out drinking. She loved the way he discussed music and books and films, taking seriously what she had to say. She loved the way he talked about London and what he would do there; he and Paul were planning to find a place together. She loved the way her took her hand when they walked back to her room after an evening out.

Now Sukey was sharing a North London flat with Tessa, who she knew from boarding school. Not too far away lived her two best friends from college; Jaz, who was now a student at a big London drama school, and Kitty, who said she no longer wanted to be an actress and worked in a pub. But for Sukey being in London meant being near Rick. The day she'd first moved in with Tessa, Sukey had written to him giving her address, and eventually a reply came. It was only after he'd been in London for ten days that he came to see her; and stayed the night.

Ten days, Sukey thought, he waited ten days. And now it's been over a week and he hasn't even telephoned. She lay on her bed, staring up at the ceiling and wished she were someone else; someone with confidence who could say witty things; someone who made an impact on others; someone solid and real. Little tears trickled down the sides of Sukey's face and she gulped slightly, not wanting to make too much noise.

'Sundays are so sad,' she whispered. As she closed her eyes, she could feel the tears hot against the lids. And the image of Ellen dying on the last Sunday of her last term at the Devon college made her turn on her side and curl herself into a tight ball.

It was July and it had rained relentlessly for nearly a week. It was the last concert of the year given by the music students and while they were playing a requiem, their conductor, Ellen, lay down and died. Sukey, there with Rick, saw the baton rise above Ellen's head. This was followed by her squirming fall as she collapsed. Edwin, the head of music, moved across, bent and took the baton, allowing the concert to continue. Someone placed a blanket over the woman where she lay.

Afterwards they all stood about in the entrance to the auditorium. Edwin came out, his white head bowed. The talking subsided and he spoke. 'I'm sorry to have to tell you that Ellen is dead.' Sukey felt sick and turned to Rick, who shrugged. He didn't stay with her that night, her last at the college; they made love and he left soon after.

When she woke in the morning, she stood watching the rain falling slow and flat. She was bereft. In a few hours she, and all the other students, would be leaving. The year was over; her first at learning how to be an adult and it had ended with Ellen's public death and cold wetness instead of warm summer.

She stood at her window, watching the weather, feeling desperately sad, thinking of Ellen, whom she'd seen nearly every day: a short, brisk, grey-haired figure eating in the cafeteria, walking between the college buildings, stopping to talk earnestly to one of the students; familiar, pleasant, round-bodied and alive. This sadness was not because Ellen was dead; Sukey had rarely spoken to her, had not been close to her. It was the death itself, its drama and timing, coming when the last college term was over and a requiem was playing, that lodged in Sukey's thinking, a motif of ending and of desolation that would not go away. Ellen's death was overwhelming because Sukey was already in mourning, regretting that her short time at the college was now over and feeling confusion and uncertainty about Rick. She wished she could have the time when she'd first met him back again and be able to do it differently.

Sukey uncurled herself and sat up. She could hear Tessa in the small kitchen that was next to her room; the clink of crockery and the gush of water from the tap, the scritch of a gas ring being lit. Making tea, Sukey thought, and she closed her eyes, thinking of spending the rest of this Sunday in the shabby flat with her boring friend. All weekend, starting on Friday night, she'd stayed in waiting for Rick to phone her.

From the kitchen came Tessa's tuneless voice singing the refrain from an early Beatles song: 'She loves me, yeah, yeah, she loves me, yeah, yeah.' The kettle started to whistle as Tessa's voice rose and Sukey decided. She needed to know what Rick wanted. Standing up and stretching, she went to peer in the mirror above the chest of drawers. She cleaned her face with cold cream on a piece of cotton wool, applied fresh eye-shadow and mascara, brushed her hair, put on shoes and wrapped herself in her cloak. Taking her bag, she ran down the stairs, looking up to say 'goodbye' when she

7

heard Tessa clumping out of the kitchen into the hallway. She banged out of the front door and almost ran to the tube station. The cold, wet streets were empty. When she emerged, two slow, rattling trains later, the rain was heavier and darkness had arrived.

Rick opened the door, raised surprised eyebrows and gave a questioning smile. Sukey smiled back, following him into the kitchen where they sat and drank tea.

'I must get on with putting the hessian on my walls,' Rick said.

'Hessian?'

'He thinks it'll look good, make the place posh.' Paul shook his head. 'He wants me to help, I've said no.'

'I'll help,' said Sukey.

'No,' said Rick.

'I want to,' Sukey put down her cup and looked at him. He shrugged.

It wasn't easy, first cutting the hessian with a pair of big strong scissors, then spreading the glue and finally pressing it against the wall until it stuck.

'It's looking great,' said Rick several hours later, as they smoothed the last edge into place. He looked at his watch. 'You've missed the last tube.'

'Can I stay?' Sukey whispered, feeling a pulse throbbing in her forehead.

'You'll have to,' Rick said, 'too far to walk.'

'You don't want me here, do you?' Sukey asked. 'You don't want me anymore.'

Rick sank down onto the mattress, folding himself up, as

if wanting to disappear. He looked down, wrapping his arms round his body.

'Well?' Sukey said, scared, feeling her heart pumping.

'It's late.'

'Is it over?'

He sighed, rubbed his forehead. 'The thing is, Sukey, it's… well, we've had a great time, haven't we?' He paused, pursed his lips, blew out air. 'But it's not the love story of a lifetime is it? Not for either of us.'

As he said it Sukey wasn't sure if it was true for her or not. She felt a yearning loss, but for what she wasn't sure. She was aware of panic, the like of which she'd never before experienced. She was overwhelmed by knowing that it was over, and there was nothing, absolutely nothing, that she could do about it. Part of her wanted to scream and yell, wanted to make Rick tell her that they were still going to be together. She was breathless. She wanted Rick: he didn't want her. And that she could not change. She shook her head, letting pain gradually take her over. She sat on the one chair in the room and started to cry.

'I'm so sad,' she said.

'I am, too. Always sad when a relationship ends.'

'Yes,' said Sukey, thinking, for me it was a first love, for him just a little affair, a filling-in-time sort of affair. She gulped, let the crying take her over. He stood, came and put his hand on her head.

'Don't,' she gasped. 'Sympathy makes me worse.' She was almost laughing as well as crying.

'Ah, Sukey,' he said and sighed. She gave in to the crying

for a little while. She heard the clunk of Rick's shoes landing on the floor as he took them off. She looked up, knowing that her eyes were swollen, her face red and wet. She sniffed loudly.

'Whatever happens we'll always remember each other, won't we Sukey?'

She nodded. Her face and head were so full of grief she couldn't speak.

'Let's go to bed now,' he said. 'D'you want first turn at the bathroom?'

She shook her head and watched him leaving the room. She sat for a time wondering if she could move. When he came back, he started to undress and his body gradually became naked. The last time, she thought. With an effort she rose, moving slowly. It was as if she had the flu. She wondered how long it would be before she recovered.

When she returned, he was lying under the bedclothes. The light was off and he'd lit a candle. She turned her back to undress.

She lay next to him and he put his arm over her and nuzzled into her neck. His hand moved to her breast and she felt his erect penis pressing against her leg.

'What are you doing?' she asked.

'Let's make love,' he whispered. Sukey lay, trying to understand.

'To say goodbye in the nicest way,' Rick murmured.

'No,' said Sukey, 'no.' She turned away, lay trembling in a sad, confused ball. Finally she heard Rick sigh, felt him turn and the room became dark as he blew out the candle.

With relief, she let herself cry again, noiselessly, despairingly.

During the night the hessian unpeeled and fell off the wall. It sounded like giant zips being slowly opened and woke them both. Sukey and Rick lay side by side on their backs. Sukey started to laugh and then stopped as Rick's fingers clasped hers in a strong grip, making her cry, and she let the tears out silently so he couldn't hear.

As soon as the alarm went, Rick jumped up. He pulled on jeans and went to examine the heap of stiff gluey material, the remains of last night's hard work, part of the process of turning this dark basement flat into a home. Sukey half sat up, leaning against the wall behind the mattress and watched him. She wondered if he'd say anything, and breathed in deeply to stop the tears coming. She must get up, dress in yesterday's clothes and go to work. Her head ached, her eyes were sore and gritty, her body limp and sad. She wondered how to cope with this new stage in her life, this unfamiliar unpleasant feeling.

'It should work,' Rick said. 'I'll get stronger glue. Don't want to waste this stuff. I spent a lot on it.' He carefully lifted the pieces of hessian and laid them on the floor by the window, pulling them flat. He stood up. 'Tea?' He asked.

'Yes please.'

'Bacon sam'ich?'

Sukey shook her head. How could he think of food and be so cheerful? She wanted to pull the bedclothes over her head, curl up into a ball and refuse to go. She thought about becoming hysterical and demanding to be looked after, cared for, loved. But that was not her way.

'Right, said Rick, gathering up the rest of his clothes, 'you'd better hurry if you want the bathroom. Paul'll be up soon. I won't be long.' He left the room and Sukey breathed out deeply, aware that she was alone for the first time since it had happened. She opened her jaw wide in a silent scream and then bent over, sobbing and gasping for air, but she did it quietly and with control. This was something she needed to do; she needed this small piece of time to let the pain accumulate, so that she could accommodate it, understand it. She could feel it in her chest, a tight balloon round her heart, real physical breathtaking agony. Part of her was outside herself, watching; part of her was saying: "Sukey's dealing with her first real boyfriend no longer wanting her. In fact, he never loved her, she knows that now."

Rick was back holding a mug of tea. 'Sukey,' he said and she looked up, closing her mouth and swallowing in an effort to stop misery from flooding out and overwhelming her. If Rick understood how sad she was, he'd try to comfort her and that would be unbearable.

'Sukey,' Rick said again, concern showing in his frown and the caressing tone he used.

'I'm fine,' she said, forcing a smile, hiding her hurt from him. She wanted him to think that she'd soon be over it and on to the next one. He put the mug on the floor beside the mattress and stood, looking at her. She continued her smile.

'We'll be great mates,' he said, 'I always enjoyed being with you.'

'Yes,' Sukey nodded, using one arm to hold the sheet over her breasts as she reached for the tea. Suddenly it seemed odd to be naked in Rick's bedroom.

Later as she was dressing, she heard him talking to Paul in the kitchen. There was a burst of laughter. Sukey almost screamed with anger. Why should she just go? Why make it easy for him?

She stood by the mattress, wanting revenge. Where were the scissors that they'd used last night? She saw them on the mantelpiece, took them, held them heavily, went to the hessian lying on the floor. She knew what she should do: wield the scissors, cut the material into tiny sticky pieces. She closed her eyes; saw herself doing it, saw herself stamping on the remains of the thick material, saw Rick coming in, looking puzzled, saw herself screaming at him, telling him how she felt. She opened her eyes, looked at the scissors, dropped them.

She wrapped her cloak round her, went into the hall, called: 'Bye,' and let herself out, closing the door gently behind her. She climbed the area steps and stood on the cold, wet pavement catching her breath. There were raindrops on her eyelashes and she thought about all those months ago, her last days at college, Ellen dying, the desolation she'd felt at the ending of that year and how the very public death had forced into focus the way she'd been starting to feel. Now the ending was complete. She should have broken with Rick on the day of the concert, made everything belonging to that time finish at once. But still, in spite of this understanding, Sukey hesitated. She turned to look down at the basement flat. Then she shook her head, sighed and walked off into the grey London drizzle.

(Many years later Sukey told a friend about Ellen. The friend thought it most strange that the concert had continued while Ellen lay dying. This surprised Sukey, she'd never considered this odd, though she'd thought about it often. For her, dramatic though it had been, the death as the requiem continued had never been an event in itself but was a symbol that gave shape and meaning to that unsettling time in her life when she was trying to learn how to be an adult.)

Chapter 2
February 1967: Minnie

The bag with the money in it was gone. Minnie stood watching as the bus rattled away up the long road. She could see its lights in the wet grey dusk, the indicator winking as it drew in to the next stop. A swish of rain, provoked by a passing car, hit her legs, soaking her shoes and her long skirt. Still staring, she blinked, squished her eyes together to see better: the bus was pulling out, continuing on. She imagined hearing the impatient ding as the conductor rang the bell, leaning out from his platform, wanting the driver to go faster, wanting to be home. Even if she ran, she could not catch up. The bus was gone, the bag was gone, all that money was gone.

Giving a deep jagged sigh, she peered round wanting to find somewhere to sit down. There was nowhere: no bench at this bus stop. She looked down at the wet pull of her skirt, tucked her arms round herself and, scarcely watching for cars, crossed the road, heading for home.

When she arrived she was shivering and she stood in the

porch fumbling with cold fingers for her key in her shabby cracked leather purse with its long fraying strap that she wore over her shoulder and at an angle across her body. It went everywhere with her and held, as well as her key, little bits of money, her tobacco, papers and lighter, the end of a broken comb, a nugget of dope wrapped in silver foil and pressed down into the back pocket. But it was too small for all those notes; those months of saved notes now probably passing through Finsbury Park in a plastic supermarket bag, its handles flapping on the top deck of the bus, or scrunched up under a seat. Unless someone had already found it, opened it, widening their eyes on seeing the contents, then running down the stairs and off the bus as it soon as it stopped, holding the bag tight and close to them before any one else claimed it, or stole it. Minnie felt her mouth turn down at the corners and start to tremble as she imagined her bag and its fate. She pulled out the key and stuck it fiercely into the lock.

In the hallway, it was dark and quiet. John and Bridie who lived downstairs had probably put their children to bed and gone out drinking. The place smelt of stale cooked vegetables and damp clothes overlaid with the sweet-dry aroma of dope being smoked. Slowly she climbed the stairs and went into the kitchen. Kitty and Dennis were sitting at the table and Malc was lying on the floor looking uncomfortable, his head, neck and shoulders pressed against the wall, his knees bent, a joint in his hand. The light from the two candles flickered as Minnie closed the door and leant against it.

'Want some tea?' asked Kitty, raising the pot with its knitted cosy, taking a heavy drag on her cigarette. Kitty was the flat's official tenant. She worked in the pub up the road, never drank, didn't take drugs of any kind. She just stole money and fags and slept with other people's husbands, of whom Dennis was one.

Minnie shook her head, went to sit next to Malc. He passed her the joint and Minnie took it. She watched her hand as it reached out; it was trembling. She took a puff, pulled the thick smoke down into her lungs. As she breathed out, she said: 'I left the money on the bus.'

'What money?' asked Kitty, her voice even more rasping than normal.

'The dealing money, the India money, the acid money, the trip money, whatever you want to call it. My money,' Minnie said and the reality of her loss pulled her head down almost onto her lap. She felt the dampness of her hair against her cheeks. 'What's Ted going to say?' she almost whispered.

'Get onto them,' Dennis said. 'London Transport Lost Property.'

Minnie sat up, pushed her back and shoulders against the wall. 'And say what? I was bringing home the money I'd made dealing and forgot it when I got off the bus. Should I say that?'

'You don't have to tell them how you got the money. Just that you've lost it.' Dennis went to the fridge, peering into its contents for another bottle of beer, which he found and opened. Minnie watched his plump lips as they sucked from the top of the bottle. He sat down again and reached for one of Kitty's cigarettes. Dennis was forty, had a wife in Battersea, four live children and another two, the youngest two, who were dead: identical twin girls, one had survived to three months, the other six. And since then, Dennis said, his wife had been slightly mad. Minnie hated his fleshy presence in the flat, his pale, disapproving, voyeur's eyes, his whining South London accent. He made her feel fastidious, vulnerable, as if she didn't belong. But then, maybe she didn't. Maybe none of them did. Except for Kitty.

Pink, fat Kitty, who kept the place almost clean and occasionally took the washing to the laundrette, thought she was making the place homely with cushions and stolen flowers. She filled the place with as many people as she could fit in, so that now in the second bedroom there were five of them sharing the space and paying some rent, whatever Kitty persuaded them they could afford. Dennis paid the most for his half of the big bedroom room where he slept with Kitty. And she made them use candles to save on bills and charged them for food, serving big vegetable stews with bread and marge. 'I could do with a couple of nice big pork chops,' Dennis had said once and Kitty replied: 'I'm not stopping you visiting the butcher.'

Kitty is why she'd lost all her money, thought Minnie. She'd left the gradually increasing pile in the safe at the alternative health food shop where she worked. It had been agreed. They all knew what Minnie was doing and no one had minded. She'd sold to them too, the others who worked there, the casuals, the managers, those like her who were more or less regular. They all wanted dope and most also bought acid when she could get it. She was not a regular dealer, just saving for a special occasion, the trip to India with Ted. The money had stayed in the safe because she didn't want it at home for Kitty to take, and she didn't want to put it in a bank in case they asked questions. And now, just when she had enough, when she'd more or less booked the plane tickets and had been going to pay for them, it had gone. She'd brought the money home because tomorrow was her day off. She planned not to let it out of her sight, put it under the mattress when she slept and then in the morning take it to the travel agency. Instead, she'd sat on the bus, leaning back with her eyes closed, tired from work, from too much dope and not enough sleep. She put the bag down when she paid her fare and forgot to pick it up when she opened her eyes and jumped up, seeing that the bus was almost at her stop.

Malc passed her the joint again and as she took a toke, she saw Dennis looking at her and wondered if his expression was lust or disgust.

'Have you any change?' Kitty asked. 'For the phone. I'll call lost property for you before I go to work. What sort of bag was in it?'

'It's too late,' Minnie said, frowning. 'Evening now; they won't be open.' She let her head droop and felt the coldness of her wet clothes soak into her skin. What she wanted to do was to sit in the comfort of a hot bath. But the tub was in the kitchen, its cover a shelf for pots and pans and piles of books that had to be moved before it could be used. Minnie felt too tired to do this and, more importantly, she didn't know how to tell the others that she needed to be alone in the room.

'Oh,' said Ted, his voice was tired and thin like the smoke he was exhaling. Minnie waited for something more, some anger, some comment on the lost money, something that she could react to. Instead Ted passed her the joint and rubbed his face with his hand.

'Sorry,' Minnie said, though why should she be? she thought. After all, it was she who'd done all the dealing, made all the money for the trip. 'Are you disappointed?' she asked Ted. He looked at her, blinking as if wondering what she meant. He shrugged, took the joint out of her hand, taking a deep draw on it before putting it in the cracked saucer they were using as an ashtray. Then he pulled Minnie to him and started kissing her. She struggled. 'I don't feel like it,' she whispered, turning her face away from Ted's.

'The others will be in soon. C'mon Minnie.' His hands were on her body. Minnie lay back, giving in, which was easier than resisting. As she felt Ted's labouring body on top of hers, she tried to make herself feel pleasure in the act, but all she could think about was the squalor of this little room, the several mattresses piled with greying sheets and limp blankets. Ted didn't notice or didn't care that she was not responding and soon after he came, he fell asleep. Minnie sat up and leaned over to blow out the candle and then lay on her back, wide awake, wishing she were somewhere else. After a bit, Jaz and Beaky, who shared the room, came in, trying to be quiet, but tripping over things in the dark. Jaz and Beaky were really John and Colin but they'd found themselves new names as they were growing up, as had Minnie, who had once been Mary Anne.

It was dawn before Malc came to bed. Minnie was almost asleep when she heard him stumble in. She turned, sighing, trying to be quiet.

'You 'wake?' Malc asked, his voice a sibilant hiss.

'What?' Minnie asked, whispering too.

'I got you some trips, acid. One each for you and Ted, free. And the others cheap so you can start saving again.'

'No,' said Minnie.

'What'd you mean 'no'?'

'I'm not going to deal again. It was a sign. We're not meant to go to India, me and Ted.'

Minnie sat thinking about the effects of acid; how it made music turn into moving colour, how it gave one idea a multitude of meaning, how it made objects look round and solid as if made of cheese. How it made everything that was said open to myriad interpretation, each interpretation spawning even more till you were stunned by possibility, immobilised by the multiplicity of what could be. How scary it could be when everything you said and felt and did was overwhelmingly significant. It wasn't that hallucination seduced you. You could choose to stay aware of what was real and what was not: the frightening part was that everything became important. This was the ecstasy as well: the fizzing feeling of exultant joy, but then that fizz could flip into its underside. That was why she'd not taken her trip that morning. She was tired, she was upset, she didn't feel clean.

'The thing is I'd think about the money I've lost. I'd be thinking about India and how we're not going,' she told the others. 'I wanted to go, find peace. I wanted a rest, I wanted to get away from the crush of London.' She sighed as she stirred the tea in her cup, watching its warm brown swirl.

'It would have been a lot more crowded in India,' Jaz said. Minnie didn't say anything, didn't see the point in replying.

Once they'd all taken their tabs they went out, heading for Regent's Park. Dennis, snorting disapproval, drove off in his cab and finally Kitty, too, left for the lunchtime shift at the pub. Minnie sighed with the pleasure of being alone and prepared for a long soak in the bath. She'd have the radio on, eat a raspberry yoghurt and plan how she would make her fortune by running the health food shop more efficiently.

'Kitty said Lost Property told her nothing had been handed in. She called them, she told me.' Minnie frowned at Dennis.

'That's what Kitty said, but she was lying.' Dennis licked his thick lips, stared at Minnie with his slightly bulging eyes.

Minnie swallowed, looked down, shook her head. 'I don't believe you,' she said, shifting in her chair and wishing that some of the others were at home. Kitty had just left for work, Jaz and Beaky weren't back from college, Malc and Ted had gone out drinking.

'I'll show you. She went down there today, got the bag, got all the money.'

'So how much is in there?'

'Haven't counted it. Lots of notes, though.'

'So you're saying that someone found the bag and handed it in?'

'Yes.'

'And that Kitty lied.'

'Yes. What are you going to do to thank me for it?'

Minnie stared at Dennis across the kitchen table. She saw little strings of spittle in the corners of his mouth and she shuddered. She remembered the photo he'd once shown her of his wife and how surprised she'd been at how beautiful she was. She narrowed her eyes; there was something pitiful about Dennis. Here he was, middle-aged, strangely living with Kitty and a bunch of students and hippies in a flat that was more like a doss house when he should be at home being a normal family man. This, Minnie thought, was how he felt about himself. He's unhappy, Minnie thought.

'Show me the bag, show me the money.' Minnie sat up, suddenly excited. Maybe the money was not lost. Maybe she'd be going to India after all. A spurt of excitement fizzled through her body. All that planning, all that dealing, all that effort, of course she wanted to go to India. She'd not let herself acknowledge how disappointed the loss of her money had made her. But now it was back. Oh please let it be back, she almost said aloud. 'Show it to me,' she demanded.

'It's in our bedroom, come with me.'

'Bring it here,' Minnie ordered.

Dennis shook his head. 'You want the money, you come with me.'

Minnie breathed out deeply, watched Dennis' fingers tapping on the table. She put her head on one side, thinking. Dennis reached out for the packet on the table, took out a cigarette and lit it, exhaled. And all the time he was staring at Minnie. 'He wants to have sex with me,' she thought, and almost retched. She wondered if she could do it, go to bed with Dennis and in return be able to take her Indian trip.

'Well?' Dennis asked, blowing smoke towards Minnie.

'OK,' Minnie said. She felt as if her heart was beating double time, and touched a little place on the edge of her forehead with the tips of her fingers as if to check that her pulse was not too fast. Dennis stood up and Minnie swallowed. She looked at the shine and the sharp crease of his Terylene trousers and the silly big patterns of white geese at the neck, sleeves and waist of his jumper. Would he look better with his clothes off? she wondered, wincing.

'Come on,' he said and Minnie followed him, out of the kitchen and up the three short steps that led to the landing and then through into the bedroom. She sat on the bed, rubbing with the palms of both hands the candlewick spread as she watched Dennis go the wardrobe and open it.

'You haven't said how you'll thank me for returning the money,' Dennis said, one hand on the door handle, gripping it tight, making his knuckles look white and knobbly.

'Give it to me and then I'll talk about the thanking.'

Dennis shook his head. 'I want you in bed, no clothes on and then I'll show you the money.'

Minnie sat for a moment, her hands still. Then she stood up and started to unbutton her blouse. She undid the zip of her skirt and let it fall to the ground. She watched Dennis watching her. She saw him swallow and heard his breathing getting louder. 'Now,' she said, 'show me the money.'

He opened the door a little wider and, fumbling on one of the shelves, he pulled out a plastic bag, a Sainsbury's bag like the one that Minnie had lost. Crumpled, too, and a little bit torn. But then London must be full of old supermarket bags.

'How do I know it's got money in it?' Minnie asked, and Dennis let go of the wardrobe door and put his hand into the bag. He took it out and showed Minnie his fist full of notes. He shook the bag: there was more inside. He put the money back into the bag, the bag back into the wardrobe and shut the door. He moved his hands to his waist, unbuckling the belt, unzipping his fly, pulling down his trousers. Minnie slipped of her blouse, undid her bra, sat down and untied her shoes. She climbed into bed wearing nothing but her thick red socks and her knickers. She pulled the coverlet over her and closed her eyes.

Dennis was kissing her. She felt his legs as they pressed against hers and the loose bulge of tummy, saggy and soft against her hip. She lay flat, unmoving, letting his wet mouth chew at her lips, she felt the thrust of his tongue and his hand hard and insistent between her legs, pushing aside the thin cotton of her knickers. She kept her eyes closed, her body still, waited for it to be over.

'Bitch.' She felt the sharp sting of his hand on her cheek

and she opened her eyes, surprised, shocked. He was sitting up, staring at her, his face red and wet with anger. 'Bitch,' he said, spitting the word out.

'What is it?' she asked, not understanding.

He was panting now. He pulled back the covers and stood up. Minnie caught a glimpse of his penis, small and rubbery below the pale insignificance of his pubic hair. Then he turned and she watched the wobble of his buttocks as he bent to find and then pull on his underpants. Slowly, as he quickly dressed, Minnie sat up and slid out of the bed. She reached for her clothes and her shoes, held them protectively against her. 'Why am I a bitch?' she asked, quietly, gently, wanting to know.

He replied, his back still towards her, doing up the buckle on his belt. 'You girls today, you think you're so much better than us. You've too much freedom: drugs, sex. It's disgusting. And then you think you're doing me a favour by sleeping with me. You insult me, the way you lie there. You should have said no.'

'But then you wouldn't have given me the money,' Minnie said, hugging her clothes tightly against her. She was shivering so much now that her teeth were chattering.

Dennis turned. He was almost crying. 'There's no fucking money. You stupid as well? Anyone finding a bag of notes would keep it. I just put some of mine and some old newspaper in the bag to fool you. Didn't really think you'd fall for it.' He gave a throaty sob. 'Now get out of the room!' he shouted.

'Sorry,' Minnie said as she crept out, not sure why she

was apologising. For a while she sat on her mattress in the room she shared with Ted, and with Malc, Jaz and Beaky. After a bit she climbed under the sheet and blankets and lay wondering what she was going to do to make things seem better. Then she started to cry, scrunched up into a ball of loss, mourning the end of the dream of the long planned trip, hating the mess and muddle of her life.

(Minnie did eventually visit India, thirty years later. Now the wealthy owner of an organic food company, she was travelling for business with a wallet full of gold cards.)

Chapter 3
March 1967: Sukey

When Sukey woke it was daytime, grey rays of wintry sun were filtering through the worn material of the thin curtains. She looked at the clock by her bed and yawned. Nearly eleven and she was still tired. She turned, pulling the sheet and blanket over her head and was soon asleep again. She woke some time later and once more went back to sleep.

The third time she woke, it was because the doorbell was ringing. As Sukey lay blinking, the bell continued to sound as if someone was leaning on it, refusing to go away. She stretched; her limbs were heavy and listless as if they'd been stuffed with kapok. Sitting up, she pushed aside the bedclothes, slowly stood and walked towards the window. She yanked it up and holding it in place, she leant out, looking down onto the street below. Jaz was there, his head bent back, staring up, one hand on his hip, the other pressed against the bell. When he saw Sukey, he stopped ringing and yelled up at her.

'I knew you were in. Are you going to come and open the door?'

She stepped back from the window and closed it. Shivering, she wondered if she'd any change for the gas meter. She bent to pick up her clothes from the floor and dressed quickly, pulling on her jumper and jeans over the T-shirt and knickers she'd been wearing in bed. She went down the two flights of stairs and opened the front door. Jaz was huddled on the step, looking cold, his arms wrapped round himself.

''Bout time,' he said, and followed Sukey back up to the flat at the top of the house (two bedrooms and a kitchen). 'Any tea?' he asked, sitting cross-legged on the floor of Sukey's room. 'Any chance of lighting the fire?'

Sukey shrugged. 'I'll see if I've got milk, and you need to put a shilling in the meter if you want the fire.'

'Toast would be nice,' Jaz said, as Sukey went into the kitchen. She filled the kettle and switched it on, opened the fridge and peered inside. Back in her room, Jaz had fed the meter and lit the gas fire. He was sitting by it, holding his hands out to the warmth.

'No milk, no bread. If you lend me some money, I'll go to the corner shop,' Sukey said, and Jaz rooted in his pocket and passed her his wallet.

'Get butter and eggs and… er marmalade,' he said, watching as Sukey pulled on boots over bare feet.

'Make the tea when the kettle boils,' she said as she took her cloak off the big armchair and wrapped it round her. On the ground floor, she used the loo, leaving the door open because the light bulb had stopped working some time ago. She wondered if Jaz would mind if she bought some toilet paper with his money; there wasn't much of the torn up newspaper left.

She stood in the corner shop looking at the shelf where marmalade was stored, trying to remember what sort Jaz preferred. She closed her eyes thinking of him sitting at a table with breakfast in front of him. He didn't eat much, cereal normally, and even though he was vegetarian, she'd once seen him with a bacon sandwich. 'Bacon is the one thing I miss,' he'd told her. She picked the Rose's Lime marmalade. It seemed the sort that Jaz would like. There was only one loaf left in the bread rack, white sliced: it would have to do. She picked out the cheapest butter, a half dozen eggs, and a double pack of loo roll. The plump woman at the counter started to ring up the purchases.

'Haven't seen you for a bit,' she said. 'Been away?'

'No,' said Sukey. 'Busy,' she said and hoped that she didn't look too unkempt, didn't smell after several days of not washing. The bathroom was in the basement, which had been pulled apart by the builders ready for a planned refurbishment that hadn't yet happened. It was filled with piles of old wood; the walls had holes in them; everywhere there were cobwebs, dust, rubble and, Sukey was sure, rats. Now that she was on her own in the house, she hated going into the basement. Worse still, the last time she'd tried for a bath, when she'd lit the water heater, it had made a banging sound and a flame had streaked out and burnt one of her eyebrows.

'There you are,' said the shop woman, smiling as she put the food into a bag. She wants to know about me, Sukey thought. She lived in the flat above with her husband and one or other of them, sometimes both, served. She had dull brown permed hair and always wore an overall: today it was blue check with a pink trim. She asked questions, too, and Sukey was certain she thought it odd that a girl of her age and with her accent was living apart from her family in a run-down house due for redevelopment. She'd once asked Sukey how old she was, and when Sukey said, 'Seventeen,' she'd raised her eyebrows. 'I thought you were even younger,' she'd said. Her husband was less curious. Not given to talking much, he would touch her hand as he gave her change and would gruntingly offer to come and fetch what she wanted from the higher shelves, needing to press close to her as he did so.

The shop woman passed over the bag and Sukey gave her some notes from Jaz's wallet. She took the change and it sat in her palm as she counted it. Enough for tobacco and papers, Jaz wouldn't mind, she thought.

They sat at the kitchen table and ate scrambled eggs and then toast and marmalade, slice after slice. Jaz stood up and put the kettle on for more tea. Sukey began to feel warm again. She couldn't remember the last time she'd eaten a meal. There'd been snacks from time to time. Yesterday she'd found a Mars bar at the back of a cupboard in the downstairs kitchen. She'd been rooting around seeing if there was anything worth having in the rest of the house.

'We're worried about you,' Jaz said as he laid tobacco on a cigarette paper.

'Who?'

'Me, Kitty. You shouldn't be alone in this house.'

'I have to stay. Just for another....' Sukey squinted, her eyes trying to remember how much longer the rent tribunal had given her to stay. 'What day is it?' she asked.

'Saturday,' Jaz said. 'Otherwise I'd be at college.'

'Yes,' said Sukey. 'I've got till next Friday.'

'You can move before then. You don't have to stay.' He was rolling the cigarette between two fingers.

'Pride. I want to make them wait.'

'And where are you going to go after Friday? You've got no money, you're not working.' Jaz licked the paper, pressed it down and reached into his pocket for his lighter. He passed the cigarette to Sukey, lit it for her and started to roll another.

'I'll get a job, find a bedsit,' Sukey said, feeling enormously tired.

'Kitty said you can come and live with us.'

'She just wants the rent money.'

'She said rent free until you get a job. You'll have to sleep in the kitchen though, all the rest's full.'

'Dennis still there, I suppose.'

'Yup. So, you going to come to us?'

Sukey looked at Jaz, his thin bony face with its too large nose and wide, thick-lipped mouth, his lank pale brown hair that had been blond when he was a child. She'd once seen an old photo of him and his family, all of them in front of their mansion, his parents and two older sisters in a line at the back and Jaz with his younger brother and sister in the front. None of them were well dressed but they still looked rich: an upper class family with left-wing leanings. Now Sukey watched Jaz bouncing his skinny knee up and down as he sat. He was always like that, couldn't be still, part of him always active, always moving. A few months ago, they'd tried to make love but it hadn't worked. There'd been no desire between them and they'd given up, lying side by side, naked. 'At least we gave it a go and now we know that we really don't want to,' he'd said, and they'd shared the joint he'd rolled and slept comfortably together in Sukey's narrow bed. He was still a virgin. Sukey sometimes wished that she were too.

'OK, I'll come and live in the flat.'

'I'll help. We can move today. The car's working now.' Jaz had an old Austin that was falling to bits. One of the doors wouldn't open and there were huge gaps in the floor that meant you had to be careful with your feet. It was always going wrong, but when his money came he usually spent a big chunk on fixing it. Jaz's parents being rich, he didn't have a student grant but instead a monthly allowance from a trust fund. He'd told Sukey this (apologising slightly, ashamed of his parents' wealth) and said that it was enough for him to live on but in the last week of each month he was almost always without money.

'Friday, I want to stay 'til Friday,' Sukey said.

When, just before Christmas, the landlord had told them that they had to move out, as they were now ready to finish the renovations, the art student from the bottom flat, who wasn't at home much anyhow, had left, and his flatmate, Ted, had moved to Kitty's flat to be with Minnie: he'd started sleeping with her soon after he'd met her. Sukey and Tessa stayed on and took the landlord to the rent tribunal. But a few days before the hearing, Tessa decided to go home to her parents and left Sukey to deal with it all. When the process started the tribunal officials discovered that Sukey was only seventeen and not old enough to take this type of legal action. But they gave her another month in the house and she no longer had to pay rent. Sukey remembered standing there in the old wood-panelled room while the men in suits and very short hair laughed at her age and audacity. She'd felt faraway and strange, as if she didn't really exist. The next day she'd stayed at home. After Christmas she'd stopped working in the department store where she and Tessa had found jobs when they'd first come to London, and registered with an office temping agency. So, because she wasn't a permanent employee, she didn't think it mattered if she stayed away from work. When someone from the agency called they sounded angry and she said she was sick. Then the phone stopped working, the bill unpaid. That had been a couple of weeks ago. Her life, Sukey thought, was becoming even more hazy and incomprehensible.

'Suit yourself,' Jaz said now, standing up and stretching. 'D'you want to come for a ride in the car? We could take some of your stuff, drop it off at Kitty's, see if anyone else wants to join us.'

'Where to?'

'Anywhere. Out of London a bit. Fill up the tank and see where we get to.' Jaz was striding round the small kitchen, moving jerkily. It was a good thing he was so short and slight, Sukey thought, as there was so little room.

When Sukey arrived back at the house it was late in the evening. Jaz had said she could stay the night at Kitty's flat. Dennis had gone to see his wife for the weekend, he told her, and he and Sukey could sleep with Kitty in her big bed. Beaky too, maybe. They did this from time to time. Sukey liked going to sleep with the press of friendly bodies round her. She liked waking up, enjoying the feeling of not being alone, nor threatened. But when they returned from their long aimless drive and they all climbed out of car – Beaky and Malc had come along, too, and Jojo, a girl Malc had recently met – Dennis had just come back in his taxi. He stood on the pavement watching as they spilled out. He shook his head: 'You lot, you're crazy, driving around in that heap,' and he spluttered a little as he breathed out. He shook his head, looking angry.

'Wife told you to piss off, did she?' Jaz asked, and Dennis turned and walked into the small front garden. He banged the door shut as he went in.

'I'll go home,' Sukey said and Jaz said he'd drive her.

'We'll all come,' Malc said. 'I think there's a party I heard of round your way.' He had his arm round Jojo. They'd been kissing in the car.

'Come to the party with us?' Jaz asked.

'OK,' said Sukey. When they couldn't find the party, they went to the pub on the corner opposite Sukey's house. She left them there just before closing time, feeling quite drunk although she'd only had two half pints, one of mild and one of cider. There was someone sitting on the steps that led up to the front door.

'Hey, Sukey,' said a voice. It was Dan. 'I've been here ages. You said you'd be in tonight.'

'Oooh, I'm so sorry, I forgot. You shouldn't have waited.'

'I've something for you.'

Sukey unlocked the door. Dan stood up and they climbed the stairs to the top floor flat. Slowly, as there were no lights. Dan followed Sukey and she could almost feel the round plumpness of his body behind hers. She tensed herself against the unspoken certainty that he wanted to sleep with her. She went into the kitchen, offered tea. He accepted, sat down, took a lump of dope out of his pocket.

'I got it for you, as requested.'

'Thanks.'

Sukey had met Dan in the street a few months ago. He was a songwriter and knew, or so he said, pop singers, writers and actors. He came to see her often, usually didn't stay long. Once he'd taken her out to dinner and another time to Hampstead at lunchtime in a taxi to the home of a famous poet. They went to a local pub and drank Barley Wine and Russian Stout and then they walked back to the poet's big house with its beautiful kitchen and little walled garden, a real home.

'My wife's away,' the poet said and the two men laughed as Dan opened a bottle of wine and the poet served a rich stew and a salad. Afterwards the poet played music and he and Dan discussed each song; often the poet would take the record off before it had finished, so eager was he to play another one, illustrate another point.

When Sukey felt the pain in her tummy that meant her

period was about to come, she leant forward, awkward and unhappy. Then she stood up. 'I'm going. Thanks for the meal and everything,' she said, and she was out of the door and running down the road. She heard them call after her. 'Don't leave me,' shouted the poet and when she heard footsteps behind her, she ran faster, all the way to Chalk Farm, with a pain in her belly and shaking legs. Dan had come to see her again the next day. Once he'd told her she was beautiful. How lovely she was with her very long, very blonde hair.

'Innocent,' he'd said, and Sukey, knowing how he wanted her, wondered why he never tried to take her to bed.

'Shall I roll us a joint?' he asked now.

'I've no money to pay for it,' she said, remembering the evening, just a day or two ago, when she'd asked Dan to get her some dope and she'd climbed into bed when he was still there and told him to go, she needed to sleep. He'd looked at her and said that was fine, and he'd have the stuff by Saturday evening. He'd left then. She'd listened to his small feet shuffling down the stairs. And here he was back again as promised.

'It's a present,' he said and smiled at her, his face round and earnest.

'I'm not going to sleep with you,' Sukey said feeling that finally she must make this clear.

'I know that,' he replied and he was still smiling; more or less.

(Sukey and Dan did sleep together many years later. By then, Dan had become sleek rather than chubby; Sukey had cut her hair, letting a few streaks of grey tone down its blondeness. Both were married to other people at the time and had just one afternoon together. It was not a great success but reminded them both of when they were young and life had seemed endless.)

Chapter 4
March 1967: Sukey

Sukey sat on the step outside the kitchen leaning against the door and slowly rolling a cigarette. She could hear Bridie and John from downstairs having a row, or rather she could hear the shout of Bridie's voice followed by a silence and then Bridie shouting again, even louder. She thought she saw a movement in the hall downstairs and leaned forward to see better. There was Dolores, lying on the floor with her eyes closed, sucking her thumb and twisting a piece of hair between her fingers. She opened her eyes and looked up at Sukey staring down. The thumb slipped out of her mouth and she sat up. Clinging onto the banisters with both hands, she started to climb the stairs.

'Hello,' she said as she reached Sukey, staring at her with big blue expressionless eyes.

'Hello,' said Sukey, not knowing what else to say. She wasn't used to young children.

'Mammy and Da are having a spat. She told me to wait in the hall and not be bold,' Dolores said. She talked a lot for such a small child, Sukey thought.

'They'll wake Baby John.' Dolores sounded just like her mother.

'They will,' Sukey said.

'And then there'll be hell to pay,' Dolores added, shaking her head. There was the sound of a bottle breaking and then a door banged and Sukey saw John striding through the hall and into the bedroom. He was followed by Bridie who slammed the door shut as she went in. Dolores had put her grubby hand on Sukey's knee and now she sat down next to her, her warm little body pressed close to Sukey. The shouting from downstairs went on and Dolores leant against Sukey.

'I'm thirsty. Can we go into your kitchen and have a drink of lemonade?' Dolores asked.

'Minnie's having a bath. I'm waiting for her to finish,' Sukey said, sighing. She re-lit her cigarette. She'd been here for just over two weeks now, moving in with Kitty and Dennis, Minnie and Ted, Jazz, Beaky and Malc; though Malc was not here very much, spending most of his time with Jojo. Downstairs was the Irish family who were noisy. And upstairs, behind their own front door, lived the landlord, who was Indian, and his wife and their two quiet little daughters. The landlord's wife did not speak English. Sukey rarely saw the landlord, his family even less. When they came in or went out they glided up and down the stairs without making a noise, the mother and the daughters with their heads bent, looking down, pressing against the walls should they encounter one of the other people who lived in the house, making themselves as small as possible as if apologising for existing. Sukey wondered what they thought of Kitty and her tenants, what they thought of John, Bridie and their constant fighting. She felt tremendously sorry that they should have all these strange activities taking place in their own house and sometimes wanted to explain to them that not all English and Irish people lived like this.

'Did you talk to the landlord about your plans for India?' Sukey had asked Minnie a few days ago.

'Of course not,' Minnie replied in her controlled way. She looked at Sukey, her face and nose sharp and cold. She pushed her lips together making them seem even thinner than usual and put her head one side, like a bird trying to fathom out the best way to tackle the worm.

'Why is Minnie having a bath in the day?' Dolores asked. Because, Sukey thought, all the others are either out or sleeping off their Saturday night bingeing and she doesn't mind telling me that she needs my room for an hour or so. But she said nothing to Dolores, who pulled at her arm and again asked: 'Why?'

Downstairs John lumbered out of the bedroom carrying a large shiny blue suitcase. He pulled open the front door and was gone. Bridie had followed him and now stood in the hallway, yelling after him: 'Good riddance and don't come back all mealy mouthed and apologetic later on.' She stood for a moment, her arms folded and then she banged the door shut and turned. 'Dolores, where the hell are you after getting to?' she called.

'I'm here Mammy.'

Bridie looked up. 'Which one are you?' she asked Sukey, who told her.

'That's right, the new one.' She laughed. 'Come down and have a coffee with me.'

'OK,' said Sukey. It would be so much better than sitting here waiting for Minnie who had already taken nearly half an hour and could be a lot longer. 'C'mon, Dolores,' she said, standing up and pulling the little girl with her.

'Have a real one,' Bridie offered an open packet of cigarettes before sitting down on the sofa opposite Sukey. She'd placed two coffee mugs on the table between them and Dolores was leaning against Sukey's chair sucking coke out of a bottle with a straw. The room was clean, warm and comfortable.

'Good riddance to bad rubbish,' Bridie said as she settled down and took a deep draw on her cigarette. 'He's a killjoy and a sourpuss.'

'John, you mean?' Sukey asked.

'The very one. John himself.'

'But, don't you want him back?'

Bridie laughed. 'Why should I? He's only good for one thing and that's putting food on the table.'

'How'll you manage?'

'I'll get onto the social, first thing tomorrer. And on top of that, I'll be able to earn a bit myself. I'll become a working girl again.' She winked at Sukey, grinning.

'But what about the children?'

'Night work, if you understand me.'

'Oh,' said Sukey, thinking that she did. 'Here?'

'Here, of course. The last time he went off, I did fine by myself; a few regulars. The ones that get it over nice and quick are the best. But John wanted us to have another go and as I was expecting the baby and beginning to show, I let him come back.'

'I don't know that I'd want to do it,' Sukey said slowly.

'If you're going to put up with it you may as well get paid for it. Don't tell me you haven't done it, hanging out with those yokes from upstairs.' Bridie leant forward, coughing, her face red from laughing. Sukey started to smile. For the first time for several weeks, she was almost happy; for months, she realised, she'd been feeling as if she was unreal and distant from other people, a physical feeling as if her blood was flowing slow and cold through her body.

'They're a strange lot your friends,' Bridie said.

'Yes,' Sukey said, wondering how she'd come to be sharing a flat in Camden Town with hippies and drug dealers, while an almost prostitute with two young children lived downstairs. She imagined her parents and how they lived, as if they were so very pleased with themselves and their large newly bought magnolia-painted house, tastefully decorated with antiques and thick rugs. She pictured her mother arranging flowers and preparing crème brulée for a dinner party, her father coming home from the office and pouring whisky into cut-glass tumblers before sitting down to enjoy the comfort of his well-looked-after home. She thought of her elder sister at university, her younger one still at boarding school, both of them planning to marry men with careers and prospects.

45

'You and that Minnie, are you sisters?'

'No,' said Sukey, sitting up straight. 'No, we're not, we're... we're not even friends.'

'Oh. I was sure you were cousins at the very least, you two are so alike.'

'Are we?'

'Not so much in looks, though you're both fair.'

'I'm blonde,' Sukey said, feeling that she could say such things to Bridie, 'and Minnie's mousy.'

'And you're both little.' Bridie raised her heavy bosom, put her hand on her cleavage and laughed. 'But mainly you've got the same sort of voices. You're both such posh girls.'

'I suppose we are,' Sukey said. She picked up her coffee cup, swirling it round and staring into it. She raised it to her lips and drank. 'I better be going,' she said.

'No need on my account. Have another fag. I've not got a dinner to cook tonight now himself has gone and I'm free till Baby John wakes up.'

'Anyone seen Malc?' Ted asked, opening the kitchen door. He came in, taking off his coat and hanging it over the back of the armchair.

'No,' said Sukey looking at the clock on the mantelpiece and wondering what time she'd be able to go to bed. Now that she had a job, a sort of job, she found sleeping in the kitchen difficult, so often one or the other of the other tenants would want to stay up late. She'd taken to getting into her pyjamas in the loo, spreading the cushions on the kitchen floor and covering herself with the blankets while two or more of them sat at the table, smoking and talking. Often she barely dozed, and when she did sleep well, she sometimes woke in the morning to the sound of Jaz and Beaky or Ted and Malc still at the table, stoned and rambling. She thought with longing of the empty house where she used to live and the long nights, often lasting well into the day, of deep, heavy sleep.

'I think Malc's more or less moved in with Jojo,' Kitty said. 'He's not given me the rent for this week.' She turned from the sink to wipe the table. Jaz raised his glass as Kitty and her cloth moved close to it. Sukey watched her plump body as she worked, thinking how nimble she was for someone so large.

'Right,' said Ted. 'Anyone seen Minnie?'

'She's gone to bed,' Kitty said as she let the water out of the sink and rinsed her cloth under the tap.

'So's Dennis.'

'Together?' Jaz asked.

'Don't be silly,' said Kitty. 'Some of us have jobs to go to. Monday morning tomorrow. Dennis has his cab; Minnie has the shop. I'm off too.' Kitty yawned, dried her hands on the tea towel and picking up her cigarettes and lighter left the room. 'G'night,' she said as she shut the door.

Ted, lifting his jumper and scratching his stomach, shuffled towards the fridge, opened its door, bent down to peer in before shutting it again and sitting at the kitchen table.

'No beer,' he said.

'No,' said Jaz.

'Any other booze?'

'No,' said Jaz.

'Dope?'

'No,' said Jaz.

Ted sighed, leant both arms on the table and put his head on them. Sukey saw that he was looking at her, where she sat, cross-legged on the floor. His eyes were half closed. If Jaz wasn't also sitting at the table, she was sure that Ted would ask her if she'd like to sleep with him in the same bored way that he used for all his brief conversations. He probably wouldn't be offended when she refused. Sukey wondered why Minnie bothered with Ted. They didn't seem to talk to each other much and it must be difficult having a sex life when they shared a room with so many others. Ted never had any money whereas Minnie worked, and it was she who had made all that effort to organise the Indian trip. Sukey sighed, leant back against the wall, wondering if Ted and Jaz would soon go to bed.

'I wanna get stoned,' Ted mumbled. 'Nobody got anything?'

'We could try smoking some of this food stuff.' Jaz stood up and opened the cupboard door. He was rooting around, 'pepper, flour, mixed spice, sultanas, semolina. No, don't think any of that would work.'

'Shall we go round to Jojo's, see if Malc or anyone's got anything?' Ted had sat up, was softly kicking the table leg with one foot.

'No,' Jaz said, 'best just all go to bed.'

'All together? In here? A threesome?' Ted sounded almost hopeful.

'No,' said Jaz. 'I know. Bananas.' He reached for the cracked bowl that Kitty used to put fruit in. It held two oranges and some wizened looking apples. And a banana which Jaz grabbed, waving it at Ted. 'Da, da, I think I read somewhere that you can get stoned on banana skins.'

'Eating them?' Sukey asked.

Jaz shrugged. 'Don't know.' He started to peel the banana, laying the skin on the table. 'Anyone want this?' he asked, his fist round the naked banana that looked both vulnerable and suggestive.

'You have it,' Sukey said and Jaz put his mouth down and licked the top of the banana.

Ted shook his head. 'Just eat it,' he said and Jaz did, gently stretching the banana skins with his free hand.

'How do we do it?' Jaz asked. He stood up, opened the cutlery drawer and took out a knife. Sitting down again he started to scrape the skins clean, piling the soft debris on the table. 'I know,' he said eventually, 'it's the inside of banana skins that you use. Sukey, come and get this and roll a joint with it.'

Sukey stood up and went to the table. She prodded the damp, yellow pile. 'It's too soggy,' she said. 'And in any case I don't believe that it can get you stoned.'

'We'll dry it in the oven.' Jaz suggested.

'OK, you do it, I'm going to get ready for bed.' It was nearly midnight and Sukey would be woken early tomorrow when Dennis and Minnie came into the kitchen, making tea and eating breakfast.

When she came back from the loo, pyjama-clad and with clean teeth, there was a slight smell of burning and Ted was busy with tobacco, papers and a little heap of brownish stuff. Sukey spread out her cushions, laid her blankets over them and watched as Ted lit the joint and inhaled.

'Well?' Jaz asked. Ted coughed. 'Bit odd,' he took another draw and then passed the joint to Jaz. When it was finished the three of them sat looking at each other, seeing if they felt stoned.

'I don't think it's worked,' Ted said.

'I do, I feel very strange,' Jaz said. 'You know what it's like when you first try dope, you have to learn how to feel the effect. It's the same with bananas. Sukey, how do you feel?'

'Odd,' she said, which was true, but how much this was just how she was these days and how much was the result of smoking the insides of banana skins, she didn't know.

'Definitely stoned,' Jaz said. 'I feel quite dizzy and overwhelmed.'

'I'm going to Jojo's, see if I can find Malc,' Ted said, standing up and pulling his coat off the chair.

'I'll come with you,' Jaz said, 'Maybe they've got more bananas.'

When Sukey moved into the Camden Town flat Kitty had told her about a man she knew who came to the pub most lunch times. He ate a sandwich, a packet of crisps and drank just one pint: never more. His name was Robin and he ran a domestic cleaning business, had clients all over North

London, and was looking for people to work for him.

'No tax, cash in hand and flexible working hours,' Kitty told Sukey, nodding as she spoke, being serious and helpful, Sukey thought.

'Right,' said Sukey.

'I've told him about you.'

Sukey raised her eyebrows.

'You can't live on nothing,' Kitty said. And what's more, you want your rent, Sukey thought. 'So he's expecting you,' Kitty continued. 'Come to the pub tomorrow, midday. If nothing else he'll buy you a drink.'

'Right,' said Sukey, wondering what Kitty would do and say if she ignored her.

'It's for your own good.' Kitty's voice had softened and Sukey nodded, resisting the temptation to say 'right' again. Kitty did try to look after them all. She might steal their money in order to be able to do it, but all of them in the flat gave in to her, let her take charge, boss them about. There was something comforting about her. She was looking now at Sukey, frowning. 'We have been worried about you, Jaz and I.'

'I'm OK,' said Sukey, not sure whether it was a lie. She thought back to September, eighteen months ago now, when she, Kitty and Jaz had met. Sukey had been just sixteen, Jaz seventeen and Kitty eighteen. She thought about that strange year at the alternative Arts College and wondered why the three of them had become friends. It had also been the place where she'd met Rick and where Ellen had died. She still marvelled that she'd managed to persuade her parents to let her go and that they'd agreed to pay for it. Years later she would realise they'd been desperate, understanding that she'd leave home in any case and hoping that this odd place might provide her with some kind of start in a career. Sukey, Kitty and Jaz had been part of a group of only a dozen drama students and at the end of the year they had come to London to live. Of the three, only Jaz was still interested in acting, having got himself a place at LAMDA.

'Well,' Kitty said now, still frowning. 'You'll be better with something to do all day.'

'Right,' said Sukey, nodding. And the next day she'd gone to the pub; she'd met the man, had satisfied him and was now working as a cleaner. Each session was a minimum of four hours, but her Monday client wanted her all day.

By lunchtime Sukey was exhausted. When she'd rung Mrs Zimmer's bell, still feeling tired from not enough sleep, the woman stared at her.

'Hello, I'm Sukey,' Sukey said. This was her first visit.

'Yes,' said the woman, looking her up and down, literally – she stood and her eyes moved from the top of Sukey's head to her feet and back again.

'For the cleaning,' Sukey said.

'Yes,' said the woman.

'Can I come in?'

'Yes,' said the woman and stepped back. All morning she followed Sukey round as she tried to improve the state of the already spotless house, going off from time to time and then reappearing. She made her clean one of the bathrooms three times, complaining that it hadn't been done properly. Sukey began to wonder if she'd be paid but finally the woman seemed pleased with the results. 'You'll learn,' she said.

At one o'clock, she sat Sukey down in the kitchen. 'Time to eat,' she said. She brought a tray and set it front of Sukey. There was a boiled egg in a cup, a triangle of processed cheese and two slices of some kind of seeded bread already buttered.

'How old are you?' asked the woman.

'Seventeen.'

'Thirteen, my goodness.'

'No, seventeen,' said Sukey, wondering if it had been a good idea to wear her hair in two long pigtails.

'Thirteen,' the woman repeated and went to open the fridge. She came back with a glass of orange juice that she placed on the tray.

'While you eat, I have my rest. Half an hour and then we start again. Very young, working at thirteen,' she said. She turned to leave and then, as if suddenly remembering, she plucked a large banana from the fruit bowl and handed it to Sukey.

'Banana,' she said. 'Very good, give you lots of energy.'

'Thank you,' said Sukey and she and the woman smiled at each other. She ate the banana along with the rest of her lunch and, when she was finished, peeled off some strands of its soft insides and chewed them slowly. She sat for moment quite still and then shook her head and threw the banana skin into the rubbish bin.

(When Sukey told her second husband that she wanted a divorce and it would be best if he left as soon as possible, he followed her round the house listing, in his whining American voice, all the things that he hated about her: one of them was the way she always completely skinned a banana before eating it. 'Poor, naked, defenceless fruit,' he whinged.)

Chapter 5
April 1967: Beaky

There wasn't any point in telling anybody how it was, how he felt about it, Beaky knew. In any case, he didn't know what it was he felt, and even if he did, he wouldn't be able to express it. What he needed to do, he thought, was to try and get away. But partly he didn't want to; mainly he didn't want to. It was great when they were all together in the kitchen. All except Kitty and Dennis who were rather like parents. Sukey had said that one night, lying on her mattress wearing nothing but a thin T-shirt and skimpy knickers. Looking at her, saying nothing, Beaky had really wanted to go and lie down next to her. He imagined being in bed with Sukey, holding her and all the rest. He wondered what it would be like to have sex with someone, especially someone like Sukey.

That had been one of the evenings when Jaz had been making joints from the inside of banana skins.

'Does it work?' Beaky had asked. Jaz had shrugged.

'The point is,' Sukey said, 'not if it works. The point is if you think it works, then you feel like you're getting stoned.'

Dennis snorted. Passed a cigarette to Kitty, took one himself and lit them. 'You lot,' he said. 'You'd smoke your own shit given half a chance.

Jaz laughed. 'Hey, Dennis, great idea, I'm just off to the loo. If I bring some back, will you roll it for us?'

'Disgusting.' Kitty said, exhaling loudly as she did when she wanted to emphasise what she was saying.

Dennis shook his head and finished his beer.

'D'you want another one?' Kitty asked.

'Nah, I'm off to bed in a mo. You coming?'

'OK,' Kitty said, and they took one of the ashtrays and left. It was then that Sukey said: 'It's like having your parents around with those two.'

'Yeah,' Ted said. He and Minnie were sitting on the one easy chair. She had her legs over one arm and he was holding her round the waist. Every now and then, his hand moved up to her breast and she would push it away.

That was the real problem, Beaky thought, remembering that evening as he finished rolling his cigarette. Sleeping with all those people, waking in the night sometimes and hearing Ted and Minnie at it.

He scratched his head and leant back. He should move out. But when he thought about it, there was a funny fluttery sensation in his chest. That's panic he said to himself, breathing deeply, trying to control it. Here he was alone in this flat, one of the few times it had happened, and he didn't really like it. Tuesday midday and everyone at work or college. Malc was probably staying at Jojo's place and Beaky was pretty sure that Ted had not been here last night. It should be the others moving out, he thought. After Kitty and Jaz, he'd been the next to move in, before Dennis and Minnie, before Malc and Ted; long before Sukey.

He'd come round when he'd seen the room share advertised in the shop window. He'd been the first and he'd liked the place, liked Jaz and didn't mind sharing. It was cheap, too, and he needed to spend as little money as possible because his student grant was small and his parents refused to help, even though they were supposed to make a contribution. So he'd moved in and it had been fine. Most of the others had been found like lame ducks and offered a bed, either by Kitty or Jaz. Sukey was OK, Beaky thought, and even Minnie, though soon after she'd moved in Ted had followed, thrown out of his place, he'd said. And Malc had just stayed once or twice after he was too stoned to go home. And then somehow he'd been there all the time, until he met Jojo. He should move in with her full time, Beaky thought.

He stood up when he'd finished his roll-up and yawned. He ought to be on his way to college: he'd already missed two lectures. Yup, he thought, better there than moping here.

The kitchen door opened slightly and Ted's head came round.

'Beak, you alone?' he asked.

'Yes.'

'Good,' Ted said and pushed the door fully open. He came in followed by a small, thin girl in a tiny skirt, high boots and a jacket so long it was only just shorter than the skirt. What he could see of her face was creamy with make up and her eyes dark and ornate.

'Hello,' she said in a small voice. Beaky nodded, watching as she came slowly into the room, her hand in Ted's. He didn't like her, didn't like the clothes she was wearing, the ridiculously long jacket, the silly skirt. He didn't like that her face was mostly hidden by her hair or the sly way she stood close to Ted as if needing his protection.

'Anyone in the bedroom?' Ted asked.

'No.'

'Ted,' said the girl in mock protestation, adding a thin giggle.

'Yeah,' said Ted, his arm round the girl now. He was grinning at Beaky.

'Dennis and Kitty out?'

'Yes,' said Beaky, frowning.

'C'mon, chick, there's a big bed waiting for us.' Ted and the girl left the kitchen, arms round each other, and Beaky, listening, thought he heard them going into Kitty's room. Not my business, he thought, but he knew he was angry and half-wondered why. It's Minnie, it's not fair on Minnie. But why should I care? he asked himself and shrugged in answer.

Minnie was in the kitchen sitting alone on the big armchair, her legs crossed and pulled up onto the seat. Each of her hands was gripping one of the chair arms and her head was pressed against the back, her chin up, her eyes closed. Once he saw her, Beaky moved quietly through the door and into the room, he sat down gently at the kitchen table and put his bag down trying not to make a sound.

He looked at her as he rolled his cigarette. Her face was very pale, there were grey rims round her eyes and her lids were slightly mauve. She had a thin, almost pretty face, Beaky thought, a small pointed nose, a straight mouth that could become firm when she was angry. Her body was little and her hair fair and silky. She was not a girl that he wanted to sleep with. There was, in spite of the delicate vulnerability she presented, something forceful and tense about her, as if she'd been forged from strong wire that was all coiled up and ready to spring.

Her eyes snapped open as Beaky fished matches out of his pocket. 'Oh, it's you,' she said and Beaky stopped himself from flinching. He stretched out the roll-up he'd just made, raising his eyebrows to ask if she wanted it. She leant forward and took it.

Once they were both smoking, Beaky realised that she was crying. Tears were rolling out of her eyes and every now and then she sniffed. He shifted in his chair, uncomfortable. He wanted to leave the room but didn't know how to do it.

'Have you got a tissue?' Minnie's voice was thick and watery at the same time.

'Oh… no,' Beaky said. 'Um, I'll get you some toilet paper.'

'Yes please,' Minnie said wiping the corner of her eyes with her fingers.

He came back and Minnie took the wadded paper and wiped her face as if she were a young child. She sighed and pushed a wisp of hair behind one of her ears. Beaky noticed that they were large with sinewy, pink rims. He cleared his throat and wondered if he should offer her another roll-up. He peered into his pouch: there wasn't much tobacco left. There wouldn't be enough left for tonight if he made them each another cigarette. He looked up; Minnie was staring at him, the wadded toilet roll still in one hand. She looked quite frightening, quite angry.

'Has Ted ever said anything to you about me?' she asked, her voice accusing.

'No.'

'Hm... Sure?'

Beaky said nothing.

'I think he's found someone else. He didn't come home last night.'

'He's done that before,' Beaky offered, hating the way his heart was beating with anxiety, hating the way he was scared that Minnie was going to create an even more emotional scene; ask questions that he might be tempted to answer truthfully. He stifled a burp, and then another.

'Yes, exactly.... You're a man, Beaky, what do you think?'

'About what?' Beaky hated the way his voice seemed to have become unbroken. He cleared his throat ready for the next thing he might say.

'About if Ted's found someone else,' Minnie enunciated clearly, as if she thought Beaky was stupid. He realised that this was the first time he'd ever had a proper conversation with Minnie. Usually there were other people about, or they didn't speak. He wondered where everyone was. Kitty had probably started the evening shift, Malc would be with Jojo, Dennis might well still be driving his taxi about; he often worked at this time, ferrying people home or taking them to bars or restaurants. But Sukey should be here, Jaz too. And Ted, where was Ted?

'Does saying nothing mean 'yes'?' Minnie asked and Beaky felt his face growing hot, knew it was turning red. He swallowed and decided.

'Yes, it does. Ted had a girl here today, a horrible girl. He took her to Kitty's bedroom.' Beaky looked down as he spoke, continued to look down as he felt Minnie's silent response. He imagined her face screwing up in anger, wondered if she'd shout at him.

Carefully, after a little while, Beaky raised his head. Minnie was staring at him, her eyes wide and glassy, her cheeks mottled pink as if someone had slapped them hard. She nodded when she saw Beaky looking at her.

'I knew,' she said, and bit her lips, which had turned hard and rubbery. 'What did she look like? Was she skinny with lots of make-up and long dark hair?'

Beaky thought for a while; was the hair dark? He just remembered it covering her face as if she wanted to hide. 'I think so,' he said. 'She had it so you could hardly see her.'

'Yes,' said Minnie, spitting. 'She's staying at Jojo's. I thought Ted liked her.' She stood up, started to walk round the kitchen, filling the space. At one point she leant against the wall and banged her head against it. Beaky reached into his tobacco pouch and started to roll a cigarette. His fingers were trembling.

'Come on, Beaky,' Minnie said and she was standing next to him. 'Let's go to bed. Kitty's bed.'

Beaky looked up from licking the cigarette paper. He felt the tobacco fall from his fingers and frowned at the waste.

'Don't you want to? Have sex with me?' Minnie asked. She touched the back of his neck with the palm of her hand. It felt cool and strong.

'I haven't any....' Beaky started, swallowing another burp.

'It's OK, I've got a cap. I'll go and put it in. See you in the bedroom.'

Beaky sat gathering the tobacco into a little pile. He pinched it up and put it back in the pouch. Then he stood up and opened his hands to look at them. It wasn't just his fingers; his whole body was shaking. He felt immensely excited at the thought of Minnie taking her clothes off, of being naked with her. And also scared, deeply scared. He should refuse: he didn't want Minnie as a girlfriend. He closed his eyes, thinking of girls he'd lusted over and had been too shy to approach, knowing they'd turn him down. He licked his lips and slowly walked out of the kitchen, up the few stairs and into Kitty's bedroom.

The curtains were closed. The room was dark and cool; Minnie's pale face lay on the pillow. He could see the knuckles of both hands where she was holding the bedclothes tight against her. He sat on the bed and took off his shoes and socks. He was still wearing his jacket and he pulled it off and then his jumper. He turned to look at Minnie. Her eyes were closed. Quickly he undid his jeans and climbed in beside her. After a bit he cupped her elbow with his hand and then slowly let it move across her body. He raised his head and looked down at her; he bent to kiss her and felt her respond. She turned to him and pressed herself against him. He moaned and began to kiss her desperately, pushing his tongue into her mouth and one leg between hers. His hand found her small breast and he kneaded it. He felt her hands go inside his underpants and he gasped, wondered how soon he could enter her, how he would do it. His head, his body, all of him was ready to explode.

'No!' Minnie was pushing him away. He tried to hold her tight to him, keeping his mouth on hers. She twisted her face away, pulled herself up so that he was forced to let go. He turned to lie on his back, breathing heavily. She had moved to the edge of the bed, and was sitting holding the bedclothes against her.

'I'm sorry, Beaky, I can't. I just can't.' She was crying now and she let go of the bedclothes so that Beaky could see her sloping shoulders and naked breasts that shook slightly as she sobbed. He wanted to touch them again, to force Minnie down so that he could lie on to top her. He blinked, watching as she cried and the desire passed. He felt guilty, almost nauseous and as if he'd had a great escape. What would have happened afterwards if they'd had sex? How would he have felt?

'It's OK,' he mumbled and slid out of the bed. He sat and looked down at his legs and the slight damp stain on his underpants. He reached for his jeans and when they were on, turned round to face Minnie. He should offer her something, but he wasn't sure what.

'I'm so horrible,' she said. 'That was a cruel thing to do.'

Beaky wasn't sure which part was the cruel part, the offer of sex or its withdrawal. He needed a cigarette, a drink. He'd go to Kitty's pub and see if Jaz or Sukey were there. He could sit with them until he felt better.

'I'm moving into the bedroom,' Sukey said. It was early Saturday evening. Kitty had cooked a big stew of white beans and leeks. Minnie had just come back from the shop and they were all sitting round the kitchen table. Kitty and Dennis, Sukey and Minnie, Jaz and Beaky. Ted and Malc had gone. The previous evening Malc had come to fetch his stuff and to say that he and Ted were now living at Jojo's. Without them the place felt, Beaky thought, more comfortable, in spite of the anger and sorrow coming from Minnie that made it hard for him to eat without getting indigestion. He'd be able to stay here, he thought, at least for a little while.

'Ted and Malc still owe me for rent,' Kitty said as she ladled out the stew. Dennis was cutting slices from a big loaf of Greek bread: we're almost like a family, Beaky thought.

'You won't get it,' Jaz said. 'It was hard enough when they lived here.'

'Stop talking about them,' Minnie said. Ted hadn't come home on the night when she'd offered herself to Beaky. The following day when Beaky came back from college he'd found her crying in the bedroom. Ted's clothes were gone, his few books, his razor and sponge bag.

'He didn't even tell me he was leaving,' she'd screamed, and then crawled across the floor to Beaky and grabbed his legs. 'Hold me,' she'd yelled, and he'd bent down and cautiously patted her back. After a while he knelt and took her in his arms, rocking her like a baby. With relief, he realised that there was nothing sexual in this close encounter and he rather enjoyed being the comforter.

(Two and a bit years later, Beaky got a first class degree and went on to do a Ph.D. He became a lecturer, married twice and tried hard to resist sleeping with his more attractive female students. The one he failed to resist became his third and most cantankerous wife, mother of most of his children. Now known as Col, he sometimes goes very slightly out of his way to pass the house where once he lived in Kitty's flat and marvels at the memory of his shy innocence and how he managed to live with such strangeness.)

Chapter 6
April 1967: Sukey

Beaky looked up as Sukey came into the kitchen. He was sitting cross-legged at the table rolling a joint, a mug and a plate with a sandwich in front of him. The sun was coming through the windows, lighting up the scratched surface of the table and the bare patches of the almost worn out linoleum just about covering the floor. There was a bunch of daffodils in a milk bottle on the windowsill and the place looked as if it had recently been cleaned. Plates, cutlery and the two large pans had been washed and were drying on the draining board. Kitty must have had one of her domestic days.

Sukey inhaled deeply, surprising herself with the feeling that was spreading almost tangibly through her: optimism, a gladness that she was who she was and that she was in this place at this time. She let out a deep, happy sigh, stroking her throat as contentment seemed to gather in her chest.

'It's great to be back,' she said. Late Sunday afternoon and here she was after a rare weekend visit to her parents.

They'd wanted her to leave later, but she'd resisted. They'd driven her to the station and her father had paced the platform as Sukey sat with her mother waiting for the train to arrive. She stood at the carriage window waving, feeling the heavy turn of the wheels as the train slowly gathered speed. Her parents waved back, her father hearty and smiling, her mother sad and confused. She said so often how she could not understand why Sukey continued to live in London and why she came so infrequently and reluctantly to visit.

Once the train had left the station, Sukey found herself a seat in a smoking compartment and celebrated the freedom of once again being apart from her parents by rolling a cigarette. They reached London with its familiar sounds and smells and, almost exultantly, Sukey had ridden the tube to Camden Town. And now here she was back in this shabby house where she lived. Her mother had told her not to be stupid when she referred to the flat as home. 'This is your home, with me and your father. And your sisters,' she'd said sharply, pursing her mouth. Sukey hadn't replied. In her head she retorted: 'When you're sent to boarding school at eight years old, you can't be expected to ever feel comfortable again living with your parents.'

'Well,' she said, sitting at the table. 'Where is everyone?'

Beaky licked the length of the cigarette paper and finished making the joint. Then he put it in his mouth and lit it before replying. 'Dunno. They've all gone out.' He passed the joint to Sukey, took a big swig from his mug and, looking down, started to eat his sandwich.

'Haven't you just had a meal?' Sukey asked.

Beaky blushed, a rather deep red. 'You know Kitty: a big pot of veg and another of potatoes. You're still hungry after.'

'Yeah,' Sukey said, and passed the joint back to Beaky. She looked at him as he smoked, one of his hands still holding the sandwich. She sometimes felt in spite of his silence, maybe even because of it, that Beaky disapproved of them all. Not Jaz, he seemed to like him, but certainly her and probably the others. She sometimes thought he was arrogant, but then she'd decide he was shy. She wondered if he fancied her; she sometimes thought he did but he never tried anything. She took the joint again and imagined what it would be like if he moved across to kiss her and how she would respond.

'There's a party tonight,' Beaky mumbled.

'Sunday evening?'

'Yeah.'

'So, tell me more,' Sukey said, leaning on the table and staring at him.

He shuffled, re-crossed his legs.

'Go on.'

'Some drama people, friends of Jaz's.'

'Are you going?'

Beaky took the joint as she proffered it to him. 'Dunno.'

'Where is Jaz? He's going, I assume.'

Beaky shrugged.

It was still early evening when Jaz and Sukey arrived at the address. A small dark girl with big round breasts and a beautiful face opened the door. 'Jaz,' she almost screamed and put her arms round him, hugging him to her. Jaz hugged her back and Sukey stood waiting as they held each other tightly, rocking back and forth. Finally, they let each other go. The girl was still smiling up at Jaz and kept a hand on his wrist.

'This is Anna,' he said. 'She's in my year at college. And this is Sukey, a flat mate.'

They went in. There were several rooms leading off a big hallway which also acted as a living area. Sukey and Jaz followed Anna as she led them to the other end of the flat and into a big shabby kitchen. A dining table was pushed against the far wall and at one end of it was a tray on which there were the remains of bread and cheese. Most of the rest of it was covered with bottles, many of which were already empty. Anna took three plastic beakers from the pile on the table while Jaz opened the wine they'd brought. The floor was sticky with spilt drinks and the place smelled of dope and sweat. Sukey took her wine and went to stand by the door of one of the rooms where people were dancing. The party must have been going on for some time, she thought, and wondered whether to just go home. There weren't many people here, but they were all already drunk or stoned and Sukey knew none of them. A man stumbled up to her and asked her to dance. She accepted.

After they'd danced, he left her leaning against the wall while he went to find something to drink. She closed her eyes for a minute and when she opened them, Jaz was there.

He leant towards her and spoke close to her ear so as to

be heard above the music. 'There's someone wants to meet you.'

'Who?'

'Come with me.'

So Sukey followed Jaz. She saw the man she'd been dancing with in the hall, talking to another girl. He's forgotten all about me, she thought. Jaz opened the door to one of the other rooms. Sukey followed, closing it behind her. It was dark and she blinked, waiting for her eyes to become used to the absence of light. She took a step forward and looked around. It was a small room. In one corner was a brass bedstead, not quite a single, not quite a double. Next to it was a chest of drawers on which several candles and a joss stick were burning. There was an armchair in another corner; Anna, the small dark girl, was curled up in it. On a heap of floor cushions against the wall by the door two men were sitting. Sukey wasn't sure what she was doing there or why Jaz had brought her.

'Come and join us,' said one of the men and Sukey turned to look at him as Jaz went to perch on the arm of Anna's chair.

'I'm Matthew,' the man said and he patted the cushion next to him. Sukey went to sit next to him, sliding down and sitting with her knees bent upwards, her arms wrapped round them. She stared ahead of her and said nothing.

'Right,' said the other man, the one who hadn't so far spoken, 'I'll go and see if I can find us a bottle.' He stood up and left the room, walking softly.

Matthew put his hand on Sukey's arm. 'Relax,' he said,

staring at her, putting his face very close to hers. He was in his twenties, Sukey guessed. He had a round face, long curling hair and sad pale eyes. He shifted his long legs and Sukey noticed how thin they were. His arms were thin, too, and his chest, but underneath that he had a little pot belly. Sukey couldn't help noticing its slight wobble. In spite of this, she found him attractive, possibly because he seemed most interested in her. He's good-looking, she thought, but I'm not sure if I like him.

'Jaz tells me your name is Sukey. I like that name very much.' His thumb gently rubbed the inside of her arm and, very slightly, he tightened his grip.

'Matthew writes plays,' Anna said.

'Oh,' said Sukey.

'I'm also a drama student,' he added.

'Final year,' Jaz said.

Matthew's face was still close to Sukey's; his hand was still on her arm, his thumb still stroking her skin. She wasn't sure what she was supposed to do or say. She wondered if Mathew wanted to sleep with her or if there was another purpose to her being brought in here.

'Don't be shy,' Matthew said and he moved his hand, pushing her back against the cushion. 'I want to look at you. I saw you coming in, and I thought how innocent you looked and how I'd like to know you better.'

Sukey lay back, stretched her legs, tried to think of something to say. The other man came in with an open bottle and some beakers. 'I think this is the last of the drink,' he said as he poured and passed round the wine.

Matthew had put his arm round Sukey. 'Someone roll a joint,' he said, 'my gear's in the top drawer.' He indicated the chest, flapping his hand loosely. It was Jaz who stood and found the dope.

Little was said until the drinks and the joint were finished. Matthew pulled Sukey closer to him. 'Would you like to stay with me tonight?' he asked.

Sukey struggled to sit up. 'Not tonight,' she said, afraid. It was too easy, always too easy these days, to sleep with someone just because they asked you. 'I like you,' she said very quietly, hoping he'd suggest they meet again.

'Stay,' he said. He was sitting up now and had one hand on her shoulder while with the other he stroked her hair. 'You're very sweet.'

Sukey shook her head, though she smiled at Matthew.

'I want you,' he said, sounding serious and very grown up. Sukey swallowed, knew she could easily accept, already she was beginning to be aroused. She wondered if she could cope with Matthew, would know the sort of things to say with him, to keep him interested. Often with men she felt flat and empty and didn't know how to behave.

'Speak to me, little Sukey, ' he said, 'say you want me, too.'

Sukey bit her lower lip. Probably, she told herself, he'd like to have sex tonight and thought she'd be easy.

Matthew pulled her to him, pressed her against his chest and stroked her head. She breathed in his scent: the muskiness of patchouli, an acid tinge of new sweat, the sweetness of dope and wine, all overlaid by the everyday smell of soap. She wondered what he was like. She felt that he thought he was significant and she wished she felt the same about herself. She was tempted to let him hold her, to give in and relax against him. Instead, she pulled away.

'Are you frightened of me?' he asked.

'A little,' she said. It wasn't so much the truth, more that she felt it was the right thing to say, as if she was following a script rather than thinking for herself.

'I'm not going to ask you again, I'm not going to beg.'

'No, I understand. I'd like to stay with you sometime, but not tonight.' Sukey could feel her heart beating fast as if amazed at this audacity. It was she, Sukey, and not he, Matthew, who was taking charge. She pulled further back, was ready to stand up. She went on looking at him.

His smile was sweet, a dimple appearing on one side of his mouth. He seemed genuinely amused. 'At least kiss me goodnight,' he said.

Sukey stood up, and so did he. She lifted her face and raised her arms, placing her hands on his shoulders. He bent and kissed her. His mouth was soft and his kiss a little slow and flabby, a little disappointing. Nevertheless, Sukey thought, if he asks I'll see him again.

She was nervous, wondering if he'd remember last Sunday and that he'd asked her to come to see him on Friday evening. He'd stood on the pavement outside the flat, watching as Sukey and Jaz walked away. He'd called: 'I'll see you soon, Sukey,' and then the door had shut.

Jaz had asked why she hadn't stayed with him and she'd told

him that she wasn't sure why not, but partly she wanted to see if he could wait. Sukey asked Jaz why he wasn't spending the night with Anna and he replied, rather scornfully, that she wasn't a girlfriend, just the favourite of his fellow students.

Sukey said: 'It's time you had a girlfriend, Jaz,' and he just shrugged.

Then he'd added: 'You need a boyfriend, but I don't think it'll be Matthew.' When she asked why not, he'd shrugged again and after a bit added: 'It's too complicated.'

Now here she was on Matthew's doorstep and hoping that it would be he who came to let her in and not Anna, or one of the other drama students who lived in this big flat.

Sukey heard footsteps coming down the hall and turned to face the street. The door opened and someone said: 'Hello.' It was the voice of the other man from Sunday, the one who'd fetched the wine and poured it out. It was not Matthew. Sukey swung round. She smiled and replied, 'Hello'.

'You were here the other night,' the man said.

'Yes,' said Sukey. 'Um, is Matthew in?'

'Oh, sure. Come in.'

Sukey followed him into the flat and waited as he stood outside Matthew's room.

'You've a visitor,' he called, knocking on the door, which opened.

'Sukey,' Matthew said, and she wasn't sure if the tone was surprise or pleasure.

'Of course I was glad to see you, of course I was expecting you,' he said later when they were in bed.

When she'd first arrived, she'd sat awkwardly in the armchair while he finished dressing, pulling on his boots, buttoning his shirt. He stood in front of the mirror and briefly brushed his hair.

'I thought we'd just go and have something to eat first.' He said, taking a jacket from behind the door. He held her hand on the way to the little Greek café where he said the food was cheap and authentic.

When they were sitting down at a corner table at right angles to each other, she could feel his foot against hers. They talked about drama while they ate and drank. Sukey told him she no longer wanted to be an actress and he said, 'What a shame,' and laughed. He told her about the play he'd written and the one he was writing. It was about a man who was obsessed by ears. Whenever he met someone the first thing he noticed about them was their ears: their shape, size, position, texture, colour. After that, he kept seeing other ear aspects, like if they were hairy or whether they moved when their owner spoke. It made it difficult for him to have relationships.

'But of course,' he said, 'the hero is also a man in love trying to win a beautiful lady.'

'Does he?' Sukey asked, having been unable to think of anything sensible to say about the ear obsession.

'Yes, but it doesn't work out.'

'Why not?'

Matthew didn't reply. 'Let's go back,' he said instead. He called for the bill and paid it and then as they were leaving, he said: 'She turns out to be the perfect woman for him. But she won't let him look at her ears. She's convinced that there's something wrong with them and that if he sees them he'll stop loving her.'

'Oh,' said Sukey, she could think of no intelligent-sounding comment: she wondered if the story he was telling was ridiculous or if the lack was in her perception. Probably herself, being unconnected to what things mean and unable to work out what's significant, she decided, rather sadly. As she tried hard and unsuccessfully to form a suitable response, they walked along side by side and in silence for a few minutes. They came to a corner and he put an arm round her. After a few steps, he pulled her roughly to him and was kissing her, holding her so tightly Sukey felt that she could hardly breathe. When finally he pulled away, he said: 'I want you so badly.'

Back in his bedroom, they made love on the floor, their clothes half off. It was too fast for Sukey and Matthew sensed that.

'Come on,' he said, 'let's get into bed and we'll do it properly. I'm sorry, it's been so long since I was with a woman.'

If she was going to be honest, Sukey didn't especially like the next time they made love, either. Now that he was no longer driven by lust fuelled by abstinence, she found Matthew almost too slow and gentle. His kisses were soft and the way he touched her felt like artifice, as if he was acting the part of a man making love. But then, she thought, he is a drama student and he does write plays. She found him less threatening and she told him she wasn't sure that he'd remembered that he'd asked her to come round. That was when he said that of course he did and that he was glad to see her. They made love again and this time Sukey came, but it was because she felt she should rather than because his lovemaking caused it. In her head she told herself to stop being so critical: Matthew was an attractive and interesting man. And she really did hope that he would want to see her again. This part was true, she wanted a boyfriend and this was a role she hoped Matthew could play.

In the morning she woke and turned her head and there was Matthew staring at her: his eyes grey, cold and sad.

'It's late,' he said, 'and I've got to be somewhere else.'

Sukey sat up. 'Sorry,' she said, wondering if at the very least he'd offer her a cup of tea.

'No,' said Matthew, 'don't be sorry. I'm sorry.' He had sat up and was rubbing his forehead with his hand. With a shock, Sukey realised that he was close to tears.

'What is it?' Suddenly bold, she asked: 'What have I done wrong?'

She watched the tendons in his neck tighten as he tried not to cry and then he gave a strangled snort and was sobbing. It didn't last long and Sukey just lay down again and waited for it to be over.

Matthew sniffed loudly and reached over to open a drawer in the chest next to the bed. He pulled out a framed photograph and passed it to Sukey. 'It's her,' he said.

Sukey sat up and held the frame in both hands. It was of a girl with big bulging eyes and a long chin. Not beautiful, Sukey thought, and there was something about her smile, distant, almost cruel, as if she was setting out to be hurtful.

'That's my lovely lady,' Matthew said. 'I thought, well I thought I was over her.'

Sukey rubbed her thumb over the photo. 'She looks a bit like Virginia Woolf,' Sukey said.

'Yes,' Matthew took the photo. 'She's mad, too. That's why we're not together. She's been in a mental hospital for over a year.' He took Sukey's hand under the bedclothes and turned to look at her. His face was open and for the first time Sukey felt that he'd stopped pretending to be whatever it was he thought he needed to pretend to be.

Then he spoiled it by saying: 'I'm in love with a mad woman and I don't seem to be able to get over her. There's something so compelling about insanity. ' And Sukey felt he was back playing a role again.

'Well, Matthew,' she said bravely, using his name for the first time. 'I don't think I can compete with that. I'll leave now.'

'Yes. I need to go and see her. I need to do that today.'

Sukey got up and dressed. She left immediately, without washing. Opening the door of Matthew's bedroom the words "another man, another failure" came into her head. She stopped for a minute, in mid-stride, waiting for the rush of sadness or some other similar feeling. Nothing came, just a flat blankness. As she closed the door behind her, she said goodbye very softly.

(Although she only spent one night with Matthew, she heard of him from time to time through Jaz. He eventually married his ill girlfriend and they lived precariously together. It was when Sukey was herself learning about insanity that she remembered him, their very short time together and why it could not have developed. She thought with disdain of Matthew's love for a woman he called mad, as she found mental illness profoundly unromantic.)

Chapter 7
May 1967: Tessa

Tessa stood with her hand on the broken gate. She made a face at the inappropriate brightness of its peeling blue paint and scratched at it with one nail-bitten finger. She thought about turning round and going back: back to Victoria station and getting on the next train home. But no, she told herself. She'd hated the last few months living with her parents and working at a boring shop in the local town, her mother not saying anything, looking at her with her eyes blinking too fast and her mouth a tight line. Tessa knew all the words that wanted to spill out and that her mother kept inside, scared that her daughter would leave home again if she said too much. Her father was as bad, worse even; coming to sit next to her after dinner in the evenings and patting her hand, telling her how lovely it was for him to have a daughter, asking her what she really wanted to do and could he help her.

'No,' Tessa would say, and shake her head in the vague way she'd developed as protection against penetrating questions. She sometimes wondered why she'd left London and then would shiver, remembering the cold when neither she nor Sukey had money for the gas, the dirty hugeness of the place and the loneliness of feeling like a little girl with few friends. She thought about the art student who'd lived on the ground floor and the time she'd gone to the pub with him and then into his bed. She'd come down to his room a few days later, given a fragile knock on his door and crept in so softly, apologising with her awkwardness for being there at all. He'd told her to go away, he didn't want her around. She'd gone back upstairs and had sat cross-legged on the floor for a long time, not feeling, just thinking.

She told Sukey what happened but as if it didn't matter. She told the story in the only way she could, with no expression in her voice, wanting Sukey to give it meaning for her. She hadn't and so Tessa had added an ironic twist to her tale: 'I only went back to see if I'd left my hairbrush there.' When Sukey smiled as if she wasn't interested in what Tessa was saying, she'd felt so tired and knew that soon she would have to go and find somewhere where living required less effort. She made the mistake of thinking that her parents' home would do.

Here she was now, back in London. She looked up at the house, with its old red bricks held together with crumbling plaster. Tessa wondered if she really wanted to be here, back in London with Sukey and Sukey's flatmates. Her letters had been full of all sorts of people and events; everything punctuated with exclamation marks and suggestive lines of dots. When Tessa had written to ask if maybe there was room for her, Sukey had replied that it would be crowded but there was a little bit of space if she didn't mind sharing with several others.

Tessa sighed heavily; this place must be better than the half-derelict house that she and Sukey had found back in July the year before. She lifted up her suitcase and went through the gate. She tried to shut it, but the catch was broken and it swung back out again, creaking and leaning at an angle. The paving stones in the front garden were covered in moss and looked as it they were always damp. There was a little round flowerbed, weedy and full of unattractive stones.

The hedge was thick and untidy; it gave off an unpleasant smell and there was rubbish and old plastic bags settled round its roots.

She stood on the front step. There were three bells by the door. Sukey's letter had told her to ring the middle one. She heard it ring inside the house, a small apologetic sound. After a while, she rang again, pressing her finger more firmly on the bell. This time she heard a door banging as it closed and then the run of feet down stairs and Tessa exhaled deeply, waiting to see who it would be.

'Oh Jaz, hi,' she said.

He looked at her, frowning, his hand still on the door. 'Yes?' he said and he clenched his lower lip with his teeth. Tessa watched as his teeth gradually slid up, finally releasing the lip. She saw his frown deepen. She waited, not moving, not speaking, wanting to see if he would finally recognise her.

'Um,' he said after a bit. 'Sukey's friend?'

She nodded, forming words in her head before she spoke them: she liked the way they strung together, thought they sounded clever and significant. 'I am she,' she said. Jaz raised his eyebrows. He didn't smile and Tessa didn't give her name.

'Come in then.' Jaz pushed the door open and turned. He ran back up the stairs and, laden with her case and a big, heavy bag, Tessa followed more slowly.

Tessa woke and lay still, listening to the breathing all about her. The window was open. Now and then a small breeze gusted through it, flapping the curtain a little; it made a faint slap of sound each time it hit the sill as the wind stopped. Day was coming and the light that crept round the sides of the curtain was growing stronger as Tessa lay in this room full of people. Sukey was next to her and Minnie in a corner, on the far side of Sukey. Jaz and Beaky shared a large mattress that was pushed into the bay window. Quietly, Tessa raised her arm and peered at her watch. It was nearly seven on a Sunday morning and she'd not gone to bed till nearly three. She turned over, pulled the bedclothes over her head and tried to sleep again. But she was desperately thirsty, needed to pee and felt uncomfortable in this room thick with sleep. And then there was the smell: sweat, tobacco, dope, stale alcohol, the patchouli oil that Minnie wore and a sour overtone that Tessa couldn't quite place. The scent of overcrowding, she told herself: underwear worn too long, unwashed bodies, human gases from nocturnal burps and farts, a submerged need for sex.

When she came back from the loo and a long drink of water, she heard Jaz whimpering as he slept. Tessa stood by the door; she was wearing white cotton socks that she'd had at school and over her knickers an old pyjama top that had once been her father's. She liked its bagginess and the colour of its pale stripes. Jaz murmured something and turned, pushing the bedclothes down his body. He was pale and bony, his skin was clammy and he had tiny nipples, dark and surprising on his white chest. Tessa could see that he had both hands stuck firmly between his legs. She hardly dared to move, scared she'd wake up one of these roommates she'd just acquired. She almost shuddered, wondering why she was here. But, she thought, it's so much better than being boringly at home and soon something exciting will happen to me.

'Hey.' Beaky was sitting up slowly, he yawned. He was looking at her. Tessa wasn't sure what to do, whether to go back to her mattress, to say something to Beaky, to leave the room again and make tea in the kitchen. She sighed, pulled down the front of her pyjama jacket, thinking about how Beaky could see how fat and wide her thighs were. She found that she was smiling at him and when he smiled back, she felt as if they were sharing a conspiracy.

The afternoon before, when she'd arrived and only Jaz and Beaky had been in, Beaky had been kind to her. She'd not known who he was at first and he'd said little, but he'd offered her a share in the sandwich he was making and gave her a cup of coffee. The others were all out. She'd followed

Jaz up the stairs and had gone through the door into the kitchen.

'Hello,' she said, standing with her case behind her and her bag over her shoulder, which was aching. A man with very dark hair and large, almost black eyes, a spotty skin and a ridiculously small nose looked up from slicing bread.

'Beaky, this is Sukey's friend,' Jaz said. He was now sitting in the one armchair in the room and was drinking from a bottle. Tessa wasn't sure if it contained red wine or Ribena. His knee was jigging up and down and he had dark rings round his eyes as if he'd not slept for a long time. She was standing by the door; quite still. She waited to see if he would use her name. Beaky was holding the knife in one hand, his other was placed protectively over the bread.

'Aren't you going to tell us what you're called?' Jaz asked after what seemed like a long time.

Disappointment hit Tessa. He should know who I am, he's met me before, she thought. 'I'm sorry I'm so insignificant that you can't remember who I am,' Tessa said, slow and ponderous, hoping to impress the two men with the way she spoke: sophisticated, she thought.

Jaz shrugged. 'I'm sorry, too, but I only met you a few times.'

Often enough, Tessa thought, for me to know who you are. 'I am Tessa,' she said, trying to sound amused and worldly. And succeeding too, she thought. 'Where shall I put my things?'

'Oh. In the bedroom,' Jaz said and he opened his mouth in an enormous yawn, showing large white teeth.

'And am I supposed to know by psychic or other talents where that might be located?' Another good sentence, Tessa thought. They should realise by now she was not a trivial person.

Jaz looked at her properly for the first time. He shifted in his seat, took another swig from the bottle. 'It's up the stairs and the door on the right,' he said. 'You'll have to put your stuff where you can. We'll sort out who gets what mattress later when everyone's home.'

Beaky put down the knife. 'I'll help you,' he said. She followed him up to the bedroom. He drew back the curtains and opened one of the windows. Then he cleared a shelf in the wardrobe and moved some stuff along a rail so that that there was a small space for Tessa to hang her clothes.

'Bit of a mess,' was all he said as he left her in the room.

After Tessa had unpacked a little, she came back to the kitchen. Jaz had gone. When she and Beaky were sitting silently eating sandwiches and drinking coffee, Sukey came in.

'Tess,' she said. 'Should have been here, sorry. But well, I went to a party last night and got stranded.' She laughed and Tessa remembered how annoying she was, with her long blond hair and naked feet.

Later, when everyone else had come home, they went to Kitty's pub for a while, before ending up back in the kitchen smoking dope and drinking whisky from a bottle that Kitty had stolen. She hadn't told them she'd stolen it, but Jaz said she had. Beaky said nothing all night, but every now and then when Tessa looked up he was watching her and twice he'd rolled a cigarette and passed it to her. Now here he was sitting up in the bedroom they shared with several others, smiling at her.

He turned away and eased himself out of bed. Tessa watched as he stood and pulled on jeans. She heard the zip closing and it sounded loud in this room full of sleepers. Beaky turned and grimaced at her. He leant down to pick up his shoes and a shirt and then carefully made his away across the room, stepping first over Jaz and then Sukey.

'I'll make you breakfast,' he whispered as he came up to her and she nodded. He opened the door and seemed to be waiting for her.

'My clothes,' she mouthed, and he smiled again and moved silently out of the room.

'Shall we go for a walk?' Tessa asked once they'd eaten toast and jam, drunk a whole pot full of tea and had made roll-ups from the last of Beaky's tobacco.

'If you like,' he said. Tessa sighed, wondering how to make more words come out of this man's mouth. She was tired and had a headache not just from the lack of sleep but from smoking and drinking too much the night before. This was her second chance at making a life in London and this time she felt she could not go back to her parents: she needed to make herself feel that she belonged. An affair with Beaky would help, she thought, fed up with being an almost virgin. With a boyfriend, she thought she would not have to exert so much effort in trying to impress people, which in any case usually failed.

They sat on a bench in Regent's Park. It was still early and warm for a May morning. The air was unusually bright and Tessa widened her eyes, enjoying the moment. The rich green of new shoots and the audacious yellow and mauve colours of spring made her feel hopeful and almost happy. She and Beaky had said little as they'd walked through the Camden Town streets that were dirty and messy with litter after Saturday night. Tessa tried to think of something intriguing to say, wondered if she'd been wrong in thinking that Beaky liked her, was attracted to her as another silent, awkward person. She sighed.

'Why did you come?' Beaky asked.

'What to the Park? Because...'

'No, I mean come to London, to the flat.'

'Sukey said I could.'

'But why would you want to?'

'I didn't want to go on living with my parents.'

'You don't seem like...' Beaky stopped.

'Like what?' Tessa asked.

'Like the sort of girl who would want to live like we're living.' He was blushing now, a deep red. Sadly, it shows up his pimples, Tessa thought. But in spite of that, the blushing made her feel warm towards him: she wanted to lean against him. It had been easy, that short exchange of words. Tessa felt that she could say things to Beaky without trying to impress him. She hoped he would take her hand, maybe kiss her. Opening her mouth a little, she licked her lips. When she realised what she was doing, she looked down and felt heat flushing up from her neck and warming her cheeks and then her forehead. She, too, was blushing and she squeezed the fingers of both hands tightly together in embarrassment.

'Tessa,' she heard Beaky say, his voice was grating and deeper than normal. She looked up and turned her face to his. He did the same and then they were kissing.

It seemed to Tessa as they sat there on the bench, kissing and kissing, that they were learning how to do it and getting better at it all the time. After a while she felt his arm round her pulling her close to him and she forgot to worry about being plump and short-legged, with a wide body and almost no breasts. She could feel her nipples swelling and longed for Beaky to touch them.

When, finally, they stopped, Tessa's mouth felt chewed and sore, but still she would have liked more. Beaky kept his arm round her, he looked dazed.

'What are we going to do?' he asked.

'Have you got any – you know?'

'No, and in any case we've nowhere to go.'

'No, we haven't.' Tessa leant against him, moved her mouth to his and they were kissing again.

He pushed her away after a few minutes. 'We could go to Hampstead Heath,' he croaked. 'There's private places there.'

'OK, but what about... protection?'

'We'll have to be careful... for today. I'll buy some tomorrow when the chemists are open.'

'Yes,' said Tessa, smiling, 'yes.'

There was no one in the kitchen when they came in and there was a silence about the place that made Tessa sure that the house was empty. Even the pram she'd seen in the hall downstairs yesterday and this morning when they went out was gone. Beaky went up the short flight of stairs and looked into the bedroom, then he walked across the landing and knocked on Kitty's door, when there was no reply he pushed it open and turned to Tessa, peering out from the kitchen.

He whispered: 'They're all out.'

'What shall we do?' Tessa whispered back. She tiptoed up the stairs to Beaky, feeling that if she made a noise the spell would break and the house would fill with people.

'Let's…' Beaky reached out and held her to him and they were kissing again. Under a bush away from the crowds on Hampstead Heath they'd lain on scrubby grass and desperately made love. Beaky had tried to pull out as he was coming but too late. They'd lain there for a long time, arms wrapped round each other and then more slowly had done it again. Beaky had slept after this and eventually Tessa, uncomfortable from the scratchy grass beneath and the weight of Beaky on top, had pulled herself away. She pulled up her knickers, feeling the damp between her legs and on her thighs. She lay down again with her arm over Beaky and drifted into an almost sleep. A cloud came over and Tessa was cold. She shook Beaky until he woke. He lay, blinking and then he sat up and looked at Tessa, saying nothing for a minute or two and then he leant towards her and was kissing her again.

'Take your clothes off,' he whispered and she'd taken off her thin jumper and bra, Beaky moaned as he rubbed her breasts with both hands and soon he was inside her again and once again failed to pull out before he came.

When a dog came nosing into the undergrowth nearby, Tessa sat up and quickly dressed. 'I'm cold,' she said. 'I'd love a bath. Let's go home.'

Beaky held her hand as they walked through the park and then back onto the streets. They bought tobacco at a newsagents and had a coffee at the café before catching the bus home. Beaky paid for everything and said nearly nothing. He yawned frequently, opening his mouth wide and screwing up his eyes.

'Are you bored with me?' Tessa asked.

'No,' said Beaky. 'I'm tired.' And he put his arm round her.

Now, it seemed he wanted to do it again. Tessa wondered how many times in a day was normal.

Later when Tessa woke lying on the mattress in the bay window next to Beaky, she felt that the house was still empty and she thought of the bathtub in the kitchen and imagined lying in hot soapy water and afterwards dressing in clean clothes. She wondered where everyone was and how long it would be before they came back.

They put a chair under the door handle to hold the door closed, cleared the pots, pans, books and other stuff off the bath cover, opened it and filled the tub. They both got in and Tessa leaned back at her end, loving the heat and the nearness of Beaky. She wondered how they would sleep tonight. Would she now share the double mattress with him and Jaz take hers? Could they do it in the night with all those other people in the room?

Tessa heard feet scuffling up the stairs and then someone stopping and trying to open the kitchen door.

'Hey,' Sukey called, 'what's going on?'

'I'll open it,' Tessa heard Jaz say. She and Beaky sat up watching as the door opened, pushing the chair to the floor with a bang. Jaz came in, followed by Sukey.

'Oh,' she said. She stood with her hand on her hips, grinning. 'Didn't take you two long to get together.'

Tessa turned to face Beaky; he had blushed bright red and was looking down.

'It might be best if we tried to find somewhere to live on our own.' Beaky said. He and Tessa were now in the pub where Kitty worked.

'Just the two of us?' Tessa asked. She felt faint with pleasure. She remembered the old word 'swooning' used to describe how a woman might react when she realises that a man is falling in love with her. She now understood what it meant: a sort of melting inside, a dizzy falling feeling.

'Yeah.' Beaky finished his drink. 'Want another?'

'No,' said Tessa. 'If we're going to find a bedsit, we need to save us much as we can. Drinking here is a waste of money.'

Beaky grunted.

'Did you mean it, about living together?'

'We do already, just might be easier on our own.'

'Yes,' said Tessa. 'I can afford the rent with my job, but we'll still have to be careful.' She was longing to be back at the flat, looking through the Evening Standard for rooms to rent. On the way home they could see if there was anything advertised in the window of the corner shop.

'I'll have another pint, last one,' Beaky said as he stood up, glass in hand.

'Oh, if you insist, get me a vodka.' Tessa said, smiling up at him: a real, proper boyfriend. It had been almost two weeks since their first time and just last night her period had arrived, five days late. Tessa had felt both relief and disappointment as she whispered to Beaky: 'I'm not pregnant after all.' He had blushed and so had she.

(Tessa had always wanted to marry young and have several children. This fate escaped her. Instead, she led a life that many would find odd, not least herself.)

Chapter 8
June 1967: Sukey

Hot. Finally it was hot and everyone at last was out and Sukey wasn't working today, had had enough of meticulous old women and probing questions. Kneeling in the bay window of the bedroom and leaning on the ledge, she was staring out onto the street and smoking one of Kitty's cigarettes – she'd left an almost empty packet on the kitchen table when she'd rushed out earlier, late as usual for work. Sukey sniffed in the smells of summer London: dust, decay, privet leaves and petrol fumes. The faint hum of traffic coming from Camden Road was a background noise to the sound of feet on the pavement and the occasional yell from a child playing in the street. Sukey yawned, finished her cigarette and stood up. She'd go out, buy a lemon to use as a rinse for her hair, maybe a magazine, then come back and enjoy being alone in the flat.

Sukey climbed over the mattresses to the wardrobe in the corner. One of its doors was missing and the other was stuck open. Now that there were only three of them sharing the room, it was mainly her clothes hanging on the rail. There weren't many of them, the dirty ones were in a pile in the alcove and it was a long time since she'd been to the launderette and even longer since she'd done any hand-washing. She chose the short orange skirt that she'd bought at Biba and from the drawer took a white top and her last pair of clean knickers. That was it. She whipped off the long baggy T-shirt she wore in bed, squirted each underarm with her deodorant and slipped on the clothes: no shoes, no bra. She stood in front of the kitchen mirror, applied eye-shadow and mascara and brushed her hair a hundred strokes. Taking only her key and her purse, she ran down the stairs and out onto the street.

She noticed them before she went into the shop: two of them, one leaning against the lamp post scratching his thigh, the other holding an open brown paper bag. As she came up to them, the lamp post leaner stopped scratching, leaned over and took a plum out of his friend's brown bag. The bag holder also reached in and took a plum, and the two of them were biting into the fruit as she went into the shop. Sukey was sure she'd seen one of them before, the one leaning against the lamppost, the one with the floppy brown hair. The other one had black curls and was very skinny.

They were still there when she came out of the shop with her lemon. She'd decided against the magazine, a waste of money, she thought, and in any case, she could always borrow one from Bridie. She stood for a moment and Curly Hair smiled at her. She turned and started to walk back up the road. At the corner she stopped to wait for the lights to change and, hearing footsteps and the murmur of male voices, she turned. The two men were just behind her. The one with brown hair smiled. Curly Hair held out the bag.

'Have a plum,' Brown Hair said and Curly Hair jiggled the bag up and down.

'No thanks,' said Sukey.

'Ah go on, they're lovely and juicy.' Brown Hair licked his lips in an obvious way.

'No,' said Sukey.

'I'll choose one for you,' said Curly Hair and he dipped his fingers in the bag, felt around, and then pulled out his hand, a plum lying on the palm. He stretched out his arm till he was almost touching Sukey. She stepped back, looking down at the palm and the purple fruit in its middle. The hand, she noticed, was covered in blotches of paint and trembled slightly.

'Take it,' said Curly Hair. Sukey looked at him. He had green eyes and long dark lashes, a wide mouth, his face was thin and his forehead broad. He made her want to smile at him; she wanted to lean against his scrawny chest and imagined his sinewy arm holding her to him.

'All right,' she said, took the plum and bit into it. It was warm and sweet and she sucked the juice into her mouth, not wanting it to spill and mark her white top.

'Right,' said the man with brown hair, skittering about on the pavement, 'now you've had one of our plums you can come and have a drink with us.'

'No,' said Sukey.

Brown hair looked at his watch. 'Still time,' he said. 'Half an hour before closing. Now do come with us.'

Sukey shook her head: 'No.' She'd finished the plum and was holding the stone, her fingers sticky. Curly Hair took her wrist between two fingers and with his other hand, which still held the brown paper bag, gently loosed the plum stone, letting it fall in the gutter. Sukey watched the stone dropping and then looked up at Curly Hair and his soft smile. She felt a gentle melting in her belly.

'I've seen you around before,' said Brown Hair. 'You live up there.' He pointed in the direction of her street. Sukey said nothing, he reminded her of a rather jumpy eager dog, a nice dog, but a dog nonetheless: a golden spaniel with a shiny coat and a desire to please expressed in its wagging tail.

'You're coming for a drink,' said Curly Hair, his fingers were still attached to Sukey's wrist.

'OK,' said Sukey, shaking her hand to loosen his grip.

'Right,' said Brown Hair and started to cross the road. Sukey and Curly Hair followed. They turned up the street and stopped outside the pub where Kitty worked.

'Oh,' said Sukey, wondering what she'd say. Then she thought at least she'd be there, Kitty, if anything went wrong.

'All right?' asked Curly Hair. Sukey nodded and followed the two men into the pub. She blinked adjusting to the dim light in the darkly painted, dingy room, which was large and almost empty of people but stuffed with ugly brown furniture and smelling of spilled beer and stale tobacco. The landlord was leaning on the counter, reading a folded newspaper. Sukey could not see Kitty, but could hear her voice, talking in her smoky way to a customer in the other bar.

'What will you drink?' Brown Hair asked and Sukey said she'd have a cider. She followed Curly Hair to a round table on the edge of the room and they sat down. He smiled at her, took a packet of cigarettes out of his pocket and offered her one.

'My name's Joe,' said Brown Hair as he joined them, carrying three glasses. He jerked his head towards Curly Hair. 'And my friend's called Sean. He's a painter.'

'A house painter?' Sukey asked.

'No. An artist. Paints pictures. And what are you called?'

'Sukey.'

'Susie, sweet Susie,' said Brown Hair, who now had to be thought of as Joe.

'Not Susie, Sukey,' said Sean. He was looking down at her bare legs and feet. He bent and ran his fingers over the roots of her toes. 'Haven't you got any shoes?' he asked.

'I can't afford any,' Sukey said. It was partly true. She had a few pairs at home: her winter boots, a collection of old sandals, some suede clogs that she'd dyed pink; but she didn't really have enough money to buy the sort of shoes she'd like to wear. She was barefoot because that was the way she wanted to be, even outside walking the dirty London pavements. That's how it had been last summer and how it would be this summer, too. She'd become used to the raised eyebrows and shocked looks and to the insults that sometimes came her way.

'Tt, tt. Can't have that. I'll buy you some shoes,' Sean said.

'So, you're successful as an artist,' Sukey said.

'He's got a rich wife,' Joe said. He was tapping on the table with one hand as if playing the piano.

'Ex-wife, Joe, remember that. Patty is an ex-wife.' Sean had poked his head forward, emphasising the 'ex', almost spitting as he spoke, enunciating it with his lips pulled back and his tongue working hard against his teeth.

'OK, Sean, OK.' Joe had raised both hands and was holding them palm up as if to fend off an attack from Sean. There was silence for a moment and Sukey leant forward to sip from her glass. Then Joe spoke again: 'Your round, Sean, and you'd better hurry, nearly closing time.'

'I'll pay, but you go and get them.' Sean lent back in his chair, pulled some notes out of his pocket and handed then across to Joe, who took them, sighing and shaking his head.

'You're a terrible man, Sean Connelly, a terrible man,' Joe said, but he pushed back his chair and went to the bar.

'He fancies you badly,' Sean said. 'When we saw you walking down the road, he said how he'd like to pull you but didn't think he was able for it.'

Sukey shrugged, said nothing.

'I told him I'd do it, I'd get you to come for a drink with us. He wants you to go home with him. He's got his own gaff, a little house by the canal.'

'Well I won't,' Sukey said. She started to tap one of her bare feet on the dirty carpet and knew she wanted to be back at the flat. She thought about washing her hair, rinsing it in lemon juice and then going out to sit in the sun to let it dry. She thought about spending the rest of the afternoon with

Sean instead and the thought frightened her a little. She wondered if she could cope with him, what he would be like as a lover.

Joe banged three glasses down on the table. 'There you are,' he said and turned so that he was facing Sukey. 'Are you a student?' he asked her. She shook her head. 'Well what do you do?'

'Nothing much, clean houses, hang around.' She wished he'd go away, leave her with Sean.

'He wants you to ask him what he does,' Sean said.

'What d'you do?' Sukey asked.

'He works in a strip club, down in Soho,' Sean told her. 'On the door. And as a by-line, he sells the strippers' underwear. That's how he got the money to buy his house.'

'Not that big a deal,' Joe said. 'I've sitting tenants, one upstairs and one in the basement. I've only got the one floor.' He paused to take a sip of his drink. 'But I've made it nice. Got a shower in there and I've built a platform for a raised bed. You can come and see it. After these drinks.'

'No thanks,' Sukey said.

'I could get you a job. You could earn a lot.'

'No thanks.'

'Ah come on, won't ye?'

She shook her head. Then she heard Kitty's voice booming across the room. 'Last orders.'

Sukey turned to the bar. 'Hey Kitty,' she called.

'What you doing here?' Kitty called back.

'Drinking,' said Sukey. It seemed strange how, though she was still only seventeen, she was never refused entry to a pub. And yet several times when she'd been out with Jaz who had just become nineteen, he'd been turned away. Kitty was coming over to their table.

'So, who are your friends?' she asked, standing with one hand on her hip, the other holding a cigarette.

'Joe and Sean,' Sukey said. 'Joe could get you a job stripping in Soho. Much more money than working in a pub.'

'Yeah?' Kitty said, suspicious, frowning. 'Well, if you want another round you'd better hurry up.' She turned and walked back towards the bar, treading heavily as she went.

'Would you have one like her in yer clubs?' Sean asked watching Kitty.

'All sorts: big, small, black, white,' Joe said. 'I could get her a job if she wanted one. Some of them like the fat ones.'

'So you really do work in a strip club,' Sukey said. She'd thought it was just a line, a way of enticing her, of making her think that Joe was interesting. 'And do you really own your house?'

'Yes, both. I'll get you another drink before they close. Will you have a rum and black?'

'No thanks. No more to drink.'

'I'll have another pint and a Jameson chaser as it's our last,' Sean said.

'Why don't you get them?' Joe asked.

Sean looked at him and then shrugged. 'If you don't hurry it'll be too late,' he said and once more Joe rose and went to the bar.

'Shoes. Did you mean it about the shoes?' Sukey asked.

'Yes. Not today, I've got to go soon… A meeting with a… gallery owner… About an exhibition. So, I'll see you tomorrow. In town, let's say midday. ' He stopped for a moment, thinking. He leaned towards Sukey and took a hunk of her hair in his hands. He pulled it gently towards him and stroked his cheek with it. Then he let it go and used both hands to pull her face toward his and he kissed her. Sukey responded, felt the pull of his lips on hers and raised her arms, letting them rest on his shoulders. She didn't want to stop.

'Sean, Susie.' There was a clink of glass on the table and Sukey felt Sean pull back. Joe was sitting in his chair staring at them.

'Her name's Sukey, not Susie,' Sean said and he leant forward for his pint.

When they'd finished their drinks Sean went to the Gents and Sukey sat with Joe, waiting.

'Are you coming home with me?' he asked. And Sukey noticed the way his eyes, brown and moist, seem to be flicking and flicking as if photographing parts of her body, bit by bit. She shook her head.

Kitty locked the door behind them and they stood for a moment on the pavement, narrowing their eyes against the brightness of the sun.

'Tomorrow?' Sukey said, facing Sean, looking down.

'Tomorrow, twelve, outside the main entrance to Harrods,' he said and touched the inside of her wrist. She looked up and he drew her to him and kissed her, pressing his bony body against hers. When he let her go, she felt dizzy from the heat, from the cider, but mainly from being so close to him. He stroked her head, turned and was gone.

'You coming back to mine?' Joe asked.

'No,' shouted Sukey, wondering how he could still be asking when he must see that if she wanted one of them it would be his friend. She turned and walked up the street, away from where the flat was, not wanting Joe to know where she lived.

'Susie,' he called. Still walking away, she called back: 'It's Sukey.'

'OK, Sukey, Sukey. Sukey, take it off again....'

Sukey ground her teeth together, exasperated. She realised that she'd have to phone Robin, tell him she was sick and couldn't do her cleaning job tomorrow. She turned the corner and stopped after a few strides, leaning against a wall. A few minutes later she retraced her steps and cautiously peered back down the street towards the pub. She sighed, relieved. Joe had gone.

'You'll be late for your Mrs Thing if you don't get going.' Kitty sucked heavily on her cigarette, put it in the ashtray and, frowning and leaning over the table, pushed the iron through the flounces on the front of a white blouse.

'I'm not working today,' Sukey said. Kitty looked up, reached for her cigarette.

'Oh? Not given up, I hope.'

'No, just a day off.'

'Second in a row.'

'Yes, well.'

'That man,' Kitty said as she bent her head over the blouse again. 'The strip man. I've seen him before, quite a few times, in the pub. Does he really work in a Soho club?'

'Yeah, I think he does.'

'Was he serious about getting us a job?'

'Dunno. Ask him next time you see him.' Sukey yawned, squinted to look at the clock on the mantle piece. Time to get moving, she thought, time go and stand outside Harrods. She sat up, stretched, drew her legs up under the chair and leant forward, her elbows on her knee, watching Kitty, wondering if Sean would be there and what they would do if he was. Would he buy her a pair of shoes? Would she go back with him to where he lived? She shivered, wondered what it would be like to be in bed with him. He was older than her, about thirty she thought, a painter, Irish. Perhaps I won't go, she thought, feeling a clench of fear inside her. But then, since she wasn't working, what else would she do?

Kitty turned off the iron, lit a new cigarette from the stub of the old one, sat down and leant over the table to raise the cosy and feel the teapot with the back of her hand. 'Still hot,' she said. 'D'you want a cup?'

'OK,' said Sukey, deciding that she'd be a little late for that morning's appointment.

As she turned the corner onto the main street Sukey saw the bus she wanted draw away from the stop. And then she had to wait over twenty minutes for another one. When it came there was a bustle of people pushing to get on and as Sukey pulled herself onto it the bell rang with an impatient 'ding ding ding.' She found a seat on the top deck and rolled a cigarette. The bus went slowly, stopped for a long time, stuck in traffic. Sukey tapped her foot, wondered if Sean would be there, would wait for her. Angry shouting came from downstairs, the conductor telling a group of people that the bus was full. The bell rang again, loud and forceful. After that, they moved quickly, ignoring several stops where angry passengers waved as the bus passed them by.

They'd slowed again as they came to Knightsbridge. Sukey decided it would be quicker to walk. A clock showed that it was nearly half past twelve. She ran for a few minutes in her bare feet, dodging between dawdling shoppers and then she slowed down for the last few hundred feet.

He wasn't there. Sukey looked inside, came out again, and stood on the pavement, looking down. She was too late. Or maybe Sean had never been there, hadn't ever intended to meet her and buy her shoes. She let the disappointment seep into her tummy and after a few minutes decided to check all the entrances just in case.

Later, travelling back to Camden town on the bus, she comforted herself with the thought that Sean may have been the one to have felt let down. That he'd stood waiting for her, looking at his watch – she seemed to remember that he'd worn one too big for his skinny wrist – and hoping that she'd be here soon. He'd have sworn, sighed and just before she arrived would have left, going home to paint a despondent picture of a shoeless girl hiding behind her long blond hair: for that's all I am, Sukey thought.

'Hey,' he called again, and again Sukey ignored him, tossing her head so that he'd know she'd heard him and was ignoring him. He called again for the third time and then was running after her. When he caught up with her, he touched her arm. Then he grasped it.

'Didn't you hear me?' he asked.

'Yes,' she said, 'but I didn't want to speak to you.'

He blinked, staring at her with his spaniel eyes.

'What d'you want?' she asked, shaking her arm free of his.

'Come for a drink?'

Sukey said nothing. She put her head on one side and raised her eyebrows. She turned to walk on down the street. She had to meet Robin by the tube station to get her money for the week. Only three day's work, so it wasn't much. She sighed. Joe was walking along with her. It almost made her laugh, this persistence.

'Susie,' he pleaded.

'Sukey,' she said, turning to him.

'Yes, Sukey,' he said. 'I know that's yer name. I wanted to see you really angry.' He was laughing. 'Look, I've got to see someone this afternoon, so I've not much time. Come and have a quick drink.'

Sukey sighed, stopped walking. 'OK,' she said. 'In that pub where we went with your friend. I'll see you there in half an hour. I've something to do before then.'

'I'll come with you.'

Sukey could see his hand hovering, wanting to clasp her arm again. 'No,' she said, and stamped her bare foot on the pavement. 'I told you, half an hour. And oh, if you see that friend of mine, the barmaid, you can talk to her about a job.

She wants to work in your club.'

When Sukey came into the pub Joe was at the bar. Kitty was leaning over it, her breasts squashed on the counter, her cleavage white and blancmange-like above it. The two were talking. Sukey watched as he offered Kitty a cigarette and then lit it. One of his feet was on the rail that ran along the bar and he was tapping it as if impatient. He nodded and waved his cigarette in the air as he talked. Sukey came to join them and he turned when he noticed her.

'A rum and black for this lovely girl here,' he said, and again Sukey saw his hand fluttering towards her as if he owned her.

'Well,' he said as they sat at a table, 'she wants a job, your friend. I said I'd look into it for her. Strippers, they make a lot of money, but you have to work for several clubs. I could get you sorted, no trouble.'

Sukey screwed up her face and put her arms protectively round her body. 'No,' she said.

'A gorgeous girl like you.' Joe licked his lips and again she felt his eyes taking her body to pieces. 'I've another friend. He does photos, you know. He'd pay to have you doing stuff for him.'

'No,' said Sukey.

'Your loss,' Joe said. 'You could be quids in, lot of money in porn. More than stripping.'

'Oh God,' said Sukey, leaning back in her chair. Maybe she should take up these offers, work for a year, make a lot of money. Posing for porn and stripping couldn't be any worse than cleaning for rich old women. She shook her head.

'Look, Sukey,' Joe was saying, 'I really do have to go.' He was very jumpy, she thought, didn't seem able to keep still, always one of his limbs moving, or his head or his eyes. He was like an older version of Jaz. 'I want to take you out to dinner tonight.'

Sukey looked at him, imagined his tail wagging.

'Saturday,' she said, suspicious. 'If you work in a strip club, how've you got tonight off?'

'Holidays, I'm on holidays for two weeks. I was supposed to be going back to Ireland but I never got round to buying the tickets.'

'Right,' Sukey said.

'So? Will I meet you here this evening?'

Sukey said nothing, watching him as he stood up, walked round his chair, shuffled his hands in his pockets. 'OK,' she said, after all she didn't have to turn up if she didn't want to.

'Seven, I'll see you at seven.' He bent over slightly and Sukey imagined he was about to pat her head. She moved away. His hand came out and pulled a strand of her hair, quite hard: it hurt.

'Ow,' she said.

Joe laughed. 'Just so you remember to be here this evening.'

'Boring,' said Jaz. 'Saturday evening and no party to go to, no shit to smoke and I spent all my money last night.' He yawned. Minnie said nothing, just looked up at him and pursed her lips.

Sukey, lying on the floor, reached for her purse. She

counted out the notes, enough to buy them all a few drinks with some left over for scoring a bit of dope. There'd be still just enough for next week's fares. She looked up at Minnie, asking: 'You got any money?'

Minnie shrugged. Her shoulders looked thin and mean as they moved forwards and back. And vulnerable, Sukey thought.

'I don't want to go out,' Minnie said. Sukey watched her swallowing. Since Ted had left the flat, her sadness had become almost solid. You could feel it as you walked into a room where Minnie was sitting and at night, in the bedroom, it made them all sleep badly. Sukey often woke with cheeks wet from tears and she'd hear one of the others crying out or moaning.

'I'm supposed to meet a man in Kitty's pub,' Sukey said.

Jaz looked up at the clock. 'When?' he asked.

'Now.'

'Will he buy us all a drink?'

'He wants to take me out to dinner. I'll get him to buy a round first.'

'Let's go,' said Jaz. 'Come on, Minnie.'

'No.'

'Just for one drink, come on.'

Minnie sat quite still, looking down. 'All right,' she said eventually, her voice flat.

'You're late,' Joe said. He was sitting at one of the tables, a half drunk pint and a whiskey in front of him.'

Sukey shrugged. 'Will you buy us all a drink?'

Joe looked first at Jaz and then at Minnie before he stood

up. 'What'll ye have?' he asked, sounding as if he'd just swallowed something that tasted unpleasant. He took the orders and went to the bar. Jaz sat down and helped himself to one of the cigarettes in the packet Joe had left on the table. Then he offered them round, lighting them with Joe's lighter.

Joe came back with three glasses. 'So,' he said as he sat down, 'you're all friends of Sukey's?' He crossed his legs and swung his foot up and down, while he played piano on his knee with one hand. Sukey wanted to lean over and hold him down.

'We all live together,' Jaz said. 'So does Kitty, the fat one over there,' Jaz gestured towards the bar. Sukey could see Joe's eyes moving from Jaz, to Minnie, to her and back again, trying, she thought, to work them all out, to suss out who belonged to who. 'Well,' he said and cleared his throat.

Jaz finished his drink and his cigarette and leaned back, looking at Joe. 'Shall we have another?' he asked.

'If you're buying…' Joe started.

'No. No money, none of us have money.' Jaz interrupted and then sighed. 'Normally I have enough, but my allowance isn't due until next week.'

Joe snorted. And then took a wad from his pocket. 'Last one,' he said, peeling off a few notes and passing them to Jaz. 'I'll have a Guinness and a Jameson. And bring me back the change.'

'Come and sit with me,' Joe said to Sukey as Jaz went to the bar. She felt obliged to; he was paying for the drinks, and now she'd have to go to dinner with him. And later he'd expect her to sleep with him. Sukey sighed and went to sit on the arm of Joe's chair. She could feel his hand as it rubbed her back, feeling its way round her body till he was holding her tight.

Later, the two of them took a taxi to Soho, to a Greek restaurant called Jimmy's. It was small, dark, crowded. There were no tablecloths, food was served on thick, white, cheap-looking plates and the menu was limited. The man who appeared to be the owner shook Joe's hand as if he were an old friend and smiled at Sukey. After she'd walked past him and sat at their table, he whispered something to Joe, who laughed. He ordered a bottle of wine and they ate lamb stew that was delicious, tasting as if it had been cooked slowly with bushels of tomatoes. There was a big green salad and Greek bread. Sweet pastries, a glass of brandy and a cup of thick coffee each ended the meal.

'We've been coming here for years, me and Sean,' he said as he placed a pile of notes on top of the bill.

'The painter, the one with you the other day?' asked Sukey.

'That one. We were at school together in Ireland. He's married to a doctor. That's how he can afford to spend all day playing with paints.'

'I thought… I thought he was no longer with his wife.'

'He just said that 'cos he wanted to get into your knickers. He's married. They've two children. His mother lives with them and takes care of them so that Patty can work.'

'Oh,' said Sukey. She knew now that Sean hadn't turned

up for their rendezvous. He was just leading me on, probably just trying to make Joe jealous. She felt a small pang of disappointment and carefully tucked it away in the dark hidden place where she stored sad and unpleasant feelings. Sighing very slightly, she wondered why life had to be so strange, why it could not be nicely controlled and ordered.

When they came out onto the street, it was drizzling. Sukey shivered, she was wearing a thin cotton dress. Her bare feet were wet and cold and she curled her toes and then warmed the sole of one foot on the calf of her other leg as they stood on the pavement watching for a vacant taxi. Joe reached for Sukey's hand and she felt his fingers squeezing hers. He seemed suddenly tentative and uncertain, as if he thought she might turn and run away. She wished she could.

In the taxi he put his arm round her and was kissing her, his lips and tongue were thick and rubbery. She felt his body pressing against hers and couldn't respond, even though she'd have liked to be able to.

He paid the taxi and then took Sukey's hand and pulled her up the narrow path, the canal was on one side of it and a terrace of little houses on the other. He stopped at one of them and took a small bunch of keys out of his pocket. Sukey followed him inside. The hall was dark and smelled of earth and fried food. He unlocked another door and they were in a big room that had once been two. He switched on the light and Sukey looked around. The place was untidy and sparsely furnished, but it had been well decorated, the floor was tiled in white ceramic and the walls were a smooth pale grey.

'This is my gaff, I'm still working on it.' He showed her the shower with its expensive fittings and the new kitchen units. In the front half of the room, a space had been opened up above the hall and steps had been built into the wall. 'That'll be the bedroom,' he said. 'Not finished yet.' He put his arms round her and led her to a mattress in the corner of the room and pulled her down next to him.

He turned on a lamp by the bed. 'You will stay,' he said and Sukey nodded, feeling for a moment that there was something pathetic about him and that it would be rude to leave now. She wasn't sure what the protocol would be for this.

'The jacks is out through the hall. Shared with the old one from upstairs. I pee in the shower but you might not want to. Himself in the basement has his own bathroom.'

When Sukey came back from the loo, which was dirty and smelly, Joe had switched off the main lights and was lying in bed under the blankets. His shoulders were naked and looked white and meaty leaning against the wall. He watched her as she undressed and as she climbed in, he pulled her to him.

It didn't last long; his hands were warm and heavy, yet somehow apologetic, as they explored her body. After a few seconds he sat up and took a condom from a packet by the bed, opened it and put it on. He entered her without saying a word and came soon afterwards. Sukey was overwhelmed by how pathetic and meaningless their coupling had been: thin kisses, no words, few caresses and an absence of feeling (by Joe as well as herself, she thought). She considered crying but it didn't seem appropriate. Soon, she thought, I'll begin to understand what's happening to me.

Joe lay on his back and Sukey thought that he'd gone to sleep. Instead, he sat up.

'Would you like some peaches?' he asked.

'Yes,' said Sukey, 'I'd like a peach.' She imagined the round velvety fruit, golden with a blush of pink. She imagined biting into it, filling her mouth with the soft taste and texture. Joe got out of bed. Naked he looked stockier than when he was dressed. He had fleshy thighs and buttocks. He walked into the other half of the room and Sukey closed her eyes. She heard the fridge door open and then Joe coming back to the bed. She felt the heaviness of him beside her as he sat on the mattress and she opened her eyes.

Joe was holding a tin and a spoon. He dipped the spoon into the tin and passed it to her.

Sukey shook her head. 'I thought you meant real ones,' she said, feeling betrayed, wondering how a man with a friend who tempted with fresh plums could bear to eat peaches sliced, covered in thick syrup and stored in a can. She turned away. She thought of leaving and felt intensely tired. She closed her eyes again, wanting to sleep. She'd stay until the morning and when it was light she'd dress and leave without saying another word.

(Not so many years later Joe was one of the first foreigners to buy a house for nearly nothing in the centre of France. It was old, built of solid brick and surrounded by an orchard of peach and nectarine. It was with wonderful pictures of his wife among these trees that he started his career as a photographer, for which he eventually became famous.)

Chapter 9
June 1967: Jaz

'Oh shit,' Sukey said, screwing her mouth up as she did when she was worried or annoyed. She was staring at the door and Jaz turned to see what she was looking at. A man had just come in and was moving towards the bar, one hand was in his jacket pocket and his eyes were flicking round the room. It was Joe, the man who Sukey had arranged to meet here and then had gone off with a few days before. When Joe saw Sukey and Jaz, he nodded and changed direction. He stood in front of them, bit his lower lip and blinked quickly.

'So,' he said, 'is this the reason you left me so quick the other day? He is your boyfriend after all.'

Sukey shrugged.

No, I'm not, Jaz wanted to say, but something stopped him, some need he felt coming from Sukey.

'Well. You both owe me a drink.' Joe said. He was looking from Sukey to Jaz and back again. He seemed both sad and angry. And confused as well, Jaz thought.

Fair enough, Jaz said to himself. But aloud he said nothing, raised his glass and took a sip.

'Oh, Jaysus then,' Joe said, 'I'll get them. What are ye having?'

'A pint of bitter, please,' Jaz said and Sukey shrugged. She never knew what she wanted to drink, Jaz thought.

'I'll get you a half of mild, Sukey,' Joe said.

'No,' she said, 'a Martini, a dry one. With an olive.'

'They don't have olives in this pub, and if they did, they'd be tinned.' Joe stuck a vindictive chin forward and stomped off towards the bar.

'What's up with him?' Jaz asked.

'Just pretend to be my boyfriend. Stop him chatting me up.'

'But you spent the other night with him, didn't you?'

'A mistake.'

'Yes,' said Jaz and put his arm round Sukey. She was prone to mistakes, especially where men were concerned. He felt a need to look after her and wished that he wanted to sleep with her.

'Don't worry about taking drinks off Joe,' Sukey whispered, leaning towards Jaz, who turned towards her, pulling a thick strand of her hair and rubbing it against his face, sniffing its clean scent of vanilla and lemon. 'He earns a fortune and owns his own house.'

Joe banged the drinks down on the table.

'That's sweet Martini and it's got a cherry in it,' Sukey said.

Joe looked at her and shook his head. He took a big swig

of his Guinness and wiped his mouth with the back of his hand. He was still looking at Sukey, both wanting her and very angry with her, Jaz thought.

'I'm meeting a friend here,' Joe announced. 'He'll be here any minute. A photographer,' he said, as if it was something to be proud of. 'He makes a lot of money, porno stuff.' He sounded even prouder. 'He might be interested in you,' Joe added, looking at Sukey.

'I don't need a man,' she said.

'I meant professionally,' Joe said. 'For his work. He's married, got two children. His wife's a potter. She's quite well known.'

The pub door opened slowly and a couple came in. He was tall and lean, and balding, although he was only about thirty. She, too, was tall, slender and beautifully dressed in plain dark clothes. She had long red curly hair and the sort of face that people would describe as belonging to an angel: heart shaped, with pale, smooth skin, a small delicate nose, huge eyes and a wide, full-lipped mouth. The two of them stood side by side as if they'd just made an entrance onto a stage and were waiting for the applause. Wow, thought Jaz and shifted in his chair, recognising that he felt both desire and envy.

Joe waved to them. 'Over here,' he called, and the man nodded.

'He's brought her,' Joe said and sounded annoyed. He stood up as the couple came up to them. 'What'll it be?' he asked and went to the bar with their orders.

'I'm Vic,' said the man, as he pulled two chairs from the

next table. 'This is Jules, my wife.' She nodded without smiling as she slipped gracefully into the nearest chair. She sat quietly, looking round, almost ignoring the rest of them.

'My name's Jaz. This is Sukey,' Jaz said as Joe came back from the bar.

Vic talked about himself almost without interruption and Jules said hardly a word. She left after half an hour, saying that she had to collect the children from her mother and then had work to do.

'She's having an exhibition soon,' Vic said when she'd gone, 'at Kailey's in Cork Street.' He said it as if it was a well-known venue and Jaz nodded as if he was familiar with it. He watched as Vic leant back and stretched out his long legs, putting his empty glass on the table.

'My round,' Jaz said, jumping up, compelled to make some kind of move.

'Thanks,' said Vic, when Jaz came back with drinks. This was a man, Jaz was sure, who accepted drinks from others, and the fact that he never offered to buy in return offended no one.

'I was watching you,' Vic said as Jaz sat down, 'I was wondering would you mind walking up to the bar again? I want to check something out.'

Jaz frowned, wished he knew what Vic was really after but didn't know how to ask.

'He'd like to look at you moving again, from behind,' Sukey said.

'Oh, OK,' Jaz said, still wondering what was happening.

'Go on then,' Sukey said.

'Right,' Vic said when Jaz came back, 'I'll need to see you in the nude and get some shots. And then maybe I'll be able to offer you some work.'

'Porno photos?' Sukey asked.

'It's for postcards. I do nude postcards. Of women.'

'But I'm a man,' Jaz said, shaking his head, worrying.

'Sure, but I do a few back shots, you know focusing on the bum, and I usually use men for them. They're normally better shaped than women, not so large and melony,' Vic said, moving his hands in the shape of a big round.

Jaz realised that he was sexually aroused and couldn't explain why. He buried his face in his glass, taking several long gulps of beer.

'Well,' said Vic when Jaz looked up.

'Yeah... I'll think about it,' Jaz said.

'I think he's what people call charismatic,' Sukey said as they walked the short distance home from the pub.

'He's also weird,' Jaz added. 'First he asked me and then he asked Kitty to pose for him.'

'So,' said Sukey.

'I'm a man and she's fat.'

'He takes photos of couples doing it. That's his main line, how he makes his money.'

'Jeez,' said Jaz. 'I need a break. Let's get some of the others together and go for a ride in the car.'

Kitty had made an effort. Her face was smoothly creamed and powdered and she was wearing false eyelashes and pale pink lipstick. She'd back-combed her hair and was dressed in a bright turquoise top that was cut low so that you could see the puffy tops of her breasts pushing out. Her black satin trousers were tight at the bum and flared widely at the bottom above inappropriate strappy sandals. And she'd even put varnish on her toenails. Jaz felt almost sorry for her, almost wanted to tell her not to bother, Vic hadn't propositioned her because she was beautiful but because he had sensed a need in her. Sukey had told Jaz this as they'd driven to Hampstead Heath the day before.

'Vic has some odd clients, and he needs people who'll do all sorts of yucky things that he can photograph and sell,' she'd said.

'How d'you know? Jaz asked.

Sukey shrugged. 'He said things in the pub. Joe's said things. You can tell.'

I can't, Jaz thought, as he looked in the kitchen mirror, combing his hair and wondering why he, too, was bothering to dress up and look good for the dinner at Joe's. In the pub yesterday, Joe had told them that he was a good cook, staring at Sukey as if she was about to contradict him. He'd also said that he'd be back at work next week, so it was a last opportunity and why didn't they all come to his place, Sunday night; he'd make a big dinner and they could discuss business.

Kitty, clearing away the empty glasses, had said she'd take the night off. It was a long time since she'd had a break. Vic had nodded, saying that he and Jules could come; their nanny or Jules's mother would baby-sit.

Now here they were, ready to go. Dennis was sitting smoking at the kitchen table and looking angry. Minnie, hearing that no one but Dennis would be in, had said, 'Oh' in a strange strangled way and then said that she was going out too, and had left soon after.

'Don't worry about Dennis,' Kitty said. 'His wife turned him down again today.'

Dennis said nothing, shuffled in his seat, looked at Kitty, frowning, his mouth petulant. Cheer up, Jaz wanted to say, but thought it might not be appropriate. How odd it was that Kitty had brought Dennis into this flat, slept with him, looked after him. But then, how odd the whole thing was. When he had made his fortune as an actor, Jaz told himself, he'd live alone in a penthouse with modern furniture and polished wooden floors, a few well-chosen paintings on the walls and friends visiting by invitation only. That was one of the visions of the future that he imagined on the rare occasions he found himself on his own and able to indulge in daydreams; the other was of being married and having six children, all beautiful, all very well behaved. There was a wife in that fantasy, but Jaz normally couldn't see her very clearly. Maybe, he thought now, as he watched Dennis being moody, his wife would look like Jules the potter, smooth-skinned, silent, calm and lovely.

Jaz imagined Vic and Jules in bed together, but they were lying side by side, not touching. He closed his eyes trying to bring passion into his picture of this perfect pair but it wouldn't come.

'What's the matter with that little faggot? Why's he

making faces at me?' Jaz heard Dennis ask.

Jaz opened his eyes and stuck his tongue out at Dennis. Horrid man, he thought.

Jaz watched as Kitty flirted with Joe. He turned to take a sip of wine and saw that Vic was watching them too, with an odd little smile bending, ever so slightly, the corners of his mouth. The main course was finished. Joe had prepared roast lamb, covered with some kind of crust; Jaz thought it looked bloody and disgusting as he refused his helping. Joe had cut him a hunk of cheese when he explained that he was a vegetarian. There were also crisp potatoes that Jaz couldn't eat, as after they had been par boiled and tossed in flour they'd been added to the roasting pan and cooked in lamb fat. Jaz had piled his plate with large helpings of the vegetables: cauliflower topped with crumbled hard-boiled eggs, courgettes cooked with milk and butter then sprinkled with finely chopped parsley, cabbage in a creamy tomato sauce. Joe was a good cook, Jaz thought, but he spoiled it all by explaining how he'd prepared the food, going into unnecessary detail. Too much to eat and far too elaborate was Jaz's judgement. There was wine as well. Kitty had brought three bottles that she said she'd bought from the off-licence section of the pub, but she'd stolen them, Jaz was sure. She often did this, although she herself did not like alcohol.

When they'd arrived, Vic and Jules were already there and were already drinking. Joe, his face red from cooking, had ushered them in, offered them glasses. Jaz took his drink and went to look out of the window. He looked down into a small basement yard. Opposite were the backs of other houses. He turned to face the room, leaning against the wall.

Vic was talking, telling about a photographic session that he'd been running a few days before with three women and two men. His three-year-old son had come into the studio when the five of them had been in action.

'Poor Seth, you should have seen his little face. I hustled him out of course, but couldn't stop the questions coming. When I got back the ... er... how should I put it, the energy I needed from the men had deflated,' Vic laughed. Jules looked at him, her face expressionless, and Jaz wondered what she was thinking.

Vic leant towards her and stroked her cheek and then cupped her chin. It was almost as if he were pinching her as he pouted, and moving closer to her, said: 'Poor Jules, don't worry, Sethie'll recover. It's only human nature after all. He's got to learn.'

Jules put her hand up to Vic's and Jaz wondered whether it was a gesture of affection or to push him away.

Vic stood up to fetch another bottle. As he passed Jaz, he reached behind him, slowly caressing his bottom, first one buttock, then the other. Jaz flinched away, uncomfortable, shook his head and went to sit at the table. He felt as if he was burning and took a big drink from his glass.

Vic, with a full bottle of wine in each hand, came back and sat opposite Jaz. He put the bottles down and winked at Jaz who didn't know how to respond. This was the sort of man who believed that he could do what he wanted and, even if it was outrageous or cruel, no one would object or challenge him. Jaz wondered whether Vic was someone whom he should admire or despise.

He looked across the table at Sukey. Vic was now sitting next to her, he had moved his chair closer and was pushing back a strand of her hair and was staring at her face. Sukey had started to blush, was trying to move back. Vic's gaze was moving down her body, taking in her breasts, her legs in their short skirt, her naked feet.

'Joe's right, Susie, I could use you as a model.'

'Sukey, my name's Sukey.'

'Sure. Tell you what, come round tomorrow, you and your boyfriend… ' Vic looked across the table, nodded at Jaz, 'and I'll try you both out. But I have to say, er, Jack, that you're too skinny for anything but standing in as a woman for my postcards.'

'He's called Jaz,' Sukey said. She was quite pink by now. She stood up and walked round the table till she was by the window. She leant against the sill, looking out.

'What about me?' Kitty asked letting out a long stream of smoke.

'Yes,' Vic said, 'I have things I want to discuss with you. I need to have people who don't worry too much about what I might ask them to do.'

Kitty nodded. 'Fine by me,' she said in her deep voice.

Soon after that, Joe served the food and he and Vic took it in turns to tell stories, Vic talking about the pornography industry and Joe about the Soho strip clubs. They ate and drank and Sukey, Jules and Jaz listened. Kitty tried to interject into the dialogue between the two men, which was a sort of duel, Jaz thought, a fight for position. Silly really, he thought; Vic was, well, Vic would inevitably be the victor. Vic sat on one side of the table between Jules and Sukey, Joe on the other side between Jaz and Kitty.

Jules said hardly a word all through the meal. Once Jaz leaned over the table to speak to her.

'What sort of pottery do you do?' he asked.

She looked up from her plate, said nothing for a minute or two. Then she smiled. 'I'm interested in objects that are not quite as they seem,' she said. 'I make big chunky things, bowls, jugs, but I do them so that they appear fragile, transient. And then I use pale, flimsy colours. It's to do with contradiction and deception.'

'Sounds good,' Jaz said, thinking that her words were pretentious and silly. 'And, er, you, er, sell your stuff?'

'Oh yes, Liberty and Harrods take my more conventional pieces and I exhibit the controversial work. I have quite a following.' She smiled again at Jaz, who said: 'Good.' I bet it's because of the way she looks, he thought, that people buy her pots. She must be hard to resist. But it's better when she keeps her mouth closed: all that conceited guff she's just spouted would put anyone off. He realised that he no longer liked Jules, no longer felt sorry for her. They deserve each other, she and Vic. He was tempted to lean back over the table and ask about their sex life: instead he poured more wine from the nearest bottle into his glass, pushed his chair back from the table and watched Kitty as she tried to chat up Joe.

'Dessert,' Joe said, standing up, wobbling a bit. Kitty lit another cigarette and smiled at Jaz. 'All right?' she almost shouted. Jaz nodded, yawned, wanted to go home, wondered if he could leave now.

Joe banged a big bowl onto the table. 'Trifle,' he said and went back to rummage in the fridge. He brought out two bottles of white wine and plonked them down before falling back into his chair. 'Somebody serve it out,' he slurred as he looked round the table for the corkscrew.

Kitty stood up to, found a big spoon and started to ladle the trifle into bowls.

'Not for me,' Jules said, raising her hand into a stop sign. 'I think we should be going.' She turned to face Joe. 'My mum's with the kids and I said we wouldn't be too late.'

'Nah, we can stay a bit longer,' Vic said.

'No,' Jules said, quietly. She was standing now and looking at Vic, her mouth pursed and hard. 'We can't.'

'You go then,' Vic said and the two stared at each other: another contest.

Finally, Jules looked away. 'All right,' she said and sighed. 'We'll stay for another little while.' She sat down, shook her head at Kitty who was passing her a dessert bowl, and bent her head. That's how she stayed for several minutes while Vic murmured to Sukey, who ignored him. Partly because she was now quite drunk, Jaz realised.

Joe reached across him with a bottle. 'Pass your glass,' he said.

'No thanks,' Jaz said. He'd drunk too much, eaten too much – he looked down at the remains of the trifle in his bowl – and now he was going home; and taking Sukey with him.

He stood up. 'Thanks for a fab dinner, Joe,' he said. 'I've got college tomorrow, so I'm leaving now, need to get to bed.' He looked across at Sukey. She looked back, her eyes moving in and out of focus. 'Coming?' he asked and she nodded. Jaz moved round table, stood with his hand on the back of Sukey's chair.

'Hey,' said Vic, 'we haven't arranged for you two to come for your camera tests.'

'No,' Jaz said, ' I don't want to.'

'Me neither,' said Sukey, standing up. 'Thanks Joe, great evening.' She took Jaz's hand and they moved towards the door.

'Don't go yet,' Joe said and he tried to rise, but gave up, slumping back into his chair.

'Stay, let me change your minds,' Vic said, but Jaz and Sukey ignored him.

'You've still got me,' Kitty said. 'I'll do whatever you want, as long as the money's good.'

Out in the hall Sukey gave a little shudder as if hit by cold. 'I hate it when I drink too much,' she said and leant against the wall as Jaz unlocked the front door.

'Wait,' Vic burst into the hall, 'you've not said goodbye properly.' He took Sukey by the shoulder and then moved his hands up to her face; he leant down and kissed her, long and hard. Jaz watched Sukey's legs as she tried to move away.

Vic stopped kissing her and let her go gently. He looked at her and said: 'You're only a little girl.' Jaz wondered what he meant. He frowned as Vic came up to him, smiling. 'Your turn,' he said.

'No,' said Jaz but Vic ignored him, pulled him close and kissed him on the mouth. Jaz felt the hardness of Vic's lips against his and the insistence of Vic's tongue pushing in. For a moment and without meaning to or wanting to, he kissed Vic back before twisting his head away and pushing Vic back. 'No,' he said again, swallowing, feeling his breath coming heavily.

Out in the little alleyway, Jaz took Sukey's hand and they walked quickly to the main road and turned in the direction of home.

'Why did he kiss you?' Sukey asked.

'That's the way he is,' Jaz said.

'He is attractive… I mean, he's got Jules and I wouldn't, but I could easily. I think I could sleep with him.'

'I think I could too,' Jaz said, the words coming out before he'd really thought them. He gasped.

'Really?' Sukey asked with genuine surprise. 'That's not because you're, you know, homo, is it? It's because Vic's so… so powerful, isn't it?'

Jaz shrugged. He didn't know what the answer was. 'Kitty's going to do stuff for him,' he said, changing the subject.

'Yup, I heard him talk about lesbian stuff and… animals. He even asked Kitty what she thought about little boys.'

'Oh shit,' Jaz said. Suddenly the whole evening, all the hours since he'd first seen Vic coming into the pub with Jules, seemed tainted and obscene. He sniffed, thinking he could smell the nastiness that was Vic's livelihood. 'I hope Kitty decides not to get involved,' he said.

(Over the years, Jaz would ponder that evening and how it changed lives, including his own. Such a trivial event: a drunken dinner party, an apparently normal Sunday evening in a London summer. He'd remember Kitty and Jules and Vic. He'd think about what happened to them later and wonder if it could have been avoided.)

Chapter 10
June 1967: Sukey

Sukey looked at Tessa's round, white, rather fat face, her pale eyes and small, slightly petulant mouth. This, she thought, was the girl who'd once been her best friend. Tessa pouted, kicked the leg of her chair.

'You don't have to,' Sukey said.

'No,' Tessa said, 'but the money, the money is so tempting.'

'I only mentioned that Kitty was going to do it.'

'If she can do it, so can I,' Tessa said. Beaky still said nothing.

'I'm not going to,' Minnie said.

'Nor me,' Sukey yawned.

'Why not?' asked Tessa as if she genuinely wanted to know.

'Because I don't want a lot of nasty old men leering at me wearing nothing,' Sukey said.

'I don't think you should, Tessa.' Finally Beaky had spoken. He looked tired and unhappy.

'I wouldn't have to do it for long, just enough to save some money.' Tessa frowned at Beaky and he frowned back.

Another Sunday, Sukey was thinking, another day which should have been pleasant but somehow wasn't even though she wasn't working. Kitty had finally persuaded Joe to come round to fix her up with a job stripping. She'd soon be home from the lunchtime shift at the pub and Joe had said he'd be over some time that afternoon. And now Tessa, who'd come for a visit with Beaky, wanted to meet Joe, wanted to know about the new opportunity.

Sukey yawned, was tempted to go back to bed. Or at least go to the bedroom and see if Jaz, who was still sleeping, would wake up and take her somewhere in his car. He probably wouldn't. Since that dinner party last week, he'd been grumpy. He'd even shouted at Sukey once when she'd asked him if he thought they should have gone to see Vic in his studio to see what he was offering and what they'd have to do for him.

Kitty had been there a couple of times already, but had said nothing about what Vic had talked to her about or what they were planning. When Sukey asked, Kitty had shrugged, lit a cigarette and then said: 'It's just a job, Sukey, another fucking job.' Well, Sukey thought, the 'fucking' is probably not just a swearword in this particular case.

'Dennis,' Minnie said as they heard loud footsteps coming up the stairs. The door opened and there he was. Come back to see what Kitty would be up to with Joe, no doubt. He looked round the kitchen, nodded at Tessa and Beaky, ignored Minnie and Sukey, strode over to the kettle, shook it, filled it and plugged it in.

'Yes please,' Sukey said. Dennis turned to look at her, frowning. 'If you're making coffee, I'll have some. What about you, Minnie? Another cup, Tess, Beaky?'

Minnie shook her head, no. Beaky looked at Tessa.

'Oh go on, I'll have one,' Tessa said, as if doing Dennis a favour, and Sukey gritted her teeth. The slow laconic way of speaking that Tessa sometimes now affected was a cause of irritation: the demise of friendship, Sukey thought.

'If we're staying, I'll have a cup, too,' Beaky mumbled.

The doorbell rang.

'Right,' said Sukey, 'I suppose I'd better answer it.'

Joe stood half turned away from the door, hunched up, hands in pocket.

'Kitty in?' he asked and Sukey shrugged.

'Not yet, but she'll be home soon.'

In the kitchen, Sukey introduced Joe to the others. 'Tessa said she might want to strip as well,' she said, and watched as Beaky winced.

'Yeah,' Joe said, taking a coffee mug from Dennis and looking round the room. Assessing us all, Sukey thought. She watched his skittering eyes and the way he bounced one leg up and down.

They all sat, waiting. Dennis had taken the loaf out of the bread bin and was making toast. He stood, leaning with his back against the sink, his legs crossed, smoking and looking disgruntled. Go home, Sukey wanted to say, go back to your wife and leave us all alone. He was nothing like her father, bore no resemblance at all, but when he was around she felt as if she was being judged and treated as her father would judge and treat her. Just the same but with the added aggravation of knowing that Dennis would like to take her to bed.

They all turned towards the door as Kitty came in, slightly breathless. 'Sorry I'm late,' she said, and then: 'Oh, Beaky, Tessa.'

She made herself tea, sat at the table smoking and asked Joe to tell them all about it. Which he did, looking at Sukey, moving his eyes up and down, then at Tessa and Minnie; he hardly glanced at Kitty. He told them how much they'd be paid, that they'd have to work five or six clubs to make it worthwhile; that's what most of the strippers did, doing a ten minute slot every two hours in each place, rushing from one to the other.

'It's hard work,' he told them, 'but good money. I've arranged to have as many of you as can make it to come down this afternoon and have a try out. But you'll be taken on, all of you, I'm sure. Now who's up for it?'

Only Kitty and Tessa offered themselves. 'Will you come with me, Beaky?' Tessa asked in a little girl voice, and he nodded at her, his eyes dark and sad.

The doorbell rang, once, twice, three times, as if someone was sending a message.

'Uh oh,' Sukey said, 'that's Malc, he's bringing some stuff for Jaz.'

'I'll let them in,' Minnie said.

When Jojo followed Malc into the room, Joe blinked and sat up straight. He watched her as she came slowly in and

136

looked round for somewhere to sit.

'What's going on?' she asked. 'Some kind of party?'

'Joe's telling us all about what we need to do to become strippers and earn loads of money,' Kitty said.

'Yeah,' Joe said, 'you interested? You'd be good.'

Jojo shook her head, smiled. 'Not my scene,' she said. 'I hate taking my clothes off unless the place is really warm. I get chilblains.'

'Shame,' said Joe. Sukey made a face at Jojo, who laughed.

Sukey sat on the floor, leaning against the wall; Jaz was in the bathtub lying back, a joint in one hand and a glass of whisky in the other. This he'd poured from another bottle stolen from the pub by Kitty, a final brazen gesture on her last night of work there. With Kitty not yet home from the clubs, once both Minnie and Dennis had gone to bed, Jaz had asked if Sukey would mind if he had a bath. During the time since Joe's visit, his grumpiness had dissipated. If anything, he and Sukey were closer, spending evenings together in the kitchen.

'You can stay with me,' he said. 'I feel like having a long soak.'

He'd run the bath, filling it almost full and adding a thick stream of bubble bath, which gave a sweet, rather cloying orangey smell.

'I must have used a week's worth of gas with all that hot water,' he'd said turning to grin at Sukey as he undressed. 'Don't tell Kitty.'

Sukey had watched as Jaz's clothes slipped to the floor, he rubbed his skinny buttocks with both hands and then climbed into the bath.

Jaz indicated that it was her turn for the joint and she stood up and went to take it.

'D'you want to get in with me?' Jaz asked and Sukey looked at him.

'Sex d'you mean?' she asked.

Jaz shook his head. 'Don't know,' he said. 'Let's see what'll happen. Just thought it would be nice to have you in the bath.'

'OK,' said Sukey. She put the ashtray and the bottle of whisky where they could reach it, pulled out another towel from the cupboard where they were kept and slid out of her clothes, just knickers and a thin, cheap dress.

'Your feet are really dirty,' Jaz said as she climbed in. Water sloshed onto the floor as she sat down facing Jaz. She stretched out her legs next to his and grinned. She reached for the joint and turned back. Jaz was staring at her breasts.

'You should feel my cock,' he said, 'it's enormous.'

Sukey felt a small stirring of almost-desire. Maybe after all they could fancy each other. She ran her free hand up the inside of Jaz's thigh and gently touched his balls with the tips of her finger. 'D'you like that?' she asked.

'Yes,' Jaz said. He reached forward and took one of her nipples, pulling at it and staring down at it. He let go and pulled back. 'I don't think I want to go any further,' he said, squeezing his eyes together in a frightened frown. 'I don't want to... do it, really.'

'OK,' Sukey said, 'Let's not.' She was relieved, she realised, not sure what it would have meant to have had sex with Jaz. She passed the joint to him and leant back, lifting her hair to stop it getting too wet.

'It's not you,' Jaz said, 'I just don't know what I feel about it all, sharing one's body with someone else.'

'What are you going to do about the size of your cock?'

'Oh that.' Jaz looked down through the sudsy water. 'It'll be all right in a while. In fact, it's already subsiding.'

'And the water's getting cold, I'm going to get out,' Sukey said.

'Wash your feet first,' Jaz said.

They were still in the kitchen when Kitty came home. The cover was back on the tub and Jaz and Sukey were dressed, but a faint scent of orange remained, mingling with the heavy smell of dope.

'Still up?' Kitty said as she came into the kitchen, yawning. Her hair was piled up on her head, a few strands escaping from the backcombed, lacquered mass. She was also fully made-up, with thick red lips and dark eyes fringed with false lashes. She sat heavily on the nearest chair.

'One of you make me tea,' she ordered, taking out her cigarettes and offering them first to Jaz, then Sukey.

'What's it like?' Jaz asked as he poured water into the kettle. They'd not seen Kitty since she'd started stripping a week earlier. Normally they were in bed when she came home and she'd left for the clubs by the time they came home from work and college.

'How you'd imagine it,' Kitty said. 'Take your clothes

off, dance, bump and grind.' She yawned again. 'Most difficult part is rushing from one place to another. Bloody exhausting.'

'How's Tess doing?' Sukey asked.

Kitty shrugged. 'OK. I've watched her a few times. She's got a slot just before me in a couple of the clubs. Bit tentative, bit wooden, not very adventurous. One of the clubs wanted a double act, two lesbians, and she wouldn't, even though it meant a bit extra in the pay packet. The club's being prosecuted for some infringement or another. They know the police will ignore them until the case and so they get more spicy than normal.'

'So are you doing the lesbian thing?' Jaz asked. He was twirling a piece of hair round one finger and chewing his lips. There were deep rings round his eyes and his face was grey and tired.

'Yeah,' Kitty said lighting a new cigarette from the butt of the old one. She exhaled deeply. 'Go to bed, Jaz, you look exhausted,' she said.

'In a minute,' Jaz said. 'What about Vic? What does Vic want you to do?'

'You don't really want to know, Jaz my love,' Kitty said as she smiled at him. She leant over and patted his arm. 'Go to bed.' It was like watching a mother and son, Sukey thought.

'Yes, Robin, no Robin,' Sukey mumbled to herself as she stood on the front door step, searching for her key. After only four hours of sleep, she'd spent the morning cleaning.

For once it was a house that really needed it. A widow with two teenage sons had suddenly decided that her house was a dirty mess and that she needed to address it. Then, as Sukey was about to leave for her afternoon assignment, Robin had rang the widow's doorbell and told Sukey that the next session was cancelled. The woman's husband had had the temerity to die the day before and she'd decided that she was too grief-stricken to entertain a cleaner.

'So,' said Sukey, 'no money for this afternoon.'

'That's the way it goes,' Robin said. 'You sometimes decide not to work.'

'But that's my choice,' Sukey said, letting her bad temper show. Having made the effort to get up that morning, she reckoned that a full day's pay was just about recompense for feeling so lousy and now she was only to get half of that. Also, she told herself, bloody Robin made almost as much as she did per hour for the work she put physical effort into, while he just sat around, organising.

Before Sukey had found her key, Bridie opened the front door. Sukey was pleased to see her, enjoyed spending time with her in her over-furnished but cosy sitting room that had become an occasional escape from the discomfort of the first floor flat.

Who you talking to?' Bridie asked.

'My boss,' Sukey said. Bridie peered round the door, shook her head, smiled.

'And so where is he?'

'In my head.'

Bridie laughed. 'Come and have a coffee with me,' she

said. 'I've got those pains in the arse from the social paying me a visit this afternoon. I need company.'

Sukey sat in the comfort of one of the big armchairs, leant back and closed her eyes, listening to the clinking of Bridie making coffee in the kitchen and the gurgling of Baby John, who was sitting on a rug in the middle of the room. He was wearing a new blue romper suit and was surrounded by a plethora of plastic toys.

There was a gentle pat on her knee. Sukey opened her eyes, there was Dolores standing in front of her, her curly hair brushed and tied with a wide satin ribbon, her dress was pale pink with puffed sleeves and white machine-made smocking. She was holding a doll under one arm and was looking intently at Sukey.

'Were you asleep?' she asked.

'Not really,' Sukey said.

'You go to bed if you want to sleep. Mammy sometimes has sleeps in the day. I stay up and look after the babies,' Dolores said. 'Baby John is Mammy's baby and this is my baby. Her name's Rosemary.'

'Hello Rosemary,' Sukey said as Dolores sat the doll on her knee.

'She comed out of my tummy. She got put there by a man's peanuts,' Dolores told Sukey.

'That'll do,' Bridie said, trying to sound cross, but she was laughing. 'You go and play in your room and leave Sukey and me to have a chat.'

'I want a chat, too,' Dolores said.

'Leave us alone,' said Bridie, 'and later we'll go to the

shops and I'll get you a treat.'

'I'll just sit quietly,' said Dolores, and dragging her doll walked behind the sofa where she sat murmuring to herself.

Sukey looked round to the room; it was so much more comfortable than the upstairs flat. It was clean, too, and smelled homely and of furniture polish. Bridie might make her living in questionable ways, but she was a good housekeeper and was probably a good mother, too, Sukey thought. She yawned.

The doorbell rang and Bridie went to open it. Sukey heard voices in the hall and then Bridie came back followed by two women, one of whom was carrying a briefcase. Bridie kept her head bent and her voice low as she offered tea or coffee. Both women refused. The one with the briefcase looked at Sukey.

'And this is?' she asked.

'My friend. She lives in one of the upstairs flats and she comes down to talk to me sometimes. It's lonely being a mother on your own with children,' Bridie almost whispered. 'You can say what you want in front of her. I'm not proud.' Bridie turned to Sukey and gave her a quick wink and a slight smile.

The women wanted to look round the flat and then sat in the kitchen to ask questions. Sukey could hear the murmur of the voices, the humble way in which Bridie responded and the occasional question from Dolores. Baby John sat happily chewing his toys.

There was a stirring in the kitchen, the scraping of chair legs on lino and the two women, Bridie and Dolores, cradling Rosemary in both arms, came into the living room. Baby John looked up and started to grizzle. Bridie bent and picked him up. She kissed his fat face and held him tightly to her, one hand stroking his plump pink thigh. He nuzzled into her breast.

'What would I do without my little ones?' Bridie said sounding pious.

'Ah Mrs McInerney, we don't how you manage on what you get. Your home so well looked after, your children so healthy-looking and so beautifully dressed,' the briefcase woman said.

'I do my best,' Bridie said, looking down, giving an impeccable performance of modesty.

'Well goodbye now,' said Briefcase and turned to the door.

When she came back from seeing them out, Bridie almost fell into a chair, laughing.

'Fecking eejits,' she said. 'They really think that I could manage on what they give me. And they believe every word I say. They asked me if I'd heard from the children's father and I told them no, not a word. I said that I thought he'd gone back to Ireland. Didn't mention the fistful of fivers he's managing to send down most weeks. Didn't tell them he's written saying when his job finishes he wants us try again, even have another baby.' Bridie was laughing so much she almost choked. 'That's worth another cup of coffee to celebrate.' She stood up, coughing. 'And I'll open some biscuits, too.'

'There was a man here yesterday afternoon, looking for

Kitty. I answered the door since none of you were in,' Bridie said when she came back with a tray holding two mugs, a glass of something fizzy for Dolores and a packet of chocolate fingers.

'Did he say who he was?'

'No, said he'd come back today,' Bridie yawned. 'So tiring, being a working girl,' she said and started to laugh again.

Sukey had just gone upstairs when the doorbell rang. She wondered for a moment whether to bother to answer it, but Bridie shouted from the hallway, 'I think it's that man after Kitty,' so she went down and opened the door.

'Hi,' said Vic, raising one eyebrow. 'I need to speak to Kitty.'

'She's not in, left for her stripping session.' Sukey held the door half shut.

Vic nodded. 'Can I come in and talk?' he asked. Sukey said nothing, wondering whether or not to let him in. He made her uneasy. Since going to that arts college over a year and a half ago now, and then coming to London last July, her life had become less and less what she, as a child, had fantasised it would be. She was not quite eighteen and already she'd had experiences that she wouldn't have been able to imagine a few years back. She knew about sex, dope and acid. And she had friends who were prostitutes or strippers or who injected heroin. Yet in some ways it seemed so normal. She wouldn't describe any of it as seedy or debauched: all of it was part of her life now.

'I don't think so,' Sukey said.

'Why not? I won't harm you.' Vic smiled as if she were joking.

'That's just the point,' Sukey said, feeling brave, aware of her heart beating fast as if to escape and of a strange tingling feeling in her throat. 'I don't think I can trust you.'

Vic groaned. 'Don't be so melodramatic,' he said. 'I'm just a normal guy, a married man with two small children and a living to make. I work hard to support the family.'

Sukey breathed out slowly, considering. She was aware of footsteps behind her and turned to see the landlord, with the landlady behind him, coming down the stairs, probably going out to fetch their daughters from school. Sukey said: 'Come in, then,' to Vic and stood aside. He pushed the door open and he, too, stepped away, leaving room for the Indian couple to exit. Vic bowed slightly as first the man with the faint suggestion of a smile and then the woman, stony-faced, looking down, hands folded in front of her, slid out of the hall and into the little front garden. Sukey watched as they turned into the street, he going first, she following, before closing the door. She sighed heavily, her head was starting to ache: not enough sleep the night before, four hours of real strenuous cleaning, too much coffee with Bridie and now a villain to deal with. A villain with charm and charisma, Sukey thought, but a villain nonetheless.

'Why do you hate me?' Vic asked as he drank the tea that Sukey had made.

'I don't,' Sukey said. She didn't, she thought as she looked at him. She could easily sleep with him, easily, but would, she was sure, regret it afterwards.

'You don't trust me, though, do you?'

'No.'

'Why not?'

'I think you're creepy. I think what you do is weird. Kitty's said a bit. Photographs with animals. Sick.'

'They like it.'

'How do you know?'

Vic didn't reply, just raised an eyebrow and sipped his tea. Sukey frowned, felt that there was probably even more that Vic did that she would find disgusting, even more that she didn't want to know.

'Look,' she said, 'Kitty's at work, she won't be back till two or three tomorrow morning. And then she's out again by early afternoon.'

'She's promised that she'll do certain things for me. We've arranged this Sunday, but I can't make it. Tell her I still want to do it, but it'll have to be the Sunday after. I phoned a few times to talk to her, but either no one answers or some kid picks up the phone and that's that.'

'It's a pay phone. We share it and it's in the hall downstairs. Dolores, the little girl who lives there, likes to answer it.'

'Train her to take messages then. And ask Kitty to call, she's got my number.'

'Right.'

Vic put down his mug. 'Any more tea?' he asked.

'No,' said Sukey, 'time for you to go.'

He looked at her, smiling slowly, his eyes narrowing. He stood up, came towards her. Sukey put her arms up; pushed him away.

'You'd like to, though, wouldn't you?'

'You're married, you said earlier you're just a normal family man,' Sukey said, knowing that the existence of his wife was not the main reason why she didn't want Vic: she didn't even know Jules, or know if she'd like her. Vic scared her; she imagined being in bed with him lying on top of her and suffocating her.

'Jules wouldn't mind. She doesn't care who I sleep with, as long as I come back to her. She even likes it when I bring – uh – friends home. That's the way we've arranged things.' Vic was still standing in front of her, too close. Sukey was still pushing at his chest with both hands. Vic grasped them, bent her arms down, leant forward and kissed her, his lips hard, insistent, mean.

Sukey squirmed away. 'Don't,' she said.

Vic smiled. 'Why don't you come and see her. Come to our house on Saturday for lunch, happy family lunch. You and that boyfriend of yours, that Jack.'

'Jaz,' Sukey said.

'Yeah, him.' Vic moved away, took a pen out of his pocket and a small notebook.

'He doesn't eat meat,' Sukey said.

Vic nodded as he tore out a sheet of paper and leant on the table to write. 'Here,' he said, passing the paper to Sukey, 'our address, come about midday. Both of you. And don't forget to pass my message on to Kitty.'

'I think we should go,' Jaz said.

'Why?' Sukey asked.

148

'Interest. See what they're all about.'

'Which one of them do you fancy, Jaz?'

Jaz shrugged, not denying, not telling.

'Maybe both of them,' Sukey said, then: 'OK, we'll go. But he scares me, you know.'

'Me too. And she does as well. I think she's a bit mad.'

Jules stood tall and slender in the doorway looking at them. It was as if she was waiting for someone to take her photograph.

'Um, Vic invited us,' Sukey started, planning to leave if it seemed that Jules was not expecting them.

'Yes,' Jules said and then she smiled. She was quite astonishingly beautiful. Sukey wondered what her pottery would be like, wondered if she was a success merely because of the way she looked.

'Come in,' Jules said, Sukey and Jaz followed her in. The hallway stretched to the back of the house and had a multi-coloured tiled floor. Each wall was painted a different colour: pink, lime-green, creamy yellow, silvery grey. The ceiling was crimson and the cornices and picture rail navy-blue. There were several well-framed pictures, all different, hanging at regular intervals down the long length of the passage and on the one narrow table, three very tall, very thin jugs. They were painted white with the occasional very small dab of pale colour. Jules' work, Sukey thought, as she admired them.

Jules led them through a door on the left into a double living room. It was sparsely furnished, the floorboards were sanded and stained pale green and the furniture looked home made, a big boxy sofa with matching chairs in dark blue wood and deep pink velvety upholstery. There was a coffee table in front of the sofa and one shelf unit against the wall, bearing more of what Sukey imagined were Jules' pots. They looked as if they were fashioned from a material of overwhelming fragility like tissue or gold leaf, not from thick, earthy clay. There were no pictures on the walls, no other objets d'art: the pots were all. At the end of the room, French windows opened onto a little paved terrace. Jaz and Sukey followed Jules through them.

To the right of the terrace was another set of French windows leading into a big kitchen where Sukey could see Vic wearing an apron. He seemed to be occupied with cooking. Beyond the terrace was a small lawned garden where a little boy and a girl not much more than a baby were playing on a rug. Happy families, Sukey thought and then, very well off happy family.

'Wine,' said Jaz, giving Jules the bottle they'd bought. He seemed overawed, out of place, embarrassed at being here. Sukey wondered where Vic and Jules worked: where were the pots made and the porn photographs shot?

'Thanks,' said Jules, 'please sit down.' Sukey pulled out a chair and sat at the terrace table that was already laid for lunch with matching wineglasses and linen table napkins. It all seemed too formal, too normal. Jaz sat opposite her and made a face, opening his eyes wide and biting his lips. Jules took the wine into the kitchen. Sukey could hear her talking to Vic. She came out with another, more expensive, already open bottle of red wine and offered them each a glass.

'I'm just going to feed the children and put them down for their rest,' she said. 'Vic will be out in a minute.'

Sukey watched her as she went and knelt on the lawn, speaking softly to her children. She stood, picked up the little girl and took the boy by the hand. He smiled shyly at Sukey as they walked past the table and into the kitchen. Sukey took a sip of wine; it had a rich taste, the flavour of blood. A small drop landed on the table and she touched it with the tip of her finger. It seemed almost viscous and she rubbed at it to make it disappear.

'Glad you decided to come.' Vic came out of the kitchen, still wearing his apron and carrying a full glass. He sat next to Sukey and took the makings of a joint out of his pocket. Good, Sukey thought, wine, dope, soon they'd all be more relaxed and able to talk.

They had just started the third bottle – the one that Jaz and Sukey had brought – when the food was served. Two home-made patés to start, one with and one without meat, then a mixed bean stew in a pale sauce with rice and salad. As they ate, Vic asked Jaz about his drama course and Sukey about what she did, as if they were all normal people living a civilised life. Sukey responded by asking about the children, how old were they, she wanted to know, and how did Jules manage to produce her pots and look after them.

'My mum helps. She's coming this afternoon to take them to her house for the night. And a nanny comes every weekday morning till lunchtime,' Jules said.

'She doesn't live here, then?'

'Oh no,' Vic said, 'we couldn't have that. Jules and I like to be on our own in the evenings. We like to enjoy ourselves.' He leant over the table and took Jules' hand in his, grasping it tightly, too tightly, making Sukey feel a little afraid. When he touched his wife, he seemed to be wanting to hurt her, or control her.

Sukey sat back, full, stifling a small burp and reaching for her glass. When this one was finished, she must not have any more, she thought.

Vic was rolling another joint. 'A bit of a smoke before dessert,' he said. 'Oh, Jules, open another bottle, would you?'

'Not for me,' said Sukey when Jules offered the wine.

'Yes you will,' Vic said. 'She needs more, Jules, just pour it.'

Sukey sighed, already a little drunk. 'All right,' she said, thinking how easy she was, how easily persuaded.

'Good,' Vic said and he put his arm round her shoulders. Then Sukey knew what was going to happen, knew what the whole lunch party had been about. She shivered, not so much scared for what was about to happen as because she knew exactly how the rest of the afternoon would pass. It was frightening to be so sure about the exact shape of the immediate future. She swallowed, looked across at Jaz, wondered what he would make of it, how he would cope. The best thing would be to leave now, but part of her wanted the experience that they were all about to have.

The children woke and Jules brought them down to eat a little of the chocolate mousse that Vic had made and then, when the adults were drinking brandy, Jules's mother arrived. Tall and beautiful like her daughter, but with grey hair, sad eyes and lines around her mouth. She was shy, didn't look at Sukey and Jaz when they were introduced, didn't talk to Vic. She disapproves, thought Sukey, as she left with the children.

Events unfolded just as she had known they would.

'I'd like to show you my studio,' Vic said making the back of Sukey's neck tingle. She looked across at Jules, who looked back, her eyes saying nothing, her face impassive. Sukey wanted to ask if she minded, but she found the other woman's cool demeanour a barrier: Jules acted as if she thought herself superior to others. She certainly thinks she's better than me, Sukey thought, more sophisticated, more talented, more beautiful.

'Shall we go?' Vic asked. He'd discarded his apron when the meal had started and had put his tobacco and dope in his pocket before his mother-in-law had arrived. Now he stood up, reached for the brandy bottle. 'Bring your glasses,' he said and led them into the living room. They walked back into the hall and up a flight of stairs. And then up another.

'While Jules works in the cellar, I have the attic,' he said as he reached the top landing and opened the door. They followed him into the studio, which was huge, covering the whole of the top floor. There was one dormer window to the front and a couple of large skylights in the roof. The walls sloped and there were little alcoves here and there. It could, Sukey thought, have been wonderfully charming. Instead Sukey felt the coldness make goose bumps on her arms.

There were a great many cameras and related equipment around, and on all the available flat spaces on the walls were photographs. The biggest one was a black and white one of Jules naked. She had a noose round her neck and looked as if she were hanging and dead.

'My God,' Jaz said. Sukey swallowed.

On the floor were two double mattresses covered in a variety of drapes and scattered about were a number of cushions.

Vic sat on the edge of one of the mattresses. He put the brandy and his glass down next to him and took the tobacco and dope out from his pocket. Jaz watched, twirling his hair, and jiggling one of his legs up and down. Sukey went to stand next to him. Vic looked up. Jules was by the dormer window.

'Draw the blinds,' Vic said and Jules did so. She turned on a few lamps, which gave a little light, and then lifted a long hooked pole, which she used to pull down thick covers over the skylights. The place was almost dark.

Jules took Jaz's hand and led him to the other mattress. 'Go and sit next to Vic,' Jules said to Sukey, who obeyed. She wished that she didn't but she did: she felt tremendously sexually aroused. She was also scared. All was just as she'd known it would be from the time, less than an hour earlier, when Vic had put his arm round her shoulder. She felt him pull her close to him. He took her glass and filled it with brandy, then he leant over and poured some for Jaz and Jules. He lit the joint, all the time holding Sukey tightly against him.

After he'd been kissing her for a while, Vic released her. 'Sit up,' he whispered, 'watch the others.' Sukey blinked, did as she was told. On the other mattress, Jules was almost naked; Jaz was still fully clothed. Now Vic was fiddling with lighting and cameras. Sukey watched as Jules took off Jaz's shoes and socks, caressing his feet as she did it, then she unbuttoned his shirt and pulled it off. All the time Jaz's eyes were closed. Jules took off her bra and knelt over Jaz letting her breasts run against his chest. She undid his fly and Jaz moaned and almost pulled away. Jules held him down. She took off his trousers and underpants, sucked his cock, removed her knickers and sat, her back to him, straddling him, playing with him and with herself while Vic took photograph after photograph. Jaz was bucking under Jules. She leaned and lifting the edge of the mattress pulled out a knife: an old carving knife with a thin, well-sharpened blade. She held it in the place where Jaz's penis and scrotum met. Sukey gasped. Jules was pumping Jaz and he came as Vic worked at his camera.

Jules crawled over to Sukey's mattress. 'Your turn,' she said, and reached for the zip of Sukey's dress with her free hand: the other was still clutching the knife. She laid this in the gap between Sukey's legs and pulled off Sukey's clothes and then pushed her until she was lying on the mattress, grasping her legs and pulling them wider apart. When Sukey felt the metal of the knife against her thigh, she struggled. She could hear the click of Vic's camera over and over. She lay limp as she felt Jules' fingers on her neck and then struggled again as the cushion covered her face so that she could hardly breath.

'Help,' she tried to scream but the sound was muffled; she could feel satin on her face and in her mouth. Then it was gone. She opened her eyes. Jaz was kneeling next to her, the cushion in his hand, fear and shame in his face. Beyond him was Vic, still taking pictures. As Sukey watched he stopped, he dropped to the mattress undid his fly and masturbated, spurting his semen over her, over Jaz and over Jules who was now lying next to her.

They lay all four of them on the mattress. The men had come, but not the women, Sukey thought. She no longer wanted to. She wanted to leave. After all that alcohol, all that dope, she felt completely sober. Limp, tired, used up and embarrassed, but sober.

Sukey pushed away Jules's arm that was lying across her body and pulled herself up into a sitting position, freeing her legs from where Vic was lying on them. 'Let's go,' she whispered to Jaz. He stared at her, seemed confused. He was lying on her dress. 'Get up,' Sukey whispered. 'Get your clothes on.' He stirred, looked down at himself, seemed surprised to find that he was naked.

'Oh my God, Sukey,' he whispered.

'You're not going,' Vic said from where he lay. 'There's lots more fun to be had.'

Jaz crawled over to the other mattress. Sukey shook out her dress, found her knickers and dressed. As she was doing up her zip, Vic sat up. His faced was creased and greasy-looking. 'Hm,' he said, shifting along the mattress. He'd been lying on the knife. He picked it up, held the point to Sukey's throat. 'Stay,' he said, 'or else.'

Sukey shook her head: the threat had gone. She was no longer scared. Vic seemed weak, stupid, and Jules, still lying naked with her eyes closed, was a poor little pathetic doll.

'We're going,' Sukey said, pulling away and standing up. 'We'll let ourselves out. Thank you for a lovely lunch. Come on, Jaz.' He was lacing his shoes, still seemed dazed. Sukey stood by the door watching Jaz, who sat for moment, his arms resting on his knees. He yawned, shook his head and stood up.

Vic clutching the knife stood too. His fly was still undone, his penis lolling out. Sukey laughed, opened the door and ran down the stairs, hearing Jaz follow her.

Out in the street she took a big breath of air. 'What did you think of that, Jaz?' she asked.

'Weird,' he said. And then added. 'I don't think I liked it.'

'Did you know that she had a knife?'

'What?'

'A knife, against your… cock.'

'She didn't.' Jaz paled, his skin so white it was almost green.

'She did.' Sukey nodded and Jaz turned and vomited into the gutter.

(Occasionally in later life, Sukey would have a premonition. It was always to do with sex, with the absolute knowledge that a man was going to embrace her, or that one would insist she sleep with him. Each time it was an undesired event and she always resisted it, remembering, as she did, Vic

157

and Jules; and she'd wonder why that first time she'd let happen what she'd foreseen, the only time when there was a threat of real danger.)

Chapter 11
July 1967: Minnie

Minnie sighed, very quietly. She didn't want to wake the others. Jaz and Sukey had come in late the night before and were both still asleep, Sukey curled up in a ball and Jaz lying on his back with his thin chest bare, his sheet and thin blanket pushed down to just below his waist. He looked like a little boy and Minnie wondered if he was dreaming about being a child again. Once more she sighed and gently pulled back her bedclothes. She knelt by the window, pushing her head behind the curtain. It was a beautiful sunny day; it made her feel sad and long for this time in her life to be over.

She turned to look at Jaz. Maybe if she woke him she could persuade him to drive out into the country somewhere: a picnic, he could take them all out for a picnic; later, maybe. But now, with luck, Dennis would have gone to make his Sunday visit to his family and Kitty would be still asleep. She would have the kitchen to herself, could take a quick bath and then go for a walk: a time to think, make some decisions about what to do next.

Minnie rummaged in a drawer for clean clothes and left the bedroom, closing the door gently behind her. Yes! The kitchen was empty. She cleared the shelf above the tub and ran a few inches of water into it before blocking the door with a chair and climbing in. She lay back for a few minutes, fantasising about a future when she would have money and could live on her own with a bathroom just for her, with thick warm towels, expensive creams and scent, as much hot water as she wanted. Next time when she'd saved a bit, it wouldn't be for some trip to India with a hippy boyfriend, it would be to start a business. One day she would be rich and she would be happy.

She washed herself and climbed out. Once dressed she made tea and toast and when she'd eaten it and washed the few dishes and tidied up, she took her leather purse and hung it round her on its long strap and left the flat.

She walked down the street taking big strides, breathing in the summer smell of London: crumbling brick, oil mixed with metal, musty pavement, dusty leaves. A year, she thought, she'd been living for a year in London. She'd just missed getting into university: 'A' level grades not quite good enough. She remembered her father's disappointment and her mother's cheery words, trying to comfort her. 'Never mind, Mary Ann, dear… There's more to life than studying. You've got Nick after all.' There was a question in those words as well as attempted solace. With her three older daughters all already married, the eldest at only eighteen, her mother was asking how serious Minnie's relationship was with Nick.

If her mother had known, Minnie thought, she'd have tried to rescue her youngest child. Naughty Nick, who'd introduced her to dope and then sex and finally to acid – perhaps the reasons for her not so good exam results. He'd been the one to suggest London, too. She'd not needed much encouragement, wanting to get away from her parents and their comments about her future. He'd driven her up in the car he'd just bought, and they'd taken over his sister's bedsit while she was on holiday. Then he'd helped her find a room in a flat, stayed with her there, introduced her to the manager of the shop where she now worked. He'd done all that and then he'd left her, gone she didn't know where.

'Your problem, Minnie,' he'd said as he packed, 'is you don't like sex, you don't like getting stoned and when you take a trip you go all still and silent. You go too far into yourself.'

Minnie had said nothing but had known with a strange shuddering feeling that he had understood her perhaps too well. She found it frightening. She'd said nothing, letting him go without asking any questions or trying to persuade him to stay. She continued numbly at her job, moved out of the flat when it became obvious that the others living there didn't really like her, and took the room in Kitty's place because it was cheap and because she'd found something comforting in the presence of Kitty. Minnie sighed remembering it all: meeting Malc and starting to deal and think of visiting India; getting involved with Ted and liking having a boyfriend again and trying to like sex as well.

Her brisk stride faltered and she turned to sit on a low

wall, looking down to avoid the glare of the sun, which was hurting her eyes. She reached into her purse for papers and tobacco and sat rolling a cigarette.

'Hey, you,' she heard someone call and looked up, squinting. There were two men on the other side of the street. One of them she knew. It was Joe, the friend of Sukey's who had wanted them all to become strippers. Minnie finished rolling her cigarette and lit it as she watched Joe and his friend skitter across the main road, dodging the traffic.

'You live with Sukey and Kitty,' Joe said as they reached her.

'Yes,' Minnie said slowly, wondering if she should stay and talk or get up and go, tell them she was busy. Joe was tapping one of his feet.

'I'm Joe,' he said.

'I know,' said Minnie.

'This is Sean,' he said, indicating his friend. Minnie looked at him. He had curly dark hair and a crooked smile. He was, she thought, the sort of man who likes to seduce young girls. She didn't understand why that idea had presented itself. And also, she didn't enjoy the feeling that he had began to engender: she was oddly and unwillingly attracted to him, drawn to his scrawniness, his sensual mouth, thin face, paint-spattered T-shirt and long fingers that she wanted to take in hers. He had what an aunt of hers had once whisperingly described with an embarrassed laugh as 'bedroom eyes'.

Minnie stood up. 'I better get going,' she said.

'Where to?' Joe asked. He was like a dog being held in check, moving around on the pavement, unable to stand still but forced to stay by an invisible lead.

'For a walk,' Minnie said, knowing that it was a weak response, that they'd try and persuade her to join them for something and that the excuse of a walk would not be strong enough to stop them insisting.

'Ah, what d'you want to be doing that for,' Joe said. 'Come and have breakfast with us. We've just been for the papers and now we're going back to my gaff for a big fry-up.'

'I've already had breakfast.'

'That's no excuse. You can come with us and keep me company while Joe cooks. And if you don't want to eat, he'll make you a great cup of coffee. Now say you'll come.' Sean's hand rested momentarily and tenderly on Minnie's shoulder and although she tried not to, she blushed.

'Ah, she'll come,' said Sean, smiling and this time his hand lingered a little longer on her shoulder. 'And she'll tell us her name, too.'

'Minnie,' said Minnie and found herself walking along with the two men.

The little house facing the canal could have been charming were it not so run down. Joe told her that he owned it, but that he had sitting tenants and so could only occupy the ground floor. This he'd turned into one big room, with a kitchen, a living area and a platform he was building to house his bed. Minnie thought that when it was finished it would be delightful. She told Joe this and then, at his bidding, went to sit with Sean while Joe grilled sausages and bacon, laid the table and made filter coffee.

Sean sat on a large beanbag and suggested that Minnie sit next to him.

'Do you have a job?' he asked her, his voice made soft and seductive by his Irish accent. Minnie told him what she did and how she was saving for her own business.

'And you have a boyfriend, of course,' he said.

'Not at the moment,' Minnie said, blushing again.

'Ahh. You won't have to wait long,' Sean leant towards her and gently pushed a strand of her hair back from her face. Minnie thought he was about to kiss her and wanted it to happen.

'You've lovely soft skin,' Sean said moving his fingers to her cheek and stroking it.

'You watch him, he's a married man,' called Joe from the kitchen area. He was melting fat in a frying pan.

'I am,' Sean said, smiling, ' but not happily.'

'And he's children as well,' Joe called over the spluttering noise of frying eggs. 'And if that won't put you off, then what if I tell you that your friend Sukey had the hots for him?'

'Just shut up, Joe,' Sean said before he gently bent towards Minnie and touched her forehead with his lips. She didn't care if he was married several times over with a multitude of children; she wanted to have sex with him. This was the first time, in spite of Nick, in spite of Ted, that she felt truly sexually aroused. She slowly raised both arms and let her hands rest one on each of Sean's shoulders. His kiss was gentle and at the same time strong: his lips pressing against hers as if investigating and his tongue moving into her mouth as if it belonged.

'Breakfast's ready,' Joe yelled and he beat on the now empty frying pan with a wooden spoon. Sean pulled back, smiled at Minnie, took her hand and helped her up.

On the table was a platter laden with breakfast food, a pile of thick cut Greek bread, a dish of butter, a bowl of marmalade, a jug of coffee and a smaller one of warm milk. It was a well-presented and well-cooked meal. Surprising, Minnie thought, that Joe should have such domestic skills. She sat down and let Sean fill up a plate for her.

When they'd eaten and a second jug of coffee had been made, she offered to wash up, but Joe said: 'I'll do it.' And he started to clear away.

'He's desperately house proud,' Sean said. His hand was now resting on her thigh as he drank his coffee. Slowly it moved to her knee and held it. Then his finger slid down her calf, reaching the end of her skirt, which it pushed up. Minnie breathed in deeply, wondering what would happen next.

Sean moved his hand away and drained his coffee. 'You're off out soon, aren't you Joe?' he asked.

'No,' said Joe, as he pulled the plug in the sink, swirling away the dirty water. He took a cloth and rinsed it under the tap, then used it to wipe the surfaces clean.

'I thought you had to meet Vic,' said Sean. Joe turned and the two men looked at each other.

'Yes, maybe I did. You and Minnie want to stay here for a bit?'

Sean nodded.

After Joe had gone Sean led Minnie to the mattress at the far end of the room and they both lay down and started to kiss. Minnie wanted it to last for ever. She held his face between her hands and savoured the sensation of his lips on hers, his tongue soft in her mouth.

Eventually Sean moved his face away and stared at Minnie, saying nothing for a little while. Leaning on one arm, he moved his other hand to her breast and pinched a nipple through her clothes.

'You're not a virgin are you, Minnie?'

'No,' she replied, almost breathless.

'You're not very experienced, then. Is that it?'

'I don't know,' said Minnie, wondering what he was talking about.

'Never mind. I want you very much in spite of that,' Sean said and he bent to kiss her. This time his mouth was hard and urgent and his hands were hard on her breasts, her thighs and between her legs.

'Yeees, I want you,' he hissed and stopped to sit up. He grasped her T-shirt and pulled it off her head, undid her bra, pulled at the zip on her skirt and wrenched it down over her knees. Minnie kicked it away as he yanked down her knickers, staring at her and then sticking his finger hard into her vagina. She gasped and suddenly she was hating what she was doing, no longer wanted to be there or to be with Sean. He undid his jeans and slid out of them and his underpants.

His penis was huge and red, dark and threatening against his thin pale hips and flat white stomach. She closed her legs together and he pulled them apart and lay between them. Soon he entered her and, crooning, he kissed her face, her hair, moved down and kissed her breasts, holding her arms tight against the mattress.

'You're an innocent, an innocent,' he said over and over. It was as if the words were hurting his throat as he uttered them. This is disgusting, Minnie thought, half struggling against him, half relishing the push of his body in her and against her. And then he came and it was over and Minnie wanted to cry and run away. He lay on her quite still, oddly heavy for one so skinny, and Minnie waited, feeling that she would suffocate if he didn't move soon.

When she stirred, trying to indicate that she needed him to move, he rolled off her, rolled over and within a few minutes he seemed to be asleep. Minnie lay crying quietly, feeling the tears go down each side of her face into her ears and resolved never to have sex with anyone again.

Sean started to snore, a gentle noise like a big bee buzzing, and Minnie slid off the mattress. She gathered her clothes together and dressed. She went to find a toilet and when she came back, stood by the mattress, bending slightly, looking at Sean and wondering whether to go or stay. And if she went, whether to leave a note. Sean stirred and Minnie stepped back. Right, time to go, no need to say goodbye.

Out in the street Minnie shut the front door quietly and went to lean on the rail by the canal. She imagined eating an orange and throwing the peel in the sluggish dirty water. She imagined its bright colour moving along with the current and wanted to take a photo of it. She shook her head. Another spoiled Sunday. But maybe if she went home the others would be up and she could ask Jaz about a drive into the countryside.

'Hi,' said Sukey looking up from her book. She was sitting at the table drinking tea and reading. Minnie slumped down in the big armchair and, without meaning to, sighed.

'What's up?' Sukey asked. Minnie shook her head. She didn't want to tell anyone, let alone Sukey, what she'd done. She felt stupid and desolate and wished that the day could begin again.

'Something's wrong,' Sukey said. 'You've been crying.'

'I wish you'd keep out of my business.' Minnie rubbed the corner of one of her eyes with two fingers and thought about the bath she'd had earlier and how it was a complete waste as she now felt dirtier than ever and needed a long soak in hot water.

'Fine,' Sukey said and turned back to her book.

'Is anyone else in?' Minnie asked after a few pages had turned.

'Sorry, no. I'm the only one around.' Sukey didn't even bother to look up, carried on reading.

Minnie closed her eyes, lay back in the chair, thought about how the day had started and the meeting with Joe and Sean. She went through the walk back to Joe's house, the breakfast cooking, Joe's realisation that she and Sean were attracted to each other, his shouting out that Sean was married and other things designed to put her off. She sat up, her eyes open.

'Sukey,' she said.

'Yeah.'

'Do you know a guy called Sean, a friend of Joe's?'

'Met him once.'

'And you fancied him.'

Sukey looked up. 'I thought he was rather attractive.'

'I just slept with him. That's where I've been,' Minnie said, and watched as Sukey's lips tightened, head went back and eyes narrowed. That had an effect, she thought, and smiled.

'Did you enjoy it?' Sukey asked.

Minnie sat looking at Sukey looking at her. It was a shame they disliked each other. It would be a lot better if they could be friends. Eventually Minnie shrugged. 'I don't think I enjoyed it. I think I hated it.'

(That was the day, Minnie recognised years later, that she began to decide that she needed to be discerning about men, to realise that there was no imperative to sleep with any of those she encountered. It was six years before she had sex again. And this time with a man of whom she approved and liked. He was a businessman who she considered sensible and solid and who she later married. It was not a marriage based on passion.)

Chapter 12
July 1967: Sukey

Sukey frowned, looked again. Yes, that was Jules sitting at a table at the back of the café, looking tired and sad. But still beautiful and as if she wasn't quite sure what she was doing in a public place drinking coffee, doing what normal people who lived mundane lives did. It was over two weeks since that Saturday and Sukey had thought about it often, discussed it with Jaz, asked Kitty if Vic had said anything about it to her. He hadn't, it seemed. Sukey turned to face the other way, sipped her drink, wondered if she should go and talk to Jules, wondered if Jules would be embarrassed to see her. She looked back and Jules was staring at her, frowning slightly. Sukey nodded and Jules' frown eased, became a smile. Then she stood up, lifted her cup, slung her bag over her arm and pushed her way through the tables, making her way to Sukey.

'Hi,' Sukey smiled.

'I do know you, don't I?' Jules asked.

'Yes. I'm Sukey. I was at your house not long ago. My

friend Jaz was there… We came for lunch?' Sukey's last sentence became a question. She wondered if Jules was joking. How could she forget what had happened between them in Vic's studio?

'Ah yes, I think I remember now… You don't mind if I join you?' Jules asked.

'Of course not.' Sukey looked at the café clock; she had another twenty minutes, even half an hour before she needed to leave for the next cleaning job. Jules sat down, moved her cup around for a bit, looked up at Sukey, smiled, stared down at her coffee, lifted the spoon and stirred it.

'Do you think we're odd? Me and Vic, I mean.' Jules was peering at the table, drawing imaginary lines on the Formica with the tip of one finger.

'Of course,' Sukey replied. The only response, she felt, to such a question. Jules had expected such an answer.

'Yes,' Jules said, still looking down. She sighed. 'I wanted a normal life,' she said. 'That's all. Do you know I hate what we do? All that extra stuff that Vic wants.'

'Why go along with it?' Sukey was enjoying Jules confiding in her; it made her feel that she was not so insignificant and unsophisticated. She liked it that a more-or-less famous potter with a glamorous-seeming life thought her opinion worth seeking and her company rewarding.

Jules shrugged. 'What else can I do? We've got the kids and that lovely house and he makes lots of money and I like having money. I like nice things.' She was sounding almost defensive.

'But if you're unhappy…' Sukey started.

'Oh unhappy. Of course I'm unhappy. I've always been unhappy.'

Sukey sat back. Stupid Jules; beautiful, talented Jules. How could she always be unhappy? 'Well anyway,' Sukey persisted, 'maybe it's being with Vic and all that stuff that's the problem. Maybe you should think about kicking him out.'

'D'you want another coffee?' Jules asked. She'd not been listening, Sukey was sure.

She looked up at the café clock. She had time. 'Yes please,' she said and Jules stood and went to the counter.

'I was only nineteen when we got together,' she said as she sat down again. 'Art school. He was the one all the girls wanted and I got him. It was wonderful to start with. It was when he got into the porn that things began to go wrong. It was only supposed to be for a little while, until we'd enough money for the house. But the thing was he started to enjoy it and it began to be part of our normal lives as well.' She paused. 'So you do think it's odd?' she asked.

'It's not the way most people live,' Sukey said.

'Look, I know that I'm the one he really wants. I mean there's all those girls around and he can have any one of them he wants. Ah, no offence to you,' Jules said, but she didn't mean it, Sukey knew.

'Why are you telling me all this?' Sukey asked.

Jules said nothing for a bit. 'I never talk about it, never. But I need to now. I don't think I can go on with it for much longer. It's getting worse.'

'What is?'

'What's what?' Jules frowned. Definitely not listening.

'What's getting worse?'

'This killing thing, the noose, the knife, using the cushion to suffocate. He's coming to love those things more than the real sex.' Jules swallowed.

'I must go,' Sukey said, thinking some of us have normal boring jobs to do. She finished her drink. 'Er, thanks for the coffee,' she added as she stood up.

'I'm sorry,' Jules said. 'What's your name again?'

Sukey shook her head, didn't bother to reply, walked out of the café.

Bridie's sitting-room door opened. She was grinning. 'I've got two surprises for you,' she whispered, widening her eyes as Sukey came into the hall. Sukey frowned, wanting to stretch and yawn; eight hours of cleaning after a night of not enough sleep and she was exhausted.

'What you on about?' she asked Bridie, who winked at her.

'Come into my room and you'll see,' Bridie laughed.

'Hello Sukey,' said Dolores, who was sprawled on the floor with her doll. Sukey blinked. Two men were sitting in the armchairs, both holding coffee mugs, both smoking, both looking a little sheepish.

'Oh,' she said. There was Rick, her very first boyfriend from what now seemed a very long time ago. And there was Dan, who used to visit her when she was living alone in the half derelict flat, taking her out from time to time and bringing her dope when she asked for it. Sukey frowned.

'What are you two doing here? I didn't know you knew each other.'

'We don't,' said Rick, who had been slumped against the back of his chair and now sat up straight.

'Just met this afternoon,' said Dan, re-crossing his short plump legs.

'I could hear your bell ringing,' Bridie explained to Sukey. Then she laughed. 'And of course there was no one there to answer it. When I peeped through the window, I saw the first of these two handsome fellows and so naturally I went to the door and told him that he could wait for you here. I knew you wouldn't be long. As soon as the coffee was ready the bell rang again and there was the second one.'

'Well,' said Sukey. 'So… have you two been introduced?' She stood by the door wearing nothing but an old and shabby short dress that she kept for the days when she cleaned, her bare feet were dirty and her hair needed washing.

'Would you like a coffee, too?' Bridie asked. Sukey nodded and went to sit on the sofa. Dolores came and sat next to her, putting one hand on her leg and looking at the two men.

'Are they your boyfriends?' she asked.

'No,' said Sukey.

'You should have that one,' Dolores said, pointing at Rick. 'He's thinner round the edges than the other one.'

'Shut up, Dolores,' said Sukey, wondering why the two men were here and how she was going to deal with them.

'Look, maybe I'll be off,' Rick stood up, put his cup on

the coffee table. 'I just came to see how you were, it's so long since I've heard from you…'

'No,' said Sukey, 'we can go for a drink. Stay for a bit.'

'I'll be the one to go,' Dan said. He too stood up.

'No,' said Sukey again. She sighed. 'I'm sorry,' she said, but not sure for what. She didn't know if she was pleased to see them and found it confusing that after several months of not hearing from either man, they'd both come to visit her at the same time. She'd seen Rick a few times since that night when he'd made it clear he no longer wanted her. They met occasionally for a quick drink, she'd never been back to his flat and he'd only been here once before and had seemed to disapprove of the place and its occupants. She'd seen even less of Dan; he'd been away for some time touring with the band he played with. He sent her postcards and twice had called round when she'd not been in and had left messages. She'd bumped into him at a party a few months ago; they'd not spoken much but he'd arranged to take her to a gig the following week. She went, but once they'd arrived at the venue, she saw little of him for the rest of the evening. Someone else had taken her home.

'Look,' said Dan, 'I just came round to say that I'll be in Edinburgh for the fringe next month, performing. I wanted to ask you if you'd like to come up for it. There's a flat I'll be staying in, room for you if you want to spend a bit of time up there. Just give me a call and we'll sort something.'

'Yeah,' said Sukey, 'that would be good.'

'Here's my number, where I'm staying at the moment. I'll be there till I go,' Dan said, passing a piece of torn paper, scribbled on with red biro.

Bridie was back in the room with coffee for Sukey.

'Not going?' she said to the two men.

'Mammy likes having men sitting in our flat,' Dolores said. 'Sometimes they get tired and they have to sleep in her bed.' Dolores was cuddling her doll close to her. 'Are you tired?' she concluded, looking at Rick. He blushed slightly, Sukey noticed and she smiled. Once upon a time, she had thought Rick the most sophisticated person she knew. Now he seemed a little dull, a little too earnest, straight-laced. He'd never been a dope smoker, disapproved of acid. He'd also been her first lover. And had dropped her. Sukey realised that she wanted to talk to him, to tell him all about Jules and Vic. She wasn't sure if it was because she wanted to hear his opinion on it all, or because she wanted to shock him or to show him how far she'd moved since their days together.

'Thanks,' said Sukey, taking the cup from Bridie and sitting up straight. 'I'll give you a call, Dan, about Edinburgh. Really, at the weekend. And, Rick, just let me have this coffee and then maybe we can go and have a kebab or something?'

'So,' said Sukey, 'what do you think?' She'd just described the Saturday that she and Jaz had spent with Vic and Jules.

Rick took a mouthful of rice and lamb curry – they'd opted for Indian instead of Greek, and Rick had offered to pay as he had a good vacation job and was earning so much more than Sukey – and shook his head. 'Should I believe you?' he asked.

'Do I lie?' Sukey asked.

'Don't know what you do these, days, Sukey-Sue,' Rick was using his pet name for her, the one he'd employed to intimate affection in the old days when they'd been sleeping together. Even at the time, Sukey had felt that it was a cop out, a poor substitute for something really loving. She put her head on one side. When she thought back to their affair that had started only about fifteen months ago and lasted less than half a year, it seemed like she was thinking about a different age, a time when she at least had been someone else. She half closed her eyes, remembering being in bed with Rick. Really, she thought, if I'd been older, I'd not have wanted him at all, or if by chance I had, I'd have known that he was never serious about me.

'These things do happen,' she said, clipping the words, making her tone a little hostile.

Rick looked up at her from his plate. He had, she thought, ridiculously long eyelashes for a man. 'I know they do,' he said, 'I do read, you know.'

'Yes,' she said. Rick had been obsessed with Durrell's 'Alexandrian Quartet' when they met, and had later introduced her to Iris Murdoch and the Marquis de Sade.

'I'm not talking of books,' Sukey said. 'I'm talking about real things happening.'

Rick sighed and put down his fork. 'Do you want another beer?' he asked.

'Yes please,' said Sukey, putting her hand down and rubbing her tummy, swelling, she was sure, from it's filling of curry, rice, popadom and lager.

After the waiter had been summoned and the drinks ordered, Rick resumed eating. He approached food methodically, ordering it neatly on his plate, each forkful conveyed to his mouth the exact same balance of rice, meat, sauce and chutney as all the others. Rick chewed, waved his fork at Sukey. 'I am worried about you,' he said. 'You seemed to have a purpose back when I first knew you. You wanted to be an actress. Now, what are you doing? Living in a dump with a group of weirdos, taking drugs, mixing with strippers and pornographers. And that woman – Bridie was it? Is she a prostitute?'

'Not really,' Sukey said. Bridie may have sex for money but Sukey thought the label "prostitute" didn't seem appropriate for her.

'I think that means she is.' Rick was saying. 'Look, Sukey. You can't go on like this. You need to make some sensible plans.'

'I like my life,' Sukey said. Well, she told herself, it's not a question of liking or not liking: it is the way it is.

'So, are you trying to get into drama school? What about Bristol?'

'Hm,' Sukey said. 'I don't like actors,' she said. 'Or at least I don't like those that teach.' She thought back to the year before, her audition at the Old Vic Drama School in Bristol, a whole weekend. Both she and Jaz had gone, staying in small ugly rooms in a damp bed and breakfast; the landlady had had a mouth disguised by thick, red greasy lipstick, a mock posh accent, swollen ankles above small feet in tight patent leather, and a curiosity about her guests that was so strong it almost smelled. Sukey had enjoyed the audition, though. Because Jaz was there she'd been confident, spoke well, made people laugh, attracted attention. On the Sunday afternoon, one of the tutors had called her into a room for an interview; told her she had talent, but that she was too young to be taken onto the course. 'Go away for a little while and learn about life,' he said in a deeply theatrical voice that seemed like parody but, sadly, wasn't. He continued: 'And then come back next year when you've experience as well as freshness and beauty to offer us.' He patted her hand and lowered his voice even further. 'We'll give you a free audition,' he concluded as if offering her a very special, very secret sexual thrill. Which he couldn't be, Sukey thought, as he was an old queen.

'Besides,' she told Rick now, 'I'm not good enough. As for Bristol, I couldn't be bothered to take up my free audition. Even Jaz is thinking of whether or not to go back to college next term. And he's really good.'

'What are you going to do with your life, Sukey-Sue?' Rick sounded sad and also rather like her father.

Sukey shrugged. 'Just now I'm going to go home. I'm tired and you won't even discuss what I told you about Vic and Jules. What's more you think I was lying, that none of it really happened.'

'All right. I do believe you,' Rick said. 'I've been letting what you said float around in my mind and I know that you couldn't have made all that up.' Was that an insult or a compliment, Sukey wondered, and did it matter, did she really care what Rick thought?

'I don't want to see you waste your life. You're clever, have you thought about studying? I can see you in ten years time as an academic. And in my opinion, you really must get out of that place where you're living. Above all, you should cut all ties with that porn couple.' Rick was frowning at her; his hand clasped tightly round his beer glass.

Sukey shrugged. 'I probably won't see them again: don't really want to. Kitty's doing some work for Vic, though. Nasty photos. I mean really nasty.'

'You not working?' Sukey said as Bridie came into the hall from her bedroom. She was dressed in a frilly, baby-blue satin negligée with nylon ruffles, on her feet she wore fluffy, silver coloured slippers with little high heels that looked too delicate for Bridie's strong, rounded legs. Her big breasts and stomach pushed against the stretch of material that covered them.

'Been busy,' Bridie laughed and yawned. 'Was just going to get myself a Guinness. Do you want one?'

'I'd love a cup of tea,' Sukey said, letting out a little burp. 'I've had too much curry and lager for anything else.'

'OK. Come on in, ' Bridie said, opening the door to her sitting room, 'and you can tell me all about those two young men of yours.'

In the small kitchen, Sukey made tea while Bridie opened a bottle and poured the dark liquid carefully into a glass. They went back to the sitting room and Sukey told Bridie how Rick had been her first boyfriend but had never been in love with her and how Dan, she was sure, fancied her but had never made a move. In the middle of telling Bridie, she gave a big sigh. Maybe Rick was right, maybe she should move from this place, get a proper job, maybe even go back to college, not to do drama, no, but to take 'A' levels, study for university. But she wondered why that sort of life would be any better than the one she was currently living. I'm tired, she told herself, and I need a break.

(When eventually she had a degree and an MA and was working towards her doctoral thesis, Sukey wondered once or twice if it was Rick's suggestion that she should take herself in hand, maybe study, that had pushed her into academia. She decided not. It had happened for the same reason that she once spent a short time with a pornographer who later achieved some small notoriety. That is, it had happened by accident, not design. And if, looking back, Sukey often framed events as if they were the result of conscious purpose, that was only so as to make retrospective sense of her life: after all, memory was more ordered than experience.)

Chapter 13
August 1967: Sukey

It was Robin on the phone. As Sukey listened to him saying: 'Hello, hello,' she could feel his anger and frustration. She almost shook the receiver as if to rid it of the moistness of his vexation. Instead, she held it away from her ear; the hellos grew fainter as if Robin himself was diminishing. And then she clumped it down firmly, feeling that the clunk, as the line was cut off, had also hit Robin like a big foot coming down on his head. She almost laughed. She was finished with cleaning. This was the fifth day she'd not turned up for her appointed jobs. Messages had been left by Robin. She'd deliberately missed their last meeting where she'd been scheduled to pay him his percentage for the last week of work. His bad luck: he took too high a cut in any case. And she needed the money until she found something else and that wouldn't be until she got back from Edinburgh.

At first, she and Jaz thought they'd go in Jaz's car. It was one reason why Sukey had asked him to come with her. Another was that she liked being with him and a third that she didn't want to go on her own: not just the travelling but being there. Dan might finally decide to make love to her if she took the trouble to go on her own all the way to Edinburgh to meet him. If Jaz was with her, this was far less likely. Last night Jaz had told her that he didn't think his car would last the journey and they had decided to hitch. As soon as he was ready, they'd go. He was now in the kitchen having a bath.

The phone rang again, Sukey lifted it, put it to her ear, heard Robin's voice, put it down quickly and before it could ring again had shuffled coins and the piece of paper with Dan's number on it out of her purse and dialled. Once again no reply. But in any case, it was probably too late: Dan must already be in Edinburgh. She'd called the number several times and Dan had never answered. No one had answered until the sixth time when a nervous voice had said: 'Hello.'

'Hi,' Sukey said, 'is Dan there?'

'No.'

'Who's that?' she asked.

'This is Dan's mother.'

'Oh,' said Sukey. She explained that Dan had asked her to call so that he could give her his address in Edinburgh.

'I don't have it.'

'Oh, well, can you ask him to call me?'

'I suppose I could. I don't see him much.'

'But,' Sukey frowned, the woman had answered the phone so Dan must live with her. This in itself was odd. She'd imagined Dan having his own place where he could hang out with his musician and poet friends, take women back and smoke dope.

'This is his phone,' Dan's mother explained in her small apologetic voice, 'in his room. It's in my house but I only come in here once a week to clean it for him when he's living here. And even then, he's not at home much.' She sounded defensive, as if she was trying to push Sukey away, stop her from making any more requests.

'Well,' said Sukey, persisting, 'do you know where he's playing in Edinburgh?'

There was no answer for several seconds and then Dan's mother gave her a name that sounded as if it might be a club: 'The Centrifuge'.

'Do you know where it is?'

A soft but insistent sigh. Then: 'No. Dan just mentioned the name in passing. He doesn't tell me much.'

'Thanks for your help,' Sukey said, being polite. 'Goodbye.'

Since then, she'd dialled the number whenever she had a spare moment but it had never been answered.

'We'll just have to go and hope we can find the place,' she'd said to Jaz.

He'd shrugged. 'OK.' They both wanted to leave London for a bit, have a break, maybe another adventure.

Right, Sukey thought, that's it. She replaced the receiver and climbed the stairs back up to their flat to see if Jaz was ready to go.

It was raining when they left the tube station and found their way to the road leading north. It was not heavy. Just a cold, grey, summer drizzle that made Sukey shiver as they stood, thumbs out, watching the cars drive past them. When the Cortina stopped and they climbed in, Jaz in the front and Sukey in the back, she was damp and cold.

'Put the heater on for yer,' said the driver in his North London accent as he pulled back out into the traffic. His hair was pale and cut so short he was almost bald. He was wearing a beige jacket and was very wide; his neck lined with rolls of fat. He was driving far too fast, his podgy fingers manipulating the steering wheel with a dexterity that Sukey felt was at odds with his plump body. He was a salesman, he told them, did a lot of travelling, loved being on the road. He was the best in the South, he said: 'Got an award, last mumf, did'n' I? Not the first time, niever... Get out the way, yer bleedin' wally!' he yelled as he overtook a slow-moving car. 'Some people. Didn't ought to be allah'd to drive.' He sniffed. Sukey realised that she was clenching her fists tight. Oh well, she thought, at least we'll get somewhere fast; that or have an accident. Jaz was rubbing a lock of his hair round one finger, but other than that, he seemed relaxed. Sukey decided to stop worrying about the speed they were going and leant back and shut her eyes, listening to the driver as he talked. He didn't ask any questions, seemed just happy to have them as an audience as he droned on and on.

When she woke up, Jaz had turned round and was staring at her from the front seat. 'Sukey,' he was saying, urgently, 'Sukey, Sukey.'

'What is it?'

'I told him we don't want to go any further. You tell him too.'

Sukey sat up. She frowned, looked out at the side of the road. It seemed that they were in the middle of the countryside. Fields stretched for miles. She had no idea where they were or why Jaz felt that they should stop.

'We need to get out now.' Jaz had turned back towards the front and was talking to the driver, whose steady stream of words was no longer monotonously flowing, and the car was going slower than before she'd fallen asleep. She could see only one porky hand gripping the wheel.

'You said you were heading to Scotland. I can take you all the way to York.' The driver was almost gasping as he spoke.

'We've changed out minds,' Jaz said. 'I've just realised I need to be back in London for my Grandmother's birthday.'

'Yes,' said Sukey, 'that's right. We need to get out now please.'

The driver gave a strange sort of yelping sigh and after a few seconds the car slowed and stopped by the side of the road. Jaz had opened the door before the car came to a standstill and was out and standing on the verge, cradling his bag in both hands.

'Thank you for the lift,' Sukey said as she climbed out of the car. The driver said nothing and was gone as soon as she'd slammed her door shut.

'Shit,' Jaz said, 'shit, shit.'

'What's the matter?'

'He was wanking. We started on the motorway and then he said he knew a short cut and pulled off. I don't know how you could sleep all the way through it. Then he unzipped his trousers and away he went. He didn't say anything: in fact, he stopped talking. Shit.'

'At least he didn't rape us,' Sukey said. She started to grin. 'It's funny, Jaz,' she said.

Jaz shook his head, fast, over and over. 'I hated it. He was horrid. I don't know if it was me or you or what. He came; just before we stopped. I feel sick.' Jaz turned and retched. For a little while he bent over, panting slightly. Then he stood up. 'We better get going,' he said.

'D'you want to carry on?' Sukey asked. 'We could always go back.'

'No,' Jaz said, 'I'm OK now.'

It was very late when they arrived in Edinburgh. And they were tired and hungry. After they'd been dropped off, they followed the directions their last driver had given them and found themselves in what they assumed was the centre of the city. They asked a few people if they'd heard of The Centrifuge Club. 'Or it could be a name that sounds like that,' Sukey explained when she saw the puzzled looks on people's faces. But no one seemed to know of it or anything like it, except for one man, who said he'd been there once, not long ago, but couldn't remember what street it was on. When they found a phone box they looked the place up in the local directory, but couldn't find it. They tried various similar names, but although there were entries that started with Central or Centre none of them seemed like clubs or venues for a music act.

'I'm too tired,' Sukey said. 'We can try in the morning

and work our way through the possibilities.'

Desperate for food they went into a fish and chip shop that was about to close and bought a portion of chips to share, a gherkin for Jaz and a saveloy for Sukey. They sat on the kerb eating.

'What are we going to do?' Sukey asked. Jaz shrugged. His face was pale, looking almost grey in the light of the street lamp, and his hair was hanging lank and greasy. Sukey shook her head. She felt dirty and gritty, wondered at their stupidity at coming all this way with hardly any money and an address that might or might not exist.

'We should find somewhere to sleep.' Jaz yawned. At the end of the street, they could see a church. 'Let's try there,' Jaz said pointing.

The church doors were locked but there was a side porch and Sukey and Jaz lay down side by side on the cold stone floor and tried to sleep.

'You canna stay here,' came a male voice with a strong Edinburgh accent. Sukey blinked against the penetrating glare of the torch and turned her face away from it.

'We've nowhere else,' she said.

'Sorry, but I have to move you on.'

Sukey sat up and, putting her hand up to her eyes to shield them from the bright light, looked at the torch's holder: a policeman. 'Jaz,' she said, gently kneading his shoulder. Jaz pulled himself into an even tighter ball, drew his hands over his head, mumbled something incoherent.

'Come on now,' said the policeman and Sukey shook Jaz, saying his name, louder and louder. Eventually he unfurled himself and sat up.

'What's happening?' Jaz asked.

'Now then, sir, I must ask you both to leave this place.'

'Where can we go?' Jaz rubbed his forehead and looked at the policeman, who shrugged. 'Where?' Jaz insisted.

'You could try the railway station.'

'Or you could arrest us and we could sleep in the cells.' Jaz said as he crossed his legs and rubbed his ankles with both hands.

'Not a good idea,' said the policeman. 'Now be away with you.'

Sukey stood up, put out a hand and helped Jaz to his feet. The policeman told them how to find the station. It didn't take them long to reach it and it was surprisingly crowded and well lit. In the ladies' toilet, Sukey washed her face, arms and hands. She thought about taking off her dress and doing her whole body, or at least putting her feet in the basin and cleaning them. She did neither.

They found seats in the waiting room and dozed throughout the night. At one point, there was enough space for Sukey to lie down on the bench and she slept surprisingly deeply for what seemed like a long time.

As it became light, Sukey woke. Jaz was now on the floor, curled up and fast asleep. Sukey stood and stretched. A fat man with a big tatty beard who had been sitting opposite them since they'd come in, winked at her.

'He's no use to you, darling,' he said, indicating Jaz. 'Come away with me, instead.'

Sukey smiled, wondered at the need men had to make some kind of advance. What, she wondered, would Fat Man do if she accepted his invitation? She sat down and waited for Jaz to wake up.

They bought a cup of tea each in the railway café and counted their money. They had very little: enough for food for a few days, but that was all.

'If we don't find Dan, then we'll have nowhere to sleep and we'll get dirtier and dirtier and it'll be harder to get lifts home again,' Sukey said.

'Hm,' Jaz was twirling a lock of hair and jigging both legs up and down. 'Seems a waste. Come all this way here and not stay.'

'Can you get some more money?'

'I could get my parents to let me have some, but I don't know how they'd get it to me. I could try cashing a cheque, but there's no money in my bank. And it's Saturday.'

'I've got a few pounds in the post office.'

'And you haven't brought your book, have you?'

'No.' Sukey drank the rest of her tea. She sniffed in the smell of bacon and her tummy rumbled. Jaz sat tapping his saucer with his teaspoon and with one bony finger was pushing a few grains of spilt sugar into a minute mound.

'Why do we do these stupid things?' Sukey asked as she watched Jaz.

'What else is there?' asked Jaz.

'There must be something that means more,' Sukey replied.

'What d'you mean by 'mean'?' Jaz looked up, keeping his finger pressed onto the tabletop.

'I don't know,' Sukey said, too hungry to be able to express herself or her feeling that somewhere, somehow, she needed to find a way of making her life significant. She sighed. 'Jaz, what are we going to do?'

'No money, don't even know if we've the address of a real place and, even if it is, don't know if Dan will let us stay with him,' Jaz said. 'We'll leave. Go back to London. We can come again another year, properly prepared.'

'Let's have breakfast first.'

'OK.' Jaz licked the tip of his finger and rubbed it over the sugar grains till they stuck to it. Then he licked it again.

Sukey slept for twelve hours. Got up, went to the loo, went back to bed and slept again. It was early Sunday afternoon when she finally woke up. She lay on her mattress enjoying the lethargy that a long sleep engenders. The others were up; both Jaz's and Minnie's beds were empty. Sukey stretched, closed her eyes wondering if she could sleep some more but soon gave up.

In the kitchen, Minnie was curled up in the armchair, reading. She closed the book as Sukey came in; she smiled.

'No one else about?' Sukey asked.

'Kitty's gone to do something nasty with Vic,' Minnie said, pursing her lips, disapproval making the words brittle and precise.

'And Jaz? Dennis?'

'Jaz said he was going to find Malc. Wants stuff. I told him Malc's probably still sleeping off last night. Dennis went to see his kids. Only just left. I think he and Kitty aren't talking. He doesn't like any of the things she's doing these days.'

'Neither do you,' Sukey said as she opened the fridge, looking for food.

Minnie shrugged, her shoulders bony and vulnerable as she raised them. 'Not my business,' she said, her voice shrill.

'Are you unhappy, Minnie?' Sukey felt compelled to ask as she put the last two slices of bread in the toaster.

'I don't know,' Minnie said. She blinked. 'It's all so difficult.'

'What is?'

'Everything,' Minnie whispered. She was crying now, softly, quietly. Sukey watched her wondering what to do, what to say. She thought of Minnie as dull, colourless, a little person of no consequence who she had never tried to have as a friend. In any case, Sukey thought, she disapproves of me.

'What's everything?' Sukey asked. A little shiver traversed her body.

'Life, men, relationships, sex, the future.'

'Yes,' said Sukey and sighed.

'When I was at school, ' Minnie said, 'I thought that I'd grow up, meet a man, and marry him. And I really did think that was the end, you know, the 'happy ever after' thing. I don't think it works like that.'

'Not for us. We've moved away from being those sorts of people.'

'The hippy life, the drugs, the sex, all that you mean?' Minnie asked. She sounded breathless, as if there was something she was afraid of.

'All that,' Sukey said. 'I didn't plan it. I didn't plan to smoke dope or take acid or sleep with men.'

'Me neither,' Minnie said. She reached into her little bag and took out the makings of a roll-up. 'I don't know how I started.'

'D'you remember the first time you had an LSD trip?' Sukey sat at the table and started spreading marge on her toast.

'Of course. It's not something you're likely to forget is it?' Minnie asked.

'No,' Sukey shook her head remembering January the year before when she was at college. Jaz had told her he had some tabs of acid and asked if she wanted to take one with him. She'd asked him to tell her what it would be like.

'I can't,' he'd said. 'It's really hard to explain to someone who's never taken it. The whole world becomes different.' He stared into the distance, thinking, Sukey presumed, of trips he'd taken. She, too, turned to look through the window. Outside in the cold of a late morning in winter it had started to snow, soft and gentle, turning the ground white below the greyness of low sky.

'I'll look after you, make sure you have a good time,' Jaz said.

He had, Sukey thought now, mostly in any case. Ecstasy had flooded her an hour or so after she'd swallowed the tiny little innocuous seeming dot; she became certain that everything around her was benign; she felt a strong desire to talk to Jaz and truly communicate. Then words formed in her head and before she could speak them the sentence altered, kept altering, not the words themselves but what they meant. So she saw that what she was going to say could be taken in so many different ways, even the opposite of what she'd intended. She let the sentence leak out, monitoring it, explaining it so that Jaz would not misinterpret what she wanted to say. But then she saw the explanation itself did not have a fixed meaning. And that Jaz's response was just as fluid.

That was the only bad bit about those long hours of mainly being deliciously in tune with herself and her world. During that time she thought that she and Jaz, both still virgins, would one day, maybe soon, make love, and then realised that the words Jaz had used did not mean that: he was thinking of something else.

The next afternoon, a Sunday, when she woke after the trip, she'd still felt good.

'I'm glad I did that,' she told Jaz. 'I'd hate to think that I'd lived my life and never taken acid.'

'Jaz and I have taken quite a few trips together,' Sukey said now, watching as Minnie finished rolling her cigarette.

'D'you want one?' Minnie asked, holding out her little tobacco bag. Sukey shook her head; she'd taken a big bite of her toast. She wiped her mouth with the back of her hand.

Minnie bent her head to light her roll-up. She took a long draw and looked up. 'Sukey, can I tell you something?'

'What?'

Minnie rolled her cigarette between her fingers. She sighed. 'The thing is,' Minnie stopped, licked her lips, continued, her voice almost inaudible. 'I don't like sex. I don't think I could bear to have sex over and over again.'

'You don't like it at all? Sukey asked.

'I haven't explained properly. I almost like it at the time, when it's being done, but when I think about it there's something revolting about it. Men are… they're… sort of invasive… their flesh is so… meaty. Even when I like it, it's almost because I find it disgusting. It's because it's disgusting that it's… compelling.' Minnie was crying properly now, big tears rolling down her cheeks. She sniffed snottily. 'I need a tissue,' she said.

Sukey went to the loo and tore off a big wad of toilet paper. Back in the kitchen she gave it to Minnie and sat at the table spreading marge and cheap plum jam on her toast.

'I like sex,' she said once Minnie had blown her nose and stopped crying.

'But not with anyone.'

'No,' said Sukey. 'Once this man chatted me up. I told him I had a boyfriend. It was when I still thought I was with Rick. It was last summer, when Rick was in Greece. The man said to me that just because you liked eating doughnuts there was no reason why you shouldn't also try eclairs. I think he was trying to say that choosing someone to sleep with was like going into a baker's shop, full of goodies and that you could buy more than one type of them.'

'Silly idea, fancy thinking of men as cakes or buns.' Minnie was giggling.

'Yeah,' said Sukey. 'The problem is that once you're no longer a virgin it's hard to see why you shouldn't sleep with whoever you want, or even whoever wants to sleep with you. There's no barrier anymore.'

'Literally as well,' Minnie said.

Sukey smiled. 'Cup of tea?' she asked.

'Please,' Minnie said. 'I want to talk about something else.'

'What?' Sukey felt a shiver of fear flicker through her and the little blond hairs on her arm stood up. Minnie was going to tell her something horrible.

'It's not that bad,' Minnie said. 'You look as if I'm about to tell you a ghost story.'

'Sorry,' Sukey said, grimacing. She set the kettle to boil.

'Mind you, it's not that good either,' Minnie sighed heavily and looked down. 'Dennis, well, he tried to have sex with me.'

'Yuck, yuck, what did he do?'

'It was after I lost the money – the money I made dealing before you were living here,' she paused.

'Yeah, I know, I heard about it.'

'Right,' said Minnie. 'Dennis pretended that he'd got the money, that Kitty had called the bus people and that it had been handed in to lost property and she'd gone to pick it up and then lied about it. He didn't actually say it, he just hinted, that he'd give me the money if I did it with him. Then when we were in bed he stopped, said I was a slut and that it was rude of me to be so obviously uninterested.' Minnie shuddered. 'I felt really dreadful.'

'But how could you go on living here after that, seeing him every day?' Sukey asked.

Minnie shrugged. 'I'm trying to save money and I don't really want to have to find somewhere else to live with a lot of new people. And in any case, I thought Dennis would go. But he didn't and I suppose I got used to it.'

'I don't know why he goes on living here, specially with Kitty stripping and all that other stuff.'

'One day he'll go back to his wife. I think he's just waiting till she gets back to normal and lets him live with her again.'

Sukey made tea and passed a mug to Minnie. It was good just the two of them here in the kitchen, talking. Sukey closed her eyes, thinking of a real home, cosiness, cleanliness and order. In some ways, she wanted to live like that again. She opened her eyes, yawned and stretched.

'Why did you come back so quickly from Edinburgh?' Minnie asked.

'We had nowhere to stay and not enough money.'

'So why did you go?'

Sukey finished pouring her tea. She shrugged. 'It seemed like a good idea at the time. We were hoping to meet a friend of mine, Dan. And Jaz and I wanted to have a break.'

'Am I in your way?'

'What d'you mean?' Sukey frowned.

'Are you and Jaz trying to get together.'

'No, not at all.'

'But you fancy him.'

'No. I like him. We have tried. You know, to do it. A couple of times. It didn't work.'

'That's the kind of boyfriend I'd like.'

'He's not a boyfriend.' Sukey dipped her knife in the jam and spread a sticky dollop on her last tiny morsel of toast.

She put in her mouth and licked her fingers.

'No, but I'd like a boyfriend who you didn't have to have sex with,' Minnie said.

'I wouldn't,' Sukey said. After a pause, she asked: 'What about Ted? Didn't you like it with Ted?'

'Yes, no, I don't know. It was a mistake me and Ted. We just got together because we were both there. I wonder what would have happened if we had gone to India together.'

'So you're over him?'

'Totally, totally over him. But what do you want, Sukey? What d'you think's going to happen to you?' Minnie took a big gulp of her tea, put her mug on the table, settled back into the chair with her legs crossed under her and started to roll another cigarette.

'I really don't know,' Sukey said.

'I'm going to be rich,' Minnie said. 'Have my own business, make loads of money, live in a beautiful place. Have everything under control. I'll be the one who makes the decisions.'

'Sounds good,' Sukey said.

'So what about you?'

'Carry on, see what happens.' Sukey shook her head.

'You need to have a plan.' Minnie sat up; the idea seemed to have excited her.

'I'll think about it,' Sukey said, not meaning it.

'You're OK really,' Minnie said.

'What d'you mean?'

'I didn't like you when I first met you. I thought you were trivial,' Minnie said.

'But I am, Minnie, that's it exactly. I can't make anything seem important.'

Minnie smiled at her. 'The point is you knew what I meant when I said it. So you're OK.' Sukey smiled back. It was like sharing a joke.

(When Sukey thought back to that time and those events: the trip to Edinburgh and back, the chat with Minnie in the kitchen, the two of them becoming friends; it seemed to her to mark the beginning of a new period in her life. Maybe, she would wonder, it was then that she started becoming restless with the aimlessness. Maybe it was those few days that saw her change and not the horror of what was about to happen.)

Chapter 14
August 1967: Jojo

Jojo took the joint from Malc and leaned back on the bench. She took a deep draw in, exhaled, repeated this twice and handed it back. She wondered if anyone in this small London park could smell and recognise the dope, or wondered why the two of them were sharing a cigarette.

'You angry?' Malc asked.

'No,' said Jojo. She couldn't remember the last time she was angry. No point, she always thought. Anger never achieved anything and it made things messy. She could be very angry with Malc if it was a feeling that she allowed: very, especially since he'd got heavily into heroin. She'd smoked it a few times – she tried all his drugs – but once he'd started to inject, she'd refused. She wondered if it was just a phase, like acid. He didn't do much acid these days, seemed to have given it up.

Even now that they had to leave the flat that Jojo had lived in for over a year –she was sure it was mainly because of Malc, and maybe because of Ted as well, that the landlord, who lived upstairs, wanted them out – even now, she was not angry with Malc, nor with Ted either. They had to move on Saturday, three days time.

'Go to the rent tribunal,' Sukey had said.

'No,' Jojo replied, 'can't be bothered. I'll find somewhere.' So now she was looking for a new flat and the others who lived with her – Malc, Joannie and Ted – were supposed to be helping. They said they were working on it, but Jojo doubted it.

'Sure you're not pissed off with me?' Malc said now, insisting, as he dropped the finished joint onto the concrete below the bench, stubbing it out with the front of his shoe.

'No, I already told you and it's time for me to go to back to work. Lunch break's over,' Jojo said.

'Right,' said Malc and he turned to smile at Jojo. He was, she thought, one of the most beautiful men she'd ever been with. He had dark hair that looked black and was almost the same colour as hers. His was longer though, straight and shiny. His eyes were navy blue and his skin a smooth brown.

'I've stuff to do later, I may be home, I may not be,' he said.

'OK,' Jojo said and stood up. Malc leaned over and, starting at the ankle, ran his hand up one of Jojo's long brown legs, right up to her short skirt and continued on it till he reached her knickers. He stuck his finger under the cotton and smiled at Jojo, licking his lips, moving his finger slowly.

Jojo pushed his hand away. 'Not now, Malc,' she said and straightened her skirt, adjusted her blouse and the collar of her thin but expensive summer jacket. Jojo loved to look good, always dressed well, was never late for work, did well at her job. She sometimes wondered how she managed it: efficient secretary by day and hippie in the evenings, with a drug dealer as a lover and several friends who she would have trouble describing to her boss and colleagues.

It was easy filling up the big canvas bag, three bottles of wine, some boxes of savoury biscuits, several packets of crisps and one of salami. Jojo was deft and nobody noticed. At the counter, she ordered two sorts of paté and a slice of Camembert. She collected apples and oranges from the fruit and vegetable section. The bananas, tomatoes and crisp cos lettuce went into the bag. She put her basket ready and smiled at the checkout man. Then she shuffled back down the shop for a loaf of bread. By the time she came back he had nearly finished ringing up her purchases on the till and she carefully added them to the goods already in her bag. She paid and left the shop. Often it helped to be tall, beautiful and smartly dressed. Being well practised was useful as well.

'Your mother rang,' Joannie said. She was sitting with her elbows on the kitchen table, her hands cupping her chin and cheeks. As usual, her face was obscured by long dark hair.

'What did she want?' Jojo asked. If she were ever to get angry, it would be with Joannie. Boring Joannie, who did nothing, said little and consumed whatever was brought into the flat: drugs, alcohol, food. Men, too, thought Jojo, remembering how she'd come home one evening to find that she'd taken Malc to her bed. Jojo forgave Malc, made very little fuss; asked him to decide which of them he wanted.

'No contest,' Malc said, kissing her over and over in front of Joannie. 'Why don't you throw her out?' Malc asked.

'She is my cousin,' Jojo said.

That had been when Joannie first came to London and was sleeping in the kitchen temporarily until the other bedroom in the flat become vacant. Jojo's flatmate at the time was a Californian. She was waiting for her parents to send the money for a plane ticket home. A few days before the Californian left, Joanne annexed Ted. Later he and Malc had both moved into the flat. That had been some months ago and now they would all be leaving.

'Don't know,' Joannie said now, watching as Jojo unpacked her bag. She leant over and took one of the bottles of wine. 'I'll open that,' she said.

'She must have said something.' Jojo stopped for a moment, put her hands into the small of her back and stretched, tired from hefting home a heavy bag full of groceries.

'Oh, yes, wanted to know if you were OK. Said they were going to be in London this weekend.'

'Bother,' said Jojo. They did this from time to time, her parents. Came to London and tried to get her to come back to live with them. This would be the fourth time since she'd finished at secretarial college the previous summer.

'You better phone them,' Joannie said. She'd managed to open the wine. 'D'you want some?' she asked Jojo, indicating the bottle and taking two glasses of their shelf.

By the time Malc came home, Jojo, Ted and Joannie had drunk most of the wine. Ted and Joannie were in bed and

Jojo was eating a bowl of cereal with a chopped up banana. She had wasted the evening, which should she have spent looking for a flat. There were now just two evenings until moving day.

'I fixed that we can stay at Kitty's,' Malc said. He was even drunker than Jojo.

'What about the other two, Ted and Joannie?'

'Don't want them there,' Malc said. 'And we're to sleep in the kitchen. Means we don't have to share with all those others. See, I got it sorted for you.' He knelt on the floor and leaned against Jojo's legs, his head on her lap. Jojo put one hand on his head and continued eating.

'Where'll Ted and Joannie go?' asked Jojo.

'Dunno, their problem. Got any chocolate?' Malc mumbled and Jojo sighed. She hadn't told her mother that she was leaving the flat, had just said she couldn't see them that weekend. Her mother, in her cool voice, had given her the name of the hotel where they'd be staying and said that she hoped to see her.

Jojo heard Malc come running back up the stairs. He'd gone down to answer the bell when it rang and had been a long time at the front door.

'It's your parents,' he said as he came into Kitty's kitchen. 'I told them you weren't here. They don't believe me. I argued with them. They insisted on coming in. So I shut the door in their face.'

'How do they know I'm here?' Jojo asked. Malc shrugged. He was reaching out for the dope tin when the bell rang again and then again. Jojo heard a door opening and Kitty's voice calling: 'I'm coming.' Jojo pushed back the blankets that she and Malc had spread over the pile of cushions that was their bed, and was at the kitchen door in a flash.

'Kitty, it's my parents. Don't let them in. They're trying to get me to go back home.' Jojo said.

Kitty stood looking at her. She was wearing a big white nightdress. She put her hands on her hips and yawned. 'Tell them you won't go,' she said.

'My parents don't work like that. I'd rather they didn't know I'm here.'

'We won't let them in.' Kitty said.

'They won't give up,' Jojo shook her head, wondered what to do. Kitty frowned, was tapping one of her big toes.

'Tell you what, Jojo. Come and hide in our bed, between me and Dennis. Malc,' she called waddling into the kitchen. 'Jojo's going to hide in our bed. You let them in and show them whatever they want. They won't find her.' The bell rang again and Jojo followed Kitty into her room. She climbed gingerly into bed and lay flat on her tummy next to Dennis. Kitty joined them and switched off the light.

Jojo heard her parents' voices coming up the stairs, her father loud and booming, her mother quieter, clipped and upper class. She heard Malc, too, and was glad he'd not been drinking that evening. He'd taken some heroin and had been smoking dope but unless you knew him well, he appeared quite normal. It was only alcohol that seemed to really affect him these days. The kitchen door opened and closed and the voices died away. Then it opened again and footsteps came up to the landing. Jojo tried to make herself small in the bed. She wrapped her arms round her head and pulled herself under the covers. She tried to hear what her parents were saying and realised that they'd gone into the other bedroom.

'Oh,' she heard her mother's voice uncharacteristically loud. She must have seen that there were three sleeping in that room: Sukey, Minnie and Jaz. Everyone had been at home that evening and had gone to bed early, even Kitty. Some Sundays she took a night off from stripping.

Jojo swallowed, she felt that she was suffocating in this bed. The footsteps were back on the landing and then the door opened.

'Switch on the light,' came her father's ordering voice. Jojo felt Kitty sit up, felt Kitty's body squash next to hers and Kitty's large leg cover her body.

'What the hell's going on?' Kitty called out and switched on the light. Jojo felt Dennis turn, squashing against her.

'She must be in here,' Jojo's mother said.

'Who?' Kitty asked, her voice loud and breathy.

'Josephine.'

'Don't know anyone called Josephine.' Kitty said. 'And how dare you come into my flat in the middle of the night. Malc, show them out.'

'She calls herself Jojo,' Jojo's father said.

'Oh her,' Kitty said. Jojo heard the snap of a lighter and smelt cigarette. Kitty was no doubt shocking her parents who would think smoking in bed uncouth and dangerous.

'She's not here, can't you see?' Kitty said.

'Maybe she'd hiding in the wardrobe,' Jojo's mother said.

'You can look, and under the bed and anywhere else you want to. But do it quickly and then go.'

Jojo was breathing as quietly as she could. She was beginning to feel sick and hoped her parents would not ask to look in the bed. There was movement round the room and then her mother spoke. 'She's not here. Are there any other rooms?'

'Just the loo,' Malcolm said.

'We'll look there,' her father said. 'And then what about upstairs?'

'The landlord,' Kitty said. 'You'll find their door locked.'

They talked about it for some days afterwards: the search for Jojo and its failure.

'Poor Bridie, they insisted on looking through her rooms, and she had a client waiting,' Malc said. He laughed. 'I rather enjoyed showing them round.'

'Why did they come here?' Kitty asked.

'The landlord at the old flat gave them the address. He was out for the evening when they went round but they waited till he came back. They told me that. As if it was something to be proud of. Maybe it was,' Malc said.

Jojo said nothing. She felt like crying, something she hadn't done for a very long time. Finally, on the Monday, her parents had appeared at her office and taken her out for lunch. They tried to persuade her to come back and live with them: 'home,' they called it.

'We've heard you're mixing with the wrong sort of people,' her mother said.

'We were dreadfully worried when we found you were no longer at your flat,' her father said.

Jojo tried to be charming, that was her way: she didn't want conflict, even with her parents. She wanted to be left alone to manage her life the way she chose.

When the dessert came, they threatened to make her a ward of court and force her to leave London.

'No use,' Jojo told them. 'I'm nearly nineteen and, as the age of majority has recently been lowered, I'm already an adult.' She smiled and the confusion in her parents' faces both pleased and saddened her.

(Years later Jojo told her daughters about their grandparents and how they'd come searching for her in London. How she'd hidden in a bed between a fat stripper and a London cabby and not been found. Her daughters laughed. They loved their mother's stories of when she'd been young, although they knew that almost none of them were true.)

Chapter 15
August 1967: Ted

Ted looked at Joannie's pale face. She was asleep with her hair falling back on the pillow and he could see her dirty skin and the spots under the old layer of the cream she used to cover it. She was snoring slightly and he wanted to lean over and pinch her nose. He didn't like her when she slept. In fact, he thought, he didn't like her at all. What he fool he was, always getting mixed up with women he didn't really want. Well he did want them more or less at the beginning, but then they got clingy and were always there and planning things. Like Minnie with India. He'd have gone if the stupid girl hadn't lost the money, but it hadn't been his idea. He didn't even remember discussing it. He scratched his thigh and yawned. He'd be off in a minute, when he'd finished his fag, going to sign on, then he was meeting Malc and doing a bit of dealing for him. Maybe he'd ask Malc if he thought he could move back into Kitty's place instead of this awful room in this awful flat where friends of Joannie's lived.

Joannie snorted and turned over. She'd been ridiculously

drunk last night and had fallen asleep in the middle of having sex. Right, Ted, thought, I'm going and I'm not coming back. He stood up, lifted down his duffel bag from the top of the wardrobe and started to fill it with his clothes. He stuffed the last of them in, he just needed his shaving things and toothbrush from the bathroom and then he'd be off.

He stood looking round the room, checking that there was nothing else of his lying around. Joannie's purse was on the table next to the ashtray. Ted flicked it open, pulled out a few notes and put them in his pocket. Then he bent to pick up a packet of her cigarettes from the floor: it was nearly full; if he was careful, it could last him all day.

The door creaked as he opened it, and as he turned to shut it, trying not to make any more noise, Joannie sat up.

'Ted,' she said.

'What?'

'Where you going?'

'Going to sign on.'

'When'll you be back?'

Ted paused. To tell or not to tell. He rubbed his chin with his spare hand. He should shave but he couldn't be bothered. He felt immensely tired: he'd woken too early but then, remembering it was his day for signing on for the social security benefit, he'd decided to get up.

'Ted,' Joannie was kneeling now, 'why've you got your bag?'

'I'm going. Can't stand this place.'

'What about me?'

Ted shrugged, decided not to reply, slipped away and into the bathroom. He scooped up his stuff and was down the hall when Joannie came out of the room, wrapped in the sheet from the bed.

'Ted,' she called, and Ted half turned. He opened the front door and was out, up the steps from the dank basement and onto the pavement. He let out a deep breath of relief and blinking against the strong light of the sun moved quickly down the street.

'No,' Malc said.

'Why not?'

'Kitty said just me and Jojo. It's because Minnie's still there. She's not going to want you sleeping in the room with her. And in any case…'

'In any case, what?'

Malc shrugged. ''nother drink?'

'Yeah,' Ted said, and he watched Malc going up the bar.

'In any case, what?' Ted asked when Malc was back.

'Jojo and me, she's…' Malc pursed his lips.

'Not splitting up?' Ted asked

'Nah,' Malc said.

'What then?'

'She wants us not to live together for a bit. She's going to find herself a flat on her own, she said. Now she's staying on at Kitty's to save money but she wants me out. And she says she wants me to cut back on my drugs and drinking. She's still allowed to do it, though.' Malc's short laugh sounded like a bark.

Ted sipped his beer, offered Malc a cigarette from the packet he'd taken from Joannie. 'What's wrong with you both staying at Kitty's?' he asked.

'You know Jojo,' Malc said. 'She's class. She wants her boyfriend to be the same. I'm going to try. Jojo's worth it.'

'Yeah,' Ted said. Of all the girls about the place, Jojo was the one he'd most like to do. She was tall and slender, wore elegant clothes that made you think she ought to be a model and her hair was like black silk. She had smooth skin that made you want to touch her and big dark eyes with huge lids. When she looked at you, she blinked slowly as if inviting you in. It wasn't just that she was beautiful. It was the way she moved, slowly, as if she was walking through honey. She neither chattered and simpered like some girls, nor turned silence into accusation like so many others, and Ted loved the soft, spicy scent that lingered round her and in the air just after she'd left a place. It was so unlike Minnie's patchouli or the dry powdery smell of Joannie.

'Well,' said Ted, looking at Malc, who sighed.

'Maybe we should get a place together,' Ted said.

Malc raised his beer mug and took a long swig from it. He put it down, wiped his mouth with the back of his hand. 'I've heard of a flat that's available,' he said. He started to smile, then he was laughing.

Ted frowned. 'What's so funny?' he asked.

'D'you want to go and see it?'

'I thought you had some business you wanted to do.'

'Yes, I'll try and sort the flat stuff for this evening.' Malc was still laughing.

'OK,' said Ted. 'Why is it funny?'

Malc smiled. 'C'mon,' he said, 'let's finish up here and get going.'

'Aren't you going to tell me a bit about it?'

Malc shook his head. He seemed to be about to laugh again.

Ted frowned. 'What's the matter with it?'

'Hurry up,' Malc said, 'we're supposed to be there by six. Don't want to keep her waiting.'

'Right,' Ted said, giving up. All afternoon he'd been doing stuff for Malc. Back at Kitty's when no one else was in, they'd cut up a weight of dope with a heated knife, weighing it into 17 one ounce portions which they wrapped in silver foil. There was a bit left once the portioning was done and that they'd keep for themselves. Malc had fished out some acid tabs he'd hidden in the back of the fridge and then they'd taken the bus to the big branch of the polytechnic, where Malc had gone off, leaving Ted in the student union with a list of names.

Gradually each of the people belonging to the names had arrived, Ted had managed to locate them, take their money and pass on their orders. He sat in one of the big old armchairs in the large shabby hall, full of people coming and going. He watched two girls sitting on the other side of the room with a pile of books and pads of paper, they were watching him, laughing from time to time. Ted was considering going to talk to them when he thought he smelled dope. As he sniffed, wondering where it came from and if he could roll himself a joint, Malc came into the room. Both girls looked up and stopped giggling.

'Time to go,' Malc said smiling at Ted, who thought that maybe his friend had been injecting heroin, as he did from time to time.

'One last customer for you,' Malc said. 'A woman with three kids.' They turned up a side street and Malc pointed out a house. He looked at his watch. 'Opening time, I'll see you in the pub on the corner.' He handed Ted a small bag and told him how much money to take.

'Aren't you coming?'

'No,' Malc said.

Ted frowned. 'Why not?'

'She's after me. Every time I go round, she tries to get me into bed. '

'Oh,' Ted said.

'Just tell her no if she tries you. I did her one time and now she won't stop. She just wants a father for those snotty-nosed brats of hers.'

The woman looked suspicious when she opened the door to Ted, but when he said that he had come with stuff from Malc, she let him in. She was skinny and small with fluffy hair, bad skin, a big nose and smelled of boiled sweets. The room she took him into was a mess, full of toys, with clothes in piles on the sofa and chair, and dirty plates and mugs on the table. A baby lay on the floor with nothing on. The door was open to a small yard and Ted could hear children's voices coming through it.

Ted handed her the package and watched as she opened

it. She sniffed at the dope. 'Seems OK,' she said, her voice surly. She looked up at Ted and smiled.

'I could give you something else instead of the money.' she offered.

'The money's for Malc, it's not mine,' Ted said. She sighed and asked how much he wanted.

Ted counted the notes, put them in his pocket and left. He banged the front door behind him, hefted his bag onto his shoulder and almost ran up the street and into the pub. He had time for one drink before Malc said that they should leave.

'We've got an appointment with the woman who owns the flat that I was talking about,' he said.

Now, it seemed, they were nearly there. Malc had slowed down. 'It's that place over there,' he said pointing. They crossed the road and went in. It was a small Greek restaurant, dark and decorated with fake vine leaves, Christmas lights and photographs of Mediterranean-looking scenes. There were not yet any customers, just one small, swarthy waiter.

'We're here to meet Mrs. Smith,' Malc said.

'Ah, yes, Mrs Smith.' The waiter smirked and indicated the table by the window. 'I get you anything?' he asked.

Ted would have liked a beer or even some of that funny Greek wine, but Malc shook his head. 'We'll wait for her,' he said. He leant back in his chair and offered Ted a cigarette. He smiled as he lit it.

The door pushed open with a jangle and Ted saw a face peering round it. It belonged to a woman of about seventy, heavily made up and with dyed red hair. The woman came in and looked at Ted and Malc. She was smiling as she walked over to them. She was small and plump, wearing a tight white dress patterned with large mauve roses and with a wide mauve belt clinched snugly round her waist. Her hands, which she held in front of her pressed against her bosom, were chunky and wrinkled, the fingers short and covered in gold rings of various sizes. A large white handbag with a big ostentatious clasp hung over one arm and her shoes were also white and remarkably high-heeled, with peep toes. Ted felt a moment of panic, he wanted to get up and leave. He could go back, he thought, and see if he could spend the night with the single mother. She'd let him stay. She wasn't that bad and he could put up with kids until he found something suitable.

Mrs Smith sat down, still smiling. She put her bag on the floor beside her, planted her elbows on the table and clasped her hands together. She nodded, looking from one to the other.

'So you are the two young men,' she said with a slight accent. 'Such handsome boys. Now tell me your names.' She licked her lips and without looking at him, she raised one arm, pointing her hand towards the waiter and clicking her fingers in summons.

'I'm Malc, this is Ted.'

She nodded, the waiter arrived. 'Get us a Meze,' she said, still not looking at him. 'And to drink, I'm sure these boys would like a beer each. I'll have a Martini. Dry, but with ice in. Don't worry,' she added, looking first at Malc and then at Ted. 'It's my treat.' The waiter slid away. Ted was sure he was sniggering, although he disguised it as cough.

Mrs Smith leant down and took cigarettes, a cigarette holder and a lighter from her bag. She sat back and smoked, questioning them: age, occupation. Malc said he was a sign writer and Ted that he was a cosmetic salesman. He didn't know where the idea came from. It sprung, as it were, fully formed into his head. He wondered what he'd do if he had to produce references, waited for her to mention them, but she just nodded and moved on to the next topic.

The drinks arrived and then the food. She ordered a bottle of wine and she asked them what they did in the evenings, and then about their girlfriends.

'None at the moment,' Malc said. Ted frowned; what about Jojo, he thought, and why had Malc lied?

'Don't you want to ask me anything?' she said as she put down her knife and fork, dabbing her crimson mouth with her table napkin. Ted looked at the white tissue staining red and felt sick. 'Well,' she said, coquettish, and Ted swallowed. He wondered if he was beginning to understand what this was all about or if he was going a little mad.

'Tell us about the flat,' Malc said. Mrs Smith inserted a cigarette into her holder and let Ted lean forward and light it.

'Very spacious. Two bedrooms, a living room, all the usual fittings and fully furnished. Nice and tasteful. Central too. Just over the road in that block.' She indicated through the window. 'Good stylish building, we own it, my husband and I. And we live on the ground floor. It's easier for him since he's in a wheelchair.'

Ted swallowed. There was no way, none whatsoever, that the two of them could afford the rent on such a place. He looked at Malc, leant towards him, mumbled: 'How much is it?'

Malc grinned at him. Mrs Smith banged a fist on the table. 'Don't be rude young man, or I'll reconsider. Whatever you want to say, say it aloud and to me.' Her accent seemed to have become stronger.

'I just wanted to know, how much the rent was,' Ted almost whispered.

'Didn't my representative tell you?' she asked.

'Yes,' said Malc, 'it was me she spoke to. I haven't told Ted. Not yet.'

'I see. And do you think he'll be interested?'

'I'm sure he will. If you are. She said that you had to approve us first.'

'Yes, well, I've done that. You'll do very well, the two of you. Now I'm going to the ladies, then I'll pay the bill and while I'm doing all that you can explain the arrangement to Ted.'

Mrs Smith rose, pushed back her chair, smoothed down her dress and waddled to the back of the dark room. Ted looked at Malc, saying nothing.

Malc smiled back. 'Well, could you do it?' he asked finally.

'You mean, let me be sure I've got this right, we do her in return for the flat?'

Malc nodded. Ted put back his head, looking up at the ceiling, drummed his fingers on the table. Thought about being in bed with Mrs Smith. He could do it, of course he could. He might even find it pleasant. 'How often?' he asked.

'Very often,' said Malc. 'That's what the woman – the one she calls her representative - said. At least once a day each.'

The flat was delightful. It was wonderful to have a fitted bathroom with a shower and huge towels keeping warm on their heated rail, to wallow in large soft chairs in the evenings, watching television, knowing that there was drink in the fridge and cigarettes in large quantities in one of the kitchen cabinets. Above all Ted loved to sleep in the big comfortable double bed all alone. He didn't even mind when he had to share it for short periods with Mrs Smith, who would arrive at around midday and open a bottle of wine. 'I knew you weren't really a salesman,' she told Ted the first time as she poured him a glass, before leading him into his bedroom and drawing the curtains closed. Most days she also came to see them in the early evening and would be gone before eight.

'We old women, we tire easily,' she'd say. And she'd laugh as she checked the fridge before leaving. 'I'll get Emily to bring you more beer and wine tomorrow.' Emily was Mr. Smith's nurse. 'She does other things, besides,' Mrs Smith told Ted.

Ted looked at Jojo and she was still laughing. Ted frowned, wondering if she really didn't mind Malc having sex with another woman. She was still laughing when Malc came from the kitchen with a bottle of champagne and three glasses. When he'd opened the bottle and poured the wine he said: 'A toast, to Mrs Smith and to all who sail in her.'

Jojo took a sip. 'You sure she won't mind me being here? Being here, sleeping with one of her boys, drinking her booze.'

Malc shook his head. 'No and in any case she needn't know. You arrive after eight in the evening, leave before ten in the morning.'

Jojo stretched out on the sofa, dangled her long legs over its arm. Ted wanted to go and sit next to her, put her silky head in his lap, lean over, give her champagne kisses, breathe in her fragile scent. He shifted in his chair, wishing that it were he and not Malc who'd soon be taking her to bed. This wouldn't do, he told himself, falling for a girl. Better off, he thought, doing it with Mrs Smith, who was rich and might be demanding, but only in short bursts. She wouldn't turn round and ask him to marry her or go to India with her. And he'd never feel about her the uncomfortable longing that he was increasingly experiencing when Jojo was around.

'Hey Ted,' Jojo said. He looked up. 'Malc tells me that you really enjoy it with your landlady. And that you're her first choice when she comes round.'

'Rubbish,' said Ted. 'Liar,' he said to Malc. He leant over and took one of Jojo's feet in his hand, running his thumb over the soft cushion of her instep. She tried to pull it back and he held on. 'I'll get you, Jojo,' he said softly and watched as she slowly folded her lids like beckoning butterflies over her beautiful big eyes.

(Some years later Ted's mother married a man who was younger than her son. She was, Ted thought, still beautiful

222

and far more lovely than most women of her age. Still it disturbed him that after the wedding she took her husband's name, referring to herself, ironically, as 'Mrs Smith'.)

Chapter 16
September 1967: Sukey

Sukey opened the kitchen door and switched on the light. 'Oh,' she said, 'I didn't know you were here.'

Jojo shook her head, once, twice, moving as if her neck was made of glass and might break if it were used. She was sitting upright on one of the kitchen chairs, her legs pressed elegantly together, still in their expensive high-heeled shoes. She was dressed in her work clothes, her hands clasped in front of her and resting on her knee. Her smart navy leather handbag was placed neatly on the table. Her eyes were huge dark shadows in a face that was so pale it was beyond white. It was if she was dead, as if her blood had drained away.

'No,' said Jojo, 'I'm not.'

'What?'

'I'm not here.'

'Has something happened?' asked Sukey. She was still standing in the doorway, not wanting to come in, not wanting to disturb Jojo.

Jojo blinked, very slowly and her head turned on its

glassy neck so that it faced Sukey.

'Not really,' Jojo said, 'just… Malc is dead.' She started to laugh. Sukey gasped.

'It's quite funny, really. It happened last night and I didn't know until I came home from work. Ted was here. He told me.'

'How?' Sukey asked. She felt sick, dizzy, and wondered how to comfort Jojo; if she should comfort her. She didn't know how to behave.

'He was run over,' Jojo said. 'Nothing to do with heroin. He went to a pub in the West End and then he was in Piccadilly Circus and he just walked into the middle of road and he lay down. A taxi didn't see him, ran over him, killed him. Ted said he'd not touched heroin for days.'

'Where's Ted now?'

'I sent him away. I told him I didn't want him around.'

'Well,' said Sukey. She closed the door and leant against it, not sure what to say, what to do. 'Shall I make you a cup of tea?' she asked eventually.

'No,' Jojo said. 'I've some wine.' She indicated the full canvas bag at her feet. 'In there.'

Sukey moved across the room and lifted the heavy bag. She put it on the table and started to unpack it. There was fruit: apples, pears, bananas; there were several cobs of sweet corn and two packets of cigarettes. Then there were three bottles of wine and a big tin of cashew nuts. 'Which one?' Sukey asked.

'Doesn't matter,' Jojo said. Sukey picked up one of the bottles and turned to look at Jojo. She was crying, making no noise, the tears were running down her cheeks taking mascara with them and Jojo's mouth was quivering. She put a finger up to her face and touched one of her wet cheeks. She moved the finger, holding it up in the air and looking at it as if surprised to see that it was damp. Jojo didn't want to be crying, Sukey knew and she turned away, rooting in a drawer for the corkscrew and taking two glasses off the shelf. She heard Jojo moving and then the ping of her lighter.

'D'you want a cigarette?' Jojo said and pushed the packet across the table to Sukey who took one and then opened and poured the wine. Jojo opened her handbag, took out a little make-up pouch and a tiny mirror and started to deal with her face. She wiped away the tears and streaks of black and then gently applied a thin foundation cream. Finally, she repaired her lashes with long sweeps of mascara. Sukey watched as she sipped the wine.

'That's that,' said Jojo, snapping her bag shut and putting it on the floor. She took a long puff of her cigarette and a deep drink of wine.

'If I'd known what had happened I'd have got gin instead,' she said.

'Are you very sad?' Sukey asked, not sure if it was the right thing to ask, but somehow wanting to know.

'No,' said Jojo. 'I'd not have stayed with Malc. Not for much longer.' No, thought Sukey, no she wouldn't. Surely the right man for Jojo would be someone rich, or famous. Malc was – had been – beautiful looking and was good to have around when you needed dope, but he was not reliable, not someone you could've imagined spending your life with.

'I always knew it was temporary,' Jojo said. 'I didn't think he had much future, but I didn't think he'd go and die so quickly, just like that.' She gave what sounded at first like a sob, but then turned into a hick-up.

'Will there be a funeral?' Sukey asked.

'I don't know, but in any case I wouldn't go.'

'No,' Sukey said. She reached for the bottle. 'Do you want some more wine?' she asked.

Jojo nodded and passed her glass. 'I don't know if he has any family. I know nothing about his parents or anything.'

'The others might want to go, Minnie, Jaz, even Kitty,' Sukey said.

'Oh,' said Jojo, 'of course, you were all his friends.' She shook her head. 'I'd forgotten. He was living here when he met me.' She frowned.

Sukey looked down at her wine, shook her head, sighed. Malc was dead. Suddenly it seemed real. Earlier when Jojo had told her what had happened she'd thought of it in terms of Jojo. Jojo's boyfriend had died. That was how it had registered. But in fact, it was Malc who was dead. Her friend, Malc, who got them dope and sometimes didn't charge for it and was kind to all of them and had lived here, slept here with them all.

'So you weren't in love with him?' Sukey asked and watched as tears started to fill Jojo's big eyes. Jojo shook her head and blinked and the tears were gone.

'Got any dope?' Jojo asked.

'No,' said Sukey, wondering how they would manage now that Malc was gone. 'We could try the insides of the banana skins. Jaz says it gets you stoned.'

Jojo smiled. 'I don't think so,' she said and yawned. 'I feel most awfully tired. I'm going to try and find a flat this weekend. I'm fed up with sleeping in this kitchen. And I'd really like to have a bath. I used to do that at Malc's place, but now….'

The kitchen door swung open and Minnie came in carrying a plastic bag full of vegetables. 'Leftovers from the shop,' she said as she dumped it on the floor and slumped into the armchair. Who's going to tell her, Sukey wondered, will Jojo or should I?

There was a silence for a bit and then: 'What am I interrupting?' Minnie asked, sitting up, her nose almost twitching as if she could smell something happening.

Sukey looked at Jojo, who looked back and then started to grin. 'Malc got run over,' she said. 'Squish, squash.'

'What?' Minnie grasped the arms of her chair with both hands. 'Is he OK?'

'In a sense, in that when you're dead you must be OK because nothing else nasty can happen to you,' Jojo said. She reached for the wine bottle and poured the last of it into the glasses. She opened her cigarettes and passed them round. Minnie accepted. Her mouth had fallen open and then shut tight. The tops of her cheeks and tip of her nose had turned pink while the skin under her nose and round her lips had paled into a pinched grey.

Minnie swallowed, holding her unlit cigarette in the air and still gripping the chair with her free hand. 'Dead?' she asked.

'Yes,' said Jojo. 'Run over by a taxi in Piccadilly Circus. Squashed into eternity.'

'Maybe it was Dennis' cab,' Sukey said.

'No,' said Jojo, 'it was a black cab. Apparently, the driver was hysterical when he realised what had happened.'

'So Malc is dead,' Minnie said as Jaz came into the kitchen.

'What?' asked Jaz.

'Malc is dead,' Minnie said. Her cigarette was still unlit, her hand still clinging to the chair arm.

'Malc?' Jaz looked round the room at the three women. 'Are you sure? How do you know?'

'Ted came and told me,' Jojo said.

'Overdose?' Jaz asked. And Jojo explained again: nothing to do with heroin or any other illegal drug. 'It was good old-fashioned booze,' she said. And then she yawned. 'I really need to sleep,' she said.

Jaz went over to her, stood behind her, leant over and put his arms around her, resting his head on hers. 'Oh Jojo, I'm so sorry,' he said.

'It's OK,' Jojo said, trying to push Jaz's arms away. She didn't want sympathy, Sukey knew. It would only make her sad, make her cry, make her composure melt away. And that Jojo could not bear.

'Stop it, Jaz,' Jojo said; already there was a watery tinge to her voice. Jaz stood up, put his hands on her shoulders and started to massage them.

'Poor old Malc,' he said, sounding dazed.

'Yup,' Jojo said.

'And where will we get our dope now?' Jaz asked. He giggled. 'Sorry,' he said, 'I didn't mean it.'

'That was mean, Jaz,' Minnie said. She was crying now, sniffing and rubbing her eyes with her knuckles. 'He was a nice man, always helped me out. Underneath it all, he was gentle and sweet.'

'Yes,' said Jojo. She yawned again.

'Jojo wants to go to bed,' Sukey said. 'And have a bath. Why don't the rest of us go to the pub and leave her.'

'Oh shit,' Jaz said, standing in the doorway. 'Look who's here.'

Sukey peered over his shoulder, narrowing her eyes, looking into the smoky pub. At a table in the middle of the room, looking like they'd been there since opening time, were Vic, Joe and Sean. 'Don't take any notice of them, Jaz,' Sukey said. 'Just go in. There's plenty of space for all of us.'

Jaz went to the bar to buy the drinks. Sukey and Minnie, ignoring the three men, found a free place in the nearest corner.

'I don't want to see Sean,' Minnie said. She had flushed red and Sukey could see delicate lines at the corner of her eyes and above her nose as she frowned and pursed her lips.

'What can he do to you?' Sukey asked. She sat back, crossed her legs and opened her arms, resting them on the arms of her chair. When Vic looked up, he saw her and waved.

Joe turned and seeing them too, stood up. He walked over to them. 'Come and join us,' he said.

'No thanks,' Sukey said. 'A friend of ours had just died and we want to be on our own.'

'Ah, come on,' Joe said. He was already quite drunk, wobbling slightly as he leant on the back of an empty chair. 'I've got to go to work soon, so it'll just be for a little while.'

'No,' said Sukey and watched as Sean, too, came over to their table.

'Two lovely women together,' he said, his eyes moving from Sukey to Minnie and back again.

'Oh go away,' Minnie almost screamed.

'There's no need for that.' Sean raised his eyebrows and went to sit on the empty chair just as Jaz arrived with the drinks. 'Now then, er… Minnie, what'll be the matter with you?'

'You couldn't remember my name. You had to think. That's what the matter is.' Minnie's voice was high and precise, pointing her words at Sean as if she wished they were knife cuts.

'Ah, Minnie, you're lovely when you're angry.' Sean turned towards her and took both her clenched fists in his and held them up to his face, staring at her and rubbing her wrists gently and slowly with his thumbs. It was as if he was trying to hypnotise her. Minnie said nothing, just stared back at Sean until she started to cry. Then Sean let go of her hands, moved his chair next to hers and put his arms round her, holding her to him and massaging her back. For a long time, Minnie let him comfort her, her sobs getting louder at first and then gradually diminishing. Finally she gave a juddering sigh and pulled away from Sean. He stayed looking at her, taking one hand and holding onto it.

'Now then,' he whispered, 'tell your friend Sean all about it.'

By then, Joe and Vic had brought their chairs and drink over and they were all crowded round the little corner table. This was not what we needed, Sukey thought as she watched Sean and Minnie on one side of her and Vic and Jaz on the other. Jaz was fiddling with his hair as he listened to Vic, who was talking to him in a low voice. Sukey saw Jaz blush and felt Joe as he pulled on her arm, trying to attract her attention.

'You haven't been to see me for a long time, Sue,' he said when she turned to him.

Sukey shrugged. 'Why should I come and see you?' she asked.

'Still playing hard to get.' Joe was looking at her but his eyes were skittering around. He was drumming his fingers on the table and his other hand was holding the arm of Sukey's chair and he was leaning towards her. He let go of the chair and put his hand on Sukey's thigh. Then moved it up under her skirt.

'Stop it!' Sukey yelled, pushing Joe away. He fell off his chair. 'Ow,' he said as he knelt on the floor. Vic was laughing and the others were now all looking at Joe.

'Piss off, Joe,' Sukey said, bending down so that only he could hear. 'I'm not going to sleep with you, so just stop pestering me.'

Once he had managed to stand up, Joe stayed for a moment, swaying slightly backwards and forwards. Then:

'I'm off to work now,' he said and left the pub, banging the door as he closed it behind him.

'I have to go, too,' Sean said. He leant towards Minnie and kissed her on her forehead. 'I'm sorry to hear about your friend,' he said, taking her chin between his fingers. He kissed her again and stood up, came over to Sukey's chair and bending down kissed her too on the top of her head, stroking her cheek as he did so. Sukey remembered that other time in this pub when she'd been drawn to him. Even now, after Minnie's story, she still found him attractive.

'Well,' said Vic after Sean had gone, 'who wants a drink?'

'Your friend Kitty,' he said when he was back from the bar, 'she's doing great work for me. Earning us money. Sure I can't tempt you two to join in?' He looked at Jaz and then at Sukey; he seemed to be ignoring Minnie.

'This is our friend Minnie,' Sukey said. 'And she doesn't want to work for you either.'

'No,' said Vic. 'Ah well.' He took a sip of his beer, seemed for once to have little to say.

'How's Jules?' Sukey asked.

'Jules,' Vic said as if wondering who Sukey was talking about.

'Your wife,' Sukey said.

'I know who Jules is.' Vic said and paused. 'Not sure if Jules knows who Jules is though, these days.'

'What d'you mean?'

'She's not been well. A few… mental problems. We'll get her sorted.'

'Why don't you just try and live a normal life?' Sukey asked.

234

'What is a normal life, then, little girl? Tell me what a normal life is?'

'You've got a home, a beautiful wife, two kids, why not try and enjoy all that? That's what I meant. All the other stuff, the porno, Kitty. None of you need that.'

Vic shrugged. 'I do,' he said. He took Sukey's hand and squeezed it till it hurt.

They drove to the funeral in Jaz's car. It was not too far and he said he thought the car could make both the journey down and the one home. There was Sukey, Minnie, Beaky and Jaz. Beaky had come to visit the day before. He had said nothing when they told him that Malc was dead. Just sat in the kitchen looking stunned, a slight frown between his eyes. Every now and then, he shook his head. When he left, he'd asked if he could come to the funeral with them. His voice was husky and Sukey thought that he wanted to cry. She went downstairs with him to let him out and stood at the front door looking up at him. She wanted to hug him but wasn't sure how. Finally as they both stood there, awkwardly, neither of them opening the door nor speaking, she'd put her arms round him and he'd reciprocated, holding her very tight and rocking slightly. She'd moved away and he'd moved quickly to the door, opening it and slipping out, mumbling: 'See you tomorrow,' as he almost ran down the garden path.

When Sukey had asked Kitty if she was coming, she said she was too busy. Jojo insisted she didn't want to be there and Ted said he would make his own way, but didn't turn up.

They'd been to see Ted at his flat on the evening after they'd learned about Malc's death. He hadn't known anything about Malc's family and eventually they found out his parents' address from the police. They lived in Guilford with his two younger siblings. His father was a solicitor and his mother a teacher. A sister was still at school, a brother at university. Such a normal middle-class family, overwhelmingly sad at Malc's death. All four had seemed small, confused and frightened at the funeral and at the gathering afterwards where relations, neighbours and a few old friends of Malc's from his school days had drunk wine and eaten sandwiches. It had been a long time since they'd seen him, all of them. He'd left for London when he was sixteen, eight years earlier and had not been in touch much since.

Sukey cried in the church when she saw Malc's coffin. She stood between Minnie and Jaz holding a hand of each of them and felt lost and forlorn. Beaky was on the other side of Minnie, all four of them with heads bent, weeping. Afterwards she'd talked to his mother about Malc, saying only good things and watching the pain flit in and out of her dark blue eyes, so like her son's.

'I don't know why it had to happen,' the mother said at one point, as if not sure that it actually had.

'I'm so sorry,' Sukey said, thinking of her own parents and how she should go and spend a little time with them.

Back at the flat they found Jojo, who was just home from work, with Ted. They were drinking and smoking a joint from dope that Ted had brought round.

'I was wondering,' Ted said to Jaz later that evening,

'would you like to move into the flat, take over Malc's room. I could introduce you to Mrs Smith, if you'd like to.'

Sukey watched Jaz as he looked at Ted; saw his face turn first white and then red, saw the puzzlement in his eyes and the frown of wonder that Ted could imagine that he, Jaz, would be able to take on such a role.

Finally, Jaz shook his head. 'Me? Me?' he asked.

'Yes, you,' said Ted, impatient.

'No,' said Jaz, 'not me.'

That night in their room Sukey woke up to hear Jaz crying. She sat up. 'Jaz,' she whispered climbing off her mattress and onto Jaz's. She lay next to him and put her arm over him. Then Minnie woke and she pulled her mattress across so that she could lie on the other side of Jaz.

'It's not for Malc,' Jaz said, raising his head from his pillow, 'I'm crying for myself.'

(Often Sukey thought of Malc: the first of her friends to die. She thought of him in conjunction with the others who had mourned him: Jojo, Jaz, Beaky, Minnie. She wondered if, had he not died that night, he'd have turned his life around and survived into good times like Jojo, Jaz and Beaky, or even found great wealth as Minnie had done. When she thought about Malc, she also remembered Kitty and Jules. She would tell herself that, had she and her friends lived less chaotically, they could have averted the events of that long ago September. At the time, though, she would think, we didn't know what was happening and we didn't have the choice of behaving differently.)

Chapter 17
September 1967: Beaky

When Beaky thought about going back to college for his second year, he wondered if he could manage it. He felt weary, drained, sick of London. He wanted a holiday but now that Tessa was stripping and making money she refused to take time off. He didn't want to stay somewhere on his own. He thought about going to spend some time with his parents. He knew he ought to, but he couldn't bear the thought of being in his old home and the way his parents treated him as if he was still a little boy. He'd have gone to Edinburgh with Sukey and Jaz if they'd asked him, but they didn't. It might have worked out better if they'd all gone together.

Beaky wished that he was back living in Kitty's flat, smoking dope or other stuff with Jaz, going to the pub, wondering what making love would be like. Instead of which he was here with a silly summer job in a boring office and living with Tessa, who was usually too tired for sex but didn't mind taking her clothes off for dirty old men.

Sometimes Beaky became angry when he thought about Tessa naked in the clubs. He'd bang his fist on the table and growl, not wanting to make too much noise in case one of the neighbours heard. Often he masturbated, alone in the bedsit, while she was out working. And sometimes he felt like crying and occasionally he did, too. He'd curl up on the bed and though he tried not to, the tears would leak out and he'd hear himself giving a curdled moan and then, scared of the strange noise he was making, he'd swallow and stop, wiping his face and sitting up on the bed, tired and wondering what to do next.

He'd loved meeting Tessa, he'd loved the sex and her soft white skin. He felt he could touch her forever. Above all, he loved the intimacy, the nakedness, being alone with her. And now she had spoiled all that, showing herself to anyone who could pay.

That morning, when it was still night but the sky was starting to lighten, he'd woken when Tessa came home and he'd watched as she'd got ready for bed. She sat at the table in the corner that was half his desk and half her dressing table and, with her mirror propped against the wall, she peered into it, peeling off false eyelashes, putting some kind of lotion on cotton-wool and using it to clean her face. She brushed her hair over and over until it fell softly round her face. Then she undressed and Beaky sat up, the better to see her pale, wide body, sturdy legs, smooth round tummy and small high breasts.

Before she'd started stripping, she'd sometimes bemoan the way she looked. 'How can you want me when I'm fat,' she'd say, or 'I've such wide hips, my legs are too short, I've no tits.' Beaky would kiss her till she stopped. He told her she had a beautiful body and that he wanted to touch her and stroke her forever.

'Tessa,' he whispered now and she looked up, wrapping her arms round her nakedness. 'Come to bed,' he urged.

'I thought you were soundly asleep,' she said and the slow measured way she spoke increased Beaky's arousal.

'I'm waiting for you,' he said, and she came and lay down next to him.

'Ah, Beaky,' she said sadly as he pulled her to him. At first she resisted and then had given in, became aroused and demanding, pulling him on top of her and wrapping her legs round him. She came before he did, loud and long. Afterwards, as they lay together, almost asleep, she said: 'Maybe we will be able to stay together after all.'

Now it was evening. Beaky sighed, thinking about what she'd said that morning and what she meant. He stood up and went to look out of the window. It had been warm and sunny earlier and was still light. The thought of the days shortening, of long, dark, cold evenings made him claustrophobic. He couldn't stand another evening here on his own. He turned to look at the pile of books on the table: holiday reading from college that he was working through. He sat heavily on the bed. He was lonely, sad, confused about Tessa and how they felt about each other. Then there was Malc's death. A waste of a good man, Beaky thought. Yes he took drugs; yes he drank, but... And here Beaky's thought stopped; he didn't know what came after the 'but'.

He wished he knew how to talk about feelings and how to deal with them. He felt overwhelmed with what was happening, the loss of a friend, the changes in his relationship with Tessa. He decided to go out, to walk the half hour or so to Kitty's place. Someone would be in, Jaz or Sukey, maybe Jojo or most likely Minnie. And if they weren't, he'd go to the pub and have a drink.

'Hi Beaky,' Sukey said. 'Come in.' She looked pale and was slightly drunk. He frowned, wondered whether to ask if there was anything wrong. She gave him a small wry smile and turned to go up the stairs. He followed.

She was going slowly and half way up stopped and turned back to Beaky. 'More bad news, someone we know has killed themselves,' she said.

'Who?' Beaky asked.

'I don't think you knew her.' Sukey had started to climb the stairs again, leaning on the banister, her head slightly bent. 'She was called Jules, married to the photographer that Kitty's doing stuff with.'

They'd reached the kitchen by now and Beaky followed Sukey in. There was one empty and one half-full wine bottle on the table. Jojo was sitting very upright on one of the straight-backed chairs and Jaz was in the armchair, leaning back, smoking what looked like a joint.

'Hi,' he said to Beaky. 'Sukey told you the latest?'

'Yes...' Beaky wasn't sure what else to say so he added: 'Terrible,' as he sat at the table

Sukey had found another glass and Jojo poured wine into

it and pushed it towards Beaky.

'We didn't know her well,' Sukey said. 'But, well, she's got two kids. I mean…' She stopped. 'She was beautiful and talented and….'

'Mad,' Jaz said. 'You have to admit, she was mad.' He took a big drag on the joint before passing leaning across and passing it to Beaky.

'It's only the insides of banana skins,' Jojo said, 'so don't go getting excited about it.' She smiled. Beaky wondered how she was coping now that Malc was dead. She was incredibly calm, but then she always was. He wondered if being beautiful and elegant made you less susceptible to pain. He took a draw of the joint. It made him cough.

'Joe told Jaz about it,' Sukey said. 'About Jules, I mean. Jaz went into the pub earlier and Joe was there.'

'Yeah,' said Jaz, 'he seemed almost excited about it. I was just having a quick drink and he came up to me at the bar and asked had I heard the news and then started on about it. She did it in the garden, apparently. Went out in the night with a razor blade and, well.' He stopped.

Sukey winced. 'It must have hurt,' she said.

'Yeah,' Jaz said. Beaky passed the joint to Jojo and took a swig of his wine. He couldn't get upset about the death, however tragic, of someone he didn't know. He considered saying this but decided against it. There was silence in the room. Beaky felt uneasy, restless, He'd have liked to have asked the others if they wanted to come to the pub; he didn't know why but being here in the kitchen with these people at the this time didn't seem right. He shifted in his seat.

What's more he didn't want to go home. But he wasn't sure if suggesting a trip out for a drink was tactful given the current circumstances.

'That's the last of the wine,' Jojo said as she shared the rest of the bottle between the four of them.

'Two deaths in ten days,' Jaz said. He was twiddling a piece of hair with an index finger and tapping one foot to some kind of internal tune. 'D'you think there'll be a third? You know everything happens in threes.'

'No,' said Sukey. 'I hope not.'

Jaz stood up, gulping what was left in his glass. 'I want to go out,' he said, moving round the small room as if in cage. 'Let's go to the pub.'

'Will Joe still be there?' Sukey asked.

'Shouldn't be. He was off to work,' said Jaz.

'Right then. I'll see if I've got any money.' Sukey stood up and went to pick up her purse that was sitting on the mantle piece

'It's OK,' Beaky said. 'I'll buy you all a drink.'

'I don't believe it,' said Jaz. 'Look who's just come out of the gents.'

Beaky turned to look and saw a tall man with slightly thinning hair take a couple of steps and then stop, standing quite still in the middle of the room, looking about him as if wondering why there were other people around him. As his gaze reached their table he nodded slightly and raised his eyebrows.

'It's Jules' husband,' Sukey said and bit her lip. Jojo said nothing, raised her glass and took a drink, watching as the man moved slowly towards them.

'I think he's completely pissed,' Jaz said. He sounded a little scared.

'Well, well, well,' said the man as he reached their table. 'If it's not my two young friends. Intimate friends.' He laughed, turned to Jojo. 'My name is Victor and you certainly look as though you need to be spoiled.' He almost bowed. 'I was just leaving but perhaps I'll join you all,' he said. He looked round again, trying to locate a chair, saw one, brought it over to the table.

'I suppose,' he said, 'you've heard the news?'

'Yes,' said Sukey, then remained silent. Jaz's face had gone dark, and he was twitching in his chair.

'Right,' said Vic. 'I suppose I should buy you all a drink in honour of the occasion.'

'It's OK,' Jaz said. 'I'll get you one. What d'you want?'

Vic raised his shoulders, spread his hands. 'What do you suggest?'

Jaz stood, said nothing, just looked at Vic, frowning.

'I know, a bloody Mary,' Vic said and Jaz turned and went off the bar.

'So, are you going to tell me who you are?' Vic was facing Jojo.

'Jojo.'

'Jojo. And though I'm the victor I'm always called Vic.' He nodded. He put his hand on Jojo's knee. She took it, raised it and let it go. Vic watched, let it flop down as if it were out of his control. As his arm dangled limply, he smiled. 'I'm in need of comfort, for my wife is not long dead. Couldn't you comfort me, Jojo, in my hour of need?'

'No,' said Jojo. Two red spots had appeared at the top of her cheeks. She was, Beaky realised, supremely angry. 'I'm leaving,' she said. She stood and was gone before anyone else could say anything; the pub door banged behind her.

Vic swallowed and started to cry, not making much noise, just letting tears fall down his face, his lips quivering. As the tears reached his mouth, his tongue came out and licked them away. 'I thought the victor got the spoils,' he said, 'instead of which Victor's life is spoiled.'

Jaz came back and stood, uncertain, holding the glass of thick red liquid. Vic looked up, blinked. 'Ah my Bloody Mary,' he said and reached out for it. He drank it one go, leaning back and gulping fast. Then he banged the empty glass down on the table and smiled, a tomato smear above his upper lip. Beaky watched, wondering what would happen next. He did not like this man; did not like the way he was behaving, did not like his treatment of Jojo. Above all Beaky did not like the way Vic seemed to assume that he would not only be the centre of attention but that he, Vic, would be the most important man in any gathering.

'Her mother blames me,' Vic said and shook his head.

'It's very sad,' Sukey said.

'Yes,' said Vic. 'I don't know if I can cope with it. And now I need another drink.'

Beaky was aware of Tessa watching him as he made the coffee, fried the bacon, put slices of bread in the old toaster.

She was leaning against the pillows; the sheet pulled up to just below her breasts. It was Sunday afternoon and tonight she would not be working. He buttered the toast and piled bacon on top of it. He took the plates over to the bed and put one on each of the side tables. Then he came back for the coffee, slipped off his jeans, and lay down next to Tessa. He put his hand on one of her breasts and pushed his knee over her thigh.

'Oh Beaky, I want to eat now. I'm amazingly hungry. I ate nearly nothing yesterday I was rushing around so.'

'OK,' Beaky sat up and reached for his coffee. 'You were really late home last night.'

'Yes.'

'Why?'

'I met some people I knew. We went for a late drink after work. I needed to unwind,' Tessa yawned.

'You're doing that more often. You weren't home till nearly six in the morning after the evening when I heard about that friend of Sukey and Jaz's committing suicide.'

'How was I to know you'd had unsettling news?' Tessa took a large bite of toast and bacon.

Beaky sighed. 'Do you still want to be with me?'

Tessa shrugged, chewed on her food, swallowed, wiped her mouth with the back of her hand. All of this done slowly and in an exaggerated way, almost as if she was on stage and acting the part of the patient woman dealing with her unreasonable boyfriend. 'You're the one who's unhappy, Beaky. You're the one who doesn't like the work I do. Have I complained about you doing that silly office job?'

'There's nothing to complain about. I go to work. I move paper about, I come home. You, though, you spend all day and half the night taking your clothes off in front of a crowd of dirty old men.'

'I earn a lot of money. I'm saving a great deal of it. Maybe enough for us to buy a house. And it's not as if I ever did anything with those men. You've got a load of girls in your office. How do I know you're not chatting them up?'

Beaky groaned. Of course he wasn't. He'd found it hard enough getting to make love with Tessa. There was no way he could entice those office girls to go out with him. They wore mini-skirts, tight tops and piles of make-up. Almost all of them were attractive and teased the men they worked with relentlessly. Although Beaky fantasised about taking them to bed, he knew he had no chance. Those who weren't already married had fiancées or long term boyfriends. When they weren't flexing their flirting skills on the men, they talked about how they were saving and their plans for the future. Beaky would not feature in any of that, he knew. He was a spotty temporary worker; what's more he was a university student and so was treated as a figure of fun rather than a real red-blooded male.

'You're blushing,' Tessa said. 'Have I hit on a truth, that you're having an affair with one of your colleagues?'

'Don't be silly… It was you who said the other morning, well you said something about maybe we could stay together after all.'

'Did I? Slip of the tongue, just that, a slip of the tongue.'

'It was more than that.'

Tessa sighed, put her now empty plate back on the side table and brushed crumbs off the sheet with her hand. 'Maybe we should split up since you're so unhappy. You can move back to Kitty's. I'm the one that pays most of the rent in any case.'

'Right,' said Beaky and lay back against the pillow. He put his arm over his eyes. He felt sad, relieved and tremendously aroused all at the same time. He wondered if he could persuade Tessa to make love and turned to look at her, moving his arm and pushing it gently round her shoulders. She smiled at him and pushed the sheet slowly down her body as she lay down close to him and slid her leg over his. Beaky grunted with pleasure.

Later when they were both finally out of bed, washed and dressed, Tessa asked: 'Shall we go round and see the crowd at Kitty's place?'

'So that I can ask if I can move back in?'

Tessa shrugged. 'Oh, Beaky,' she said, 'what is it you really want?'

Beaky wasn't sure what to say. Did she want him to say that it was her she wanted? With a house and marriage. He thought about saying that he'd like her to stop stripping, but he realised that it no longer bothered him as much as it did. And this, he thought, was a sign that he was not as keen on being with her as he had been only a few months ago. He sighed, knowing that their relationship was coming to an end. He said nothing.

(Soon after he started his affair with the woman who would become his third wife, Beaky told her that his first girlfriend had been a stripper. His future wife said: 'That is so typical of you, Col. You and your overdone sexuality.' He'd tried to explain that it wasn't like that. He and Tessa, he said, had found each other because they'd both felt left out of the sexual games that had been playing all around them at the time. He told her that what had united them had been their ordinariness, their plainness even. He tried to tell her about Vic and Jules, their strange life together and the tragic ending to their story, and how people like that and the events they engendered made him feel normal, drab and boring. She had laughed at this image of Beaky and he, grateful for the changes the years had brought, said nothing.)

Chapter 18
September 1967: Tessa

'That was nice,' said Stevie as he pulled back from Tessa, 'shall we do it again?'

'If you like,' she said and put her arm round his neck.

'Gently,' he said and giggled. 'This is all new to me.'

Tessa let her arm slip so that it was on his shoulders and moved her mouth to his. He had lovely mobile lips and a hard, muscled body that she liked to lean against. But above all, she enjoyed kissing him because she believed that she was in control. It would not, she felt sure, go any further.

'Oh my,' Stevie said, breaking away and then coming back for more. Tessa felt his hand on her waist, clutching her tightly. She was aroused and a little drunk and overwhelmingly tired and she should stop now and go home. She shifted slightly, feeling the rough material of the banquette rubbing unpleasantly against her thighs. Stevie's other arm was round her now, he was pressing himself against her. She raised her head, pushed herself away from him. He moaned; his eyes were shut and his face was marked by the slack look of desire that reminded her of Beaky when he was making love to her.

'Stevie,' she whispered.

He opened his eyes slowly, blinking and looking at her. 'I think I want you,' he breathed.

Tessa shook her head. 'No,' she said, 'I should go home now, it's late.'

'What am I going to do?' Stevie asked. He pulled her against him again.

Tessa could feel the press of his erection against her leg. She shifted slightly. 'It was just supposed to be a kiss. You said just a kiss so that you'd know what it was like with a girl.'

'Now I do and I want more.'

Tessa sighed, looked round the seedy room of the club, a place for drinking after hours: dark, shabby, badly decorated, cheaply furnished in spite of the high bar prices that were charged. There weren't many customers now: it was after five in the morning.

'We've nowhere to go,' Tessa said. And in any case, she thought, this was not what was supposed to happen.

'We can do it here,' Stevie said. 'Just don't make too much noise.'

'No,' said Tessa.

'Yes. Sit on me, move over and sit on me.'

In the taxi on her way home, resting her head against the glass of the window, half looking out as the day began and morning people started to emerge onto the streets, Tessa thought about what she'd done with Stevie, whether she should feel guilty, and how she would now behave with Beaky. She wouldn't tell him, 'that's for sure,' she said to herself. This thing with Stevie, it wouldn't last, it couldn't. She swallowed. She had found it enormously exciting, though. Mainly because it was so unexpected. There she'd been feeling safe. 'Sex was not on the agenda,' she whispered to herself. And then they'd been doing it, coupling in public. She shivered, re-living the surreptitious pleasure of being with Stevie.

She'd met him at the club the week before. She and Kitty with some of the other girls occasionally went there after work. You were supposed to be a member but the manager let the strippers in without fussing too much. Often their drinks came cheaper, too.

Stevie was the little brother of Janice, a tall, blonde woman who'd been working the Soho strip clubs since she was seventeen. She was now in her mid twenties and still lived with her eight-year-old daughter, her mother and two younger sisters in a small council flat in Leytonstone. Just lately Stevie had moved in with them.

'He's been in Amsterdam for I don't know how long, working as a bleeding fire-eater, if you don't mind. And he's a bloody poof,' Janice had told Tessa as they both sat in a squashed dressing room applying make up in front of the mirror.

'Why's he come back?' Tessa asked.

'Split up with his latest boyfriend and homesick as well, he said. Wants to see if he can find work here.' Janice laughed. 'I don't know as there's much call for fire-eaters in London. Anyway, I'm meeting him for a drink after work. You can come along if you like.'

Tessa had done so. He'd been sitting on his own in a corner. He waved when he saw Janice.

'So this is your beautiful brother,' Tessa said when they reached him. He was, too: tall and blonde like Janice, with big blue eyes, long lashed in a perfectly shaped oval face.

He pursed his lips and patted the seat beside him. 'Flatterer,' he said, 'you can come and sit next to me.' Tessa did. He asked her about how she liked being a stripper.

'It's just a job, but a very well paid one,' she said. 'I'm saving the money. I won't do it for ever.'

'I strip, too,' he told her. 'I do all sorts.'

'Janice said you were a fire-eater.'

'I am, among other things. I juggle, swallow swords, a bit of acrobatics. I'm an all round entertainer, really.' He giggled. 'I'll do anything for money.' He emphasised the 'anything' and raised his eyebrows.

Later in the evening, he touched the inside of Tessa's arm. 'You've beautiful soft skin,' he said, turning her arm over, holding it palm up with one hand and stroking it with the other.

Tessa found it extraordinarily sensual and leant back, closed her eyes, enjoying the sensation. She was liking Stevie, liking being with him. 'You're wonderful at doing that,' she said as he continued to softly move his hand up and down her arm. 'Maybe you should add masseur to your list of talents. I feel safe with you, it's nice to be with a man when you know that you don't have to worry about sexual attraction.'

'Don't be so sure,' Stevie said. He was giggling again. Tessa opened her eyes.

'Just teasing,' he said.

Through Janice, Stevie had found a job in one of the clubs; doing stuff behind the scenes, helping with costumes, tidying up. 'Just 'til I can make contacts, find myself something more in line with my skills,' he said to Tessa the second time they met in the club after work. This time it was just the two of them sitting close to each other and, Tessa reflected now as the taxi turned into her street, doing a lot of touching and what she would have thought of as sexual teasing had it not been with Stevie.

Then earlier this evening he'd said he wanted to kiss her, just to try, see what it was like. And then… The taxi came to a halt and Tessa shuffled in her seat, wondered if Beaky would smell the sex on her. He'd be asleep, she hoped. Lately though he'd been waking when she came in. Wanting sex, even wanting a conversation. She scrambled out of the taxi, paid the fare, let herself into the house and slowly walked up the three flights of stairs to the bedsit. She paused outside the door wishing Beaky was not there, feeling bad about that wish and wondering what had happened to the joy she'd experienced when she and Beaky had first made love, when he'd asked her to live with him.

'I want to do it again with you,' Stevie said, pouting.

'But you… you only like men. That time was, just a one off,' Tessa said.

Stevie shrugged. 'I've changed. In any case, it's easier

socially to be involved with women than men. And I don't want to be dismissed as just a one night stand.' He tossed his head.

He was, Tessa thought, still very poncy. He looked like a homosexual, dressed like one, talked like one, gestured like one. She almost said this to him but decided he would be offended. 'Gets easily offended like one,' she said to herself. 'It's such a dilemma.' She sighed.

'I thought you enjoyed it, Tess.' Stevie took her hand, was rubbing the fleshy part under her thumb with his index finger and she knew she wanted him.

'Not in here again. I don't want that.'

'You can't come back to mine. There's no room. You'll have to get rid of that boyfriend of yours. Or… tell him you're bringing me back and see what he says.'

'No,' said Tessa, feeling scared. She'd been thinking of finishing with Beaky but, now that it seemed to be a reality, she wasn't sure that was what she wanted. She didn't want to be on her own and she didn't think that this… this liaison with Stevie would last.

Beaky stared at her, his eyes big, dark and sad. He looked as if he might start crying and his skin was flushed, making his spots more visible.

'What if I refuse?' he asked.

'I don't know,' Tessa said. 'It's not us finishing. It's just we need to be on our own for a bit, to see what it's like. See if we really do want each other or not.'

'Living at Kitty's is hardly being on my own.' Beaky was

picking at the nails of one hand with the thumb and index finger of the other. He was looking at them as he spoke.

Tessa said nothing; thought about asking what Beaky wanted. He stood up, walked to the window, looked out.

'I think you've found someone else,' he said, his back to hers. 'And you're not sure about it yet so you don't want to split up permanently.'

Yes, thought Tessa, he's right. She breathed in deeply, pressed her lips together and decided. 'You're very perspicacious,' she said, feeling vertiginous, knowing that it was a mistake as the words came out. Beaky wheeled around. She saw his Adam's apple going up and down in his neck.

'You little bitch!' he cried out. Tessa cringed; it almost seemed as if he would hit her.

'Right. I'm going now and don't ask me to come back because I won't.' Beaky went to the bed and dragged his suitcase from under it. He yanked open the drawers one by one, pulling their contents out, throwing them on the bed, and then slamming the drawers shut. He started to fold his clothes and put them in the suitcase.

'And I'm not going to Kitty's place.' Beaky stopped for a moment. Stood in the middle of the room, looking down, looking sad and lost. 'I'll go and stay with my parents until term starts. I'll leave their number; you can call me if…. Well, if anything changes.' He went back to his packing and Tessa thought she heard him sniff.

'He's a homosexual,' she said.

Beaky stopped again and turned to face her. He was frowning.

Tessa took a deep breath. 'The someone else. He's a fire-eater and he's a poof.'

Beaky started to laugh. He collapsed on the bed, shook his head and went on laughing. After a little while he stopped, sat with his head bowed and then he wiped both eyes with the back of his hands, stood up and continued with his packing.

Tessa brought Stevie back that night and a few days later he moved in to live with her. Janice thought it was both ridiculous and hilarious. 'It won't last,' she told Tessa, who didn't bother to reply.

(Years later, thinking about her life, each stage of which had somehow surprised her (stripper, escort, companion to a transsexual, wife of a criminal, madam), Tessa realised that swapping Beaky for Stevie was the first of many senseless decisions. She told Beaky this when he contacted her, having read a review of her ghost written autobiography: 'Boarding School to Brothel'. 'Any possibility of a second chance for you and me?' Tessa asked. 'Absolutely not,' said Beaky. But he laughed, congratulated her, took her out for dinner and bought her champagne.)

Chapter 19
September to October 1967: Dennis

Dennis knew as soon as the alarm went that there was something different about the room. He yawned, closed his eyes again, pulled the bedclothes further up and turned, stretching out his arm to Kitty. He frowned, stretched further. There was no warmth in the space beside him and there was certainly no Kitty. He opened his eyes and sat up. He shivered a little. It was cold and he could hear the regular splashing of rain from outside the window. He thought of the wet, leaf-strewn, slippery streets and knew he should get up and get out. It was a day for a cab driver to make money. What with having to give so much to Paula for her and the children he needed all he could earn.

Where was Kitty? Maybe she was in the toilet, but her side of the bed felt as if it had not been slept in. It was unlike Kitty not to come home. The others, that superior Jojo and the other two girls, Minnie and Sukey who shared the other room with that skinny apology for a boy who called himself Jaz, they often stayed out all night, but not Kitty, not since

Dennis had been sleeping here. Even on the few nights when he'd gone to see Paula and had stayed over, Dennis was sure that Kitty had been at home. Even now that she'd become a stripper. Apart from the few occasions when Dennis had worked late and had driven her home, she always took a taxi, had no choice as public transport was no longer running when she finished work. Odd, he thought, Kitty as a stripper. He'd found it slightly disturbing when she'd told him the possibility of that sort of job and he'd hated meeting Joe and hearing what working the Soho clubs entailed. But Kitty had taken it up, insisted on it. That was over three months ago now and he'd got used to it. And some of her stories spiced up their sex life. Not, Dennis thought, that he'd taken up with Kitty for that reason. He leant across the bed for his cigarettes and lighter, plumped his pillow up and sat up, leaning against it smoking.

He replayed meeting Kitty in the pub that first lunchtime after Paula had told him she wanted him to move out. He'd been very close to tears after his seventh beer, and when Kitty's shift finished she'd brought him home and made him tea, listened to more of his story and told him he could stay with her. She'd put him to bed and gone back to the pub for the evening shift. He slept and only woke when she came in and told him that she'd brought them Chinese takeaway. Later he'd gone back to bed and she'd come with him and held him to her so that finally he had cried while she stroked him and rocked him and whispered to him, just like a mother might, he thought. But then, after he'd sat up and blown his nose and they'd both had a cigarette, sitting side by side in the big bed, she'd turned to him again and kissed him, almost seduced him, Dennis smiled, remembering. Where the hell was she? He should go to work, but felt uneasy, didn't want to leave until he knew where she was.

Dennis stubbed out his cigarette, got out of bed and dressed. He could hear movements on the landing and stairs, the others getting ready for work and college. He went to the window and pulled aside the curtain, looking out. All he could see was greyness and rain.

Minnie and Sukey were sitting at the table eating toast. Jojo's cushions and blankets had been neatly stacked in their corner. Minnie looked up as Dennis came into the kitchen. He still almost winced each time he saw her, and she still blushed. It had been months ago now, that stupid time when he tried to have sex with her. At first, he'd thought to move out of the flat, but what would he tell Kitty, and where could he go? Minnie will leave, he thought, but she hadn't. Once he'd asked her: 'Why you still here?' She'd looked at him with those accusing eyes of hers. 'Why are you?' she'd retorted sharply.

Then Sukey had said something one time when they were in the kitchen, that time just before Jojo and that sad case Malc came to stay for a short while, and she'd been talking to Jaz. She'd said that Minnie was saving again, trying to get enough money together to buy a business. The one where she worked. So that was why she stayed on here, Dennis, thought, cheap rent, like the rest of us.

He shook the kettle to see if it needed filling again. 'Just boiled,' Sukey said and he turned it on and spooned instant coffee into a mug.

'Any bread left?' he asked. Sukey stood up, sighed, and grabbed the remains of a sliced loaf from behind the toaster. She passed it to Dennis.

'Why is it that men can't see what's in front of them?' she asked Minnie who shrugged. Once, Dennis thought, he was sure that these two had been enemies, but now they seemed to be almost friends. There was often just the two of them here when he came in from work and he'd seen them together in the pub, the nearby one where Kitty used to work.

'Have you seen Kitty?' Dennis asked.

'She'll be still sleeping,' Minnie said, as she carefully pulled the crusts off her slice of toast before starting to eat it. She reminded Dennis of the mouse his eldest child had once had as a pet. He wondered why he'd bothered to try and seduce her. Sukey, now, she was a different matter. No chance there boy, he told himself.

'No,' he said, 'she's not. She never came home last night.'

Sukey stopped chewing; looked at him, frowning. 'She always comes home. She's, like, well, her not coming home is like my mother staying out all night. As if. You sure she's not curled up in bed?'

'I don't think I could mistake Kitty in bed,' Dennis said. He lit a cigarette and when his toast popped up out of the toaster, scraped the last of the marge onto the two slices, his cigarette held tightly between his lips. He took a deep draw on it, removed it from his mouth and said: 'We need food, hope she's back in time to do some shopping.'

'Maybe she's got a new man,' Minnie said, her voice high

and light, irritating Dennis. He snorted.

'Maybe she has, Dennis,' Sukey said.

Dennis sat down, stubbed out his cigarette in the ashtray and started to eat his breakfast.

'No, I know I suggested it, but I don't think she has,' Minnie said. She sounded a little frightened. 'Things come in threes: first Malc, then Jules, now Kitty. It's been a really bad September.'

'Don't be silly,' Dennis said, cutting his second slice of toast into four small squares and putting one into his mouth. Something didn't seem right, there was a strange sensation in his tummy, in his chest, in the very front of his head, but he wasn't sure what it meant. He chewed quickly and swallowed the toast. He didn't know if he was angry or scared or unhappy. He was unable to describe how he felt. He shuddered, oddly sure that something dreadful had happened or was about to happen.

He finished his toast, drained his coffee mug, jumped up and ran to the toilet, wanting to be on his way, out working. He'd already spent too long this morning getting up, talking in the kitchen, thinking about Kitty.

He went back into the kitchen to fetch his jacket from behind the door. 'She'll be back, don't you worry,' he told the two girls and then was off down the stairs, jingling his keys in one hand and trying to whistle.

'There's no fucking bread, no fucking marge, no fucking jam and no fucking Marmite,' Jaz was saying. Dennis stood in the doorway, listening. He took off his jacket and hung it

263

behind the door. He didn't want to go into the bedroom just yet, didn't want to find the evidence that Kitty had not been home. Even if she had been, she'd have gone by now, starting work as she did in the early afternoon.

'And there's no fucking tea, either,' Jaz finished. He pulled out the chair at the top of the table and sat on it, crossed his leg, tapping one foot and swinging the other backwards and forwards. He scratched his ear with a bony finger from one hand and drummed on the table with the other. 'Anyone any fags, any tobacco?' Jaz sounded like a cross little boy and Dennis had to clench both fists to stop himself from walking across the room and hitting him.

'Why don't you just go and buy what you need?' Dennis asked, clenching his teeth as if to keep his tongue in check.

'Because,' said Jaz, 'I don't have any money. It's nearly the end of the month and my allowance arrives on the first. And I pay Kitty every week for rent and the food she's supposed to provide. All there is in the fridge is half a bottle of milk and an old carrot. And there's nothing but two black bananas in the fruit bowl.'

'Stop whining,' Dennis said, reaching into his pocket for his packet of cigarettes. He stood leaning against the door, smoking, watching Jaz staring at him.

'S'OK, Jaz, you can have some of mine,' Sukey unfolded herself from the big chair, took her tobacco and papers out of a pocket and passed them to Jaz. 'Make one for me. I'm too tired to do anything. Horrible day at the office.' She yawned.

Dennis moved to the sink, filled the kettle with water. 'There's still coffee,' he said.

'Make us all one, Den, please,' Sukey said. 'It'll have to keep us going 'til tomorrow. When I've got the energy, I'll make a shopping list and leave it for Kitty for tomorrow.'

'What about eating tonight? Who's got money?' Jaz asked.

'I might have enough for chips and something cheap for you and me, Jaz,' Sukey said. 'Sorry, Den, not enough for all of us. And Jojo may have some stuff when she gets in.'

Dennis poured hot water into the three mugs and added milk. He measured four teaspoonfuls of sugar into his, passed the drinks and sat at the table. Kitty, he felt sure, had not been home. He'd go and work again in a short while. If he found himself in Soho, he might ask at one of the clubs where Kitty stripped, if anyone had seen her. He thought about Paula at home with the children and felt a wave of longing to be back with her, back with the family, shouting at the kids, complaining about the mess, stomping out for a beer at the local, coming back and making love to his beautiful wife. He sipped his coffee and as he put down the mug, a deep sigh escaped.

'What's up, Den?' Sukey asked. He wished she wouldn't call him that but when he asked her not to, she just laughed. He frowned, not wanting to answer Sukey's question.

There was silence. Jaz had sat back and was winding a strand of hair between two fingers, his leg was still jigging up and down.

'Say, Dennis, d'you think Kitty came back today?' Sukey asked.

Dennis looked at her, shook his head. 'Dunno,' he said.

It was time to stop, Dennis thought as he dropped his fare in Kentish Town. He looked at his watch, just after midnight. He'd be home in a few minutes and then he could have a few drinks and wait up until Kitty came home.

He parked and took the plastic bag from under the front seat: six cans of beer, two packets of fags, chocolate, crisps and a pork pie. If any of the others were up he'd just eat and drink and smoke in front of them. He slammed the cab door shut, locked it and walked the few steps to the house and up the short garden path. The upper parts of the house were in darkness, but both of the downstairs windows were lit, that bloody Bridie at it all night. He let himself in and heard murmurs and a muffled gasp coming from the front bedroom of the downstairs flat. He banged the bag on the newel post as he reached the stairs and the murmuring stopped for a moment, followed by a giggle.

'I am so tired,' Dennis said to himself, 'I am exhausted.'

All four were in the kitchen, Jaz and Jojo at the table; Minnie on the big armchair and Sukey sprawled on cushions on the floor. They were smoking a joint, Dennis saw, and he let out a breath in disapproval.

'Don't be so accusing,' Sukey said. 'You smoke, you drink, what's wrong with other drugs?'

Dennis couldn't be bothered to answer. He sat down, rummaged in the bag, opened one of the cans and took a long swallow before pulling the wrapping off the pie and biting into it. He hadn't eaten anything since his early lunch. When he finished the pie, he started on one of the bags of crisps and when that was finished he stopped for a minute, thinking, chocolate or fag next? Chocolate won.

'I've got the munchies,' Minnie said. Dennis looked at

her, his mouth full. He might have given her a couple of squares of his Cadbury's fruit and nut bar had she been on her own.

'It's my tea,' he told her. 'I'm starving.'

'You can't have the munchies, Minnie,' Sukey said. 'It's not dope we've been smoking, silly. Just the insides of banana skins. Again.'

'I wish Malc was still alive, I wish he still lived here,' Jaz said.

'Just so that we'd have better access to dope and acid and stuff, I suppose,' Sukey said. Dennis heard Jojo breathe in sharply.

'Yeah, but I miss him too. I think I miss him. Sorry, Jojo, I keep forgetting, but we do all miss him, you know.' He paused. 'That banana mush does work. I feel really woozy.' Jaz took a puff on the joint and leaned over to give it to Minnie.'

Dennis swallowed the last of the chocolate. 'You kids, you're mad,' he said. He looked at his watch. Kitty should be home in an hour and a half, at the very latest. Should he go down and pick her up? He could go into the club where she did her last show and wait for her. Yes, he decided, that's what he'd do, but he had time for another beer, maybe two before he had to leave. Pleased at the idea he opened a new packet of cigarettes and offered them round the room.

Joe was on the door wearing his spiv suit and one of those silly big flowery ties. Dennis remembered how much he'd disliked Joe when he'd first come round to the flat. He'd noticed the way Joe's eyes had skittered round the kitchen, lighting on the girls, especially Sukey. He'd look somewhere else and then start all over again. Sukey, Minnie, Sukey again, even Tessa, but not Kitty. Then Malc had come in with Jojo. Joe had jumped up and his hands flapped even more, his eyes seemed to have almost swollen and Dennis imagined them popping out of their sockets and jumping across the floor to Jojo where they'd hop up her legs and into her lap. Dennis had shaken his head then, feeling foolish. It must be all the drugs around the place, he thought, making him think such stupid thoughts. He remembered Joe shrugging when he realised that the only one of the women who wanted to be a stripper was Kitty; possibly Tessa, but not the others, certainly not Sukey, certainly not Jojo, not even Minnie with her grasping need to make and save money.

'So what's wrong with Kitty?' Dennis had wanted to ask but hadn't. On top of that Joe had seemed not to see him, ignored him when he spoke, handed fags round to the girls but not to Dennis.

'Hey, Joe,' Dennis called now. It was raining again, drops falling fat and slow, keeping people off the streets and giving the lights of cars and taxis a watery sheen as they swished down the street and round the corners. Joe had his shoulders hunched, was smoking, and was moving up and down as if dancing. 'Joe,' Dennis called, louder now, and Joe looked up, shaking his head. When he saw Dennis, he beckoned him to come closer.

'I want to come in and wait for Kitty,' Dennis said.

Joe looked at him, shook his head, frowned. 'You'll have a long wait,' he said.

'Why?'

'She's not here, that's why. She's not been here all day. And she never came yesterday either. Where the fuck is she? You're her man aren't you? You should know where she is.'

Dennis turned and ran through the rain to his cab. He sat for a little while, hunched and shivering. Finally he gave a heavy sigh and put the key into the ignition.

Five days. It had been five days since Kitty was last at home. She'd been lying in bed, asleep on Tuesday morning when Dennis had left for work. That was the last time he'd seen her. When he'd gone to the police station on Thursday to report her missing, they'd made fun of him.

'Hey, Trevor,' the desk sergeant had called to a work mate in a back office somewhere, 'there's a geezer here wants to report a missing stripper. Been gone since, ooh a long time, since yesterday. Maybe the day before.' He'd started to laugh.

'She's not like that,' Dennis said. 'She's reliable. She wouldn't just disappear. Something's happened.'

'I believe you,' the sergeant lied when Dennis insisted he take down details. He went on laughing as he wrote down the description that Dennis gave. He hated having to tell them that she was a big lady.

'Fat stripper does disappearing act. Maybe it was a very effective way of dieting,' he heard one of them joking as he left the police station.

Now it was Sunday, early evening. Dennis was in the kitchen thinking about the morning he'd spent with Paula and the children. Maybe she'd let him come home soon. It no longer seemed right staying here with no Kitty. Even the others, Sukey, Minnie, Jojo and Jaz were subdued and worried. No one was speaking, they just sat around, drinking tea and smoking.

The doorbell rang and they all looked up, looked at each other.

'I'll go,' Jaz said. He was already standing and left the kitchen as he spoke, banging the kitchen door open and running down the stairs.

Dennis, straining, heard a female voice. Not Kitty's: not deep enough, husky enough. In any case, he thought, she wouldn't have rung the bell; she'd have her key. He heard Jaz say: 'Hi,' and then another male voice and footsteps coming slowly up the stairs.

'Hello all,' Tessa said as she came in and looked round. 'Playing happy families without Mummy,' she added in the slow breathless voice that made Dennis want to slap her. The deliberate way she spoke, as if measuring out the words, made him curl up his toes inside his shoes. She was probably the least posh of all the girls who'd stayed in the flat at some time or another but she was the one who made Dennis most aware of the privileged families they'd left behind. He could not understand why they'd given up all that: big homes, not having to worry about money, foreign holidays no doubt, flash cars and lots of rich chinless wonders as prospective husbands.

Tessa stood by the door, leaning against Stevie and holding his hand. 'Sorry, probably not the most tactful of remarks. We just came to see if you'd any news of her, of Kitty,' she said.

'No,' said Sukey.

'Oh, well. Any chance of a cup of tea since we're here?'

'So, she's not shown up for work at all?' Sukey said as she put the kettle on and fished teabags out of their packet. Tessa had pulled Stevie into the room and was now sitting on his knee, playing with the fingers of one his hands. He looked bored, Dennis thought, and theatrical, with his short hair, blond and permed, and that way he had of flicking his head every now and then as if to rid it of nasty thoughts.

'Has anyone else from the clubs gone missing?' Minnie asked.

'Not so you'd notice,' Tessa said, and Dennis wondered why she couldn't just say 'no', why she always tried to make things mean more than they really did. He sighed and as they continued to sit, silently, drinking tea, he thought, I've got to move on. He lit yet another cigarette. Even if Paula won't let me come home, I'll find somewhere else, he thought. I can't go on living with this bunch of beatniks.

There was a gentle knock on the door; no one got up, no one said anything. The knock came again and Dennis looked round the table. It was probably the landlord, wanting his rent. Kitty had always paid him on Saturdays.

'Answer it one of you,' Dennis said.

'Why don't you?' Minnie asked. Dennis watched the tip of her nose and the tops of her cheeks turning pink. He stood up and went to the door, opened it. He was right; it was the landlord.

'Hello, good morning… er good afternoon,' the little Indian man said, he stopped, coughed, looked up at Dennis, blinking, waiting for a response.

Dennis scratched his head, still holding the door midway between open and closed.

'I was wondering,' the landlord said, 'is Miss Kitty here? Normally, she is paying the rent and now it's Sunday.'

'No,' Dennis said, 'she's not here, we don't know….'

'Shut up Dennis!' Sukey shouted. She stood and came to the door and pushed Dennis away.

'Hello,' she smiled at the landlord. 'Come back in an hour, we'll have the money for you then.'

The landlord nodded, looked at his watch. 'Yes,' he said, still nodding, sounding uncertain.

'In an hour,' Sukey repeated. Now she, too, was nodding. The landlord turned and was walking up the stairs to his flat. Sukey closed the door.

'If you tell him that Kitty's not here, he might throw us out; she's the one with the rent book,' Sukey was almost hissing.

Bossy little number for all her fey ways, Dennis thought, pursing his lips, angry. 'So,' he said, 'how are we going to pay?'

'We'll pay what we normally pay. After all, I'm pretty sure that Kitty's got it organised so that she lives here free. Do you know where the rent book is?' Sukey asked Dennis.

He shook his head. 'No, but there's a drawer in the

bedroom full of her documents. It's probably there.'

'Oh,' said Tessa, 'there's another reason I'm here. Beaky wants to move back in. Now that Stevie's taken over from him.'

'Is he still with his parents?' Minnie asked.

'Yes,' Tessa said, 'but he's coming back tomorrow. He telephoned, wanted to know if I'd come to my senses.' She paused, smiled. They all looked at her. 'I told him I was staying with Stevie. That we were engaged.' She wriggled in Stevie's lap. He giggled. She wriggled some more and added in her slow voice: 'So then Beaky asked me to ask Kitty if he could come back here, at least for a little while. I think he's still a little upset about my betrayal.'

'What did he say when you told him Kitty was missing?' Jaz asked.

'I forgot to mention it,' Tessa said. Silly little bitch, Dennis thought, once more wanting to slap her. If she'd been his daughter or his girlfriend, he'd have given her a good shaking.

Dennis poured brown sauce over the chops, mashed the beans into the potato, felt the gurgle of his stomach as it rumbled. Thank God they'd all gone out leaving him in peace to cook and eat his tea. He went to the fridge for a beer. He felt the bottle, not that cold; he daren't leave them in the fridge when he wasn't in the kitchen for fear the others would take them. In spite of what he'd said, the threats he'd issued. They wanted him gone, Dennis knew, and because of that, he'd changed his mind about moving on. He would stay. All that fuss about the rent, insisting he pay half as he had one whole bedroom to himself. And that Sukey: 'If you don't like it, Dennis, then you can share. You and Jaz and Beaky, when he comes back, can have our room and Minnie, Jojo and I'll take over yours. Or you can just leave,' she'd said in her high posh voice. Still, at least she'd organised things.

He'd come back into the kitchen with the rent book and she'd taken it.

'Bloody Kitty,' she said as she looked at the pages in the book. 'She's been making a fair bit from our share of the rent.' Sukey calculated how much they all should pay and Dennis had argued that while the others were all paying less than before, his share would be more. It seemed that Kitty had treated him favourably. And now she was gone and Dennis wondered where she was and if she would ever be back.

He finished his food, burped, took another beer from the fridge and sat back, smoking. He'd go to bed soon, an early night and an early start in the morning. Kitty would not be back; not today, not ever, he decided, and wondered if he was missing her or just the way she looked after him and made his life seem a little better than the mess he felt it to be just now.

(Years later, when he was terminally ill in hospital, Dennis started to dream about his months in the flat in Camden Town. Waking, he'd wonder if it had really happened. One evening as she sat by his bed knitting something for one of their grandchildren, he asked his wife Paula if he'd ever lived with a woman called Kitty, and watched as she walked out of the ward without a word. It was the last time he saw her: he died that night.)

Chapter 20
October 1967: Jojo

It was hard with Malc dead. Not just his death but having to keep it all together, acting the calm and collected person she expected herself to be. Not showing that she was sad. Jojo had woken in the early morning every night since he'd died and had lain confused for quite a long time, scared almost to breathe, wondering where she was. Then gradually she'd remember: she was lying on a heap of cushions spread on the kitchen floor in Kitty's place. Alone. And realising she was alone, she'd let a few sobs shake her chest, but still she wept quietly and with restraint. Just in case.

She'd been happy during the day that had ended with her hearing that Malc had died. Happy and pleased with herself, too. At lunchtime, she'd gone to see a flat that a colleague, Anne, was moving out of in a couple of weeks. One small bedroom and a large room combining living and kitchen areas. It had its own bathroom and, best of all, it was on the ground floor and had a little west-facing garden. It was just right and she felt, given the way she minimised her daily expenses, that she could afford the rent. And she'd have to pay even less if she let Malc move in with her and he contributed. She opened the French windows and stood outside on the tiny patio, imagining the two of them sitting at a little table, enjoying the evening sun and sharing a bottle of wine.

'Will the owner let me have it do you think?' she asked Anne.

'I'm pretty certain he will. He's asked me to find someone I could recommend. He hates using agencies and putting an ad in the Evening Standard gets too many replies. He's sure to like you,' Anne replied and when they were back at the office she'd phoned and arranged for Jojo to meet the landlord at the end of week. Jojo wondered whether to try and contact Malc to tell him about it and ask him if he'd like to live with her again. It was time, Jojo felt, to have him back. He'd said that he wasn't doing heroin much anymore, and if they were together in their own place he'd drink less, she was sure.

There was no answer when she dialled Malc's number and so she decided to wait until the flat was hers. She imagined opening the door to him and showing him the place, seeing him like it and then telling him he could move in with her if he wanted to. She imagined his smile coming slowly and the way he pushed back his hair from his face when he was pleased. And then, when she got back to Kitty's place after work, there was Ted in the kitchen, looking so pale and tired that Jojo had swallowed, knowing something was wrong, but not guessing what it might be. She sat down opposite him at the table and he said nothing for a bit, just looked at her. Then he bent his head so that he could no longer see her, rubbed his face with both hands and started to tell her a story of some kind.

'Speak up,' said Jojo. She couldn't hear what Ted was saying. Or rather, she thought she'd heard but knew she must be mistaken.

'I'm sorry,' Ted said. He was almost crying as he repeated what he'd already told her. Jojo sat upright, let the eddying world settle round her as she felt her breath slow down while her heart squeezed tight somewhere inside her and a drum beat stupidly in her head.

'Will you say it again?' she asked and he did. The fourth time he said it she realised that it must be true. And she couldn't help letting out a sob.

'I'm sorry, I'm so sorry,' Ted said. He was standing now, in front of Jojo, twisting his hands together and shaking his head as he stared at her. She sat perfectly still waiting for the strange awfulness of what had happened to Malc settle down and become true. And to think, she thought, I was happy today, making plans for us when all the time he was lying in a morgue, cold and alone, and he would never see me again and he'd never even know that. She let another sob escape.

'What can I do for you?' Ted asked.

'Nothing,' Jojo said. 'Maybe you should go.'

'I can't leave you all alone.'

'You can. That's what I want. I want to be on my own.' She spoke slowly, it was hard to get the words out, her mouth was frozen and her tongue felt too big for it. She sat and listened as Ted told her more about Malc's death, how he'd not been doing much in the way of drugs. He said all sorts of other stuff that he must have thought she'd needed to know. Or maybe it was because he needed to tell someone: he needed to let it all out so that it was no longer poisoning him.

'Please go,' Jojo said when Ted paused. 'Now.'

'No,' he said.

'Please, please, please will you go now,' Jojo insisted.

'All right,' Ted almost shouted and he'd left quickly, slamming the door behind him. Jojo heard him running down the stairs and she continued to sit immobile in the kitchen, which, after a little while, began to get dark.

That had been over a month ago, very early in September. Jojo had decided not to go the funeral: Malc was dead, she knew he was dead and she needed to work hard to get used to it. A funeral was about being sad, and she didn't want to be sad.

At least I have somewhere to move into, she'd told herself. But on the day she was supposed to meet the landlord, she realised that she no longer wanted to live there. When she thought of the place, she felt claustrophobic. She imagined being in the small garden, locked in, unable to get out, and she began to hyperventilate. She didn't go to the meeting at the flat and she didn't cancel it either. Anne told Jojo that the landlord had phoned asking what had happened to her and suggesting that she must be unreliable.

Jojo shrugged. 'I don't want the place anymore,' she said.

Anne had looked at her, her mouth tight and angry. 'You

should have told me,' she said. 'It's made me look foolish.'
For several days after that, Anne only spoke to Jojo when she
needed to, asking or telling about work related issues. Jojo
enjoyed it, she liked the sharpness of the few words when
they came and Anne's brisk walk out of her office refreshed
her. It was like sucking a peppermint to take away an
unpleasant taste. She stopped thinking so much about Malc.

Now it was October, days were shorter and colder.
Somehow, probably because that was when the school year
started, Jojo had always associated autumn with change and
new beginnings. She told herself that the tragedy of Malc
dying had been superseded by Jules' suicide and Kitty's
disappearance, and it was now time to find herself a flat. It
was late Saturday morning and she sat in the kitchen in her
pyjamas drinking coffee. Outside the sun was shining,
showing up the dirt on the windowpanes. Kitty had been
gone for nearly two weeks and although she rarely saw her,
Jojo missed her. She thought of Kitty on Sunday afternoons,
her big hands in rubber gloves, pink like her face, a bucket
on the floor and Kitty kneeling beside it cleaning the floor
with a big old scrubbing brush. She smiled, remembering
Kitty sitting up in her wide saggy bed, hiding Jojo from her
parents, turning their middle-class, middle-aged assurance
into uncomfortable uncertainty. Kitty's absence had deflated
the flat; it felt greyer, and in a strange way smaller, given that
Kitty had filled it with her bulk and energy.

Jojo stood up and stretched, wondering if there was any
point in using the rest of the day to find somewhere of her
own to live. Dennis and Minnie had left for work that

morning and the rest of the flat's inhabitants were still sleeping. Jojo thought about making tea and taking them all a cup, suggesting that they get up and go for a drive somewhere. She was restless and needed something to do.

When the bell rang, she went slowly downstairs. Dolores had opened the front door. She stood on tiptoes, one hand stretched up still on the latch. She was wearing a thin nightdress, her hair was un-brushed, a limp naked doll dangled from her other hand and she was looking at Ted who stood, embarrassed, peering down at the child, his arms across his chest.

'Hello,' Jojo said, and Ted looked up and smiled at her. 'Let him in,' Jojo said to Dolores, who let go of the door, pulled her doll into her arms and pouted.

'I'm coming up with you,' the little girl said. 'Mammy and baby John are resting and I need a biscuit.'

'Can't you get one from your own kitchen?' Jojo asked. She was never sure how to treat Dolores, who she found oddly precocious and worldly wise.

'I can't,' said Dolores emphatically, 'because we haven't got any.'

Jojo shrugged, turned and went back up the stairs followed by Dolores and behind her, Ted. In the kitchen, she made coffee for Ted and a jam sandwich for the little girl in the absence of biscuits.

'I need orange squash as well,' said Dolores, but accepted weak, milky tea when Jojo told her there were no soft drinks. She sat at the table, her doll on her knee, eating and drinking and watching Jojo and Ted.

'So,' said Jojo, 'how're things in the flat?' She'd not seen Ted since he'd told her about Malc's death.

'I've got to move out, I can't do it any more. I got a friend to move in after....'

'Yes, after Malc died,' Jojo said, looking at Ted, holding his eyes with hers, stopping them from sliding away.

'Yes,' he said and coughed. 'But, well, he left, couldn't take it for long. And she wants me out now. It's all been too much for her – and me – and she wants a fresh start.'

'Yes,' said Jojo, grinning. 'Fresh meat,' she added, and Ted shook his head almost imperceptibly, then grimaced. 'Well,' she said, 'who've you come to see, or are you here to ask if you can move in?'

'No, I can't move in, not with Minnie still here. She is, I suppose?'

'Yes.'

'I came to see you. I thought you might like to come and spend some time at my flat. Mrs Smith's away for the weekend.'

'And you're off duty,' Jojo laughed.

'Well?'

Jojo thought for a bit. 'Why not?' she said eventually. 'Can I have a bath there?'

Ted nodded, he smiled, leant across the table and touched Jojo's hair. 'But I'd like to get in with you.'

Jojo looked down. Part of her felt angry that so soon after Malc's death he was chatting her up; part of her told herself not to be so silly, she had worked so hard not to feel sad about Malc, had striven to remain normal. She felt Ted's hand on her hair, felt it move down and stroke her neck. He left it there, two fingers gentle just above her throat.

'You're beautiful when you're wearing just pyjamas,' he said.

Jojo looked at him, swallowed. 'Malc was your friend,' she almost whispered.

Ted nodded. 'Yes, it's not too soon, is it? You know I fancy you.'

Jojo shook her head, but she wasn't sure what she was trying to convey by that gesture. She took his two fingers in her hand and moved them away from her neck. Still holding the fingers, she leaned towards Ted, he leaned towards her too and they kissed. For Jojo it was a test: she wanted to know how it would feel to kiss someone who wasn't Malc. It was not that she was heartless or cruel or unfeeling. It was because she was young and attractive and needed to know that all her effort at not being overwhelmed by the death of a boyfriend was worth it. She felt nothing as she moved back from the kiss, but this was better than being revolted or moved to tears. It was a start: something could develop from nothing.

'Why are you kissing?' Dolores asked. 'Do you want to have a rest together?'

Jojo looked at the little girl. She had jam on one of her cheeks and a curl of her hair was sticking to it.

'I asked you something,' the child said, pouting.

'No,' Jojo said, 'we're just friends.'

'Mammy's got a lot of friends,' Dolores said. She pushed the last of her bread into her mouth and chewed.

'It's time for you to go back to your flat,' Jojo said. She stood up and rinsed a dishcloth in the sink, squeezing it out and using it to wipe Dolores' face and hands. The little girl squirmed in her chair.

'I want to stay here,' she said when Jojo had finished.

'You can't, I want to dress and get ready to go out. So off you go.' Jojo lifted Dolores from her chair, carried her to the door, which she opened and put her down outside before firmly closing and leaning against it. She raised her voice against the noise of Dolores shouting to be let back in. 'She can be a bloody nuisance that child. You know she came up here once when everyone must have been out and stole Kitty's Dutch cap. Bridie found it and brought it up the next day. She thought it was hysterical... Oh,' said Jojo, realising that Ted probably knew nothing of Kitty's disappearance, 'she's been missing since last Tuesday. Did you know?'

The shouting stopped, followed by a few seconds of Dolores banging on the door.

'Who's been missing?' Ted asked.

'Kitty.' Jojo took a couple of steps back into the room as she heard Dolores' slow footsteps plodding down the stairs.

'Probably just moved on to another man,' Ted shrugged. 'Are you going to get ready?'

'I won't be long. Wait for me outside.'

Ted opened his mouth.

'No you can't stay,' Jojo said.

Jojo held her breath as Ted unlocked the door to the flat and pushed it open. She wondered if there'd still be anything of

Malc's around. She didn't really want to ask. She followed Ted in.

'My bath,' she said, swinging the small bag she'd packed with clean clothes and her sponge bag.

'D'you want a drink first?' Ted opened the fridge, lifted out a bottle of champagne. Jojo shook her head.

'Can I come with you?'

'No, I just want to get clean.'

'You know where it is,' Ted said. He'd sat down and lit a cigarette.

Jojo nodded, turned and went into the bathroom. She locked the door behind her and breathed out, as if for the first time since entering the flat. She put down her bag and swallowed. She couldn't help herself; she started to look around, moving things on the shelf to see if anything of Malc's was there. There didn't seem to be. She opened the cupboard under the basin and inhaled sharply. There was his toothbrush, one she'd used sometimes when she'd stayed without planning to and hadn't brought her own, and there was his razor. She lifted it out. There were dark hairs still caught in the blade and Jojo squeezed it tight. She sat on the edge of the bath and let herself cry, very quietly, very sadly, for a long time.

When she stopped she leant over and put in the plug and then she turned on the taps, pouring in bubble bath from one of the bottles on the shelf.

Ted knocked on the door. 'You're taking your time,' he called through the keyhole.

'I need time,' Jojo called back. She put the razor in the

little ledge at the end of the tub, turned off the taps and took off the clothes – the ones from yesterday that she'd put on quickly before coming here – and climbed into the bath. She leant to pick up the razor again and rubbing bubble bath into her armpits gently shaved away the thin growth of hair.

When she woke in the early hours of the next morning, Jojo, as was usual, wondered where she was. When she realised she was in bed with Ted she turned over trying to decide if she really wanted to be there.

They didn't get up until late on Sunday.

'When is Mrs Smith back?' Jojo asked.

'Not till Tuesday. You can stay if you want.'

Jojo sat up, pulling at the bedclothes so that they covered her chest. She folded her long legs together. She could feel the softness of Ted's hip against hers, knew that he was watching her, wondering about her. Last night she'd realised how much he'd been wanting her. It made her feel better. She had decided to sleep with Ted because he was – had been – a friend of Malc's. It wasn't because she thought that that would bring her closer to her dead boyfriend. That couldn't happen; she knew that. It was because she liked to have a man in her life and since it couldn't be Malc, it was best that it should be someone who knew him. And Ted had known him, lived with him, shared so much with him.

'What are you doing for money, these days, Ted?' Jojo asked. There was no reply. She felt Ted's hip move away and turned to look at him. He was on his side, his arms over his head, curled up. 'Tell me,' Jojo insisted.

'I've gone straight. I've got a job,' Ted mumbled, ashamed.

'A job!' Jojo was surprised. Since she'd known Ted he'd never worked in the traditional sense, he'd done some dealing for Malc, probably some other bits and pieces she didn't know about. The image of Ted getting up early on a Monday morning and dressing for work made her smile. 'What sort of job?'

Ted sighed. 'I've given in, given up sort of... It was after... Malc... I went to see my father and he... I don't really want to talk about it now,' Ted finished. He turned over and sat up. He put his arm round Jojo and pushed back her hair. He started to kiss her face, little loving kisses, and Jojo knew that he wanted to tell her that he loved her, but that he wouldn't, because he wasn't quite sure of how to do it. She'd not known that Ted could be so soft and delicate.

Later Jojo went back to Kitty's flat to fetch more clothes so that she could stay with Ted until Mrs Smith returned. While she was out Ted cooked them a meal and that evening as they smoked what would be the last joint of the day, Ted said, sounding casual: 'We could find a flat together if you like. I mean, I need to move out and you don't want to go on sleeping in Kitty's kitchen.'

'OK,' Jojo said. 'Now tell me about your job.'

'Nothing, it's just work. In my father's firm, you know, boss's son, learning the ropes.'

'If we're going to live together, you'll have to carry on with it.'

'I know,' Ted said. 'Malc used to talk about you

288

sometimes.' He took a big draw of the joint and passed it to Jojo, not looking at her. 'He said you needed… well, he said that he'd have to get himself together if you were going to stay with him.'

Jojo felt the tears coming, felt them making a lemony taste in her throat. She shook her head not wanting to cry in front of Ted. She didn't want him thinking she was weak.

'Too right,' she said, pulling on the joint, her head back, her eyes half closed. She exhaled deeply and took another big puff. She passed the joint back to Ted and smiled at him. The moment of danger was over: she was back in control.

(Thinking about that time, Jojo realised it was a turning point for Ted, the start of his success as a businessman. He never stopped smoking dope, and later took up cocaine, but that didn't impinge on his developing ability to make money (legally) from the enterprises that he became involved in. As for her, it was the beginning of her move back to normal middle class life. She was able to introduce Ted to her parents and he was accepted. They separated – Jojo had never been really in love with him – when she met the man she was to marry: a barrister.)

Chapter 21
October 1967: Sukey

As she let herself into the house, Sukey wondered if maybe Kitty would be back. It was over three weeks ago that she'd disappeared, but it seemed far longer. So much had changed since she'd gone. Sukey was working again, for another temp agency: a boring normal job, but it was better than cleaning and she earned more. Jojo was moving out the next day, Saturday. She and Ted had found a place in the next street. Beaky, even more silent than before he and Tessa became a couple, had moved back into the flat. Last week he and Jaz had enrolled for their second year at their respective colleges, both were taking it more seriously than previously, or so Sukey thought. There was less staying up late, less sitting in the kitchen enjoying doing nothing.

It was more than just people moving in, moving out, starting term, finding new jobs. The atmosphere – being there – was different. The flat had begun to feel as if it were a temporary place, just somewhere to sleep and eat in the absence of anything better. Once, Sukey realised, it had been more or less home. But now, she was no longer sure that she belonged there and on the few occasions when there was just her and Dennis in the kitchen, she felt restless and uncomfortable. Last night she'd confronted him, told him she knew about Minnie.

'Minnie said you tricked her into getting into bed with you; you pretended that she could have that money back, the stuff she'd lost, if the two of you had sex.'

Dennis turned from the sink where he was washing the dishes from his evening meal. That was another thing, since Kitty had gone they rarely all ate together. Even when she'd been at the pub working or lately stripping in Soho, she'd prepare a big pot of soup or vegetable stew for them to heat in the evening. On Sundays she'd cook a meal for all of them, sometimes with chicken, or minced beef, often with a cake to have as pudding.

He went back to his washing-up. He'd said nothing, but Sukey could see that she'd angered him. He noisily scrubbed a pan, scratching it quick and hard with wire wool before banging it down on the draining board. He raised both hands and then splashed them down into the sudsy water, scrabbling round for what was left.

'Well?' asked Sukey.

'Well what?' he said.

'What are you going to say?'

'Nothing,' the word came out long and hissing. Dennis dropped the last of the cutlery next to the pan and jerked the chain that held the plug so that the water swirled out. He put his hands on the edge of the sink, leaning on them, bending over, his head bowed.

'Why did you do it?'

Dennis turned to face her; he wiped his hands on the back of his trousers. His face was red, his bulgy eyes were puffy. He licked his lips, leaving them damp with saliva, and then he shook his head at her. 'It's none of your bleeding business.'

'She's my friend and you weren't nice to her.'

'No? She wasn't nice to me either and I've not noticed the two of you being that pally.'

'We weren't, we are now.'

'Leave it out, will you?' Dennis asked. He took a beer from the fridge and subsided into a chair. He sighed and lit a cigarette. 'D'you want one?' he said. He was sad and deflated and for a moment, Sukey felt sorry for him. An ordinary man in the wrong place with the wrong people. He'd go home if he could, Sukey thought, as she smoked the cigarette he'd given her and said no more.

Now it was Friday evening as Sukey climbed the stairs to the flat. She wondered if Kitty might be there, if any of the others would be in and if there were plans for the evening.

They were all there, all bar Kitty: Jaz, Beaky, Minnie and Jojo, even Dennis, who was smoking as he ate, a bottle of beer in front of him. Ted had come around as well, looking unlike his old self, still wearing a suit and tie from work. It was a long time since Sukey had seen him in the flat, and she glanced at Minnie. She was sitting hunched up, her small face was closed and wary, but then she often looked like that. And she'd told Sukey that she had recovered from Ted and what seemed now, she said, 'an unsatisfying and rather silly affair'.

'Hello,' Jojo said. 'Come and sit down, this is my goodbye meal.'

On the table were bread, cheese, grapes, a plate of ham, salami and other sliced meats, as well as jars of pickles and bowls of nuts and olives. There were also two open bottles of wine and another couple on the shelf above the bathtub.

'Right,' said Sukey, taking it in. Jojo had done well, she thought. At first Sukey had been amazed at how much food and alcohol Jojo contributed to the flat. Not all the time, but when she felt like it. After she'd accompanied Jojo to the shops a couple of times she began to admire her skills as a shoplifter and had helped once or twice, but had never done it on her own. She did not want to be caught, which she was sure she would be, not having the panache and serenity (nor the height, nor the beauty, Sukey told herself) with which Jojo bewitched the shopkeepers.

Sukey sat down and Jaz poured her some wine and passed her a plate.

Soon after, Ted left. 'My last evening of duty at the flat,' he said, making a face as he went out.

'We'll be at the pub, see you later,' Jojo said.

When they'd finished all the wine, Jojo brought out a bottle of brandy, Dennis offered the last of his beer around and Jaz rolled joints from what was left of his cache of dope, adding the insides of the skins of two bananas to make it go further.

'Want to try it?' he asked Dennis who shook his head,

saying: 'Pah,' showing disgust. But he didn't go to work: he stayed with them, drinking with them, saying little, but watching and listening. When Jojo decided it was time to wash up, Dennis helped her and he came with them to the pub. Something he'd done rarely and never since Kitty stopped working there.

It was drizzling and dark when they left the house. Although it was cold and damp, the pavements slippery under their feet with the falling leaves and greasy London rain, Sukey felt a surge of optimism, as if all their lives were going to work out well. Kitty would return, having been on holiday with a millionaire who wanted to spend even more money on her and her friends. Dennis would be allowed go home to his family. Ted and Jojo would marry. Beaky and Minnie would fall in love and she and Jaz... Ah well, she wasn't sure what would happen to Jaz and even less sure about what would happen to her. But just at that moment, it didn't really matter.

In the middle of the pub Vic was sprawled at a table, on which there was an overflowing ashtray, several empty tankards and glasses, as well as two which were still half full with what was probably whisky. He looked up, watching them as they passed the table. Then he pulled himself into an upright position. 'Hey,' he called as they reached the bar. Sukey had taken her purse out, offering to buy them all a drink.

'Hey,' Vic called louder, gesturing with both arms: 'Come and join us.'

Sukey shook her head as she took the orders from her

flatmates, transmitting them to the barman. By the time she'd finished and paid, the others had found a table nearby and were drawing up chairs around it. A man came from the men's loo and walked passed them to the bar. It was Sean. He bought drinks and took them to the table where Vic was sitting. Sukey watched Minnie watching him.

He sat down, his back to them, and Minnie turned to Sukey. She shook her head. 'Do you think he recognised us?'

'I don't care,' Sukey said, before she realised that Minnie was close to crying.

'I think I'll go home,' Minnie whispered.

'No,' Sukey said. 'Don't let him chase you away.'

'It's not him really. He was sort of nice to me the last time we saw him. No, it's not Sean. I just want things to be ordinary,' Minnie said, 'I want to feel normal.'

Sukey sighed. It would be another of those start-of-the-weekend evenings when possibilities would seemed endless and wonderful and then would gradually deflate and fade until it was Sunday afternoon with time having passed once more, yielding nothing more than an empty wallet and a grey, used feeling, like a dropped and melting ice-cream lying dirty in the gutter.

'I'm going,' Minnie said and stood up. As she walked passed the table where Vic and Sean were sitting, Sean looked up, looked straight at her for a moment saying nothing. Then he turned to talk to Vic again. Soon afterwards Ted came in, had one drink and left with Jojo.

'He's changed,' Sukey said to Jaz.

'Yeah,' said Jaz, twirling a piece of hair with his finger. 'I think he wants to be a grown up.'

'Nothing wrong with that,' Dennis said leaning towards them. 'You've all got to grow up sometime.'

'Why?' Sukey asked and grinned when Dennis spluttered into his drink.

Later, when it was almost closing time, Sukey looked up to see Sean leaving and Vic coming towards their table. Earlier he'd seemed very drunk, but now it was as if he'd spent the hour or so they'd been in the pub becoming sober. 'I'll join you now,' he said. 'Get you all a last drink.'

'So,' he said to Dennis, once he'd placed his order at the bar. 'You're the boyfriend of the famous Kitty.'

Dennis went red; he shook his head, making his cheeks wobble and looking even more damp and flustered. 'Why did you mention Kitty?' he asked, belligerent and vulnerable.

'Why not,' said Vic. 'Don't you want to know where she is?'

'Yes,' Dennis said. 'Do you know?'

'Me? Why should I? I only saw her a few times.'

'A few times too often,' Dennis said. He swallowed.

Sukey thought he looked as if he might start to cry. The idea horrified her. 'Let's go home,' she said.

'No,' said Vic, 'let's go on somewhere. There's bound to be a party going on. Or we could go to a club. You, Jack,' he turned to Jaz, 'you don't want to go home, do you?'

'Where could we go?' Jaz asked, jiggling his foot and stroking his chin as if he were wearing a long beard.

'There's a guy at college having a party. He lives quite close,' Beaky said softly, almost as if apologising.

'Right. Off we go,' Vic said. He poked Dennis in the stomach with one of his long fingers. 'Are you coming too?'

Dennis said nothing for a bit, blinked his pale gooseberry eyes. Then he shook his head. 'No,' he said. 'I'd be right out of place.'

Because they knew the landlord from the time when Kitty had worked there and because he'd never suspected that she'd been the one stealing from the till and from the stock, Jaz managed to persuade him to sell them a bottle of cheap Spanish wine even though the off-licence section was now closed. They left the pub, hearing the doors lock behind them, and followed Beaky as he tried to remember the exact address of the party. The rain was falling more heavily now and Sukey wished she were wearing more. She had no coat, just a thin jacket, and she started to shiver. Vic put one arm round her and another round Jaz and they walked clumsily along together, Beaky slightly to one side.

By the time they found the basement where the party was being held, Sukey wished they'd gone straight home. The woman who let them in was staggeringly drunk and someone had been sick just outside the front door. Most of the booze had run out and the kitchen was a sticky mess, full of empty plastic beakers and soggy cigarette butts, some in ashtrays, but most on the floor or the table. Loud music and the sweet smell of dope came from one of the two other rooms. Jaz opened the bottle and passed it round. Still clutching the bottle, he made for the dope-and-music room and Sukey followed him. It was dark and they found a space next to each other on the floor. Joints were being passed round and Sukey accepted one when it reached her, took a few deep drags and passed it on.

She peered round the room looking at its inhabitants, all drunk, stoned or (most of them) both. She'd always thought of parties as places to meet men. Often she'd find herself being chatted up, but rarely by someone she wanted to spend time with. Not if she was honest. She thought of Jojo with Ted and sighed. It was time she had a proper boyfriend. She leant back against the wall and shut her eyes.

When she woke up she was leaning on Jaz, who was leaning on Vic. Vic had his arm round Jaz's neck, and his hand was fondling his throat. Sukey sat up. The music had stopped but the room was still full of people, some of whom were asleep, though one or two were kissing. As she blinked, she realised that the woman on the sofa was naked and that she was lying across the knees of three other people, one of whom was stroking her breasts.

'Jaz,' Sukey whispered. He struggled slightly and Vic moved his arm, pulling him closer. Then Vic started to kiss him and Sukey closed her eyes again. She felt Jaz next to her as he moved away from Vic and she heard his soft sigh, but didn't know what it meant. She felt her arm being shaken and she opened her eyes.

'C'm on,' said Jaz. 'It's time to go.'

'What about Beaky?' she asked as they stood up.

'We'll find him.' Jaz said and he peered round the room. 'He's not here,' he added.

By now Vic was standing, too. 'What are you doing?' he asked.

'Going home,' Jaz said.

'Deserting me. You all desert me,' Vic said. 'Jules left me, Kitty went and now you're going, too, Jaz.'

'He got your name right,' Sukey whispered.

'Yes,' said Jaz. He touched Vic's arm and shook his head. Sukey followed him as he walked out into the hall. Beaky was sitting on the floor, leaning against the wall, asleep.

It had stopped raining and the air was soft and almost warm. Sukey stood on the pavement waiting as Jaz and Beaky came slowly up the steps from the basement. She breathed in deeply, sniffing in early Sunday morning London. Mingling with the sour smell of damp overused earth was the aroma of old petrol fumes, soggy leaves and a bitter overlay of grit, grime and grease. Beaky seemed to be half-asleep and he stumbled as he reached the pavement.

Back at the flat, he went straight to bed. Sukey peered into the kitchen, not wanting to wake Jojo if she were there, but the room was empty. She went in and sat in the big armchair, no longer feeling tired. Jaz followed her. He stood yawning and stretching, raising his arms high above his head. Sukey saw his jumper ride up exposing the thin white flatness of his tummy in which his small protruding navel, grey and gristly, didn't seem to quite fit.

'There's some brandy left,' Sukey said.

'And I've got a tiny little bit of dope, too. I kept it specially.'

They sat smoking and drinking, not saying anything until the joint was nearly finished. Then Sukey asked: 'Why did you let Vic kiss you again?'

'Oh… He started before I realised what was happening. And then…'

'You liked it. As you did the last time.'

'Yes,' Jaz said, quite simply. He looked up at the ceiling, as if there was something of great interest there that he needed to study. Sukey shuffled in the chair. She really should go to bed quite soon.

'Sukey,' Jaz said and she looked at him. 'I think… well, something's happened.'

'What is it?'

'Don't tell anyone else. Not yet anyway.'

'OK, go one, tell me.'

'I think… no I used to think, now I'm sure. I like men.'

'You mean you want to have sex with men?'

'Yes I do.'

'Like Vic?'

'No, not Vic. Not really Vic. I mean I want to but I don't want to.'

'Yes,' said Sukey. 'Look, if it's Vic that you fancy, it's not because he's a man, it's because he's like that. We've talked about him before. He's the sort of person that other people kind of… They want to be with him and even have sex with him. Even though he really is not a nice person, he has that sort of effect.'

'I know,' Jaz said, he had his elbows on the table and had cupped his face in both hands. He was rubbing the tops of his cheeks and the side of his nose with the ends of his fingers. He looked desperately tired with almost blue rings under his eyes and his skin was papery and flaky.

'So?'

'So it's someone else. But, it's wrong.'

'It's OK to be homosexual.'

'Yes, it's not that. I kissed a man who's living with someone else. I wanted to do more than that, so did he. But, we didn't.'

'Not Ted!'

'No. It's Stevie. He's so beautiful. I mean I almost gasped the first time I saw him.'

'Tessa's Stevie?'

'Yes.'

'But when?'

'They came round once. I was the only one in. Sunday afternoon a few weeks ago. And then she went off to buy some fags and we were alone. We'd been watching each other in any case; both times they visited before that day. We sort of noticed each other from the moment we met.'

'Does Tess know?'

Jaz sat up, clasped his hands together. 'No. The thing is Stevie's had loads of men. Tessa's his first girlfriend. He wants to make it work. He says he wants to try being heterosexual.'

'Doesn't sound to me like it's working.'

Jaz sighed, rubbed his hands through his hair, started to twirl one strand of it between two fingers.

'Look, if you want to do it with a man, find someone else,' Sukey said, moving upright.

Jaz looked at her, his eyes big and exhausted. 'But it's him I want.'

Sukey stood up and went to him. He leant against her and put his arms round her waist. Soon he was crying.

'Let's go to bed and cuddle,' Sukey said.

(Sukey and Jaz are still friends, so many years later. Once, when she was between marriages, he suggested that they have sex together. 'It didn't work when we were young and it won't work now,' Sukey said. 'And in any case you're gay.' (The term had come into use by then.) 'But I'd like to see what hetero sex is like,' Jaz insisted. Sukey told him that it was too late. 'Back in 1970 was when we were trying things out, ' she told him. 'Then anything went. Now I'm trying to live more normally.' Jaz asked her what 'normally' meant and she laughed because, she said, she still didn't know the answer to that question.)

Chapter 22
November 1967: Ted

Jojo had left a note for him. Ted saw it when he came in and went to the fridge. She'd taped it to the bottle of beer nearest to the front and Ted laughed when he saw it. She knows me so well, he thought. Then as he was opening the bottle, he panicked. Why a note? Was she leaving him or had she left him even? Clutching the beer in one hand and the note in the other, he moved quickly from the small kitchen back into the main room, where they lived, ate, slept, made love. He looked round; as far as he could see all her things were still there. Her books and ornaments on their shelves. The three occasional lamps that she'd bought and whose shades she had restored were in their normal places. The old sewing machine and the wickerwork box, which stored her needles, thread, scissors and such like, were still on the antique side table she'd brought from her parents' home, and the several pot plants were still dotted about the room.

He opened the wardrobe door and there were all her clothes with her boots and shoes neatly ranged underneath.

He breathed a sigh of relief and took a deep swig of beer. He sat down, lit a cigarette, leaned back and unfolded the paper she'd written on. So that's it, he thought as he read it: "Ted, I've gone round to Kitty's flat. The police have found her. Her body that is. Sukey called me soon after I got home and I thought I should go. You could come over too if you want to. Love Jojo XXX"

He finished the beer and decided on a second one. He changed from his office clothes into his home clothes, and rolled a joint, which he smoked as he drank. Then he decided to go round the corner to what was once Kitty's flat. He wasn't sure what he felt about the fact that she was dead, and wondered how it had happened. When he'd first read the note, he'd assumed she'd been murdered, but Jojo hadn't said that. He put some dope in his pocket to take with him and then changed his mind. There might be police there.

Sukey answered the door when Ted rang the bell. She opened her eyes wide at him, as if telling him how strange and at the same time exciting the situation was, and told him to come up. She didn't seem at all sad. Once in the kitchen he saw that everyone was there: Jaz, Beaky, Minnie, Dennis. And of course, Jojo. They were smoking and drinking. Bridie from downstairs was in the armchair, the baby on her knee sucking from a bottle and staring around at everybody. The little girl was sitting on the floor cross-legged with a mug of what looked like milky tea.

Jojo came over and put her arms round Ted. And then she led him to a chair. She pushed him down and then perched on his knee, her long legs folded back and half wrapped round his. Sukey poured him some wine before filling everyone else's glass. Dennis was sitting at the end of the table, his head bent. He lit a cigarette from the stub of the one he'd been smoking, took a gulp of wine and let out a big sigh.

'Dennis went to identify the body,' Sukey said. 'First thing this morning. And then he had to "help the police with their enquiries", didn't you Dennis?'

He nodded, looked as if he might be sick. 'I told them, you could hardly recognise her. It's been, what? Six weeks since she's been gone.'

'So... where was she... er... when they found her?' Ted wanted to ask how she died but was a little scared of seeming churlish. None of them, not even Dennis – though he did seem to be in an odd shocked state – were acting as if they were mourning Kitty, but they were all subdued.

'In the garden of a house that the council had bought. It was boarded up and when the builders started work on it yesterday there she was, it seems,' Sukey said. 'They did a post mortem to see how she died. A mixture of suffocation and strangulation.'

'So, she was murdered,' Ted murmured. Partly he wanted to go home with Jojo, have a meal, more beer, a few joints and then go to bed. Partly he wanted to stay, find out more about Kitty and what had happened to her. He frowned. Kitty was dead. He couldn't say that he felt anything for her. He had when Malc died. He'd felt quite sad and churned up when that had happened.

'I don't think you can suffocate yourself,' Jojo said. Ted shrugged. He was used to her sometimes slightly acid remarks, always made in a tone of sweetness. He thought of her tongue licking his skin and her eyes narrowing as she looked up at him. He shuffled slightly, wondering what he was doing there.

'Three,' Minnie said, 'three deaths. That should be the end of it.'

'I hope so,' Jaz said. 'What are we going to do for the rest of the evening?' he asked. 'Can we pretend everything's normal?'

'No,' said Dennis.

'The police have spoken to us all,' Sukey said. 'They came round early this morning just before I was going to leave for work. They've even been up to see the landlord and his wife and they spent a fair bit of time with Bridie.'

'Are you all murder suspects, then?' Ted asked.

'Only Dennis,' Jaz said.

'No I'm not.' Dennis' face flared red.

'Sorry,' said Jaz. He made a face. 'Actually I think they think it's something to do with her work. They're going to talk to all the people at the strip clubs.'

'That's probably it,' Bridie said. 'If you want to do that sort of work, you should do it from home.' She laughed, struggling to stand up, the baby under one arm. 'I better be going down, I've a friend coming soon and I want the children in bed before he arrives. Come on Dolores.'

'No,' said the little girl. 'I'm staying here. I want to be here when Kitty comes home.'

'She won't be coming here,' Minnie said. Her face was higher and thinner than normal, thought Ted, looking at her pinched face with its pink-tipped features and hiding eyes. He wondered why they'd spent so long together, nearly six months. Laziness had kept him with her. She turned to face him, must have felt his stare. She continued to watch him, her expression enigmatic, and then she allowed a small smile. Ted smiled back, not sure why, but it seemed the right thing to do.

'Where will she go?' Dolores insisted. No one answered.

'Come on, child, Kitty's gone to heaven,' her mother said eventually. 'And I hope she's enjoying it there,' she added briskly.

The door banged behind Bridie and the children and Jaz said, his voice surprised: 'I hadn't thought about it, but there'll be a funeral. Will we have to organise it? Or what?'

'Her mother. The police will contact her mother and she'll be in charge.' Sukey said.

'But we should go,' Jaz said. 'We can't not go to Kitty's funeral.'

During the week following the discovery of Kitty's body, Jojo was oddly quiet and Ted did not understand why. On Saturday night he wanted to ask her what was going on with her and if there was a problem between them, but he didn't know how to. He mumbled something about Kitty as he lay on the floor smoking a joint, but couldn't finish what he was trying to say. Jojo didn't reply. She was concentrating on mending an old silk blouse that she'd bought at a second hand shop that afternoon.

'So,' Ted said, 'Kitty'll be buried next week and will you, I mean, after the funeral, will you feel better?'

She looked up from her sewing, stared into the distance. 'I wasn't really close to Kitty. She did some good things for me, like letting me stay in the flat and hiding me from my parents. She was a bit like a mother, only one that let you do the things you wanted to do. But, well, she's dead, that's it. I just wonder what's going to happen to the rest of them living in the flat.'

'D'you think that Dennis murdered her?'

'No,' said Jojo. 'Sometimes, Ted, you can be really stupid.'

Finally, Ted began to wonder, after it had been a week and she still didn't want to make love, if Kitty's murder had reminded Jojo of Malc and made her think again of his sudden death. He had no idea of how to ask this and was scared that he was going to lose her. One night when he was very drunk, he told her that he loved her. He held her to him, stroking her thigh and buttock, backwards and forwards, backwards and forwards, saying over and over again: 'I love you, I love you.'

(Ted never stopped thinking about Jojo. Years after they'd separated a picture of her – tall, dark, beautiful, inscrutable – would often slide into his imagination when he was sitting watching television or alone in his car. He would conjecture that, if Kitty hadn't so carelessly and messily died, he and Jojo might have stayed together. When he was being honest, he would recognise that she would have gone in any case.

She never loved him as he loved her. It was good, however, when he was feeling down, to be able to blame Kitty for the loss of his lovely Jojo.)

Chapter 23
November 1967: Sukey

'We should go to the funeral,' Jaz said. 'You and I, Sukey, if not the others. We've known her for longer, since college.'

'It's so far away, we'll have to pay for a bed and breakfast and the train fare and everything.'

'I'm going,' he said, tapping with a bent fork on the table. He looked grey and worn. Sukey wasn't sure if it was because of Kitty's death, his unrequited obsession with Stevie or just because the days were growing shorter, colder, darker and Jaz was tired. Sometimes she wondered if he were ill. He was small and slender and seemed, even when rested and well fed, fragile somehow.

'I'll come with you,' Sukey said, deciding. She didn't want Jaz going off on his own, travelling up to Lancashire and spending hours with strangers.

'Maybe Dennis will want to come.'

'No,' Sukey said. 'How would he explain himself?'

Their time in the small Lancashire town where Kitty grew up was like a dream, an unpleasant one. Before going there

Jaz drove his car to his parents' and he and Sukey stayed there the night. They were kind and loving towards Jaz. And his younger brother and sister were like puppies, frolicking round him, unable to leave him alone, following him down the passage when he went to the loo, still talking to him when he was inside.

In the morning before they left, borrowing a car that was in far better condition than Jaz's, Sukey heard his mother say: 'You should treat a girlfriend like that well if you want to keep her.' She didn't hear what Jaz said in reply, it was just a quiet murmur.

At the funeral, there was a small assembly of family: an aunt, two cousins and Kitty's mother. She was like a ghost. She was thin, pale, aloof and as unlike her daughter, Sukey thought, as it was possible to be. She didn't appear to understand what was going on and she greeted them back at the house as if she had no idea why they were there. She didn't ask who they were or how they knew Kitty. She seemed to care about nothing, and for the first time Sukey felt sad and wanted to cry for the loss of a friend.

They drove back to Jaz's parents that day, arriving late in the evening. It was better than staying in that grim small town where Kitty had lived as a child and where she was now buried. They left early the next day, though Sukey could sense the family's disappointment that they hadn't stayed for lunch. It was a Saturday and they could have delayed their departure. But Jaz wanted to leave and that was that. He told her that he needed to be at home. The funeral had been enough without having to deal with his mother as well.

'But where is home?' Sukey asked. 'The flat doesn't seem right anymore.'

'It'll be better when they find who murdered her,' Jaz said. 'It'll be really over then.'

Vic was in the pub that night when they went in, sitting on his own, once more at a central table. He did not appear to have been there for long – he was not as drunk as he had been the last time they saw him. That was before Kitty's body had been found. He looked up and watched them as they walked across to the bar: Jaz, Sukey and Beaky. Vic's eyes were red, he hadn't shaved and he looked as if he hadn't slept for days. What's happening to us? Sukey thought. We all seem to be worn down, worn out, tired, falling to pieces.

'Well,' said Vic as they passed him, 'Madame Sue and her entourage. Are you going to join me?'

Sukey stopped, looked at Jaz and then at Beaky, raising her eyebrows as a question.

'Why not?' Jaz said. 'But it's your round,' he added, turning to Vic, who blinked.

'OK, you get them though.' He pulled some notes out of a pocket and passed them to Jaz. 'I'll have a Guinness and a whiskey chaser – Irish.'

Sukey felt restless as she toyed with her cider. She didn't really want to be here, wasn't in the mood for drinking. She re-crossed her legs, shuffled in her seat, tried to concentrate on what Vic was saying. He was rambling on about how difficult it was to work, now that he was the main one responsible for the kids. The nanny had left after Jules died and he was finding it hard to get another one who was suitable.

'Why the hell did my sweet wife do what she did?' He sounded as if he were angry with Jules for killing herself, almost as if she'd done it to inconvenience him.

'Where are the children?' Sukey asked. 'How can you get out so much?'

'What?' asked Vic, turning to face her. Sukey shrugged. He'd heard. He was playing a game of some sort.

'Where are your kids?' Jaz asked. He too was shifting in his seat. Only Beaky seemed untroubled and that was probably because he'd spent years practising how to sit silent and unnoticed in social situations. Sukey imagined them all living in a big terraced house, sitting comfortably with a coal fire burning, music playing on the hi-fi and the smell of a meal being prepared coming from the kitchen. Outside they could hear the cold rain falling and through the curtains, the silhouettes of trees bending in the wind were just visible, lit by the pale light of street lamps. She closed her eyes the better to imagine the internal warmth and comfort and its contrast with the external cold and damp. She shivered. The room she was picturing was too much like her parents' living room. And that was disconcerting. She did not want to have the kind of life they lived, but just now, she would love some order and stability.

'Wake up, Sukey,' she heard Vic say and she opened her eyes.

'Since you seem so interested in my children, would you like to be their Nanny? All sorts of additional benefits as well as a nice place to live and a decent wage. At the moment, Seth and Beatrice are spending a lot of time with my mother-in-law. Ex mother-in-law, I suppose I should say. Not good for them as she's in a real state with what happened to Jules. So, Sukey, want the job?'

'No thanks.' Sukey paused. 'I want to go home. We were at Kitty's funeral yesterday,' she added, and saw Vic flinch and put down his Guinness.

'I spent a lot of yesterday talking to the police about her,' he said raising his glass again and taking a long drink. He put it down, wiped his mouth with the back of his hand and stared at Sukey. 'Someone told them that she was working for me. And so now I'm being questioned.'

'Oh, I can't remember if I mentioned your name or not,' Sukey said. She felt her face warming. She must be blushing, she thought. She felt guilty, as if she'd somehow let Vic down, betrayed him. But why she should feel like that she didn't know.

'I gave them your name,' Jaz said. 'They wanted me to tell them about everyone she knew and might have seen recently.' He shrugged. 'No harm done. As long as you're not guilty.' The last few words came out as a squeak and he started to giggle.

'It's difficult,' Vic said, slowly, angrily. 'How do I explain to them what Kitty was doing at my place?'

'The truth,' Jaz said.

'I don't think they'd like that,' Vic said. He was leaning towards Jaz, almost threatening him. Jaz shrugged, pushed his chair back, seemed to shrink, as if he was pulling in his

317

extremities in, like a snail retracting into its shell.

'You shouldn't have mentioned my name. What's her death to do with me? They took a lot of my stuff away to look at: photographs, equipment, documents. It's very inconvenient. I told them they couldn't but they'd got themselves a search warrant.'

'Sorry,' said Jaz, still sitting small and hunched up.

'It's not Jaz's fault. If you're ashamed of what you do then you shouldn't be doing it,' Beaky said to Vic with a sudden spurt of authority.

Vic turned to him as if he'd only just noticed that he was with them. 'What do you know about anything? Especially when it comes to women and sex and what people really want. Oh and I think it's your round, mate.'

'No,' Sukey said. 'I think we should go home. Let's see if we've enough money for a bottle of something and go home.'

'OK,' Jaz said, unfolding himself. Beaky nodded.

'What about me?' Vic asked. 'Am I invited round to your place?'

There was silence.

'I'll buy a bottle of whiskey and you can share it with me.'

'No,' Jaz said loudly, and 'No,' said Beaky more quietly.

'Please, I'd like to treat you all,' Vic said.

He was, Sukey realised, very alone and also scared, worried in some way. She frowned. This was not right. This was pathetic: Vic offering them booze in order to buy their company. Vic the confident, Vic the successful, Vic the man of the world and beyond, almost begging for the company

318

of three insignificant teenagers. Had losing Jules, and in such a way, diminished him so much? Had his charisma been merely a reflection of his being with Jules: a result of his marriage to a beautiful and talented woman?

'Well?' Jaz asked, looking at her and then at Beaky, who shrugged, as if to say: why ask silly little me?

'Up to you, Jaz,' Sukey said. 'But we want a bottle of wine as well, if we say yes.'

'OK,' Jaz said, standing up. Vic just nodded, as it he knew they'd let him come with them in the end.

When they got back to the flat Sukey knocked on Bridie's living room door and asked her to join them.

'Why don't you all come into mine?' she asked when Sukey had explained that they had drink and cigarettes and there'd be a large packet of chips when Beaky came in. He'd run down the road to buy them. 'As long as you've not got any of that Maryannie stuff, I have to draw the line somewhere,' Bridie laughed. Once Sukey had asked her to share a joint with her but after a few puffs, Bridie had given up. 'I don't like the taste. And in any case it's illegal,' she'd said. 'I do have children to think of.' She'd winked at Sukey.

It was warm in Bridie's living room. The fire was lit and, crammed as it was with a three-piece suite and a couple of extra easy chairs, it was comfortable for all of them. Bridie fetched thick tumblers, wineglasses, plates for the chips, a salt and pepper set, a bottle of vinegar and one of tomato sauce. She put an ashtray on each of the occasional tables and sat back on the sofa next to Sukey, crossed her legs and lit a cigarette.

'So,' she said, 'how was the funeral?'

Sukey shrugged. 'Horrible.'

'The police were back here yesterday, but none of ye was in,' Bridie said.

'What did they want?'

'Asked where you all were. I told them. As far as I could. They'll be back.' Bridie leaned forward to take a handful of chips. 'Strange how hungry working can make you. I've already had a couple of jobs this evening.' She laughed, leant her head back, opened her mouth wide and filled it with the chips. When she'd finished eating she turned to Vic. 'So, you're the yoke she was doing all that porno stuff with?'

'Photography,' Vic said.

'In the nude, though.'

'Yes.'

'What else, what else did you have her do?'

'Do you really want to know?'

'No,' said Bridie, sitting up suddenly, tightening her mouth. 'I don't think I do.'

Later when Vic left the room to go the loo, Bridie looked round at them all. 'I don't trust him,' she said, using a loud stage whisper and widening her eyes. 'I'd say he was the one that done her in.'

'No,' said Sukey, 'he may be weird, but he wouldn't have done that.'

'Why not?' Bridie asked.

'Because we're not the sort of people who know murderers,' Sukey said.

'Little Miss Posh,' Bridie said, mimicking Sukey's accent.

'We don't take tea with murderers, or strippers, or whores.' She laughed and hit Sukey on the knee, showing that she meant the teasing kindly.

Later still, when a man rang Bridie's front door bell, the others went upstairs, taking the rest of the whiskey. When that was finished, Vic rolled a joint and asked if he might stay the night.

'No', Sukey said. But he was still in the kitchen with Jaz and Beaky when she left them to go to bed. When in the late morning she woke and went to make some tea, he was asleep, wrapped in the blankets and lying on the cushions that had been Sukey's bed when she'd first come to live in the flat.

Sukey filled the kettle and plugged it in. She put tea leaves in the pot and checked to see if there was milk in the fridge. There was. She went and stood looking down at Vic, her arms folded. He was lying on his back and was so still that she wondered if he was dead. She kicked him gently with her naked foot and he let out a muffled sound and turned onto his side. Sukey thought about what Bridie had said the night before. Could this man asleep in the kitchen of Kitty's flat have killed her? She kicked him again, harder, and then again until he woke up. He sat up, rubbing his face. He yawned and swallowed, didn't seem to know where he was.

'If I give you a cup of tea, will you go home after you've drunk it?'

Vic said nothing, just leant against the wall, looking around the room, his eyes vacant.

'Tea?' Sukey almost screamed and he nodded. 'Then you'll leave?'

'Yes,' he said. He looked at his watch. 'I suppose I'd better fetch the kids. Take them home.'

No, thought Sukey, definitely not a murderer, just a pathetic man whose wife's dead and without whom he was finding living difficult. She thought about offering him breakfast, but decided against it. When he'd gone she'd go and buy the Sunday papers; with luck she might have the kitchen to herself and be able to have a bath.

'Sukey, Sukey.' She heard her name being called and turned, unable to locate the caller. She stood, her paper under her arm, looking round. It was a cold November Sunday, but there was no rain and few clouds. The sun was a pale disc in the sky, giving a grudging light and making Sukey feel almost hopeful about herself. She started back towards the flat. She must have imagined she'd heard someone calling her name.

'Sukey, it's me, Dan.' She saw a short, plump figure on the other side of the road, its arm raised, waving at her. She stopped, waved back, waited as Dan made his way across the road, dodging traffic.

'I was coming to see you,' he said when he reached her. 'See how you are.'

'It's been a long time. I thought you'd forgotten all about me.'

'I've been busy, very. Involved in gigs and stuff. A lot of writing. I stayed up in Edinburgh after the festival. '

'Yes,' said Sukey. 'We came to see you there, but we couldn't find you. So we came home.' She laughed. It seemed such a long time ago, such a silly thing to have done and so irrelevant now given recent events. 'Never mind,' Sukey said, as she saw the questioning look on Dan's round face.

'Well,' he said, walking along beside her. 'Come and have lunch with me, that's what I was coming to ask you. I've a new place, not too far away and I've food. I'd like to cook for you. And there's wine and dope...' His voice trailed away.

'And a bathroom?'

'Yes.'

'Could I have bath while you make the lunch?'

Dan laughed, sounding pleased. 'Of course,' he said.

Sukey closed her eyes and lay back, pushing her legs against the end of the bath. It was the perfect length, just right for her to lie in comfortably. She lent forward to turn the tap, filling up with more hot water. Then she ducked down till the water was over her face. She sat up again and reached for the shampoo. She lathered her hair and then rinsed it under the spray.

There was a knock on the door. 'D'you want me to bring in a drink: gin or something?' Dan called.

'No, I'll be out soon.'

When she was dressed, her wet hair wrapped in a towel, Sukey left the bathroom and joined Dan in the big living and dining room. A record was on the turntable: beautiful guitar music and a soft song that she thought was probably one he had helped to write. The table was laid for two and on it were a green salad, a bottle of red wine and a bowl of Parmesan.

'Spag bol,' Dan said from the kitchen area. 'Will that suit?'

'Thank you,' Sukey said as he poured them each a glass of wine.

'So what've you been up to?' he asked.

'Well,' she said, pulling out one of the two dining chairs and sitting down. 'Rather dramatic really. A friend killed, run over when he lay in the middle of the road. Another person we knew killed herself. Her husband did porno photography, I don't know if that's why. And then Kitty – you know the one whose flat it is, where I live now? – she disappeared. And then just over a week ago they found her body and it seems that she was murdered.' Sukey frowned, looked up Dan's face, almost laughed at its expression. His mouth was open in an almost perfect circle and his eyes too, were round. It was almost as if he was mimicking astonishment.

'Is that all true?' he asked. 'Or were you testing my credulity?'

'True,' Sukey said. 'Now you'd better tell me what you've been up to.'

'No, tell me more about your life.'

Sukey shook her head. She didn't want to. Telling Dan like that, in one go in a few short sentences, had made it seem real. Up to now it had almost been as if she were dreaming, watching a play or film, listening to a story. She had kept herself apart from it, she now realised, and didn't know if she wanted to acknowledge that all this violent death was part of her every day life.

She touched the towel on her head and unwound it, shaking out her still damp hair. She stood up to take the towel back to the bathroom.

'OK, you don't want to say any more,' Dan said. He served the lunch and chatted to her, getting up every now and then to change the music.

Afterwards he made coffee and they went to sit on two big chairs by the window. He had put some chocolates in a dish and smiled as he passed it to her.

'That was a lovely meal. This is great,' Sukey said, leaning back, meaning it. The pleasure of the soaking in a tub in a real bathroom, of washing her hair without being rushed, of eating good food prepared with care, of relaxing in a comfortable room almost empty of other people seemed so delightful and so unlike all her recent experiences that Sukey realised she was about to cry. She blinked trying to stop it coming. And then she just gave in. Dan came and sat on the arm of her chair and held her while she sobbed.

'Sorry,' she said, as the tears subsided, and she wiped her cheeks with her fingers. She pulled herself upright and out of Dan's embrace.

He stood up, looked down at her. 'I'm not trying to seduce you,' he said.

'I know.'

'But, you seem to be…heading nowhere. What are you going to do next?'

'I don't know.'

'Are you working?'

'Yes, office temping.'

'You could do more than that.'

'Yes,' said Sukey. She was reminded of the last time she saw Rick. He, too, had been worried about the way she was living and its lack of direction. 'One day I will, Dan, I will. But, everything's fine, really, apart from a few people getting rather dead. I just needed to have a cry and now I feel better.' And that, Sukey felt, was the truth.

(Dan wrote a song for Sukey about a lost girl in a violent world. Sukey heard it from time to time being played on the radio but, not registering that it was one of Dan's compositions, she took little notice of it. Years later he rescued it, re-wrote it as a poem and sent it to her. It evoked that period in her life, that Sunday at Dan's flat, his kindness to her. Remembering all that and the friends from that time who had disappeared, it made her cry.)

Chapter 24
December 1967: Jaz

After the police left they all sat in the kitchen. Jaz was aware of his whole body trembling, he felt as if his limbs had lost most of their power. He remembered once having a blood test when he was in his early teens and his parents had become worried at his lethargy and ability to sleep for over twelve hours at a time. He had been summoned to the surgery to discuss the results and had been surprised when the doctor said: 'Everything is normal. There's nothing to show any unusual internal functioning.' Jaz had leant forward slightly to look at the sheet of paper on the desk with its strange foreign-seeming words down one side of the paper, the rest covered with columns of figures. It meant nothing to him, but what it showed, and what the doctor's words had indicated was that inside him Jaz had blood that was moving around as it was supposed to do, doing all the things that blood was designed for. That was what had surprised him. Up till then he'd imagined himself as a sort of doll made of rubber, had somehow discounted the existence of ordinary internal organs, such as a heart, lungs, liver and kidneys, all working together inside him and keeping him alive.

Jaz, sitting at the kitchen table, looking down at the floor, recalled the surprise he'd felt at understanding that he was a real flesh and blood human being. Now he felt as if that blood was congealing, that flesh was contracting, all the bits and pieces that made up his insides were standing still, waiting for a signal to start working again. He swallowed slowly: there was still saliva in his mouth. He wished this news had not come today, not after the wonderful twenty minutes from earlier that afternoon. He looked up in the silence to see what all the others were doing, how they seemed to be reacting to the information the police had given.

Dennis was pale. He was staring intently at the floor, resting his chin in the palm of one hand, the other holding a cigarette. Beaky was sitting upright, his eyes moving round the room, resting on each of them for a few seconds before going on to the next one. He had no expression in his face, almost as if he'd deliberately put on a blank look, but Jaz could see that he was clenching the edge of the table with a tight fist. Minnie was leaning back with her eyes closed and her lips pressed thinly together. She was cross-legged and open armed, her hands placed palm up on the sides of the big comfortable chair She looked as if she was meditating.

Sukey, who'd been sitting with her head bowed, each of her naked feet pressed close against the outside legs of her chair, suddenly jumped up and ran out of the room, banging open the kitchen door and leaving it swinging as she rushed into the toilet. Jaz could hear her retching and he let out a long sigh.

'What do we now?' Beaky asked as they heard the sound of flushing and Sukey came slowly back into the room. She went to the sink and filled a glass with water.

'What can we do?' Minnie said, her eyes still closed. 'Kitty's gone. We know who killed her. So that's that.'

'It might not turn out to be murder, though. They said maybe manslaughter. He told them it was an accident,' Sukey said.

'He still killed her. That man, that disgusting man, took her life,' Dennis said. His hands were shaking as he lit another cigarette.

'Yes,' Sukey said. 'Vic killed her. He admitted he killed her.' She paused. 'Those kids, what's going to happen to his kids?'

'D'you think she knew she was dying?' Jaz asked. He thought about what the police had told them. He thought about Kitty lying naked in Vic's studio, while Vic took photographs. He imagined Vic putting the noose round her neck and pulling it tight; going to take a photo, coming back, making the rope even tighter, another photo, then the cushion, the body struggling, more photos. Then Vic coming back, moving the cushion, seeing that Kitty was dead. Vic loosening the noose, touching the bruises, seeing the tongue swollen and lolling out of the mouth and the eyes glazed and bulging. He saw Vic trying to revive her, trying over and over again to make her breathe, saying her name, shaking her; finally realising that she was dead and that was that. And then, not wanting to waste the event, taking the last few pictures of the sprawled and naked body: Kitty, plump, pink, smooth-skinned and dead. An image, it seems, that someone would find exciting and for which they would be willing to pay a great deal. Then Vic would have gone down to the kitchen to think, have a drink, a joint, decide what to do.

Jaz understood why Sukey had been sick. He remembered their afternoon in the studio: the sex, the knife, the cushion. That time he had vomited. His mouth filled with the taste of bile. His insides must be working again. They had survived: Kitty hadn't.

'It must have been hard getting the body out of the house and over the wall into that derelict garden,' Minnie said. She was still in the same position with her eyes closed. She hadn't moved since sitting down as the police were leaving.

'Yes,' said Jaz. After he'd made his decision, Vic would have gone back to the studio. It had happened on a Monday afternoon and the children had been staying with their grandmother. The police had told them that. They'd told them matter-of-factly when and where and how Kitty had died. They'd said that although Vic had been charged with murder and had admitted killing Kitty, he insisted it was an accident. They warned them all that they would probably need to take more statements; especially from those that, it seemed, had known Vic quite well. That meant him and Sukey, Jaz knew.

He watched in his head Vic going slowly up to his studio. He saw him look down at Kitty and check again that she was really dead: really, really dead. He thought of Vic waiting till it was dark and then waiting again until it was midnight, the pubs closed, few people out in the streets. Jaz imagined that long day and how Vic managed it. He might even have gone out at some point, had a few drinks, he'd have come back home, phoned some friends, had easy-going chats, laughed, made arrangements to meet.

Eventually he'd have gone back to the studio, hoping that there would be no one there: no body on the floor several hours dead. Maybe when he saw Kitty this time he'd have gasped with horror, or cried out in shame. Maybe all he'd felt was how inconvenient it was of her to die like this. Then he'd have pulled her by the arms along the floor out onto the landing. Would he have pushed her, carried her or dragged her down the stairs? Once he had the body on the ground floor, would he have covered it before taking it out into the night, carrying it down a few streets, heaving it over the wall into the deserted garden? Probably he'd gone out and checked to see if there was anyone around. It would have been about one in the morning by then. Yes, Jaz thought, he'd have crept out, made sure the area was deserted and then, fuelled with adrenaline, he'd have carried the heavy lump of dead flesh through the dark streets and once it was despatched, run home, slammed the door behind him, poured a drink and waited until he could relax into sleep.

'What must it be like,' Sukey asked, 'to know you've taken away someone's life? How could you live with that?'

'Vic didn't seem worried,' Beaky said. 'He carried on as normal.'

Dennis stood up, his stomach was rumbling. 'I'm sorry but I'm hungry,' he said. ' I fancy a kebab. Any one else want one? I'm not paying, but I'll go and get them.'

Only Beaky said he felt like eating.

A couple of hours later when Dennis, who said he couldn't face working even though it was a Friday evening and a profitable time for cabbies, had gone to bed, Beaky asked: 'Shall we go to the pub?'

There was no answer for a few minutes. Minnie yawned. Sukey looked up at the ceiling, bending her head back so that her long blonde hair flowed down, a pale stream, almost to the floor. Jaz realised that he was ravenously hungry. He'd had no breakfast, just a packet of crisps at lunchtime – he'd had to spend hours in the library finishing his term dissertation on the plays of Terence Rattigan that had been due to be handed in that afternoon, and had had no time to eat before the brief meeting in the pub with Stevie. Once with Stevie, he'd not felt hungry. And of course, he'd eaten nothing that evening, what with the police visit and its aftermath.

He still felt weak and his limbs were not working properly, but now he thought, it's from hunger and tiredness rather than from thinking about Kitty and how she died. He slipped from his chair and lay down on the floor, stretched out. 'I need food,' he almost whimpered. 'Just because there's been a disaster doesn't mean everything stops.'

'No,' Sukey said, sitting up. She went to rummage in the fridge and then in the food cupboard. 'D'you fancy a bowl of rice with some peas?' she asked. 'That's about all there is.'

'Let's go to the pub,' Beaky said, 'and call in at the chippy on the way.'

'Yes,' Sukey said, 'Let's get back to normal. After all, we've known that Kitty's been dead for weeks. All that happened today is that the police told us how she died.'

'And we know that we made friends with a murderer,' Jaz said from the floor. His voice sounded strange: echoing. He started to giggle. 'But after all – life must go on,' he declaimed theatrically. He was tempted to tell them all his other piece of news, the good news, as he thought of it. He decided not to. Sukey might feel she needed to protect Tessa. Beaky and Minnie would wonder why he was so pleased about a date with another man. And in any case, he didn't want to contaminate the pleasure of looking forward to Monday with the horror of what they'd been told today.

When Jaz woke the next morning, it was still early for a Saturday; light was beginning to filter through the curtains. He sat up, looking round the room; all the beds were empty, the others must already be up. He yawned and stretched. Then he lay down again and thought about what to do with his day. He wondered if the police would be back, wanting more information about Vic. He shuddered, thinking about the time in the studio and if they'd question him and make him tell. He felt his face grow hot at the idea of describing the events of that afternoon.

He turned over, scrunching up into the foetal position, pulling the blankets over his head. He tried to think of something pleasant that would chase away the image of him talking to the police, telling them about him and Vic, Jules and Sukey and how Jules had made him come, while Vic took photos. I'll think of Stevie, he thought, and pictured him sitting, so beautiful, in the kitchen. Jaz remembered the slight pout and the widening of the eyes as Stevie looked at him that first time they'd met. How they'd smiled at each other while Tessa went on slowly talking. He though about the smile, the way he wanted Stevie and the certainty that Stevie also wanted him. Then later that kiss, followed by the meeting yesterday, when neither seemed able to speak, silenced by sexual longing. He thought again of their kiss, groaned at the memory, wanting more. But without warning, the image of Stevie transformed into Vic. Jaz squirmed in the bed and then sat upright. Time to get up, he thought; time to stop all these horrid thoughts.

Sukey was alone in the kitchen eating scrambled eggs on toast and drinking coffee.

'I got up early, went shopping,' she said, indicating with her knife the fruit in a bowl and the groceries still piled on the draining board. 'It's nice to wake up on a Saturday and know you've got the whole day to do things in and no hangover or anything. Shall I make you some breakfast?'

'I'll do it,' Jaz said. He rooted in the cupboard, looking for a frying pan. As he lit the gas, he asked: 'Do you think we're growing up? Friday night and just two rounds of drink and no joints. Is this how we're going to be from now on?'

'No,' said Sukey. 'I think we were all exhausted. Bad news can be tiring, you know. '

'I've been offered some LSD. It's ages since we took a

trip. D'you fancy one? I can get the stuff today.' Jaz turned to look at Sukey. He wondered if she'd say 'yes' and if she did how he'd feel. It probably wasn't the right time to be taking acid, he thought.

'It's not a good idea, Jaz, just now. You know that. With Kitty and everything… It could go really wrong.'

Jaz nodded, smiled at Sukey, pleased at what she'd said, as if she'd passed some sort of test.

'Maybe when, well, when we've all got over this we'll do it,' Sukey added.

'You're right, bad time for tripping,' Jaz said. He turned and reached for the eggs, cracked first one and then another into his pan and put bread into the toaster. There was a soft knock at the door, so quiet he wondered if he'd imagined it. It came again and Sukey called: 'Come in.'

The landlord slid round the door, thin and apologetic. 'Good morning,' he said, nodding.

'The rent,' said Sukey standing up.

'Yes,' said the landlord, he bowed his head. He was clasping his hands tightly in front of him. 'And something else.' He cleared his throat. 'Police came to see me yesterday. Just before coming to you. They told me about Miss Kitty… Since she's been dead I been thinking about the flat.'

'You want us to leave,' Sukey said.

The landlord moved his head from side to side, wringing his hands, shuffling his feet. 'It was Miss Kitty who was tenant,' he said.

'Can we become the tenants?' Sukey asked. In spite of being slender and very much younger than the landlord, she seemed somehow to have become larger and older than him: larger, more assured and in control. 'We have been paying the rent, after all. It's been over two months since Kitty disappeared.'

'Yes, yes,' said the landlord. 'Problem is, house. I want to sell. Too much, too much er…. I sell. I buy elsewhere. Wife wants to move to suburbs.'

The toast popped up and Jaz turned. He took a plate from the shelf and stuck a knife in the butter (real butter instead of marge, he noticed), prior to spreading it on the toast. He slid the spitting eggs from the pan and sat down to eat. He'd let Sukey deal with all of this rent and flat stuff, he thought, as he took a mouthful of food.

'I see,' Sukey was saying. 'Fine, that's fine. But you must give us time. There's only three weeks till Christmas, and that's a bad period to be moving. You must give us proper notice. A letter. And we'll have to check with the rent tribunal, see what our rights are.'

'Rights,' said the landlord as if he did not understand. He cleared his throat. 'But you not tenant.'

'No, we're not. But we still need time.' Sukey turned to Jaz. 'Maybe we should all consider moving in any case. What d'you think?'

Jaz shrugged, finished his mouthful. Then he nodded, not looking at either Sukey or the landlord. 'I think I'd like to find somewhere else to live. This place doesn't feel the same anymore.' He felt excited at the idea. A better flat, his own room, a real bathroom. Stevie coming to visit; or better still, sharing with him. He looked up at Sukey, wondering if he was blushing.

She frowned a little, must have seen something in his expression that told her more than Jaz meant to impart. She turned back to the landlord: 'OK. We'll go, but not until we've somewhere else to live.' Sukey passed him the rent book with the notes stuffed in it. Once they'd accepted that Kitty had gone and might not be back, she'd taken charge of collecting everyone's weekly share and made sure that the landlord was paid every weekend.

The landlord checked the amount, slid the notes into his pocket, initialled the book and passed it back to Sukey. 'So you will go, soon, but I let you stay till you find another place,' he said, nodding again as he left the room.

'Well,' said Sukey, sitting down. 'Shall we spend today flat hunting?'

Jaz pushed aside his now empty plate and started to roll a cigarette. 'Do we all want to go on living together?' he asked.

Sukey shrugged. 'Not Dennis,' she said.

'Let's wait,' Jaz said. 'We'll see after Christmas. Things might happen – change – over the next few weeks.' Again he thought of Stevie and wondered whether to tell Sukey that he was meeting him on Monday evening at the studio where he lived. It was all planned, Tessa would be at work and Stevie had taken the night off to spend with Jaz.

(Afterwards Jaz found it hard to disentangle his relationship with the man who'd killed Kitty and his first fully fledged sexual experience with a person he believed he loved. He wondered if this was the cause of his continuing inability to

337

remain intimate with one person for more than a short period. He was sure, though, that the juxtaposition of the two events had made him a better actor: he knew, he told himself – and others, when they'd listen – what constituted drama.)

Chapter 25
December 1967: Sukey

Dennis was sitting with his legs crossed, leaning on the table, jiggling his foot up and down and smoking, inhaling heavily. He sighed, rubbed his face, yawned. Sukey wished he'd go. He'd said he was going to spend the evening making money with his taxi and then had sat there, not saying anything, lighting cigarette after cigarette.

'Are you staying in then?' Sukey asked.

'What?' Dennis looked up her, his eyes were bleary, not focusing properly and his skin seemed to have softened and stretched so that his face looked larger and vaguer.

'Thought you were going to work,' Sukey said. She reached across the table and took one of Dennis' cigarettes out of his packet. 'Don't mind do you?' she asked.

Dennis shook his head. 'No,' he said. 'You lot found a flat yet?' he asked.

'No,' said Sukey. 'No one seems to want to live together any more. Jaz says definitely not. Minnie thinks she might be able to move into a room above the shop where she works.

Beaky's just miserable. I think he's hoping he might get back with Tessa.' Sukey twirled a piece of hair between her fingers. 'You should be going, Dennis, all that money you're not making,' she said.

She wanted the place to herself, not just to have a bath but so that she could wrap the presents she'd bought for her family and pack ready for the short trip away from London for Christmas. Three days, she thought, with parents and sisters, grandparents visiting and Boxing Day with her father's brother and her four teasing boy cousins.

'What are you going to do, Dennis? About living, I mean, when this flat's gone.'

Dennis lit another cigarette. 'She's letting me back for the holidays. And if it works out for those few days then she says I can stay for a longer trial period: partly at home, partly here. And if it all works out, I can move back full time end of January. Going to have to be on my best behaviour.'

'Does she know about Kitty?'

'Nah, not all of it. Enough.'

Sukey wondered what Dennis felt about, thought about his now dead lover. He'd said little since her body had been found and not much more after Vic had been arrested for murdering her. What he had said had been about the awfulness of the way certain people lived; he'd hardly mentioned the loss of Kitty. In the days since the funeral, no one had said very much in any case. Jaz had been out most nights, coming home very late and going straight to bed. Minnie had been busy developing her plans to take over the shop where she worked. Beaky had spent several evenings sitting in the kitchen smoking joints and saying little. And in a few days, they'd all be going away for Christmas and Sukey wasn't sure what was going to happen when they came back.

'Ok,' Dennis said, finally standing up, 'I'm off.' Sukey sat back in her chair and watched as he left the room. He clattered up the few stairs and into his bedroom, which he left after a few minutes, clomping down to the ground floor. Sukey heard the front door opening and Dennis saying something, sounding surprised. A man's voice replied. The front door slammed shut, followed by footsteps coming back up the stairs.

'Oh shit,' Sukey whispered and Rick walked into the kitchen. 'Oh shit,' Sukey said again, louder.

'So you're not pleased to see me?' Rick smiled: a small, tight curling of the lips and a slight lightening of the eyes.

'Should I be?' Sukey asked, feeling weary. Here was the first man she'd slept with, a man she'd imagined being in love with, a man who'd ended their relationship, but not in an easy way. The way he'd done it had been to just stop coming to see her and he'd only admitted that it was over for him when she'd confronted him. Here was a man she hadn't seen for nearly six months. The last time he was here, he'd taken her out for a meal and lectured her about getting her life better organised. Since then there'd been no contact; not that she wanted to see him. But she did wonder how he thought that he could turn up when he felt like it and expect to find her there; and assume that she would be pleased to see him.

Sukey suddenly felt a sharp squirt of anger and she shouted: 'What the hell are you doing coming to see me after all this time? What d'you want?'

Rick raised his eyebrows. 'I'd like to take you out – a meal would be good – and to wish you "Happy Christmas" and all that. I thought it would be nice to see you.' He sounded tentative.

'You paying?' Sukey asked.

'Yes, I was planning to.'

'OK, then.'

'Very gracious,' Rick smiled at her, ducking his head.

'You're lucky I'm free to see you.'

'Yes, ma'am.'

'Stop laughing at me.'

'Oh, I'm not, Sukey-Sue, not at all.'

'And don't call me that stupid name.'

'OK, OK. Now d'you want to go and change?'

Sukey looked down at what she was wearing. Shabby black boots, a long black skirt, a loose pale blue jumper over a pretty flowered blouse. It seemed fine to her. 'No, there's nothing wrong with what I've got on.' She looked up at Rick, raising her chin.

'No, of course not,' he said.

In the restaurant, Greek this time, one that Sukey chose, she told Rick all about Malc and Jules, Kitty and Vic. She told him in bits, letting out pieces of shocking information and watching his reaction. They were drinking wine and at some point Rick ordered a second bottle.

'Sukey,' he said as he poured her a glass, 'I don't know what to say to you. You really must move out or on or something.'

'It's OK, we have to leave the flat. The landlord wants to sell the whole house. After Christmas I'll be looking for another place.'

'Well,' Rick said, 'You could share my place. Paul's moving in with his girlfriend after the holidays. He's just told me and so I need someone for his room.'

'Oh,' Sukey looked at him. Was that why he'd come to see her, looking for a person to share with him? 'So that's the reason for your visit,' she said.

'No,' said Rick, 'no. I just thought of it.'

Sukey thought about sharing with Rick. She'd have to pay more rent, but then she was earning more now and she'd have her own room and a place to study if she decided to take evening classes. And Rick living next door. No, she thought, no. He'd not like it when she smoked dope and he'd certainly try to prevent her taking trips. Although just at the moment, she wasn't sure if she wanted ever to be on acid again. He'd probably also disapprove of any men she might bring back to the flat.

'No thanks, Rick,' she said, 'I don't think it would work. But one of the others might be interested. Jaz or Beaky, I'll ask them if you like.'

'Yes,' Rick said, 'you're probably right. It would be too tempting for us to be sleeping next door to each other.'

'What?' Sukey frowned at him. What was he talking about?

'Sex. We might be tempted to want to have sex together if we shared a flat.'

Sukey shook her head: 'I don't think so.'

'I'd still like to sleep with you, you know. Just at the moment I'd very much like to.' Rick reached over the table and took her hand. He stretched out his legs so that they touched hers.

'No,' Sukey said, pulling back her hand, pulling back her legs. 'You dumped me, not nicely at all and now you're doing this.'

'But I always fancied you. I just didn't want a … didn't want to be tied down in a relationship.'

'And I did,' Sukey said. Holding her wineglass tightly by its stem she raised it and took a short sip.

'I thought you were sort of, looking for something serious.' Rick said, almost whining.

'And now I'm not.'

'You've grown up a bit, well a lot.'

'Enough to know that sex is OK but permanent stuff isn't?' Sukey wanted to slap Rick's face; more, she wanted to scratch her nails down his cheek and leave lines of blood. She wanted to pull his hair until he screamed and kick him between the legs until he doubled up in pain. She felt the fury in her body and wondered how to control it.

'Oh, oh, oh,' she let out little puffs of exasperation. And then one long exhalation: 'Ooooooh!' She started at Rick. If he was laughing or mocking she'd walk right out of the restaurant, wait for him outside and then... she'd do something: something to hurt him badly. But he was looking serious and sad. He blinked and his long eyelashes fluttered.

'I'm sorry,' he said.

Sukey wasn't sure why he was apologising; was it for breaking up their relationship all those months ago, for propositioning her just now, for making her angry? She shook her head. 'I suppose you had a girlfriend until recently and you've just ended it and you're looking for a bit of comfort.'

Rick blushed and looked down. She was right and she'd not seen him looking so unsure before. She thought about saying how she'd never enjoyed being in bed with him or something about him being a terrible or selfish lover. But that, she thought, would be trite and silly. Also, it would not be true.

She thought about telling him that she, too, would like to sleep with him tonight and offering to go back to his flat with him. She closed her eyes, thinking about what she wanted to do. She was a little drunk and still in that shaky, glazed stage of post-anger. It would be very easy to sleep with Rick, to make love to him fiercely, to take control and have him moaning underneath her: to have sex in a way that they had never done in the six months of their time together.

No, she thought, tiredness emerging, it would be another mistake to make love with Rick tonight. Or ever again, she added in her head.

'I'd just like to go back to my flat,' Sukey told Rick. 'I'll make you a coffee and then you can go home.'

'OK,' said Rick weakly.

Later, in the flat, they sat squashed together in the big armchair with their arms round each other. Sukey turned her face to Rick's and they kissed gently. Sukey felt a stir of desire for Rick but had no need to develop it. And he seemed to understand. It felt, finally, like a good ending to their affair. She slept well and deeply that night.

Two days later, the evening before Christmas Eve, Dennis was working, Beaky had gone back to his parents for the holidays, Minnie was out with the owner of the shop celebrating the signing of a deal they'd made. Only Sukey and Jaz were in the kitchen. They made a meal together. Jaz was tired and remote, saying little. He chopped onions and carrots when Sukey asked him to. He grated cheese slowly, smiling to himself. Once the bowl of thick soup was simmering on the stove, he went downstairs and Sukey heard him murmuring on the phone. She wondered who it was. Jaz was in love, or in lust, or something like that. He'd lost that spiky energy that made him move and twitch and jerk even when he was trying to sit still.

Sukey stirred the soup, laid the table, sliced bread, put the cheese into a bowl and sat waiting, rolling and then smoking a cigarette. She heard Jaz coming up the stairs, a gentle bumbling sound, and then the gradual opening of the door. He smiled as he came in but there were big rings under his eyes and his thin face was pale. He wore, as well as a soft look of happiness, a strong twist of worry.

'What is it?' Sukey asked. Jaz bit his lower lip with his teeth and rubbed his head, making a lock of hair stand up. He came to sit down and Sukey served the soup.

'Aren't you going to tell me who it is?'

'What?' Jaz asked, stopping his spoon half way to his mouth.

'It's obvious you've got a lover. Is it that Anna girl from the party? Or have you finally decided that it is boys you like?'

'It's not Anna.' Jaz paused. 'I didn't realised it showed so much.' He sprinkled more cheese on his soup and ate without speaking for a little while. He stretched for a slice of bread and after he'd taken a bite, and with his mouth still full, he said: 'It's difficult.'

'Why?'

'Because…' he sighed. 'It's going to make a friend of yours unhappy. Really unhappy.'

'You mean Tessa, I suppose.'

'Yes.'

'So you have been seeing Stevie after all, Jaz.'

'Yes. I'm in love with him and he's in love with me.'

Sukey sat back; put down her spoon. 'Silly, silly Tessa,' she said. 'It's quite obvious to anyone that Stevie likes boys.'

'Yes, and me specially,' said Jaz. He couldn't help smiling, Sukey noticed.

'So why Tessa?'

'An experiment. You know, try everything.'

'Right,' said Sukey, not knowing how to feel. Should she be sorry for Tessa; angry with her for being stupid enough to fall for an obvious queer; pleased for Jaz; worried in case Stevie might hurt Jaz?

'You don't mind that I'm that way, that I like boys?' Jaz asked, looking down, a little shy.

'Why should I? It means we can be friends without any of the other stuff spoiling it. Unless one day we both fall for the same man.'

'No,' said Jaz, 'I think we like different types.' He sounded serious and grown up and sure of himself. He hadn't understood that Sukey was joking because he was, she felt, so absorbed in, so much enjoying this new stage in his life: this defining time. Sukey smiled, pleased for him.

(Although Jaz and Sukey remain good friends, Sukey never saw Rick again, but she thought about him often. Years later she tried to find him via the Internet but was unsuccessful. She continues to think that they might meet each other again one day, as she would like him to see what she has become now that she's grown up.)

Chapter 26
January 1968: Tessa

She'd known, been sure almost from the point of conception, that she was going to have a baby. But now the doctor had confirmed it: Tessa was nearly three months pregnant. How delightful, she said to herself, thinking of part of Stevie growing inside her. But now it was work time: twelve hours of stripping and rushing between the clubs. She'd buy a bottle of champagne in one of her longer breaks and tonight she and Stevie would celebrate. And he'd be nice to her again.

Since the time when they'd learned of Kitty's murder and that Vic, the awful friend of Sukey and Jaz, had killed her, Stevie had been acting strange. They'd hardly made love since then. In fact it was only once, Tessa thought, on Christmas day when they'd been drunk, and afterwards he'd cried and wouldn't let her comfort him.

Soon after, he'd gone out, slamming the bed-sit door and she'd opened the window and called to him as he walked away down the holiday-empty street, away from her. But he'd not looked up and had started to run. She closed the window and sat down, looking at the mess of the remains of their meal and the jumble of bedclothes where they'd recently been lying. She was shivering. She was wearing nothing but a thin silk dressing gown and cold had come in when she'd opened the window. She started to cry and wished there was someone she could go and see, but all her old friends had gone back to family for Christmas. She felt deeply alone and curled up on the bed. Later, after she'd fallen asleep and then had woken up, she saw that her mascara had run, leaving a deep dark stain in the pillowcase.

Stevie had been in a better mood when he'd come home, but he hadn't wanted to talk. He'd sat watching the television that she'd given him as a present and had opened the last bottle of good wine and had drunk most of it.

Tessa sighed, a mixture of sadness, remembering Stevie being distant, and of happiness at knowing how pleased he'd be about the baby, and how he would become loving towards her all over again.

'Stevie,' Tessa whispered as she let herself into the bed-sit, coming straight home after her last strip. She tiptoed over to the bed. He was there, curled up, asleep. She knelt by him, stroked his hair, whispered his name again. He grunted a little and turned over. Tessa yawned. She was exhausted: soon she'd have to give up working. But that was all right, she'd saved money, quite a lot of it, and Stevie earned enough to keep them. Enough for three, she thought, smiling, adding to herself, oh my big delicious secret. She stood up; she'd let him sleep. She put the champagne in the fridge. They could have it in the morning. She yawned, undressed and slipped into bed, too tired to take off her make-up. Stevie was lying with his back towards her. She pressed herself close to him and put her arm over him, pressing her hand against his tummy button.

As she fell asleep she felt Stevie stir, felt him take her hand and push it away, felt him wriggle away from her to the very edge of the bed.

'Stevie,' she murmured, heavy with sleep.

'Leave me alone,' he said, speaking softly but as if he was gritting his teeth.

'What's the matter?' she asked, the words slurring out of her mouth. There was no reply and as she tried to ask the question again, sleep silenced her.

'Wake up, wake up.' Tessa opened her eyes and blinked. It was early morning, still dark outside. Stevie had turned on his bedside light. He was sitting on his side of the bed, fully dressed. He was frowning.

Tessa smiled, stretched remembering her news. 'Stevie,' she said, trying to make her voice soft and seductive.

'What?' Stevie asked, screwing up his face. 'You should see yourself, Tessa, your face is a mess, there's black all over your cheeks and everything's splodgy.' He sounded angry.

'Stevie,' Tessa said again, sitting up, reaching out to touch his hand. He jerked it away, scowling. She caressed his knee instead, and he stood up, turned away and went to the window and half raised the blind. He stood looking out at the darkness, leaning against the sill.

'I've some good news for us,' Tessa said. 'Why don't you get back into bed while I tell you about it.'

Stevie shook his head.

'Come on, Stevie,' Tessa said.

'No,' he said. He turned to look at her, but then his eyes skidded away from hers. 'My news first.'

Tessa blinked, watching Stevie's face, which he'd made hard and cold. He was staring not at her but at the wall above her head. He was standing up straight as if to attention. She felt a bite of fear in her chest as if someone was nipping at her heart. Licking her lips, she put her hand to her throat and exhaled: 'Oh'. She breathed in deeply; she knew what was about to happen, what Stevie was about to say. I could be wrong, she told herself in panic, swallowing, tasting bitterness under her tongue.

'Yes,' said Stevie, 'I've something to say, too. I'm in love with someone else. I don't want to be with you anymore.'

'No,' said Tessa, 'you love me.'

'Not anymore. I don't know if I ever did.'

'Give me a chance, let's try again. What do you want me to do to make it work again?'

'You can't. It's not your fault, it's just… wrong for me. I wanted to have a girlfriend but, but…' Stevie shook his head.

'It's a man? You're in love with a man?' Tessa sat up straighter. She shook her head; she pulled the blankets tight round her and put her hand on her belly. The baby was crying inside her, she was sure.

'I'm sorry Tessa,' Stevie said, crumbling. He came back to sit on the bed and looked at her, his eyes watering and sad. He was clasping his hands tightly together and looked so vulnerable and young that Tessa couldn't help reaching out to put her arm round him. He pulled it off, but gently. Crying, he told her that he was sorry; it was his fault, he should never have thought that he could be in love with a woman, he hadn't meant to hurt her.

Tessa's life was falling to bits. In her mind, she could see herself breaking up into little pieces. She felt unable to move, to let herself feel, to think beyond the current moment. She felt oddly calm and distant, as if she were not there in reality but was just watching herself from a distant place. Maybe, she thought, she should ask if they could wait a bit, talk about it, see if Stevie could change again, love her again. Somehow the words wouldn't come. The baby, she began to think about the baby. When Stevie knew about the baby, he'd change his mind. He'd forget about the man, he'd want to be with her: a family, him, her and the baby.

'That's it, then, Tessa. And I am sorry, truly. But I can't help it.'

'No,' Tessa said. 'There's more, it's not the end. We're having a baby. I've been thinking that I was pregnant for some time and yesterday the doctor confirmed it.'

'No.' Stevie had jumped up, was shaking his head. 'No,' he said again.

'Yes. There's a baby. Our baby. Aren't you happy about it?'

Stevie said nothing. Just stood looking at Tessa, his face creased into confusion.

'It makes a difference, doesn't it?' Tessa said finally.

'No,' Stevie said, 'no. I can't be with you, baby or not. And… Are you lying? Are you saying this just to try and keep me?'

'No, it's true,' Tessa said.

'I have to go,' Stevie said, 'I can't stay here any more. I can't breathe. I can't… I'll… Sorry, Tessa. I can't cope any more.'

He was gone. The door banged shut and Tessa heard his quick footsteps running down the stairs. She sat in the bed, not knowing what to do. There were no tears, which surprised her. She tried to imagine that it was true, that Stevie had left her, and examined how she felt. Just numb, she decided. What, though, if he came back to her, had just gone to be on his own and think about things, her, the baby, this new lover of his? Maybe he'd realise that she was more important than whoever it was he'd been seeing. He'd come back to her, of course he would, he wouldn't be able to resist the idea of being a father and he'd miss her: he'd miss her dreadfully. She wondered whether to cling onto this idea or to give in and accept that the affair with Stevie was over.

An hour later she had drunk a cup of tea and had showered and cleaned her face. She sat in front of her mirror ready to put on make up for work and, looking at her big, round, pale face staring back at her, she started to cry. It lasted a long time, and left her weak, with swollen red eyes, phlegm filled sinuses and an enormous hunger that she felt she'd never be able to fill. Shuddering she went back to the bathroom to blow her nose and to wash her face in cold water and then she sat again at the mirror and applied her make up.

Tessa left the flat, going slowly down the stairs as if she was swimming. She was no longer sobbing but tears kept sliding out of her eyes, making her mascara run. In the local café she ordered a big breakfast that she ate, aware of the café owner and the other patrons looking at her: a heavily made-up woman eating a great plate of food while crying silently. On the bus going to work, she continued to cry soundlessly, and she cried while she repaired her face before her first strip. The only time she stopped crying was when she was on stage. As she left the tears silently started again and continued as she dressed in street clothes, walked to her next session, donned her stripping gear, once again repaired her make-up. When the other girls asked what the matter was she told them softly: 'Stevie's left me for a man and I'm pregnant.' When they tried to pursue the subject or show sympathy, Tessa told them that she couldn't talk about it, she wanted to be left alone.

When the long hard day was over she went home and held her breath as she walked up the stairs to her bed-sit, wondering if Stevie would be there. He wasn't. The room felt cold and empty. She looked in the wardrobe and the chest of drawers but none of his clothes had gone. Where was he, she asked herself, and what was he going to do? 'I can't live here on my own,' she said out loud, and decided to see if she could move back to Kitty's flat while she thought about the next steps in her life. It's not that I've given up on Stevie, she told herself, but we need time even if we do get back together.

It was early evening and Tessa was just leaving the stage, more or less naked, when one of the girls told her that Stevie was waiting to see her. He was sitting in the crowded dressing room while the girls fluttered around him, getting ready for their acts or putting on street clothes for the move to their next club.

Tessa looked at him. 'Why are you here?' she asked.

'We need to decide who stays in the bed-sit,' he said.

'You can have it,' Tessa said. 'I'm going to move back into Kitty's flat. I'll sort it out tomorrow. It's my day off.'

'Oh.' Stevie looked uncomfortable. He scratched his cheek.

'What is it?'

'It's Jaz,' he said.

Tessa frowned; what was he talking about? 'What?' she asked.

'Me and Jaz,' Stevie said.

'Oh,' Tessa said, understanding, and then she slapped Stevie hard on the face. He lifted his hand to touch the red patch that was forming and Tessa did it again, on the other side. Then she kicked him, first on the shin, and then again between the legs. He fell against the wall, almost screaming in pain and she pushed him down and grabbed his hair with both hands, pulling it hard, not letting go until he was crying. Then she gave him one last kick and went back into the dressing room.

He was still there, scrunched up against the wall when Tessa came out, wearing a coat and carrying her costume bag. She stopped to look at him: 'There's more than just the bed-sit to talk about. There's the baby as well and how you're going to support him.' He shuddered and swallowed but Tessa didn't wait. She opened the street door and went out. She was feeling strong and almost hopeful as she strode along to her next venue.

(Tessa continues to spend time with men (and not quite men) that do not make her happy. Now she's older and more experienced Tessa knows that relationships like this are mistakes and, even though she's in her fifties, she continues to think and hope that living happily ever after is a viable option.)

Chapter 27
January 1968: Sukey

Sukey pushed the kitchen door open firmly and loudly. 'Right,' she said, 'you two, time's up. This is a communal room after all. It's Sunday morning and I want to have breakfast.'

'We weren't doing anything,' Jaz said. He and Stevie were lying curled up together on the cushions that they'd made into a double bed. This was where they'd been making loud and lengthy love for the last two nights, since Stevie had come round and told them all that he'd left Tessa and needed to be with Jaz. The noise had carried into the bedroom Sukey was now sharing with Minnie and Beaky.

Stevie had been almost crying that evening when he'd come round. He'd sat with Jaz on the easy chair and told them all about what had happened. 'And she says she's pregnant,' he'd finished, his voice rising, almost hysterical.

Sukey looked at Beaky. His face was red, his head bent and he was gripping onto a teaspoon as if it could save his life. He didn't say anything. She saw him swallow, his

Adam's apple moving big and violent in his throat. He's angry and upset, Sukey thought, and he doesn't know how to deal with it all.

'I don't want you both sleeping in our bedroom,' Minnie said, her voice thin and imperious. 'You'll keep us awake with all that disgusting sex.'

'We'll have the kitchen, then,' Jaz said. 'Or maybe we can kick Dennis out and have the double bed. He's hardly here these days in any case. I haven't seen him since before Christmas.'

'Dennis is only sleeping here occasionally now. He told me that his wife says he can move home after a trial period,' Sukey said.

'So we can have his room,' Jaz said

'No,' said Sukey, 'he uses it some nights. He's not going to want to come home and have to share with you two.'

'Kitchen'll be fine,' Stevie said. 'Only till we get a place of our own.'

Beaky stood up. 'Going to the pub,' he said, picking his jacket off the back of his chair. He slammed the door as he went out.

Stevie made a face. 'I think I've upset him,' he said, sounding complacent.

It hadn't been easy with Stevie in the flat, though he hadn't been there very much. Last night he'd come home and had cried in the kitchen. 'Tessa attacked me,' he'd almost screamed. Later he told them that she was moving out of the bedsit, so he and Jaz would be able to live there. 'Tessa wants to come and stay here again. She's coming over tomorrow. Jaz and I'll move out and she'll move in.'

'How do you think Beaky's going to like that?' Sukey asked.

Stevie shrugged. 'Maybe they'll get back together again.'

Sukey shook her head. She was angry, with Stevie very much, but also with Jaz. He had changed, was so absorbed in Stevie that he seemed to have forgotten all the other parts of his life, especially his friends. Sukey wished that she had somewhere to go where she could be on her own and cry.

Now it was Sunday morning and here was Sukey in the kitchen looking down at Jaz and Stevie, who were both smiling up at her.

'If I make you tea and toast will you get up?' she asked them.

'Can't we have it in bed?' Stevie asked.

'No,' said Sukey, 'and when is Tessa coming round?'

'She didn't say, she was too busy kicking me to communicate further.'

'Right,' said Sukey. She put the kettle on and put bread in the toaster. 'I'll go and see her. You two can go off for the day. Oh and take all Jaz's stuff with you. Your car's still working?' Jaz nodded and Sukey sighed, wondering why she felt obliged to take control of the situation. Probably because no one else would and because Tessa was her friend from long ago and she felt responsible.

Sukey could hear movement in the room. She wondered whether to knock again. Then she heard Tessa call: 'I'm coming,' and there was the sound of a key in the lock and the door opened.

'Oh,' said Tessa, 'what are you doing here?'

'Stevie told us all about it,' Sukey said as Tessa moved aside and let her in.

'You can sit down it you want to,' said Tessa and Sukey did so, watching her friend, feeling the anger and a seeping sadness that filled the place. Tessa was pale and her eyes were sore, her lips cracked, her hair hung lank and greasy. She stood wearing a soiled and creased dressing gown, thin and silky. She was quite still, her arms at her side, her sturdy legs slightly apart. Sukey was aware of a sour smell in the room, which was untidy and dusty.

'You can't have tea or coffee as there's no milk. Unless black'll do,' Tessa said.

She hates me, Sukey thought. And felt guilty, as if what had happened was her fault. 'No thanks, nothing to drink…Tess?' she said.

'What?'

'Stevie said…' Sukey paused. 'He said you wanted to move back with us.'

'I don't want to,' Tessa said, her face reddening, emphasising the word 'want' as if it was something disgraceful. 'It's not what I want. I have no choice. I can't stay here alone. I can't. And there's nowhere else.'

Sukey sighed. 'We're all moving out, but you can stay till then. It's not going to be easy for Beaky, though, you know. And maybe we can look for somewhere together, you and me.'

'Did darling Stevie also tell you about the baby?' Tessa asked. She'd moved her hands: they were now on her hips.

'Yes,' said Sukey. 'What are you going to do?'

'What do you mean?'

'Well… keep it or not.'

'I'm not going to have an abortion. I want it. Stevie would have wanted it too, if he hadn't got… stupid.'

Sukey wanted to say it wasn't a question of being stupid. It was because he was a homosexual, but decided that that would make Tessa even angrier. 'Please stop being so cross with me, Tess,' she said instead, feeling worn out with all the emotion stored up in this little room.

Tears started to trickle slowly out of Tessa's eyes and she drooped, her hands let go of her hips and her arms dangled, looking useless. She stood wavering for a minute and then took a few steps and sank down in the chair opposite Sukey.

'My life's gone all wrong,' Tessa wailed and sniffed loudly. Sukey looked round for tissues and saw a roll of loo paper beside the bed. She went to fetch it, tore off a large wad and passed it to Tessa, who took it. But rather than blowing her nose she held it one hand, clamped tight. She sniffed again. 'S'not fair,' she said and started to laugh while the tears still flowed.

'No,' said Sukey, laughing too, 'S'not.'

Tessa gave a big phlegmy sniff. 'What am I going to do?' she asked.

'First we'll pack your stuff and take it round to the flat. Then we'll think about it all.'

'What about Stevie? What about Beaky?'

'Stevie's gone off for the day. I'm seeing him this evening in the pub. I'll give him the key and stuff. As for Beaky, you'll have to sort that out with him.'

Sukey took the chicken out of the oven, holding the pan with the worn-out kitchen gloves that Kitty had once bought, or maybe stolen.

'D'you think it's nearly ready?' Sukey asked Minnie and Tessa, who were both sitting cross-legged on the cushions that had recently been a bed shared by Jaz and Stevie. She ignored Beaky, who was sitting on the big armchair with his eyes closed, a bottle of beer in one hand and a roll-up in the other. The only words he'd said since Sukey had arrived back earlier with Tessa and her belongings had been when Sukey asked him if he'd like to share the roast dinner she was planning to cook. She'd bought all the food the day before, wanting, in a strange way that she didn't quite understand, to bring them all together before they finally left the flat, separated, started new lives apart.

'I've invited Jojo and Ted. Minnie says she's no problem with Ted these days. Dennis can eat with us too, if he's home. I might even see if Joe wants to come round,' she'd told Beaky. 'So are you joining in?'

He'd swallowed. 'I suppose you thought that Jaz and Stevie would be here,' he'd said.

'Yes,' Sukey said. 'I was even going to make a cheese and onion tart for Jaz as he doesn't eat meat, but I won't bother now.'

'You've got Tessa instead and she's a meat-eater.'

'Right, so are you on or not?'

Beaky sighed and turned his head, thinking. 'Yes,' he said reluctantly.

Now here was Sukey wondering how you knew when a chicken was cooked, especially such a large one as this.

'Stick a fork in it, see if blood comes out,' Tessa said, sighing. She took a deep draw of the joint she was smoking and then passed it to Minnie.

Sukey put the hot pan on the table and leant over it. She took a fork from the draining board and poked the chicken with it. Hot juice spurted, slightly tinged with pink. Not quite ready, she thought. She peered at the potatoes. They were brown in parts and when she turned them, the underneaths were crispy.

'I'm going to make gravy,' she said. 'That's one thing I know how to do. I always did it for Mum when I was living with my parents.' She stood up straight and stretched. Three pans of vegetables stood waiting on the top of the stove. Carefully she put the chicken pan back in the oven. 'I'm off to the pub,' she said, 'to give Jaz Tessa's keys.'

Tessa looked up. Her eyes filled and tears started to drip down her face again.

'Stop crying,' Minnie said. 'He's not worth it, none of them are.'

Tessa sniffed and wiped her face with the back of her hand. She took the joint from Minnie and sucked on it. 'You're right, Minnie, but I don't plan all this weeping and wailing. It just emerges.'

Beaky stood up. 'I'll come with you, Sukey,' he said.

'I'm not going to have a drink,' Sukey insisted, she was buttoning up her coat that had been hanging on the back of the door. 'I'm just delivering stuff.'

'I'll still come.'

Sukey shrugged.

When Beaky came home from the pub the meal was almost finished. The bottles of wine that Jojo and Ted had brought were finished and Joe was just opening the brandy that was his contribution to the evening, when the kitchen door swung open and Beaky almost fell into the room.

Sukey turned to look at him. 'You're late,' she said, 'but there's still loads left.' She stood up. 'You can have my chair, I've finished.'

Beaky staggered to the table and sat bent over, his arms folded while Sukey fetched a clean plate and piled it with food. She put it in front of him together with a knife and fork and he started to eat, looking down, saying nothing. No one else said anything either. They sat and watched Beaky as he diligently moved large portions of chicken and cooling vegetables from his plate to his mouth.

Joe passed round the brandy glasses. Sukey took one and went to sit in the armchair. The food had been good. Jojo's wine (stolen, Sukey was sure) tasted better than the cheap stuff they normally drank. It hadn't been a bad evening – even Dennis had been almost convivial – until Beaky came in. Not a bad evening, Sukey thought, and the first time there'd been a good shared meal since Kitty died, but Tessa had cried through much of it. She still managed to eat and drink well though. And smoke a fair bit of dope, too. Sukey wondered if it was bad for the baby growing inside her. Another joint was passing round the table. Beaky took it as it reached him and put down his knife and fork while he smoked it. He passed it on, took a big gulp of brandy, went on eating.

Sukey closed her eyes. Soon she would go to bed; tomorrow was a work day. In a strange way she was looking forward to the start of a new week: the getting up, dressing in office clothes, travelling to work, talking to her colleagues as if she lived a normal life. And above all, she must start being serious about looking for a place to live. She and Tessa would probably share, at least until the baby arrived. And she'd need to help Tessa find a normal job. She'd talk to the temp agency tomorrow; arrange for Tessa to go and see them.

'Let me out, let me out, I'm going to vomit.' Sukey opened her eyes as she heard Tessa almost shrieking. She was standing up, trying to push her way past the table, squashed in as she was, at the back, with Dennis and Ted blocking her path. Both of them were moving out of her way. Tessa squeezed past their chairs and into the middle of the room, making retching noises, her hand over her mouth. She almost made it to the door before she was sick. It landed on the floor with a squelch and splashed against the wall. Moving to the sink, Tessa leaned over it as all the food and wine that she'd taken in that evening came heaving out, stinking and noisy.

Sukey's stomach, too, heaved. She let out a loud burp,

hoping that she would not be sick. The sight and smell of it often made her join in, in sympathy as it were. The others were all looking at Tessa and at the mess she'd made. Do something, Sukey wanted to shout, but instead she went to the pile of old newspapers that she'd shuffled into a corner of the room and started to clear up, retching as she did so.

Jojo came to help her and Minnie joined them. She'd got the bags that had held the wine and was opening them for Sukey to put in the soiled paper. Jojo took the cloth from the draining board and more or less wiped up the last of the mess. That too went into the bag.

Tessa now was panting, still leaning on the sink. She seemed to have stopped vomiting, at least for the time being. Minnie leaned over her to turn on the taps, letting the water flush the sick down the drain. Sukey heard the sound of a lighter and looked round to see that Dennis was sitting at the table again, smoking.

'Right,' said Joe, 'I think I'd better go.' He came up to Sukey and for a moment she thought he might be going to kiss her. She shook her head and he scratched his.

'Well,' he said, 'I'll see you soon.' Sukey nodded and he left, walking carefully over the now more or less clean patch of floor by the door.

Ted stood leaning against the wall as if wondering what to do. Beaky was still at the table; he'd finished eating but was re-lighting the abandoned joint with Dennis' lighter. Jojo was rubbing Tessa's shoulder and the back of her neck and Minnie was busy clearing up around the sink.

Sukey was exhausted. 'That's the last time I cook a

Sunday dinner,' she said, trying for humour.

Tessa turned to look at her. 'I'm sorry,' she said. The expression on her wide pale face was so sad that Sukey felt a tremor of genuine sorrow for her. For the first time, she realised that Tessa was suffering, was in a mess and that it was real. She needed someone to look after her. Sukey was suddenly afraid. She shivered, scared of responsibility.

The moaning woke Sukey. She'd been deeply asleep and when she opened her eyes, she lay still for a moment in the dark, pulling the blankets up to her chin against the cold. The moaning started again. Tessa, Sukey thought and was gently annoyed. 'Please stop, Tess,' she whispered. 'I've got to go to work today.'

'I'm hurting,' Tessa said. 'In my belly. Ow, ow, ow.' The moaning had turned into crying. 'Ow,' Tessa almost screamed. Sukey heard Minnie push back her bedclothes and stand up. She heard her pad across the floor and the click of the light being switched on. Sukey scrunched her eyes against the brightness and slowly re-opened them. She sat up. Minnie was by the door, wearing her sensible pyjamas, her arms wrapped round herself as if to keep herself warm. She was staring at Tessa who was huddled into a small mound on her mattress. She was groaning now.

Sukey sat up. 'What is it Tess? Are you going to be sick again.'

'It's the baby, I think it's... not right.'

Sukey crawled over to Tessa, put her hand on her forehead. It felt hot and sticky.

'I think there's blood,' Tessa said.

Sukey didn't know what to do. 'Are you having a miscarriage?' she asked and Tessa started to cry again. She pushed back her bedclothes and tried to sit up. 'No, no, I don't want the baby to go,' she wailed. But Sukey saw, on the dingy sheet on which Tessa had been lying, a large dark stain. She gasped. 'Minnie, I think we need an ambulance. Tessa's bleeding.'

After Tessa had been taken to hospital, Minnie put the kettle on for tea and she and Sukey sat in the kitchen. They whispered as they spoke, for Beaky was lying asleep on the cushions on the floor; he was gently snoring. When finally, the evening before, the clearing up had been done and Tessa had been sent to bed, Beaky had said: 'I don't want to share a room with her. Her and her brat. My turn to sleep in the kitchen.'

'What about the smell?' Sukey asked, almost retching again, breathing in the odour of vomit which still lingered. Beaky shook his head and said nothing. He was, Sukey realised, still quite drunk.

Now, at four in the morning, Minnie poured water into the mugs and reached into the fridge for milk. The brandy bottle that Joe had brought was on the table. Sukey stretched for it, lifted and shook it. 'Shall we have what's left in our drinks?' she asked.

'I don't know that it will go with tea,' Minnie replied.

'Why should that worry us?' Sukey asked. 'We seem to drink and smoke anything that's around, regardless of whether it's appropriate or not.'

Minnie sighed. 'Yes,' she said and passed her mug for Sukey to add the brandy. 'In less than two weeks it'll all be over. Life in Kitty's flat... You've not found anywhere to live?'

'No,' said Sukey.

'You can share with me,' Minnie said. 'I'm having the second floor above the shop. There's a spare room. Luxury, Sukey, a bedroom each. No living room, but a big kitchen like this one. Only nicer. And a real bathroom.'

'What about Tessa?' Sukey asked.

'What about Tessa?'

'I said I'd share with her.'

Minnie was silent. She swirled the liquid around in her mug and then took a swig. 'I don't want Tessa in the flat and if you're going to choose between us, you'd be better off with me,' she said finally. 'Time to move on, Sukey. Tessa's a mess.'

'But I promised...'

'Look at her record: she takes up with Beaky, becomes a stripper although he didn't want her to; then finds a new man who's never going to stay with her, gets pregnant.'

'She's my friend.'

'OK. Room's there if you change your mind.'

'Can I afford it?'

'Yes.'

Tessa was sitting on the armchair when Sukey came into the kitchen. Her face was grey and strangely naked without the layers of make-up she'd taken to wearing since she'd started stripping.

'I went to visit you in the hospital,' Sukey said. 'They told me you'd insisted on leaving.'

'Well, it's over now. The baby's gone.' Tessa sighed deeply. 'I would be crying but I don't think I've the energy for that anymore.'

Sukey stopped herself from saying that she thought the miscarriage was just as well under the circumstances. She wondered if Stevie knew yet. Tomorrow evening she'd maybe go and see Jaz, tell him that he no longer need worry about his boyfriend being a father. She felt a pang of longing for the days when she and Jaz were friends, best friends almost. She wished herself back in the time before they met Vic, before the deaths of Malc, Jules and Kitty. It seemed now, looking back, like an era of innocence: in spite of the drugs; in spite of the sex; in spite of their rootless, aimless ways.

'What?' asked Sukey. Tessa had been saying something, but she'd not been listening properly.

'I said I've got to save my energy for getting back to the clubs.'

'You're not going to carry on stripping, are you?'

'Why not? I make a lot of money and it's something I know how to do.'

'I thought we were going to share a flat, make some changes in our lives.'

'We can still live together,' Tessa said.

'Maybe,' Sukey said, knowing that she didn't want to.

'Right then,' Tessa said, 'we'd better start looking for somewhere.'

'Please, Tessa, stop the stripping thing. There's loads of other jobs you could do.'

'Why should I?'

'It... Doesn't suit you. It's not just the work, which is bad enough, getting naked in front of a lot of horrid men, it's the life that goes with it.'

'So your life is better is it? Acid trips, booze, dope, sleeping with whoever comes along, mixing with pornographic murderers.' Tessa winced and sat back. 'I still hurt inside,' she said. 'All the same I'll help find us a place to live.'

'No,' Sukey said, 'this is not what I want. I don't want to live with you while you're still grinding away in Soho. I spoke to my agency and they have plenty of work. Filing clerk, OK? After everything's that happened to you, to all of us, don't you want to do something different, live differently?'

'Sometimes Sukey you are so pompous,' Tessa said, sitting up, colour appearing in her face.

Sukey said nothing, just stared at Tessa, not giving up on her, but recognising that just because she, Sukey, wanted to live in a particular way it didn't mean that all her friends would want to move in the same direction at the same time.

(It was the collapse of Tessa and the need for someone to take control of events that finally propelled Sukey into a new life. She was almost aware of it at the time. And later, once

373

she'd obtained 'A' levels through a year of evening classes and as a result, a place to read for a degree at a London Polytechnic, she recognised the role that her friend had played, even though she had not succeeded in persuading Tessa herself to change. Sukey's own move towards a different way of being had started with the disappearance of Kitty and in Sukey's involvement in ensuring that rent was paid for the flat. She found that she was not a drippy hippy flop of a person, but an organiser, a person who could make things happen and make them happen efficiently. Later in life, this has sometimes annoyed some of Sukey's friends and lovers who advocate 'going with the flow'. Sukey doesn't care about the irritation she causes such friends: she knows some of the nasty places where the flow can go.)

Chapter 28
January 1968: Sukey

'Have another one,' Bridie said, standing up. 'It's your last chance to have a decent cup of Irish tea. I won't be inviting you down once John gets here.'

'So, it's really happening then, the two of you getting back together?' Sukey asked.

'It is. Tomorrow evening he arrives and then end of next week he's booked for us to go home to Dublin.' Bridie sighed. 'I'll put the kettle on then,' she added, stooping to pick up the tray.

Sukey followed her into her kitchen. 'Are you glad?' she asked.

Bridie laughed, but somehow it didn't sound the same as her normal laugh. 'I am and I'm not,' she said. 'I can't carry on like this with Dolores getting older. But, I'll be losing a bit of freedom. I suppose that's what it's all about. There again, we'll be buying our own house.'

'Does he know, John I mean, about what's been going on?'

'And what has been going on?' Bridie smiled at Sukey, raising her chin and putting her head on one side. She winked.

'You know, Bridie.'

'Course he doesn't. And he never will.'

'What if... if Dolores says something?'

'I can handle that. I can invent an explanation for anything she might come out with.' Bridie emptied the teapot and poured in hot water from the kettle, swirled it round, then heaped tea leaves into it. 'You're all set, then, you lot upstairs?'

'Yes. Minnie and I are moving into the flat above her shop. It's being redecorated, should be finished before we have to leave here. Beaky's got himself into a big place with loads of other students. He's only got a bed in an alcove in the hall, but he seems to think that's OK, as far as I can tell. He's moving on Saturday.'

'And that Tessa woman?'

Sukey sighed. 'She wanted to share with me. But... Anyway, she's moving in with a woman she works with. Only temporary 'til her husband gets out. You know, prison. And Dennis' wife's having him back. He's hardly here now in any case.'

'And that Jaz, there's a turn up. I always thought it would be you and he in the end... You've no boyfriend at the moment?'

'No,' said Sukey.

The kettle boiled and Bridie poured water onto the tea leaves. 'Ah well, Miss Posh, I expect you'll find yourself a decent man sometime. Not like some of those yokes you've been mixing with. It's been very strange all that going on up there, sex and murder and I don't know what. Not how your parents expected you to live, I don't imagine.'

Bridie laughed, it sounded more like her this time: as if life was and would continue to be a source of great amusement, and Sukey felt compelled to put her arms round her and rest her head on her shoulder. Bridie hugged her back, still laughing, while she stroked Sukey's head.

'That's my Mammy.' Sukey felt a hand pulling on her leg. She broke away from Bridie and there was Dolores, standing in her nightdress holding her doll with one hand and rubbing her eyes with her other one. 'I woked up,' she said and yawned. 'What are you doing with my Mammy?' she asked.

'Just saying goodbye,' Sukey said. 'You didn't mind, did you?'

Dolores stared up at her. 'No,' she said after a bit. 'We can share Mammy. She likes to be shared.'

Bridie raised her eyebrows and laughed again.

When Sukey came home from work on Friday evening, the flat was empty. She'd been aware as she let herself into the downstairs hall that John had arrived home. She could his voice and Bridie's laugh coming from the front room. In contrast, once she climbed the stairs and went into the kitchen, she shivered, feeling that strange still emptiness that fills a place when there's no one at home. She hung her coat behind the door, put the kettle on and rolled a joint.

When it was done, she took it and her mug of tea and climbed the few stairs to the bedroom. She stood in the doorway looking round: three mattresses and far less of the clutter that had once filled it. Tessa's two large suitcases stood in the window, looking fat and packed. Right, Sukey thought, she's ready to move out.

She crossed the small hallway and knocked gently on the door of the bedroom that Dennis had once shared with Kitty. When there was no reply she slowly turned the handle and opened it. She switched on the light and drew in her breath. Dennis had been gradually moving his clothes and other belongings, so now this room had become again Kitty's.

Sukey, motionless, wondered that none of them had moved any of Kitty's things. On the dressing table was her hairbrush, comb and hand mirror, a basket full of make-up, bottles of scent, another of hand cream, a tray containing various jars, some tweezers, a bag of cotton wool, a little bundle of emery boards, a layer of dust. On her bedside table was her alarm clock, an expensive one that had been a present for her eighteenth birthday; two paperback books one with an old photo poking out of it, probably acting as a bookmarker; and more dust.

Softly Sukey walked into the room, went to look in the wardrobe: Kitty's clothes hanging on one side, the other almost empty, just one pair of Terylene trousers and a blue nylon shirt hanging in Dennis' space. Gently swinging on the hook on the back of the door that led into the room was Kitty's frothy pink negligée.

Why, thought Sukey, had none of us done anything about all this stuff? Why had Dennis not even kept the place clean? She'd have to deal with it, Sukey decided; over the weekend she'd pack everything up and take it to a second hand shop. She turned to leave the bedroom and as she did, passed the two books sitting on the bedside table. She read the titles – romances, not her sort of novel at all. Her finger touched the corner of the photograph and she pulled it out, holding it up to look at it. 'Oh,' she said aloud. It was her and Jaz when they were at college together, smiling at the camera, arms round each other, wearing silly woolly hats. In the background was Jaz's old car and although there was snow on the ground, the sun was shining. We look so much younger, she thought and yet it was taken… She screwed up her eyes, trying to remember the day… It was a few weeks after the return from the Christmas break, January 1966: only two years ago, a long two years ago. Sukey sighed and holding the photo – she'd keep it, she'd like to show it to Jaz but she'd keep it for herself – she went back to the kitchen.

'I'm going back to the grindstone,' Tessa told them a few hours later. She'd not long walked into the kitchen. She was fully made-up and was wearing a pair of tight, black suede high-heeled boots that looked new. Minnie, recently home from work, and sitting at the table eating a cheese sandwich with a joint ready to smoke in the ashtray next to her, turned to Sukey and raised her eyebrows.

'Soho?' Minnie asked.

'Stripping, I suppose,' Sukey said.

'Both. Stripping. In. Soho.' She must be recovering, Sukey thought. Tessa was once more using that slow emphatic way of speaking that Sukey was sure she'd adopted to try and make what she said sound important.

'But you've not fully recovered from the... er... miscarriage.'

'No?' Tessa sat on the armchair, crossed her legs and started to pull off her gloves slowly. All she needs now is a cigarette in a holder to complete the image, Sukey thought.

'How are you going to manage when you're still bleeding?' Minnie asked, whether from genuine curiosity or to make a nasty point, Sukey wasn't sure: her face was bland, impassive.

Tessa pouted. 'Be assured, I can manage a little inconvenience like that. And another thing,' she reached into her handbag and took out a packet of real cigarettes and a lighter, 'I'm moving on Sunday to my new place. It's better for getting to work, nearer to the centre of town and I'm welcome there, too.'

Tessa lit her cigarette and inhaled deeply, her lips becoming a thick red pout. 'So, shall we all repair to the pub, as it's my last free evening before I leave this place?

'Beaky will be there most probably,' Minnie said.

'Why should I care?' Tessa asked.

So they went.

The place was oddly quiet for a Friday evening. Tessa went to buy a round while Sukey and Minnie sat at a small round table. Sukey shivered. It was cold, dank and gloomy. The worn patterned carpet smelled musty and Sukey thought about the years of beer that had spilled and settled into its fibres. The chipped veneer of the table, marked with cigarette burns, the large ugly un-emptied ashtray at its centre, the cheap and dingy paintings on the dark smoke-stained walls oppressed and irritated her. Once, she remembered, she'd liked the fact that the pub was seedy, she'd enjoyed the feeling of debauchery it had engendered.

She leant back, trying to grasp how she was feeling. She was aware, oddly she thought, of being happy and sad at the same time. The past felt like a long time ago, but at the same time as if it was still happening. Here was where Kitty had worked, here she, Sukey, had come when she'd first met Joe, who had then introduced her and Jaz to Vic and Jules. She remembered the first time that couple had walked into the pub and had stood by the door as if waiting for applause.

Tessa came back to the table carrying three gin and tonics. Sukey sat up, shook her head, smiled. She raised her glass when Tessa suggested that they toast each other and the future.

'And here's to your new life, Sukey. Your change, devoid of sin and naughtiness,' Tessa added.

'Oh no,' Sukey said. 'That's not it. I'm not going to give anything up, not all the fun stuff. I'm just going to live more comfortably and… make decisions about what I do.'

'More control,' Minnie explained.

'Control, I see,' Tessa said, sounding dubious.

Beaky stood in the kitchen with his suitcase by his side. He seemed unsure of what to do next.

'You will come next Friday, won't you?' Sukey asked. 'Our last evening here. People are coming over. The usual lot: Jojo, Jaz.'

Beaky shrugged.

'Well have a cup of tea before you go.'

'No… Come and have a drink at the pub.' Beaky rushed the words out and then blushed.

'OK. '

They sat at a table in the middle of the room.

'This'll still be your local, even at your new place,' Sukey said.

'Yeah.'

Sukey took a sip of her cider. 'Will you miss us?'

'Yeah,' Beaky was blushing again.

'And you'll come over to see me and Minnie in our new place?'

Beaky raised his glass and hid behind it as he took a long swallow, finishing the beer.

'Well?' Sukey asked.

'I think so,' Beaky said. 'I'd better be going.' He stood up and didn't move, his hands dangling by his sides, looking at Sukey.

Sukey swallowed. She felt like crying; she'd never been close to Beaky but he'd been there, an almost unnoticed part of her life for so many months. Even when he'd been living with Tessa he'd often come round to Kitty's flat or had been in this pub. He, too, Sukey was sure, felt sad and a little lost because of the parting that was about to happen, and he understood its significance: an important part of their lives was ending.

Sukey opened her mouth wide, she often found this was a good way to stop herself crying. She closed it again, tightening her jaw. 'So it's goodbye Beaky, I suppose.'

Beaky took in a deep breath, nodded, bent to lift his case and walked to the door. Sukey watched to see if he would turn to look at her before he left. He did.

Sukey woke and turned over, luxuriating at being alone in a big double bed. She had decided to spend her last night in the flat in Kitty's old bedroom. She stretched her legs wide, enjoying the space, wondered what time it was and then decided it was too early to get up. She pulled the bedclothes up so that they almost covered her head and settled herself for more sleep. The next time she woke lines of hard light were coming in through the sides of the curtains. This time she sat up blinking and looked at her watch: nearly ten already and today she was moving out of this flat and into their new one. After work Minnie was bringing home the van that her business had recently acquired, and before that Sukey had to finish packing, tidy and clean the place up after last night's little party.

There was not much mess: it had been a quiet well-behaved, short-lived party. Jojo and Ted had arrived with their usual quota of wine; Jaz had come without Stevie who was working. Even Dennis had made an effort to turn up. He'd arrived just after Joe had left, heading for another session at the doors of a Soho club. He'd only been at the flat for half an hour and hadn't said much. Sukey wondered why she'd bother to invite him.

'I've come to say goodbye to you all. Not stopping for long,' Dennis said. He accepted a glass of beer.

'Now, Den,' Jaz said, 'I want you to share a joint with us, just so you can say you have.'

'You must be bleedin' jokin'. I've only just got back into the wife's good books, the last thing I want is to turn up all squiffy from those drugs you smoke.'

'Go on, do,' Ted said. He was the one rolling the joint. 'Do it in memory of our good friend Malc.'

No one said anything as they all thought about Malc and how he'd died. Sukey took a sip of her wine and looked at Jojo. She was staring into the distance.

'I tell you what,' Jaz said, breaking the silence. 'If I do one with just the insides of banana skins in, will you try that, Den? It's not real drugs.'

Dennis was opening a second bottle of bear. 'Well, you lot, you're the strangest crowd I've ever run into, but all right. I'll give it a go.'

Jaz rooted in his bag and pulled out a bunch of bananas. 'I bought these specially,' he said. 'My goodbye present to the flat.'

After Dennis had taken a few puffs of the ersatz joint that Jaz had made, he stood up. 'That was disgusting. I always knew I was right to refuse your stuff. So… it's time for me to go. Cheers all of you and it's been… different.' He stood at the door for a moment and then waved. They heard his feet clumping down the stairs and then the slam of the front door, echoing eerily in the emptiness of the downstairs flat: Bridie and family had left the day before.

'I thought he might say something about Kitty,' Jaz said.

'Like what?' Sukey asked. 'What is there to say?'

Jaz shrugged.

'Let's go to the pub,' said Ted. 'It's…' He shook his head.

'Yes, isn't it?' Sukey said.

'But what if Beaky comes and we're not here?' Jaz asked.

'He won't,' Sukey said.

'We'll leave a note on the door just in case,' Minnie suggested.

It had been a strange, low-key evening, Sukey thought as she washed the glasses in the sink. She turned to pick up the two dirty bowls that had held the ice cream she and Jaz had eaten when they'd come back later. There'd been just the two of them by then. Just like the old days, she'd thought as she rooted in the freezer compartment of the fridge, teasing out of the ice a carton of vanilla and one of Neapolitan. I must defrost that later, she told herself.

'Do you miss Kitty?' Jaz had asked.

'No,' Sukey said. 'It almost seems like she's always been dead. When I think about her, even long before, I can't think of her – say at college, or working in the pub or stealing stuff – without knowing, even though we weren't aware of it at the time, that she'd be dead soon. So… d'you miss her?'

'I don't know.' Jaz had stopped eating for a moment and then he licked the back of his spoon, turned it round and licked the front. 'When Ellen died – you remember Ellen from college dying on our last day? Well at the time I thought of it in relation only to myself, you know, endings, death, saying goodbye.'

'So did I, still do, I think,' Sukey said.

'But now I don't know. How do you assimilate Malc dying and Jules killing herself and then Vic murdering or manslaughtering – or whatever you call it – Kitty? How do you fit all that into your life?'

'Do you have to be able to explain it?' asked Sukey

'Probably not.'

'The main thing is, for those of us who are still alive, is that we are the ones who survived. So far.'

'Right,' said Jaz, 'and now I'm going to roll us a last joint of the insides of banana skins. But I'll put in some real dope, too, just in case it's only a myth about banana skins getting you stoned.'

Sukey cleaned the kitchen, the loo, the hallway, both bedrooms. She wandered through the unlocked rooms of the downstairs flat. At one point the landlord came down, knocking apologetically on the kitchen door and nodding with what Sukey thought was appreciation when he saw how clean the place was.

'We'll be gone this evening,' she told him.

Everything was ready by the time Minnie came with the van, and they loaded it with their cases and the boxes of bed linen, books, leftover groceries and the few household items they owned. They stood in the bedroom they'd shared with so many others. Sukey went to stand in the bay window. She drew the curtains back and she and Minnie looked out onto the greyness of London lit by the regular dim glow of street lamps.

'I've food in the flat, and wine, and I've scored a nice piece of Lebanese black: it smells good,' Minnie said. 'And then, if you're interested, I've been promised some acid tabs. For when things are right. OK?'

'OK, for when things are right,' Sukey echoed. She smiled. 'Let's go,' she said and led the way through the door and out of the flat.

Epilogue

Arriving back in London early in the twenty-first century, on her way to stay with an old friend, Sukey is in a taxi going from Kings Cross to the street near Hampstead Heath where the friend lives. The taxi drives past the house where the old flat was. She strains her neck for a last glimpse as the taxi moves away eager to take her to her destination.

Although almost all the area around it has changed, the house remains the same: three stories, semi-detached and dingy. The brick is dirty, the little front garden sour and neglected, the hedge enclosing it mean and ragged. Sukey sighs as the taxi speeds away. That house holds so many months of her past: a significant time she never wants to forget.

That evening, the friend's four-year-old grandson explains a picture in a book to his little sister. 'Look, Tilly,' he says, pointing, 'that's a boat and that's a coastguard.' He pauses for significance, or maybe just to collect his thoughts. 'See that man? When you're in trouble he will save you from your life.'

Sukey and her friend laugh and laugh. Soon there are tears in Sukey's eyes. She's thinking of the house she saw today, she's thinking of when she was very young and believed that whatever happened and in spite of it all, she would never need to be saved from her life.